The First Man

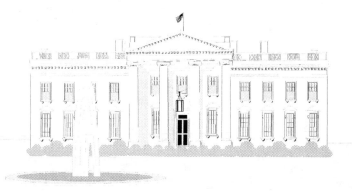

To Be First Lady

Clarke Allan

'2001'

The First Man *To Be First Lady*

Clarke Allan

Copyright © 1999 by Allan Paul Wiley

ISBN 0-7414-0157-6

Cover design by Christopher A. Master
Published by:

PUBLISHING.COM

Infinity Publishing.com
519 West Lancaster Avenue
Haverford, PA 19041-1413
Info@buybooksontheweb.com
www.buybooksontheweb.com
Toll-free (877) BUY BOOK
Local Phone (610) 520-2500
Fax (610) 519-0261

Printed in the United States of America

Printed on Recycled Paper

Published October-1999

I'd like to dedicate this book to my Grandma, who said,

*"I'm going to talk to your Guardian Angel and have her pull a
few strings for you.
And I don't mean the one's on her harp neither."*

The strings were pulled. Thank you Grandma, and thank you,
Guardian Angel Gurt.

Grandma has always been a hard one to say no to.

ACKNOWLEDGEMENTS

A dear friend said, "You can never repay a gift of love with money, or with anything money can buy." And you know what? She's right. Although she could use a good cosmetologist, she's got what it takes on the inside. Always has.

I would like to give my heart-felt thanks and appreciation to my editor and new found, wonderful friend, Cherie Tucker of GrammarWorks.

A never-ending thank you to Karen who, in a time when floral arranging was not a Letterman's sport for adolescent boys, always cheered me on. And still does.

A special thank you to JO, who has always encouraged me to write, right.

An extraordinary thank you to Cousin Sheila, she's always there for me. Period.

A delicious thank you to Sergeant Tracy Adams. She taught me how to sauté up a smile and whip up a grin.

An incredible thank you to Cheryl Anne, who taught me how to verbally yank folks by the hair and twirl them like a Texas twister, and put them back down where they belong.

A gracious thank you to Michelle, Bridgett, Sandy, and Mary Gail, a quartet of ladies who do not sing together, but together, have put a song in my heart.

A most distinguished thank you to White House Historian Edward R. Wiley. His knowledge and devotion to his historical studies, has the fictional characters of this book actually walking the halls of the White House. You will be impressed with the knowledge you attain while reading this book. The Eisenhower China really is gold.

An edificational thank you to George Ray of KCTS TV Seattle, Washington. You taught me how to learn just by watching.

A great big thank you to Ms. Larue, she is Scarlet with a red pen.

A very loving thank you to my best friend and 'Super' Grandma. She's never been shocked at anything I've ever admitted to, or come out of. Grandma said it best when she said, "I know about these things, I watch Oprah Winfrey."

Thank you Oprah. You make my life a whole heck of a lot easier.

For the first time the press could remember, the First Lady wasn't drunk when she left the White House. Everyone knew the First Lady was an alcoholic. She had gone through rehab so many times even Betty Ford wouldn't have her back. Nonetheless, she hated the President and wanted to be sober for her last official duty as First Lady. She made sure every news network was present, live, with cameras rolling, when she barged through the doors of the Oval Office. With a rehearsed attitude, she threw the divorce papers down in front of her husband, the President of the United States. Although millions enjoyed the live show, not too many were surprised. Ironically, the President had seen to it that the First Lady's alcoholism was made public, in order to hide her illegal drug addiction. In his re-election campaign, the President boasted to the religious right, "The White House wine cellars are locked and no 'sinful booze' will be served on the grounds of the White House."

It had also been rumored the First Lady and the former Vice President were having an affair. No one ever denied it. The First Lady, the unknowing subject of a top secret FBI criminal investigation for possession of illegal drugs, was finally arrested while doing those same illegal drugs with the former vice president.

The world heaved a collective sigh of relief when the vice president was safely behind bars. He resigned his office in

1

return for a lighter prison sentence. It all seemed unbelievable, like a really dumb late, late show. But there it was, on primetime, every time you changed the channel, read the newspaper, or heard anyone talking.

America hadn't seen the First Lady since the day she had been acquitted, threw the divorce papers at her husband, and the former vice president was handcuffed, sentenced and thrown in prison. The world wondered where the First Lady was. She was never seen in public or at social functions. America prayed she was safe in a rehab center. Everyone thought the President had hidden her, or worse. But even he didn't know where she was and publicly said he didn't care.

The United States was glad it was over. It seemed the only thing left in America was bigotry among the fundamentalists and a strong military. All America needed was one small spark to jump-start the nation. Suddenly, like the roar from a once-dead engine, America could see it right before their very eyes. No one could believe it.

Was he a wish come true? A twinkling star? Was there finally a glimmer of hope? He was the nation's nominee to be appointed to the office of vice president of the United States. He was all the televised excitement of an election year ticker-tape parade. The excitement wasn't for the man going into the White House, but rather hope that the man IN the White House would resign and get OUT once and for all.

Congress had narrowed their choice for vice president down to two men who were, at that very moment, debating in front of Congress, behind closed doors. Televised coverage continued with raw, sarcastic enthusiasm for the other candidate for the office. He was presently the Secretary of Defense and a weasel of a man. He selfishly kept the military big, strong and well armed. He had the biggest defense budget in history and it kept growing. It was only a matter of time, he was sure, before he would conquer the world. Hank considered himself a 'good ole boy' and his attitude said Congress would appoint him vice president hands down.

Without coverage of the debate between the appointees for vice president, television news was the same boring old thing. The President had been caught doing this, evading taxes on that. It was proven he offered political jobs in exchange for sexual

2

favors. It was the same old shameful routine in every newscast. Not only was America tired of it, so was the rest of the world, who looked to the United States for hope. The United States needed a breath of fresh air, and the nation's nominee for vice president was breathing life into the world with each breath he took.

The news broadcast continued with the same old, tired question: "Who would become the First Lady for the world's most eligible and most powerful bachelor?" Clarke hit the mute button. He was tired of hearing that question over and over and over. He tousled Barney's head then gently petted him.

Clarke thought about the question for a moment. It was a fair one. If appointed vice president, Michael would be the world's most eligible bachelor. Just thinking about the people's choice for vice president made Clarke smile from ear to ear. Michael was an enviable six-foot-seven inches tall, a strapping man of 257 pounds, broad shoulders, small waist, size 14 shoes. And boy, could those shoes dance!

Newscasters always commented on his professional credits. It was a list the length of your arm: Bachelor's degree in political science from the Naval Academy; law degree from Harvard; he loved all sports and had been the quarterback for the Naval Academy football team. He had been sought by the pros, but went Navy full-time as a fighter pilot. And he proudly smoked a pipe.

To this impressive list, Clarke added his own personal list. He started to count on his fingers, adding another finger every time he said the word 'he': he's left-handed; he hates wearing a tie, but does—he even ties his own bow tie, but not too neatly. He doesn't like to wear a tuxedo, but will when it's appropriate; he works out daily, running five miles before breakfast. He doesn't lift weights; instead he chops wood. He spars to keep his black belt in Karate. He doesn't cook, but loves a home-cooked meal. Clarke smiled. Naturally, his favorite vegetable was French fries. Clarke laughed out loud. He even likes fruitcake during the holidays. If ever there was a perfect example of 'opposites attract' it was the two of them. They were the perfect couple. One would describe Clarke as a fine gentleman. He had that certain something you couldn't quite put

3

your finger on, but whatever it was, it fairly illuminated the entire room when he walked in.

Clarke was on the school board and was everyone's favorite substitute teacher. He was a volunteer fireman and the first in with the hose. If there was a kitten up a tree, he was on his way up the ladder. If there was a party, Clarke was invited; a committee, he was asked to head it up; Founder's Day parade, he was Grand Marshal. Clarke didn't like the attention, but he handled it like a gentleman sipping a fine cup of tea. Some people just have that quality naturally inbred.

Clarke was a well-built man himself: broad shoulders, small waist; that perfect 'T' only seen in trendy male magazines. He was down-to-earth, with a unique voice that everyone enjoyed. It wasn't masculine, and it wasn't feminine. It was just Clarke. Even though Clarke was of average height, he was dwarfed when he stood next to Michael.

Clarke smiled and shook his head, thinking, "If only the world knew." It was high-tech's best-kept secret and Clarke was determined to keep it that way. No doubt about it, it was hands-down who should and would be vice president. Clarke watched all of the congressional hearings just so he could see Michael. Michael Arthur Kent. His friends all called him MAK. Clarke grinned as he wondered, "If Michael gets appointed vice president, would they call him Big MAK?" Clarke looked at the TV, noticing that Michael looked great, although just a little rumpled around the edges. That was normal when Clarke wasn't around to spruce him up.

The House Painted White By The Sea

Clarke was used to not seeing the man he loved very often and they cherished whatever time they had together. Clarke stared at the TV. On the one hand, Clarke was so proud that Michael was the people's choice for vice president, but on the other hand, he knew it would be almost impossible for them to see each other if Congress did appoint him. A commercial break interrupted Clarke's thoughts and he left Barney lying on the edge of the bed still staring at the TV. Barney was a great dog and Clarke's best friend. He wondered if Barney really understood what he was watching or if he watched for the same reason Clarke did.

Dressed in sweat pants and a tank top, Clarke left his bedroom, with a thumpity-thud of suede and fleece slippers against hardwood floors, to start his daily workout. He lifted weights, watched what he ate and religiously yanked out any gray hairs. Clarke hummed a tune as he bounced down the stairs of his magnificent home. The stairs spread gracefully to a grand foyer lit by a brilliant crystal chandelier. The house was as spectacular on the inside as it was on the outside.

It was a traditional sea captain's home, built with the world's finest imports: hand-cut marble from Turkey; stained glass windows from Europe; silk fabrics from the Orient; priceless rugs from Persia. The house was topped by a widow's walk, perched high above the third floor and framed by an elaborate wrought iron railing, rumored to have come from the ruins of a castle in Germany. The salt air kept Clarke busy scraping and painting. The house was painted white and trimmed with its original 'gingerbread', delicious with color. Clarke made sure it was always in tip-top shape, both inside and out. He basked in his rewards: simply rocking on a porch swing and enjoying the sunset.

The house was as unique as the person who lived within its walls. The estate should have been registered with the National Historical Society, but Clarke loved his privacy. It was far off the beaten path, proudly nestled on several acres, on its own peninsula, facing the sea—the furthest point west in the continental United States. The clouds of Northwestern Washington were never gray to Clarke. They were glistening silver.

The main highway was hidden by acres of vintage fruit orchards and fields dotted with wild blackberry bushes. The estate had been his Great Aunt Naomi's home since the day she was born and now it was Clarke's. Clarke had been orphaned at a very early age and was sent to live with his only living relative, the debutante of Washington State, Great Aunt Naomi.

She willed not only her lavish home to Clarke, but also her class, charm, and quick wit. In her day, fine parties and cotillions were her family's pride. Aunt Naomi, with her special flair, made Clarke a 'debutante in trousers', as she so proudly joked. She taught him about the finer things in life and loved him for who he was. She made him promise her that he would never change.

The estate was bequeathed to Clarke with one stipulation—it would continue to be a place of elegant cotillions and festive parties. Like a fine wine, the house was getting better with age. The furnishings were as original as the house, but enhanced with Clarke's sparkle. He walked into the parlor and placed another log on the fire. Michael had chopped a lot of wood the last time he was home and Clarke had watched him split each log.

An elaborate mantel clock, trimmed in rare blue-marble, chimed the quarter-hour. Clarke looked at the clock then at his watch. He reset his watch. The beautiful clock kept perfect time. Of all the ornate antique one-of-a-kind pieces in her home, this mantel clock had been Aunt Naomi's favorite. Clarke looked back at the clock and ran his fingers along the gold carvings. The clock held many treasured memories for him. The house wouldn't be his home without it.

Clarke turned and walked out of the room and down the hall. The house was a mansion in itself, although smaller than most, yet it had a feeling of home far larger then the rest. Clarke had a flair for decorating and the house was ablaze with color. *Architect's Magazine* wanted to do a spread on the lovely old house by the sea, but Clarke refused. His life was private and that's the way it would always be, period.

Clarke looked around and suddenly realized he was alone: Barney wasn't at his side. Clarke began looking for his dog. He looked into various rooms and scanned the hallways and finally found Barney at the front door. He wasn't barking, just staring at the door as if he had just treed a squirrel. As Clarke walked closer, Barney started to point, just as he had been trained to do at obedience-hunting school.

Clarke had acquired Barney as a puppy—a gift from Michael, of course. The owner of the litter insisted that all of the Springer Spaniels he allowed to leave the litter, Barney included, go through the 'proper schooling'. But today was the first time he had ever seen Barney point. Just as he was ready to say, "Good Boy" and pet him, as he had been trained to do by the obedience school, Clarke instead found himself asking Barney what was wrong. Not only was Barney Clarke's best friend, he was also a great watchdog. Suddenly the front doorbell rang. It rang over and over and over as if the doorbell had its own emotions and had suddenly gone hysterical.

The sudden ringing of the doorbell startled Clarke. He had learned at a very early age to count to ten before showing any emotion. Not only did Clarke count to ten, but also rambled out any fears quietly, to himself. A product of Great Aunt Naomi's teachings, Clarke would always outwardly show the composure of a fine gentleman.

As the doorbell continued to ring, thoughts raced through Clarke's mind. He knew it wasn't the staff from the fields because they always used the back door. Not that they couldn't come to the front of the house, but Clarke's office was just off the kitchen. Whenever they needed him, he was just a gentle tap on the window away.

People from town would have announced themselves first. The drive to the house was beautiful, but defiantly off the beaten path. Clarke looked at his watch. It was way too early for the mail carrier. His was the last house on her route, and besides, she always honked as she came up the driveway. The driveway itself was almost hidden. Many invited guests had missed it over and over again, but this time, Clarke was sure, no one had been invited. He hadn't prepared for anyone. Clarke looked down at himself. He certainly hadn't dressed for guests.

It really didn't matter what Clarke was wearing. In this small seaside village, where everyone knew everyone else, it was still Small Town, USA. Clarke could get everything he needed on Main Street as long as he shopped before 6:30 p.m., Monday through Friday, and before 5:00 p.m. on Saturday, and never on Sunday.

The village wasn't a place to hide, but to enjoy life. A few hours away lay the big city, offering an airport with every-other-day commuter air service. The big city also had a mini-mall with a catalog store from J. C. Penney and, of course, a Wal-Mart. Clarke's little town was still America's best-kept secret. And with a Wal-Mart a couple hours away, the town's people were satisfied to keep it just the way it was.

The insistent ringing of the bell finally interrupted Clarke's ramblings. Without even thinking, he opened the door and his heart immediately sank. There stood a woman, flanked by two men, all dressed in professional black suits, staring gravely back at him. Instantly, Clarke was sure it must be morbid news about Michael and immediately asked them. They assured him it wasn't as the trio flashed Secret Service badges. Clarke wished he had his eyeglasses on. He couldn't read what the badges said but it didn't matter anyway; the woman immediately took command.

"May we come in?" She pushed past Clarke with all the grace of a tank headed for battle. The men followed. Clarke, stunned, followed them with his eyes, his hand still clutching the doorknob. Barney carefully sniffed each one of them, then gave Clarke the "all clear" bark. Barney's actions reassured Clarke: that sniff of approval was never wrong.

Michael had been involved in politics for a long time and often joked with Clarke, saying that cooperation was the only way he could ever get rid of the Secret Service. Okay, Clarke would go along with the joke. He relaxed and, remembering his role as host, offered his guests a cup of coffee as he shut the door. The black-clad trio was obviously surprised that someone had offered them genuine hospitality. They looked at each other and nodded.

Like soldiers in formation, the trio in black followed Clarke down the hallway to the kitchen, their shoes tapping on the marble floors dotted with Persian rugs. Off the hallway was a music room where a grand piano proudly sat in front of a bay window, encompassing a breathtaking view of the sea.

Their walk continued, past gilded cabinets filled with sterling silver, polished to a mirror shine. Fine china from all over the world was displayed with a decorator's touch. Crystal chandeliers cast prisms of color as the morning sun shone through leaded windows resplendent with beveled designs. The black-clad trio walked through the house as though they were walking through a museum. They gave knowing nods to each other and commented to Clarke how beautiful the house was.

"Great Aunt Naomi had impeccable taste," Clarke said in a "thank-you" tone. He continued walking, occasionally looking back at his uninvited guests, who all seemed totally awestruck. They appeared to be shocked that this was Clarke's home and not a five-star resort. Clarke thought they were a little annoying, but seemed genuine. They reached the kitchen and they stopped in the doorway.

A stove from the turn-of-the-twentieth-century still performed its duties from its original post. It stood proudly on Queen Anne legs and was topped with large rounded ovens set off to the side. The entire piece was trimmed in polished nickel and accented in the popular blue from its era. It was truly a work of art. A large pot rack, suspended from the high ceiling, was filled with copper pots polished to a mirror-shine.

Off the kitchen was a laundry room. A vintage wringer washer relaxed in a corner, its brand name proudly written in shiny chrome. A modern washer and dryer could be heard as they hummed on duty behind louvered doors. Shelves of home-canned food lined the pantry. Off the kitchen, in the other direction, was Clarke's office, complete with a view of the sea and pictures of Michael and Barney. A computer was spouting, "You've got mail."

They could tell immediately that Clarke was completely at home in the kitchen. He walked past a double-door refrigerator decorated with a collection of clever refrigerator magnets and opened a cookie jar, then gracefully placed home-baked cookies on a silver tray. Then he walked to the huge, over-sized sink, took the pot from one of the two identical coffeemakers that sat on the counter next to it. Clarke put it in the sink under the running tap and nonchalantly looked out the kitchen window,

9

waiting for the pot to fill. Suddenly his heart skipped a beat. He couldn't believe what he was seeing. He pulled back the checkered curtains so he could get a better look. There was a team of men, dressed much liked the ones inside the house, keeping an eye on nothing, just enjoying the fresh salty air.

Clarke quickly turned around and stared at the woman dressed in black, who was obviously the one in command. His stance said he'd had enough. Clarke refused to go any further with the joke. Arms folded across his chest, Clarke demanded, "What is this all about?"

"I'll finish the coffee," A black-suit said as he reached for the coffeepot. The man poured out some of the water that Clarke had absently let run over in his concern.

The woman walked towards Clarke and calmly said, "Maybe we should talk." She looked quickly at the men she commanded, then looked back at Clarke. "Privately." Clarke silently led her back down the hallway, the woman professionally scanning the house as they walked to the front parlor. Barney never left Clarke's side. The woman was watching Clarke with more than a professional eye, making him think that if she had been a dog, he would have been sniffed for a tracking scent.

He invited her to sit down then sat across from her in a winged-back chair that welcomed him like a throne. Clarke was framed by a floor-to-ceiling bay window facing the sea. He looked almost regal. The woman looked beyond Clarke and out the window. The surf was wild, waves swelling then crashing into the rocky shore. She seemed so entranced by the view she appeared to have forgotten where she was for a moment.

Clearing her throat, the woman in black struggled to regain her composure. She looked Clarke straight in the eye then smiled. She looked around the room, "Your decorator is incredible."

By now, Clarke was getting seriously annoyed with the woman's attitude. He knew she was trying to throw him off-guard by getting him comfortable on his own turf. "I don't have a decorator, a tailor, or a seamstress." He paused then continued with in a smooth but quick tone. "I decorated this house, designed and sewed the slip-covers and installed the drapes ALL BY MYSELF. NOW," Clarke paused once again. He calmed himself without having to count to ten and again became the gracious host. "What may I do for you?"

"You have a really beautiful place." Her sincerity caught Clarke off-guard. She paused, looked down at the lush carpets, then back up at Clarke. She took a deep breath and got right to the point. Her voice deepened. "The Vice President-Select has asked you to come to Washington for the swearing-in."

Clarke looked a little puzzled. "The swearing-in? Has there been a decision made on the vice presidency?" He asked.

"Yes," she replied.

Clarke looked at his watch and realized with disappointment that he had missed the official announcement. He had been looking forward to seeing Michael's expression when reporters interviewed him for the first time as the Vice President-Designate.

The woman continued, "Congress made their decision and it was announced moments ago on all the networks. The Vice President-Select wants you in Washington and we have been sent to get you. Our plane will take off as soon as we get to the airport. I, along with a select few, know all about you and the Vice President-Select. Enough said?"

Clarke nodded. Calling Michael Vice President 'SELECT' was enough said. The *proper* title was Vice President-*Designate*. This woman should have known that.

"How do I know this is on the up and up?" Clarke demanded.

"We showed you our badges when you invited us into your home."

She was right. Clarke was silent. He had missed the official announcement. Clarke looked at his watch again and finally forgave himself, then looked back at the woman. He wasn't going to argue with her.

"You have hidden it well," she said with a cocky attitude. "Our investigations never put you and the Vice President-Select together."

Clarke looked her straight in the eye. "Because one enjoys one's privacy doesn't mean one is hiding anything." He calmed himself and once again became the polite host. He looked at her hand. Clarke didn't see a wedding ring. "Miss...?"

"Jones, and it's Ms.," She said, as common as her last name.

Clarke gave her a nod as if he were saying, "Pleased to meet you", but what he really meant was, "Of course it's *Ms.*"

She continued, "The Vice President-Select wants you in Washington. Like I said, there's only a few of us who know and he's keeping it that way. Again, enough said?" She kept repeating herself as if it made her more powerful to think she knew a great big secret. Then, to Clarke's surprise, she leaned forward, crossing her legs. Ever so gently she rocked her foot. She cocked her head to one side as her silky hair flowed. Her smile broadened and her eyes widened. "Besides," she batted her eyelids, "if I wanted to take you, you would already be bound and gagged!" She brought her hand to her face and rested her chin on it in quite a lady-like gesture. Her nails were perfectly manicured. This woman was going to win the battle with whatever ammunition she had, up her sleeve or loaded in a gun.

Clarke returned her stare, trying not to laugh at her attempt at seductive intimidation. Then he turned and looked first at the men in the kitchen, then at the men outside. Clarke sighed in amusement. She was right.

"You don't have any choice but to come with us." She raised her eyebrows. "Peacefully or not."

Clarke didn't appreciate her tone. His smile was edged with an angry expression. He knew she was right, but at that point he didn't care. There was a long silence. Clarke was ready to fight and *Ms.* Jones definitely would not win this one. Suddenly her attitude changed. Fast. She knew without a doubt that Clarke wasn't going to be bullied. If this were to be a successful mission, she would have to play nice guy in a black skirt.

Clarke was ready to be a bad guy in trousers and reduce this wench to ruin. Men like Clarke didn't fight with their fists but rather with a sharp tongue that could slice you in two, long before you noticed you'd even been scratched.

"The Vice President-Select thought you might be a little uncomfortable about all of this so he gave us a code. I don't understand what it means but he said you would. And I quote, 'By the way.'"

Clarke grinned from ear to ear. Ms. Jones realized that this was all the reassurance he needed. "This is going to take some time." Clarke was blushing.

"We will meet with your in-house staff and work around them. Out of their way, of course." She smirked.

"I don't have an 'in-house staff'." Clarke said flatly, then smiled back at her smirk. She looked a little puzzled. Clarke was very matter-of-fact. "I take care of this house myself." Clarke was a little annoyed—she had the same look everyone else always did: *"You're a man and you know how to vacuum?"* This country had come a long way toward equality for women but still had a ways to go for a man who cooked and cleaned. "The grounds have a staff. You can meet with them. Outside." Clarke had just put this woman in her place, out back, down the sandy path.

"That won't be necessary. We won't be in their way. Our staff is here to watch the house and the grounds while you're gone. This is all routine." As Clarke knew very well, this was far from *routine*. Michael was always full of surprises. They were always good ones—even if they didn't seem like it at the time.

Clarke thought about it for a moment, then turned and looked out at the sea. For some reason, the crashing waves helped him decide. Clarke had all the faith in the world in Michael. If this is what he wanted, then it was best. The blue-marble mantel clock chimed the hour. Clarke and Ms. Jones looked toward the fireplace then at each other.

"I can be ready within the hour." Clarke said as he politely excused himself.

The woman watched Clarke as he left the room. Barney stayed downstairs, performing his duties as watch dog.

As Clarke showered, he thought about the Vice President-Designate. Michael wanted him in Washington for the swearing-in. What a tease, Clarke laughed. Any time Clarke was invited to be in the audience, he and Michael were not together. That was understandable. Michael knew Clarke didn't want to be in the limelight. And why should he be? He was there to support his man, even if that support came from the back of the room. As long as Michael knew Clarke was there, he had the wind beneath his wings. It didn't matter if he was acres away, they would still be together for the swearing-in.

13

Clarke packed his suitcase. He didn't wear a suit too often but always had a silk button-up vest ready for any occasion. Clarke dressed like a fine gentleman from the turn of the 20th century. Matching vest and trousers, tie in a perfect knot, French cuffs and cufflinks with just a spot of 'pizzazz'. They had been Great Aunt Naomi's vintage rhinestone earrings and Clarke had them made into cufflinks. He packed his tuxedo and clothes for a week or so. Barney's shift of guard duty was over and he was sitting on the edge of the bed, licking his whiskers. The suited man downstairs, Barney's new best friend, had given him a cookie.

Since Clarke didn't know what was appropriate to wear for a kidnapping, he decided on a royal blue linen suit with a double-breasted vest and matching jacket. He always sported spectator shoes. Few men dressed like Clarke but then Clarke wasn't like most other men. He had his own style, his own quick wit, and his own incredible charm.

Clarke zipped up his garment bag and clicked the matching suitcase shut. Then he promised Barney he'd be home in just a few days and assured him that the nice guys in black would take good care of him. Clarke picked up his eyeglasses from the dressing table, looked through them at arms-length, then put them on. He did a once-around-the-room, making sure everything was in its place, then picked up his luggage and walked down the stairs. Barney trotted past him, then looked up at Clarke from the bottom of the stairs with a "HA, HA, I beat you" look.

Ms. Jones did a double take as he came down the stairs. Clarke was flattered. She continued to look at Clarke with an arched eyebrow. Her expression said he looked great and passed inspection. Ms. Jones caught her breath as she watched Clarke from across the hall.

With a blushing thank-you smile, Clarke put his luggage next to the front door, nodded to Ms. Jones, then turned and walked to the laundry room. In one easy motion, he opened the louvered doors, took the clothes out of the dryer and set them in a wicker basket. The washer had stopped and he lifted the lid and tossed the wash into the dryer. He shut the dryer door, turned the dial, and gently closed the louvered doors.

Clarke folded clothes as he gave a few instructions to the men who were going to stay at the house. The most important instructions had to do with what Barney was supposed to eat as opposed to what Barney *wanted* to eat. Clarke showed the men where the fresh linens were. He invited them to enjoy the contents of the fridge and the rest of the cookies. He had packed a few dozen of his homemade chocolate chip cookies in a Tupperware container for Michael.

Clarke stopped at the front door and looked around his home, almost as though he was seeing it for the first time, and maybe the last. He smiled to himself as he looked at the people dressed in black and put the Tupperware container full of cookies in his suitcase. Another man dressed all in black took the luggage as Clarke walked out the front door. He paused on the grand porch for a moment, then walked down the stairs to the circular cobblestone driveway. There was a large black car, not a limo but certainly as shiny, waiting with the motor running.

As his luggage was put into the trunk, Clarke petted Barney good-bye and looked back at his house. Window boxes in bloom stood guard below each window. White wicker furniture with plump yellow cushions dotted the wraparound porch. The porch swing swayed in the breeze. This was his home.

Clarke turned and looked out at the sea. The salt air comforted him. He bent down and gave Barney a big hug. Barney caught Clarke off guard and licked him. The man who had put the suitcases in the trunk opened the car door for Clarke. Clarke got in and the woman followed. Clarke was told to fasten his seatbelt as the man shut the door. Clarke suddenly felt trapped as the locks automatically bolted.

The day seemed to smile with approval as the car drove down the driveway. The field staff waved goodbye. The men in black just stood there. A suited man threw a ball toward Barney. Clarke saw Barney grab the ball, run to the man, drop it and run in the opposite direction.

After a long, silent ride, the car stopped alongside a huge Boeing 727 sent from Washington. Armed guards stood on alert at checkpoints marked by bright orange cones. The Secret Service agent sitting in the front seat talked into a walkie-talkie and a large door swung open on the side of the aircraft. Stairs unfolded like escalators at a fine department store.

Ms. Jones motioned to Clarke and they got out of the car. As Clarke stretched and nonchalantly commented that it felt good to stand up, he was suddenly sandwiched between her and a male Secret Service agent. In quickstep, they hustled him up the stairs and into the plane. The shiny black car drove away. Armed guards picked up the orange cones, stacking them one into the other. Aircraft engines screamed—takeoff was imminent.

Clarke noticed that the crew was busy putting things away and shutting overhead bins. When he looked back at the doorway he had just walked through, a man dressed in a pressed uniform was already shutting the door. Suddenly, Clarke felt he had been tricked and started to breathe heavily. Ms. Jones immediately noticed how uneasy Clarke was and began to brief him as to where his private quarters were located, which Clarke thought odd.

The steward, a handsome man with red hair and a 'boy-next-door' look, immediately invited Clarke to have a seat. Clarke sat down in the oversized airline seat and buckled the seatbelt. He reached in the seat-back pocket in front of him for the Emergency Evacuation Card and followed along as the steward gave him a private safety briefing.

The plane taxied down the runway then raced into the sky. When the 'fasten seat belt' sign went off, Clarke was given a tour of the aircraft. He looked at his private quarters. It was a small area, with a private lavatory, a closet and two overstuffed easy chairs complete with seatbelts. There was even a bed. It looked a little too secluded, so Clarke went back to his seat.

When he sat down, the steward handed him a telephone and politely said, "It's for you, sir." It was the Vice President-Designate calling over a secured line. Clarke congratulated Michael, then Michael told Clarke that everything was okay and he could talk to anyone on the plane. They were all well aware of the appointed Vice President-Designate's lifestyle and how important the man they had gone to pick up really was. Clarke blushed. He would still guard every word, but the cat was definitely out of the bag. With any luck, Barney wouldn't chase it all over the yard.

"How's Barney enjoying the flight?" Michael asked.

Clarke looked at the telephone as if Michael could see his look, then he spoke into the telephone, "Why would I bring

Barney to Washington? I'm only going to be gone a few days. Besides, Barney's having a good time with the men dressed in black." Clarke looked at the woman sitting across from him. She seemed more relaxed and actually cracked a smile at Clarke.

Michael could tell Clarke wasn't comfortable talking on the telephone, so he quickly said his good-byes with a special, "By the way." Clarke almost melted and said a breathy "by the way" back into the phone. Clarke handed the telephone back to the steward with a thank-you and looked back at Ms. Jones.

The flight to Washington would be about five hours. Clarke was offered lunch, but only took coffee. It wasn't very good coffee. Clarke was used to Seattle, where the whole world sent their best coffee to be savored. He requested a glass of water with lemon.

The woman who kidnapped Clarke finally relaxed, urging Clarke to do the same. "First off, we didn't kidnap you. You came of your own free will." They both smiled. That relaxed Clarke a bit, but he would continue to guard each word. The Vice President-Designate and Clarke had something very special. Clarke wasn't about to share that with anyone.

Ms. Jones wanted to chat, girl-talk—Clarke could see that look a mile away—but first she had some official duties to perform. Once that was finished, Clarke knew she had some questions, 'off the record'. Clarke knew girl-talk, at its best, has never been 'off the record'. There were many forms for Clarke to fill out and she asked him questions from each page. Clarke answered them honestly as she filled in the blanks. He knew this was for a security clearance. She insisted it was all 'routine', but Clarke knew very well it wasn't.

With all the paperwork finished and Clarke fingerprinted, he knew it was time to talk, 'unofficially'. For some reason, Clarke was surprisingly comfortable with this woman and began to talk as he wiped his hands. The goop they give you to get all the ink off never gets all the ink off. She wanted Clarke's footprints but Clarke refused with a smile and said, "THAT will take a presidential order." The woman smiled. It was a genuine smile this time.

With all her paper work put away, a soda pop on the rocks in her hand, Ms. Jones asked Clarke how he and the Vice President-Select had met. Clarke loved that story. It was a story everyone who was there in the theater that night knew. Clarke put the towel away, picked up his glass of water with lemon and smiled as they sat back down. Clarke was going to relive his favorite real-life fairy tale.

In the Beginning

"Ten minutes to curtain everyone." The overture began. Regardless of how many times an actor performs, butterflies still applaud. In the theater, when you're nervous, butterflies don't flutter in your stomach, they applaud. That was Clarke's sign for good luck. He knew it was going to be a good show.

Clarke took an acting job while working his way through a dissertation entitled, "Auditioning, A Disappointment." His research included auditioning for a part in Disney's *Beauty and the Beast* while secretly interviewing his fellow hopeful actors. Clarke's research questions included why the actors wanted the part, then when another actor was chosen, was the anticipation worth their disappointment? To his utter amazement, Clarke got the part. With his professor's urging Clarke continued his research with a twist, on stage.

Clarke loved Disney's *Beauty and the Beast* and brought it to life with the Broadway show. "Be Our Guest" was the number America came to hear. Ever since his theater days, Clarke loved to entertain, and used that song as his motto. The show was live, performed as rehearsed. Clarke's character, Lumier, captivated the entire theater. "It's just the character in costume." Clarke had told reporters. He was so convinced it was true, no one ever thought Clarke had an attitude about his success. He was genuine and shone like the flames in his candlestick. Actually, Clarke was the candlestick.

As he went on with his story, he relived every special moment and, by the tapping of his feet, every single dance step. It was Clarke's big solo and those applauding butterflies had become a squadron, flying in formation. Ms. Jones smiled at Clarke's metaphor as his thoughts took him back to the stage. Just as their attack was imminent, Clarke began to sing his big number, "Be Our Guest." Those butterflies broke formation and started to dance right along with him.

Clarke blushed with a bit of embarrassment as he continued the story. "Just as the dance number started, the candelabra costume gave way. You know, the part that holds the candle?" Clarke asked.

"I follow you," Ms. Jones said anxiously. Clarke was amazed she was so into their story.

"Anyway," Clarke continued, "It flew off my costume toward a dancing plate doing the can-can." On stage, Clarke, as the candelabra played to the audience, who was hysterical with laughter. He simply pretended that his costume falling apart and flying across the stage was part of the script.

Clarke was a real pro. He made the whole mishap look like a choreographed move. He kept dancing, dodging the twirling plates with theatrical flamboyance. Just as he bent down to pick up the candleholder part of his costume, he paused and looked over at Ms. Jones. He started laughing so hard tears came to his eyes. "Wouldn't you know it, that dancing plate 'can-canned' it right into the audience." Ms. Jones broke into a smile then started laughing with him.

Clarke stopped laughing and said, "I must have given a dazed look to the dancing plate. She looked back at me with a look that said, 'Get over it.' All I could do was take my surprised look to the audience, who burst into laughter. I knew the dancing plate had accidentally kicked it, but that far into the audience? I sang right along with the beat of the orchestra. What else could I do? The audience batted around that piece of costume like it was a balloon at a little kid's party. Just as the song was about to end, someone from the audience must have thrown the costume part back toward the stage. Suddenly my costume part flew back on the stage, whirling end over end just as the song was almost over. I saw it coming my way. The orchestra leader also saw it whirling my way and suddenly gave the orchestra a new ending to the song. The musicians' eyes were glued on the conductor. The conductor's eyes were glued on me. The audience was convinced they were enjoying the best live performance theater had ever offered. The orchestra continued to play the final note, the French horn and timpani playing in a duet while I continued singing the last note. Dancing plates were still. All the theatrical fantasy was quiet. It was a miracle. I was so nervous, it was as if the entire world had gone into slow motion as I reached up and the candleholder slid right back onto my costume, just as it had flown off."

In exclamation to fabulous live theater, Clarke bowed his head with the final note from the orchestra. The audience went wild with a thunderous ovation as Clarke stood with outstretched arms, poised as a candelabrum. Clarke knew he was surely surrounded by angelic help and that night's performance proved it. With his head bowed, Clarke noticed the players in the orchestra giving each other high five's. "They were the most talented musicians I had ever worked with." Clarke said, shaking his head in amazement.

Clarke raised his head and looked over at Ms. Jones. "I remember during all the applause I looked to the heavens and said a, 'thank you' to my Guardian Angel." He started laughing again. "There was a man on the catwalk who thought I was saying, 'thank you' to him and yelled a, 'you're welcome,' back."

Clarke was so touched by the audience's reaction, he could still hear the cheers. Clarke just stood there, on center stage, humbled, along with the rest of the cast. The director quickly had the curtains closed as the orchestra played the chorus again. The curtains opened for an encore and then closed for a very early intermission. The audience continued with the longest ovation ever heard in the Kennedy Center for the Performing Arts.

"To make it even more exciting, that live performance was being taped for television." Clarke thought about that for a moment. "I don't think it was ever on TV." Clarke laughed with relief. "Anyway, getting back to your question of how the Vice President Designate and I met—after the performance there was this big formal party, by invitation only. We, the cast, were asked to meet with the guests, mostly political people, and powerful political people, the Vice President-Designate among them; well, he wasn't the Vice President-Designate then," Clarke said with a grin as he looked around the plane that had been sent just for him. "I was still in costume."

"It sounds like trick or treat." Ms. Jones flatly interrupted. She was annoyed that Clarke still hadn't answered her question as to how he and the Vice President Select met.

"It had that ambiance to it. We all like to dress up and be something we're not every once in awhile." There was Clarke's style: Put them in their place with their very own words.

"So then what happened?" Even though she wouldn't admit it, Clarke could tell Ms. Jones was eager to hear the rest of his romantic story. She was sitting on the edge of her seat, ready for even the smallest detail. Clarke couldn't wait to tell her.

"The Vice President..." Clarke paused.

Ms. Jones quickly interrupted. "Yes, I know. He wasn't the Vice President Designate then," she started laughing, and with a wave of her hand said, "go on."

Clarke smiled. The woman actually called Michael the Vice President Designate. Clarke was still amazed that she was so genuinely interested in hearing their story. "The Vice President Designate came up to me and introduced himself. It was hard for me to shake his hand, since I was still in costume, so I said I owed him a rain check for that handshake. We, the cast that is, were invited back to the party after we changed out of costume. I went back for the rain check and the rest," Clarke paused, "is history."

It seemed totally out of character for her, but Ms. Jones seemed to genuinely love Clarke's romantic story. Maybe she had been alone for so long that loneliness was her best friend. Clarke was a matchmaker at heart, but didn't know anyone who could match up to this one. Clarke noticed that she didn't seem surprised to learn that he was in the theater. He guessed that her investigations must have revealed that Clarke was a Tony Award-winning actor. He had done some TV, made a good sum of money, which he obviously invested well, then suddenly dropped out of the limelight. Clarke's aunt was dying of cancer. He gave up his career to take care of her. Ms. Jones slowly shook her head from side to side as if to say, "What a man."

An overhead announcement interrupted their conversation. The steward announced that the initial descent for landing had begun. There was a bit of bustling around the aircraft as the steward put things away and shut overhead bins with a click. Clarke took a walk to the men's room. Fellow passengers became quiet as he walked past them. Their looks were nice, but their silence was annoying.

Clarke went back to his seat when the fasten-seatbelt sign came on and quickly buckled his seatbelt. The landing was bumpy. The aircraft taxied off the runway. Clarke looked out the window as the plane came to a complete stop. They were parked right next to Air Force One. Clarke looked a little awestruck.

Ms. Jones said, "Welcome to Andrews Air Force Base." She released her seatbelt, got up and walked towards the front of the aircraft, talking into her walkie-talkie. Suddenly another shiny car, almost a twin of the one that had taken them to the airport in Washington, the state, was there to take them to Washington, the city. The Washington's weren't confusing. One had the Space Needle; the other had the White House.

The roar from the aircraft engines almost knocked Clarke down as he was escorted down the front stairs of the aircraft still sandwiched between Secret Service agents. As they got into the car, Clarke felt the trunk slam. Ms. Jones turned to Clarke and said, "Congratulations. Your luggage made it, too." That was her idea of a joke. No one laughed. No one said a word. Clarke looked back at the airplane. The stairs were retracted and it sounded like it was getting ready to take off.

The silence was deafening as they drove into the nation's capital. They arrived at a beautiful hotel that seemed hidden among tall buildings and bushy trees. Clarke was assigned a fine suite with room service at his beck and call. Ms. Jones presented Clarke with an agenda: where he could go, how he could get there, and whom he could talk to.

Clarke was asked what he would be wearing for the next couple of days. His wardrobe was met with an arched eyebrow and a "that will be just fine." Clarke wasn't in the mood to go shopping, so it would have to do. He was going to wear a simple dark blue, double-breasted suit, silk vest and tie. His vest appropriately accented his suit. If Clarke took off his jacket he would still look well dressed. Clarke made sure his cufflinks had pizzazz but didn't sparkle too much and, of course, he wore his spectator shoes.

Clarke received a handwritten note from Michael. To Clarke's disappointment, the Vice President Designate wouldn't be available that evening. Clarke would be able to see him first thing tomorrow afternoon. Clarke began to tingle inside. It was signed, 'By the way'.

"This is all routine." Ms. Jones said, but Clarke knew very well that it wasn't.

The swearing-in would take place on the White House South Lawn at the base of the stairs of the South Portico. Ms. Jones informed Clarke it was the side of the White House with the rounded porch. Clarke nodded. Even though her attitude was condescending, she was trying to be helpful. It would be a beautiful backdrop. Clarke would be in the crowd. He would be so far away that he probably wouldn't even see Michael take the oath of office.

Clarke was lonely. He felt as if he had been hidden for the night. He ate dinner in his room, alone. A Secret Service agent was on guard outside his door. The telephone had been taken away. Clarke tried to settle in with a good book, but finally gave up and turned off the light. He tossed and turned and finally fell asleep. Clarke woke up early and worked out in the gym, almost alone. It was only he and a few Secret Service agents watching him. Clarke just kept lifting weights, wishing there were an aerobics class to take his mind off the men in black. They just stared at him with a blank expression. They wouldn't talk. They wouldn't work the weights. They just stared.

Ms. Jones and her radio kept Clarke to his schedule. Of course, she was wearing another dark suit. "Is that all these people wear?" Clarke thought. He went back to his room, showered, and dressed. Clarke couldn't wait to see Michael. He practiced in the mirror—he wanted a look that said a professional, 'Hello, Mr. Vice President' not, 'Hey dude, I got a mattress strapped to my back.' Clarke laughed. He didn't know what he was laughing at, his joke or the fact he was practicing saying, 'Hello, Mr. Vice President' with shaving cream frosted on his face.

Clarke dressed in everything but his shirt and tie. He wore his trousers and a tank T-shirt, revealing his bulging muscles. He packed his suitcase, then fluffed the room a bit, even though the hotel had a housekeeping staff that would sanitize the room once he left. Clarke wrote a thank you note to the maids, acknowledging them for the royal treatment. Clarke smiled. He really felt like a queen.

A knock on the door let Clarke know that it was finally time to go. He was relieved and quickly finished dressing. He put on his shirt, buttoned it, and tied his tie in a perfect knot. He buttoned his vest and adjusted his ensemble in front of the mirror. He carried his coat. He didn't want it to wrinkle.

Clarke was escorted to yet another shiny black car, the woman who had 'kidnapped' him leading the pack. A bellman followed with the luggage. Clarke was once again sandwiched between Secret Service agents and, again, had to sit in the middle of the back seat. He was going to the White House! Ms. Jones briefed him on what was going to take place, where he would go and where he would stand.

Clarke interrupted her. Her look said that no one had ever done that and he better not do it again, but at this point Clarke didn't care. "If I've been invited to the swearing-in, then why am I going to be in the Blue Room to meet with the Vice President AFTER he's sworn in?"

"This is where the Vice President Select wants you. I don't have the answers, just my orders."

The bitch is back, Clarke thought. "Of course," he said with a bland tone. The drive was silent after that. There was a small TV in the back for security surveillance, but for right now it was tuned to the Network News. Clarke liked Tom Jennings. He was America's favorite news anchor. America trusted Tom Jennings. In the midst of tragedy, he kept the country calm, just by reporting the facts. It was simple. When Tom Jennings talked, people listened. Always. Clarke looked at Ms. Jones then back to the TV. Clarke's mind wondered to politics. It seemed the White House was full of drab old men with ideas that needed airing out like a mothballed closet in a moldy basement.

The country was not represented in the White House unless you had blue hair and a walker. Even though the senior populace was growing with every year, it was the younger generation that was paying for and taking care of them. That younger generation's voice was getting louder and needed to be heard. Family values were a virtue but had lost their patience. The Bible was used for hatred instead of love and for bigotry instead of righteousness. Clarke could only agree the Vice President Designate's day had come.

The vice president would be appointed, not voted for or selected by the people. This was the second time in America's history such an event had occurred and the first time America was happy about it. The Dow Jones hit its highest trading mark in history when the Vice President Designate was announced.

Michael Arthur Kent was the most eligible bachelor in the world and every woman wanted him. He was everything a man wanted to be and a woman wanted to marry. The country was excited about youth, their future and, above all, every matchmaker across the nation wondered about the woman the Vice President Designate would marry.

Clarke looked away from the TV. He would be enjoying the ride if he could see out the windows but he was sitting in the middle of the back seat. He was bored and began remembering all the devilish things he used to do as a child if he had to sit in the middle. Carsickness came to mind. Clarke smiled at Ms. Jones.

Ms. Jones talked into her radio. The main gate opened. Slowly the car drove straight ahead towards the White House and the gate shut behind them. Ms. Jones handed Clarke a pair of sunglasses that looked like the ones she and the men she commanded wore. "Put these on until I tell you to take them off." Clarke removed his own glasses and did as he was told. She handed Clarke a radio. "Hold this like you know how to use it. It's not connected to anything. And for God's sake, don't 'say over and out'."

Clarke felt like he'd been handed a great part in a movie. He took the radio and acted as if he would be nominated for an Academy Award. Clarke did as he was told without even thinking about it. The car stopped and everyone got out. No one said a word. Clarke was escorted through the East Wing of the White House, surrounded by the Secret Service, through crowds of people. The press thought Clarke was just another Secret Service agent and he realized what a great decoy the sunglasses and radio were. The woman in black suddenly became friendly. She had delivered her charge safe and sound. Ms. Jones held out her hand. "The sunglasses please."

Clarke pulled off the sunglasses and placed them in her hand. She put them in her pocket as Clarke put on his real glasses.

"The radio, please." She held out the same hand. Clarke gave her the radio. He was just beginning to have fun with all the toys, but someone said 'bedtime' too soon. Clarke put on his jacket and pulled down his sleeves to expose his cufflinks. As he buttoned his jacket, the light caught the sparkle from his rhinestone cufflinks and a smile from Ms. Jones.

She looked at Clarke, apparently ready to give her next command, when Clarke saw something out of the corner of his eye and almost pushed Ms. Jones out of the way.

Clarke shrieked, "Barney!" Barney ran down the hall. He knelt down and Barney jumped right into his arms. Barney kept licking Clarke and squirming around. "How... what did... where did you come from?" Clarke couldn't make complete sentences. He didn't count to ten, he just babbled on.

"The Vice President Select sent for him as soon as you left the aircraft yesterday." Clarke just looked at her. He petted Barney for his own comfort, not knowing what else to do. "He's already seen the Vice President Select." Ms. Jones said. She was handed a leash, but it wasn't connected to anything or anyone.

Clarke wondered, "When do I get to see the Vice President SELECT?" By this time Clarke was so irritated by hearing her say 'Vice President SELECT' he bobbed his head, thinking the word, 'SELECT'. Clarke hugged Barney. Right then any hairy beast would do, but Clarke wanted Michael. So did every woman in the nation. Clarke took a deep breath and tried to relax. As he looked around the room, he noticed that the carpet was worn and the walls were drab. The White House? Drab? But then he remembered how this administration was.

Clarke and Barney were escorted into the Blue Room—at least that was the color it was supposed to be. Ms. Jones told Clarke where to stand, and not to move. The room was crowded. Clarke noticed two well-dressed women pointing at him and Barney. The women laughed, then turned and talked with a man in a dark business suit. The man smiled and gestured with personality. Obviously not a Secret Service agent, Clarke thought to himself. Clarke stopped looking around the room and did as he was told. He just stood there petting Barney.

A podium decorated with the presidential seal was set up with what looked like hundreds of microphones sprouting from it. A television camera was poised directly in front of the podium. Monitoring equipment was on the other side of the room, attached by a long cord that wouldn't let it get away. Clarke watched the monitor. Michael took the oath of office for

Vice President at precisely twelve o'clock noon, on the South Lawn, as the bells from the National Cathedral struck the hour. The Vice President shook hands with the President.

The Vice President made way. The President went to the podium and promptly resigned his office. With his resignation came the loudest ovation ever heard in his political career. The Vice President calmly positioned himself to take the oath of Office of President of the United States.

Clarke just stared at the monitor. "My God. Michael is the President of the United States." Clarke started to breathe heavily. He broke out in goose bumps and started to shake, but then got hold of himself. He was so proud of Michael. "And he wanted us here," Clarke said to himself. Barney looked up at Clarke then back to the monitor.

Clarke was safely hidden in the Blue Room. No one knew who he was. Just the way it had always been. Clarke felt selfish when he realized he would probably never get to see the man he loved again, at least not until his administration was over. Clarke would settle for just a few moments alone. Then he would fly back to the West Coast and wait. "If it's worth having, it's worth waiting for," Aunt Naomi used to say. Clarke sighed. That old saying wasn't very comforting.

Clarke was in shock. He just stared at the monitor. He seemed to be the only one who hadn't expected it. Michael looked powerful, his right hand extended, his left hand on the Bible his mother carried down the aisle on her wedding day. The Bible was as cherished as the memories of his mother.

After the oath, the announcer said, "Ladies and Gentlemen, the President of the United States, Michael Arthur Kent." Thunderous applause seemed to vibrate the room. The new President gave a rousing speech to more thunderous applause. The President shook hands with the dignitaries seated next to the podium, then he walked to the stairs.

Clarke took a deep breath, then let it out. He rubbed Barney's head, not taking his eyes off the monitor. Clarke couldn't see what was happening from inside, since it was happening right below them.

Ms. Jones leaned toward Clarke and said, "The President is on his way up." Clarke was ready to be handed the sunglasses and radio.

News commentary was heard as the President walked up the stairs of the South Portico. In a low, hushed voice the news anchor continued, "The President's speech of America climbing together is symbolized as the left-handed President walks up the right side of the South Portico of the White House." There was a repeat of the President's speech. "Together America will climb and together we will reach the top. All of us. Together."

Tom Jennings continued as television cameras followed the new President up the stairs. "America is coming back with leadership and justice for all. The nation is excited to watch a young President not ashamed to smoke a pipe or salt his food." The anchorman smiled, "Or tell the world he enjoys a good beer every now and then. Who will be his First Lady? Will she be a fine princess with a pillbox hat? A debutante everyone wished their daughter would be and their son would marry? Will she have long silky hair and wear fine clothes? Will there be babies born in the White House with the nation as the Lamaze coach, yelling, 'push', and arguments of will it be a boy or girl, Democrat or Republican?" There were a lot of stairs for the President to climb and the news anchor irritatingly took advantage of it.

"Not only will the country have leadership again, they will also have something handsome to look at. Everyone can share the President's youth. If you don't have it anymore, you had it once and can remember what being young felt like and Ben Gay was something funny at the drugstore, not a way of life. Young Americans can look at their future and know what they want to be when they grow up." It was there on every channel, being watched in every home across the nation.

Tom Jennings had a political analyst standing by. Since it was taking a lot of air time to show the President walking up the stairs, Tom Jennings introduced his guest, asking him to predict who the President would choose for his Vice President. The political analyst talked like he knew President Kent personally.

"The new President has been very private about all matters. He doesn't even let his closest advisors know anything until the time is right." It was obvious the political analyst had no idea *who* the new President would choose for his vice president.

Tom Jennings went on, "This man, the youngest ever to hold the office of President of the United States, not voted into office by the nation, but appointed to the office of Vice President and is now President, is about to enter the Blue Room." Clarke looked away from the monitor and could see Michael enter the room and walk towards the podium.

Clarke's heart began to pound. He gently held Barney by the collar. Even though the Blue Room was uncomfortably warm, Clarke felt like someone had poured ice down his spine. Michael made eye contact with Clarke and nodded with a twinkle in his eyes. Clarke broke out in a cold sweat.

Clarke couldn't take his eyes off Michael. Even with the chills, Clarke had a hot flash and his glasses steamed up, so he removed his glasses and put them safely away. Michael reached in his breast pocket and took out a piece of paper that had been neatly folded. He spread it out in front of him. Clarke knew there was going to be another speech. He could hear the news anchor from the monitor, "It is speculated the new President will make the announcement of his selection for vice president." Tom Jennings looked down at his monitor, watching history in the making.

There was a pause, so Tom Jennings went on with more jovial ad lib. "Camelot is alive in the Cinderella story. The man in the White House is everyone's American dream."

Hometown local pubs and sports bars were packed with customers. Televisions were tuned not to sports but to live news, as history was in the making. Ironically, several drinks had been named after the former First Lady. The recipe was exotic. Mix everything you've got together and garnish with a straw. Patrons felt patriotic when they drank one and today, with the swearing-in of a new President, they were two for the price of one. "Hey, turn it up," someone yelled as pool players chalked up for another game.

School gymnasiums were crowded as children all across the nation watched the live swearing-in of the vice president. Many news channels were covering the story from America's heartland full of homemade apple pie, secretly bought at the grocery store.

Churches were just as packed. For the first time, large screen TV's had been set up behind the pulpit as parishioners watched history unfold. They personally felt they had flushed out the old administration with their loud political voices. Their prayers had been answered and this was truly a day for 'one nation under God'. The vice president, who was now President, was a churchgoer, though non-denominational. This was a great political move, but he had always attended a community church. He wanted the teachings of God, not the teachings of some group who said, "God loves *us* more than anyone else."

Americans, along with the rest of the world, were glued to their TV sets. A President left in shame with the happiness of the nation at his back and a new President climbing to the top. Promise and hope graced the screen. The world felt safer and America was ready to become a great nation once again.

"This is a great day." Tom Jennings continued. "And all of this with the swearing-in of one incredible man we all want to follow." News anchors were just making idle chitchat, waiting for the new President to speak once again.

"Now, children, be quiet," school principals hushed. Customers in local bars were motionless. People at home were shushing at each other as the handsome man who just took office was about to speak. Preachers were finally quiet, church organs silent.

Tom Jennings continued with a blow-by-blow account, repeating himself. "The President has just entered through the French doors of the Blue Room, where it is speculated he will announce his selection for vice president. The President will speak once everyone following him has entered the Blue Room." A few select people were invited to follow the President but were several stairs behind him.

There was much speculation as to whom the President would select. Everyone was waiting to hear who that would be with great anticipation. Congress would go into an emergency session to approve, or disapprove, his choice. The President already knew they would approve this one.

Clarke was to the side and far right of the President. The Blue Room was crowded with more people, but there was plenty of room for Clarke and Barney. No one seemed to be crowded next to them. Clarke was so proud of Michael. Barney stood close to Clarke and seemed to feel the moment, not trying to wiggle away or get petted by hands across the room. A big red light came on over the television camera. A man directing the technical crew pointed to the President.

"My fellow Americans, it's time we get down to business and make our country the great nation we want it to be. And we will. Together." There was applause. "I would like to make the announcement for my selection for vice president. But before I do, I would like to make a very special, personal announcement." There was a pause. Then the President smiled. "Many questions have been asked as to who is going to be your First Lady. At this time, I would like to thank all of those who wrote in requesting the position." Laughter echoed around the room.

The President continued, "As my first act as your President, I would like to introduce you to my spouse." There was such fanfare. Everyone imagined they heard a drum roll as they looked around the room for a lady who could measure up. The President reached out his hand, "Ladies and gentleman, my husband, and your FIRST GENTLEMAN, Clarke."

A hush slammed into the nation.

School assemblies stilled. Customers in local bars were dumbfounded. Churches stunned. News anchors were unprofessionally speechless. The camera zeroed in on Clarke. He looked like a deer staring in the headlights of a mountain traveler. His eyes bulged. His mouth dropped. He just stared into the camera. It was obvious that Clarke was more shocked then anyone else in the world.

His dazed look was seen all across America. The world was quiet, numbed with the news. America stood speechless, staring at Clarke staring back at them. Barney just sat there wagging his tail. Ms. Jones politely pushed Clarke back into reality. Clarke walked to the President's side as Barney trotted along.

Without so much as a blink the new President continued with his choice for vice president. "Ladies and gentleman, Olivia Longley." Clarke smiled as the President motioned for her. Without being politely pushed, she proudly walked towards the podium and stood on the other side of the President.

History was being made with every American watching. The President appointed the first female vice president, a retired Army General, an African-American woman who was adored by millions. Congress would approve her hands down. She had a military career 'and could shoot with the best of them' is how the press described her. Her figure said she was proud to be a woman and that she also enjoyed a candy bar every now and then. She had never been married and raised her only child alone, a son now in the ballet. Someday she hoped to be a grandmother.

She adored Clarke and the President. She protected them with every word. Not only was she a political advisor, she was also the President and Clarke's long-time dear friend. She always knew Michael would someday come to power. She was one of the few people who knew about the President's lifestyle and respected his privacy. To Clarke, she was divine.

The President's speech was inappropriately interrupted when he was suddenly called to the Oval Office by the Joint Chiefs-of-Staff. Clarke saw the look on Michael's face. It was a look of power and retaliation. Clarke almost felt sorry for the person who gave the order to interrupt the President's speech. President Michael Arthur Kent politely excused himself. There was a White House staff member on every corner to escort him. Clarke was at the President's side, with the Vice President Select following a step behind them. Barney felt at home, calmly trotting along. Clarke had no idea where they were being led and tried to make a mental note of where they were, so he could get back.

They walked briskly down a wide staircase to the Ground Floor Hall, then out a set of French doors, along a pillared colonnade, past the Rose Garden, where Barney decided to enjoy a bush. A Secret Service agent said he'd take care of Barney. Clarke noticed it was the same man who had been playing ball with Barney when Clarke left his house in Washington, the state.

It was also the same man who walked Barney down the White House hallway when Clarke first saw Barney in Washington, the city. Barney had a new friend. Clarke knew Barney was safe and caught up to the President who was ready to go through another set of French doors to the Oval Office. Network news went back to Tom Jennings in New York.

"What a surprise." Tom Jennings said. He looked stunned, just like the rest of the nation. The political adviser said, "WOW! I'm shocked." His look said it all.

"The whole world is shocked," Tom Jennings said with an approving smile.

33

"THE FIRST MAN TO BE FIRST LADY?" He repeated himself like he couldn't believe what he had just said. "THE FIRST MAN TO BE FIRST LADY. The President is gay?" His attitude said *how could this be?* He went on with fact about the President's masculinity. "He played football for the Navy. My niece wants to marry the guy." It was all ad-lib shock speaking. Truth was the cornerstone and the President was building the nation.

"What do you make of this?" Tom Jennings asked the political adviser sitting next to him.

"The President would have had my vote, gay or straight. I for one feel he will bring this country back and we will climb together, just as he said."

"No," Tom Jennings said, "The choice for vice president."

"Oh. She's the perfect choice and no one ever thought of her. The President is gay? We've never had a gay President."

"How do you know?" Tom Jennings asked. The political analyst was stumped; he didn't know. How did anyone know? No one did. President Michael Arthur Kent was the first President in history to be out of the closet, openly gay and proudly introduced Clarke as the nation's First Gentleman. Tom Jennings looked into the camera. "The President has just been called away to the Oval office after introducing his husband, Clarke, the First Gentleman, who is the FIRST MAN to be First Lady."

Clarke was speechless. He didn't say a word to Michael. The French doors were opened to the Oval Office by gloved White House staff. Michael asked for Clarke to excuse him. He had that look that Clarke knew meant 'later.' When the President had the doors to the Oval Office shut behind him and his Vice President Select, television cameras took the viewers to Andrews Air Force Base to watch the old administration leave. Most networks used that time to go to a commercial.

For a brief moment, Clarke stared at the closed door and thought about what just happened. His husband was the President of the United States, and that made him the First Lady. The First MAN to be First Lady. "No," Clarke corrected himself, "that makes me the First Gentleman."

Out of the corner of his eye, Clarke could see a television camera poised in front of a reporter who was talking into a microphone. "The President has just entered the Oval Office after introducing the world to Clarke, the First Man to be First Lady." She shook her head as she announced, "American History is being made here today."

Clarke counted to ten. The only American History Clarke could remember was Bess Truman doing her White House bedroom in plum and Mrs. Roosevelt wearing a hard hat. Clarke hated plums and could see Mrs. Roosevelt singing with the Village People. Clarke swallowed his panic. He looked over at the man who had escorted them to the Oval Office. With a commanding smile Clarke asked, "Where is my office?"

The man looked Clarke up one side then down the other. In a condescending tone with a stereotypical flip of the wrist said, "The First Lady doesn't have an office in this wing."

With a deep, authoritative voice Clarke growled, "He does now." In one condescending comment from a staff member, Clarke realized how Nancy Reagan earned the title of Dragon Lady. Clarke imagined himself exhaling fire as his nostrils flared. Clarke stood up straight. He puffed out his chest. Clarke's smile deflated as he took a deep breath.

Almost terrified, the man quickly ushered Clarke into a briefing room which another staff member respectfully referred to as the Roosevelt Room. Several people followed Clarke, taking their assigned seats. Clarke looked around the room. He was the only one who was still standing. Everyone else was seated, waiting for instructions from the new First Lady, who just happened to be a man. Clarke looked around the room in disbelief. He was on stage and someone just threw him a candelabrum. Clarke counted to ten as he removed his jacket. A White House usher reached for it and Clarke handed it to him with a thank you, then took his seat.

In the Oval Office, all the Joint Chiefs-of-Staff were already seated, waiting to advise the President about what actions they would be taking. Threats had been coming in from the Middle East for some time and now attack was imminent. The world wanted peace and looked to the United States for hope.

The President would do what was right. He listened to what the military leaders had to say, then calmly gave them their orders. The Oval Office was silent as the President spoke. Moments ago, he was the man you most admired and wanted your daughter to marry. He was still the man you most admired.

Back in the Roosevelt Room, Ms. Jones handed Clarke a stack of folders. Each was stamped, TOP SECRET, WHITE HOUSE. These were White House files, one on each person in the room. In proper order, the Chief of Protocol's file was always on top. The next file was on another woman, rather friendly with her. Clarke had seen them in the Blue Room, talking and pointing, thinking they were blending in and not being seen. Clarke could see right through them. Barney wasn't the only one who could sniff out a bitch. Separating these two files from the rest was a piece of blank letterhead. It was the White House stationery. At first glance it looked like a thoughtful gesture. A sample of what all correspondence that left the house would be printed on. Clarke picked up on the subliminal message Ms. Jones was giving to him on these two women. She was there to serve and, above all, to protect. She was going to protect Clarke.

Clarke put his glasses on. As he was introduced to the people around the room, he opened a folder and could review all the facts about them at a glance. Clarke didn't have X-ray vision, but he could read. He didn't mention what was in the folder or make conversation from it. He was interested only in what the staff had to say, who was what, when, and where. In depth, the files would tell him how each person in the room got where they were today.

While looking through the folders, Clarke immediately sent for Ms. Deverough. She was Clarke's modeling coach and dearest friend, who just happened to be the best kept secret on the socialite front. Clarke looked at Ms. Jones. "She will need a White House clearance." The woman nodded. Clarke called for the White House steward, who introduced himself as the White House Chief Usher. Clarke nodded a "Pleased to meet you."

"I understand that you and the White House staff are at the pleasure of the President. Isn't that correct?"

The Chief Usher nodded in agreement.

"Very well." Clarke continued with sleeping arrangements for the President and himself. "The President will sleep in the Lincoln Bedroom."

The Chief Usher looked at Clarke, "And for you, sir?"

"I am the President's pleasure. I sleep with the President." Clarke looked at him. The Chief Usher gave a nod of understanding. There were giggles from a few members of the staff. Clarke slowly looked around the room. "What goes on between the President and me behind closed doors is our business. Period."

Clarke was very matter-of-fact. He made eye contact with the entire room. "I am the spouse of the President. The only difference between any other First Lady and me is that I am the First *Gentleman*. I DEMAND the very same respect any woman received while in the position of First *Lady*."

Clarke repeated himself as it all started to sink in. "I am not the First Man To Be First Lady, I am the FIRST GENTLEMAN, married to Michael Arthur Kent, the President of the United States of America." Clarke's voice grew louder and deeper. "Ladies and Gentlemen, savoir-faire has returned to the White House." There was thunderous applause. That caught Clarke off guard but, surprisingly, gave him the boost he needed to handle his new position.

Clarke turned back to the Chief Usher. "I need to see what is scheduled for the White House and all documentation covering it, from menus to table linens to china patterns to what we do with the empties."

"Many arrangements have already been made," the Chief Usher looked at a woman sitting across the room. Then he looked back at Clarke with an attitude designed to put Clarke in his place. "Arrangements have been finalized."

"Arrangements are not finalized until 'I' finalize them." Clarke's attitude put the entire room in its place. "I will see all menus, guest lists, drink orders, table settings, and floral arrangement ideas." Clarke stressed 'ideas'. "I will meet with the culinary staff in the morning, along with the in-house maintenance staff. You will be in attendance at all meetings, isn't that correct." It wasn't a question. The Chief Usher nodded. Clarke knew exactly what he was talking about and clearly knew how to be a proper First Lady.

Clarke continued with momentum. "The apartment where the President WAS living will be packed up and delivered to the White House. He does not live there any more." Clarke was making a list as he talked. "The President enjoys chopping firewood. He does this as a hobby and to relieve his tension." Clarke looked at the Chief Usher. "I would like to have logs sent in for the President. I believe the pits where former President George Bush used to pitch horseshoes are still on the grounds." Again, it wasn't a question. The Chief Usher nodded.

"That will be the perfect place for the President to chop. We will also need a few axes. Please make sure they are made in America." As Clarke continued, items were written down and tablet pages turned so quickly that the White House was falling in order with a stroke of a pen. Clarke was handed a ledger with times the White House was open for tours, what, and whom to expect.

A woman stood. She walked towards Clarke. Ms. Jones was ready to pounce. "A man cannot handle this position." She shook her head in a condescending wiggle. "This is a mockery of everything this country stands for. I will not be a part of it."

"Then I trust I will have your resignation within the hour," Clarke said.

"*You* can't fire me." She looked down at Clarke as if he were something she should scrape off her shoe.

"No, but I can," the President said as he came into the room. Everyone stood at attention like a squadron of military soldiers. Everyone but Clarke.

An eerie silence fell over the room. Clarke looked over at the Secret Service woman who was clearly waiting for her first official order from the new President. The President said to Ms. Jones, "See to it that she is escorted off the grounds and her White House clearance is taken away. Immediately. If she is seen on the grounds for so much as a White House tour, she is to be arrested." The President motioned for everyone to sit down. The room did as it was told.

The ex-Chief of Protocol didn't put up a fight when Ms. Jones escorted her out. She knew the Secret Service were trained to take anyone down who needed it, and she also knew that Ms. Jones would love the chance to perform for the new First Couple. The woman in custody glared at Clarke.

The Secret Service woman tightened her grip as she led her away. Ms. Jones ripped the ID badge off the woman's dress with relish and tossed it to a man holding a radio. His gun was in full view. The ex-Chief of Protocol's desk had already been cleaned out. A Secret Service man was holding a box of her personal items and her purse dangled off his wrist. The ex-Chief of Protocol was so hot Clarke thought her cosmetic surgery would melt.

She turned and yelled at Clarke, "You will burn in hell for this."

It was a tense moment. Clarke turned back to the room and looked down at the stack of folders. He was embarrassed by such an ugly incident. Then, with an apologetic look at the people around the room, said, "At least I'll know someone there." Everyone burst into uncontrollable laughter.

Many in the room would have jumped for joy. They had always been afraid of this woman. She had the pull to make or break an administration. She had run the White House while the former First Lady abused her substances. Her escort was always the ex-Secretary of Defense. He resigned the position when Congress did not select him to be appointed vice president. Now she could join him in the unemployment line.

"She is the Chief of Protocol and will make a mess," someone said boldly.

"WAS the Chief of Protocol," the President reminded them. "And if she makes a mess, then we will clean it up." We have 1,000 days left of this administration and I will not tolerate bigotry or hatred within my staff. And that goes for race, religion, sex, or SEXUAL ORIENTATION. Have I made myself clear?" Everyone around the room nodded.

The President looked at Clarke and almost swallowed him with his eyes. "I came to see if you needed any help, but I guess I should have stayed in my office." The President excused himself as everyone again sprang to attention. Everyone but Clarke. The President walked out the way he walked in. Clarke watched him walk away and remarked how uncomfortably warm the room was. He regained his composure as everyone took their seats.

"Who is my speechwriter?" Clarke continued. He knew that all the First Ladies had speechwriters. His favorite author of all time was Liz Carpenter, Lady Bird Johnson's speechwriter.

"I am." A well-dressed woman stood, taking control of the room. Clarke could see right through her. She was transparent as tape and just as sticky.

Clarke invited her to sit back down and said, "I would like to meet with you, and explore with you, my ideas along with my style of speaking. I can write my own speeches, but I will not give the press any ammunition to destroy this administration. That's where your expertise comes in. I have a voice that will be heard upon request."

Clarke knew his speech was irritating this woman, so he went on. "I would like a speech that correctly says what I have to say. I want the world to know me, not what the stereotypes say I should be, but who 'I' am. To sum it all up, I would like your expertise in catching the embarrassing moment before it happens." She agreed with a nod. Clarke noticed that this woman was shallow. She was a snake, coiled, ready to strike.

Clarke looked around the room. "This administration is not about being gay. It's about what is right for the nation and the world. My husband is the President of the United States. His job is to take care of the country. My job is to take care of my husband the President of the United States." Clarke paused with that comment. He noticed that Ms. Jones was back from escorting her prisoner off the grounds. "We've been sitting here for some time. Why don't we take a fifteen-minute break? Is that OK with everyone?" Everyone politely agreed as they rose from their seats.

Clarke and the woman who would be his speechwriter walked towards each other. Clarke extended his hand, personally introducing himself. She followed his lead. They talked idle getting-to-know-you chitchat. She didn't like Clarke. Clarke sensed that from her laughter and finger pointing when he and Barney were escorted into the Blue Room.

Her demeanor was sappy sweet. Fake. President Truman said, "If you want a friend in Washington, you get a dog." Clarke and the President had Barney. "Thank you for the opportunity to work so closely with you," the woman chirped. She looked away; her voice dropping to a whisper, "I lost my brother to AIDS."

Clarke couldn't believe she was using that one on him. AIDS is not a homosexual disease, but if you wanted to hit a gay man right where it counts, bringing up AIDS was the way to do it. She probably thought it would give her the edge she needed. "My brother had an alternative lifestyle. I could never accept it. I

never got a chance to talk with him, to say I was sorry. He died."
She paused. Clarke noticed she was trying hard TO cry. She went
on, "He died alone. I can never forgive myself." Her voice
cracked.

Clarke knew what she was doing. In past administrations
if you wanted a name, you yelled sexual harassment. She was
going to use Clarke's vulnerability, his empathy and willingness
to comfort someone emotionally hurting. She would misconstrue
Clarke to the press and make him out to be a sexually abusing
man and make a laughingstock out of the administration.

As she looked to Clarke for sympathy, he turned and
looked at the Secret Service woman. "Ms. Jones, I want this
woman out of here. Now." Clarke was professional, to the point
and loud. When those who had left the room heard Clarke, they
scurried back in and took their seats. Clarke walked back to his
chair and sat down. "See to it her White House clearance is taken
away."

The room went morbidly silent. The woman just looked
at Clarke. Ms. Jones grabbed her and hauled her away. Clarke
had read her file. She was an only child. The only family she had
left was an uncle in a nursing home, out of her way, somewhere
in upstate New York.

Clarke looked about the room, again making eye contact
with each person there, making each of them feel important, but
not more important than what he had to say. "I will say it once
again, and for the last time. I will not tolerate bigotry on my staff.
If anyone has a problem with the President and me being in love
with each other, please leave. If I am treated like this again by
any one of you, I will see to it you will never work in the United
States Government again. Have I made myself clear?" Clarke
looked at each person. They looked back at him with a nod. If
anyone had needed a potty break, it was too late. Clarke scared
the excrement right out of them.

"Now," Clarke smiled, bringing the room back to a
comfortable level, where people could smile back. "I will ask the
question again. Who is my speechwriter?" No hands went up.
There was no one there who had ever written a speech for the
First Lady.

Clarke noticed there was a woman who hadn't spoken
but was very attentively listening to Clarke's every word. Clarke

noticed her hidden grin when the Chief of Protocol was taken out, then her broad smile when the next woman followed in the same manner. It was a smile of relief. This woman was genuine. She dressed professionally on a budget and was concerned more with her job than her hairdo.

Clarke asked her to introduce herself. She was very nervous. Not scared—nervous. "I would be interested in hearing your credentials." Clarke said. The people in the room sat on the edge of their seats.

She introduced herself as Daffney Velaflor. She had a journalism degree and a graduate degree in political science. She had been published on a small scale in various newspapers and occasional magazines, but didn't feel qualified to be the speechwriter for a First Lady. Clarke promoted her on the spot.

As the meeting went on, more arrangements were made. Appointments were penciled in, then set in stone. It seemed like a dark cloud was passing from over the White House. All the people in the room wanted to make a difference, but still needed that potty break more than ever.

In the Oval Office, the President was briefed on the first news story about the new President. "The President calls for the Joint Chiefs-of-Staff." The world knew the Middle East was at it again. In his first speech as President, Michael said, "This administration will not do what is right for politics but what is right for the United States of America and the world." The country was leery. The President was a man of his word but the United States had met with slogans of "read my lips". They'd rather sink ships. This President wasn't interested in being elected to office. If he didn't say that out loud, introducing Clarke to the world certainly did.

The President ordered deployment of troops and the Navy's fleet was sent to the Persian Gulf. The military was on stand-by and the draft was ready to be re-activated if necessary. The President stunned the Joint Chiefs-of-Staff when he ordered women to sign up for the draft, the same as men.

Congress would have to debate if women could be in combat, but the draft was another story. Women were as able as men and the facilities within the Armed Forces had been designed to handle just as many women recruits. If women couldn't go to battle, they could be behind the lines serving their country.

When that hit the airwaves, America almost forgot about the First Man To Be First Lady. The President's popularity surprisingly soared to new heights. News commentators publicly said, "It's about time." Women were the first to say, "Right on!"

The only opposition came from the Commandant of the Marines. The President made it very clear. "If this is against your policy, then I will take your resignation. I am your Commander-in-Chief and this is my policy. You will carry out my orders and THAT is a direct order." The Marine Commandant resigned. President Kent called for the Secret Serviced to remove the ex-Marine Commandant.

When the doors shut behind them, the President stood. Like a drill sergeant with an attitude, he called the men comfortably sitting around the room to the military position of attention. Immediately the men sprang to their feet. They stood motionless as if made of stone. "I am giving you all a direct Presidential Order: under no circumstances do any of you hold enough rank to interrupt me while I am speaking to the people of the United States." He looked at each man standing before him. "Have I made myself clear?" No one in the room moved. The President smiled. Of course, they couldn't move. The military men were at the position of attention. President Kent took his seat, then said, "At ease. Take your seats." The men took their seats but remained silent, waiting for their Commander-In-Chief to give his next order.

The President appointed a new Marine Commandant. The best person for the job was a woman. She was an American of Asian descent and perfect for the roughest position the military could offer. For the first time in the history of the United States Marine Corps, a woman was Commandant.

Clarke's meeting had been adjourned. His staff had been excused and had been escorted off the grounds. Routine. The Chief Usher had already briefed the White House staff; Clarke was the First *Gentleman*. The title would be shown the same respect as any woman who held the title of First *Lady*. Period.

The Chief Usher escorted Clarke to the second floor of the White House, the First Couple's private quarters. It was huge, but very worn. Barney was already there, sitting with the same

Secret Service man, chewing on a tennis ball he found while he was snooping around the grounds. The Secret Service man petted Barney good-bye, then excused himself.

Clarke could see the private quarter's day had come and gone. The furniture was worn, the colors faded. It had been covered up pretty well, but it needed some tender loving care and someone to call it home. The Chief Usher showed Clarke how he could ring for the White House staff. There were concealed buttons only noticeable once they had been pointed out.

Clarke's luggage had been placed in the Lincoln Bedroom. Wardrobe boxes filled with the President's clothes had been delivered from Michael's old apartment. Clarke couldn't believe it. He had just asked for the President's belongings to be sent over, and there they were.

Clarke started to move the luggage to a vacant bedroom. The Chief Usher waved him off, saying "Sir, you have a staff for this and your staff is at your pleasure." They smiled at one another. "While this is taken care of, may we continue our tour?"

As they walked out of the room, Clarke glanced back at the luggage and all the boxes. They went first to their private kitchen. It was big. There were four wall ovens, two dishwashers and a lot of counter space.

Their tour continued to the third floor. It needed painting. It had taken a lot abuse but then, abuse was the motto of the last administration. The laundry facilities looked like an upscale dry cleaner on Fifth Avenue. Clarke asked for instructions on how to use the equipment.

Clarke was informed which staff members took care of that, who cleaned the quarters, and did the dishes. Clarke couldn't believe it. There was staff to do everything. Clarke was a little bewildered. There was even a staff member to escort Barney to his private bush. "That really isn't necessary," Clarke said as they made their way back down to the second floor. Clarke looked for Barney. The Chief Usher informed Clarke the Secret Service man had taken Barney for another walk. Clarke was amazed.

"We are at the pleasure of the First Couple." The Chief Usher was proving his point. "What can we do to make your first night special?" The man really wanted to be of service.

Clarke thought about it for a moment. "Yes. A fire in the fireplace." Clarke nervously laughed. "Of course, where else would it be?" The Chief Usher didn't laugh at Clarke's joke. Clarke was a little embarrassed. It all started to sink in, again. Clarke's husband was the President of the United States and that meant that Clarke was the First Gentleman. He was feeling overwhelmed. He was ready to run far away, and fast. But then he remembered Michael. They would finally be together. "If I could only see him," Clarke thought.

"Sir?" The Chief Usher was trying to get Clarke's attention. Clarke apologized for his rudeness. He wasn't comfortable giving orders. Clarke usually did things himself. He did it ALL himself. Clarke changed his tone. "This is a special night. A crackling fire and champagne. The President hasn't eaten all day and the kitchen isn't well stocked."

"I can take care of that, Sir. What would be the First Couple's pleasure?"

"At this point, whatever you have."

"This is the White House, Sir. We have whatever you would enjoy." The Chief Usher was just trying to get an idea of what the President and Clarke would like for dinner.

"The President will be really hungry." The man waited for Clarke. "A hearty dinner for two. I will ring for service when we are ready." Clarke was falling right into place. Just what the White House staff needed. What they weren't used to was a sincere 'please' and 'thank you.' Clarke walked over to the Lincoln Bedroom and opened the door. He looked lost. He had opened the door to the Queen's Bedroom by mistake.

The Chief Usher smiled and said a very sincere, "Welcome home," as he opened the door to the Lincoln Bedroom.

Clarke blushed as he laughed a "thank you." He walked into the room and the doors were quietly shut behind him. A fire was already dancing in the fireplace. Of course, where else would it be? He laughed and looked from side to side. The boxes had been removed and relocated in a bedroom down the hall. Two fluffy bathrobes had been placed at the foot of the bed.

There was an inlaid wooden box on the mantel. He opened it and discovered it held stick matches. Clarke took a match and lit the candelabra that proudly stood on each end of the mantel. Clarke hadn't yet been alone with the man he loved but he had seen him and he took his breath away.

"The President is in quarters," boomed a male voice.

Clarke could feel his heart beating heavily. He turned around and there was Michael. The doors were shut behind him. Clarke couldn't move. The President stared at him. Clarke couldn't control himself any longer and ran into Michael's open arms. The President grabbed him and held him tight. Clarke hugged back tighter. It was a grip that should have broken the two men in half.

"My God, Clarke," was all the President could say. Then they kissed passionately. Together they were one. Clarke thought he would never breathe normally again. The President pulled Clarke away and just looked at him. Clarke gazed into his eyes. "Clarke, I am so sorry to 'out' you like that, but I can't do this without you." He paused, "Please don't leave me."

Clarke was stunned. Michael was worried about outing him? Begging Clarke not to leave? The President of the United States, whose first act as President was to tell the whole world he was married to a man? Married to Clarke.

"Darling, I am your husband. My place is at your side. I will never leave you." The look on Clarke's face held deeper promises. "I will do whatever you want me to do. I'll go wherever you want me to go."

Michael interrupted Clarke, pulling him closer. He caressed the back of his head, comforting them both. "Clarke, just be the man I married and do what you've always done. I need you." Clarke pulled himself away. He smiled an 'I'm all yours' kind of smile. Michael embraced him tightly and they kissed again. The President sat down on the Lincoln bed. He loosened his tie, then removed it. Clarke reached for the tie, rolling it so it wouldn't wrinkle.

"Shall I ring for dinner?" Clarke asked, proud of himself for remembering where the buttons were to call the staff.

"No." The President was hungry for passion and starving for Clarke. He pulled Clarke down on top of him, then rolled him over. They made love like it was created only for the two of them. Passion exploded like a shaken soda pop can and ran over the top like an uncorked bottle of champagne. They lay there, breathing heavily, paralyzed by their consumed desire.

In the stillness the fire danced. The glow from the candelabra embraced the darkness. Clarke couldn't remember where he was. He looked over at the man he loved, then remembered: he was in heaven. The President was asleep. Clarke knew that when Michael woke up, he would be hungry. Clarke would fulfill his appetite many times over, but first they would have to eat.

Clarke carefully got out of bed. He took one of the fluffy bathrobes left by the staff, pulled it around him and tied a neat knot. He picked up the clothes they'd scattered around the room. He neatly folded them and laid them over a chair, then pushed the button the Chief Usher had shown him.

A quiet knock sounded at the door. Clarke opened the door to a uniformed man pushing a cart. Clarke put a finger towards his lips and motioned that the President was still asleep. The sheets were pulled up only to his waist exposing a furry, well-built, powerful man with a childish grin on his face. The room smelled of sweat and fresh sex. Clarke was apologizing to no one. The uniformed man looked at Clarke with a subservient smile.

"Thank you. I'll take it from here," Clarke whispered. The man nodded and shut the doors behind him, never turning his back on Clarke.

The smell of good food woke Michael. His eyes followed Clarke as he wheeled the cart near the fireplace and set chairs at each end of it. It was a drop-leaf cart that unfolded to a beautiful round table. Clarke rearranged the dishes and then went to his suitcase and pulled out the Tupperware container full of his home-baked chocolate chip cookies, attractively arranging them on an extra plate. The wine had been opened and set to breathe. They hadn't even had champagne, Clarke thought to himself.

Clarke smelled the fresh flowers as he remarked softly how beautiful they were. Michael loved to watch Clarke. Clarke could make a TV dinner elegant. And here they were in the White House, with Clarke putting his finishing touches on dinner and making it grand.

Clarke had his back to the President, but knew he was being watched. "Darling," Clarke said, pausing, then looking at the President and gesturing with his hands, he announced, "Dinner is served." Clarke wasn't sure what was for dinner but it smelled great. He peeked under the silver dome. It looked great. The President got out of bed and tied his fluffy bathrobe as he walked towards Clarke. There was a patch over the right chest. It was the Presidential Seal. Michael gently caressed Clarke, who almost purred. Then he motioned for Michael to sit down.

"Our first dinner as President and First Gentleman," Michael said. Clarke removed the silver domes and placed them under the table as he sat down. This was all a dream—a grand, never-forget-it-as-long-as-you-live kind of dream. Suddenly Clarke woke up. He looked at his plate. His dinner had been served on the Lincoln China. He was sitting across from the most powerful man in the world and Clarke was his First Gentleman.

The President poured the wine. He lifted his glass. Clarke followed. "To the First Couple." Clarke chimed in, "To the First Couple." Their glasses clinked in exclamation.

The next morning came early. Even with lack of sleep, surprisingly, the President and Clarke felt refreshed. Barney was curled up in front of the fireplace still chewing on his tennis ball. The sun barely poked its first light when the President dressed in his suit trousers and dress shirt. He would finish dressing after breakfast. Clarke tied the President's tie and placed it over the wooden hanger holding Michael's suit jacket.

The staff prepared a wonderful breakfast for the First Couple. When the President finished, he asked if there were any more cookies left. Clarke gave him the bad news: "They're all gone", but promised in the same breath that he would bake some more. The President left the table with anticipation and went back to the Lincoln Bedroom. After he finished dressing, Clarke walked him to the stairs and watched him walk down. Michael turned and smiled at Clarke before he disappeared off the landing.

Clarke took a deep breath and let it out then turned and walked back to the Lincoln Bedroom. To the left of the bed was a door that opened to a hallway leading to a dressing room and bathroom. Clarke showered. He realized he didn't have a complete wardrobe for such a position and wondered where the nearest J.C. Penney was.

The staff cleaned the Lincoln Bedroom. Fresh candles were placed in the candelabra. Clarke was going to unpack, but his suitcases were already empty. He went looking for his clothes. The bedroom the First Lady traditionally used had a huge walk-in closet. All of Clarke's clothes were freshly pressed and hung in order. The small amount of clothes made the closet look a lot bigger. Clarke didn't dress in a traditional suit but rather in a silk vest and tie. He looked at his watch. He was right on time. He had several meetings scheduled and the first one was with the Chief Usher.

He came down the hallway with a pad and pen in hand. The Chief Usher was waiting with his own pad and pen poised, ready. They sat in front of a big arched window in a room Clarke learned was the West Sitting Hall. He still marveled at how bad everything looked. The State Rooms looked okay but, as a whole, the White House needed help.

As Clarke and the Chief Usher talked in the private quarters, Ms. Jones appeared with a summons from the President. Clarke's presence was requested in the Rose Garden immediately. Clarke excused himself, like a fine gentleman. He wasn't worried or concerned, just did as requested.

The new vice president had been appointed, hands down. Congress had been given so many bills to pass, the easiest thing to do was to have the Vice President appointed. She would be sworn into office with a simple ceremony in the Rose Garden. The President didn't take the oath of office at the Capitol; neither would the Vice President. There were no military bands, no high rise bleachers, and no mouth-dropping surprises. Television cameras were in place. The Vice President's son was in attendance. Tears streamed down his face as he watched his mother raise her right hand. She proudly took the oath of Office of Vice President. "Ladies and Gentlemen, the Vice President of the United States." Amidst the applause, she received a handshake from the President.

Clarke offered her his congratulations with a handshake along with several other political people in attendance. She hugged her son. A Secret Service agent escorted him to the Protocol Office. The President and his Vice President walked back to the Oval Office. Clarke went back in the White House. He had a lot of work to do. The President was certainly a handful.

Only Twenty Four Hours

As Clarke walked down the Grand Hall of the White House, he thought about what was happening. Twenty-four hours had passed and America still had a gay President whose husband was the First Gentleman. That very morning, Clarke had watched the President give his first televised speech, sitting behind his desk in the Oval Office, complete with pictures of Clarke and Barney proudly displayed on a credenza behind him.

The President spoke of bills already sent to Congress. He urged pressure from the American people at home. Elected politicians were going to answer for what they promised— Congress would finally do their job "for the people." The President had thought of everything in order to get his way. Local political parties had agreed to televise postal and e-mail addresses as well as toll-free telephone and fax numbers of that state's congressional members. The people at home would know exactly whom to call and whom to write. There were absolutely no excuses, right down to a postage stamp. If you didn't have a stamp, local post offices would give it to you and bill the elected official.

Republicans had always been known as the friends of big business and this President was no exception. He proposed the biggest tax cut in history to corporations that offered daycare to their employees as a benefit and an education grant to those employees who couldn't afford it.

For those not working for a big business, low-interest education loans were available. Not only were loans offered for a higher education, but also included clearing many of the student's financial liabilities. This way, the students could focus on the classroom and not on their rising debt. The check was to be written to the establishment that had lent the money, not to the person borrowing it. This money was to clear debts. Period.

Once the credit card or bank loan was cleared, it remained on the person's credit report; no other loans or credit cards could be obtained until the government low-interest loan was paid off. This was made very clear to anyone applying for the loan. A large fine was levied on both the borrower and the lender if the agreement was violated. It was clearly stipulated on every contract and was announced on every credit report.

The President wanted every American to have medical benefits. He would never give up on that one. The President knew it would be a bitter pill to swallow, but the first change in healthcare would be with the medical insurance companies. He would sign into law a new policy that any insurance company accepting federal funds at any level must comply with. Fourteen percent of all money brought in to an insurance company had to go to medical research.

The insurance company could use the money for research of their choice under two conditions: It had to be medical research and something their insured had submitted claims for. Americans citizens didn't need a spoonful of sugar to help that medicine go down. Why insurance companies would pay for a pregnancy and the delivery of a newborn, but not for birth control pills was mind-boggling. Another law ready to be signed by the President made birth control pills completely covered. Insurance companies would save millions.

Welfare reform brought the biggest applause from Americans since John F. Kennedy said "Ask not what your country can do for you, but what you can do for your country." The President signed into law, "What you will do for your country." Welfare reform hit an all new high. 'YOU WORK, YOU GET PAID' was the name of the bill. Those on welfare had to perform community service in order to receive a check.

For those who couldn't work but could read, they could earn their checks by reading to children in daycare or to the elderly in nursing homes or to shut-ins. If people felt they couldn't work because of health reasons, doctors who were providing services in lieu of paying back their student loans gave them a complete physical, free of charge.

If you didn't work, you were in school getting an education, with at least a "C" average and 97 percent attendance rate. If not, you were cleaning up America the beautiful by picking up trash or painting over graffiti. For the first time since President Johnson activated welfare, people were running to the want ads looking for work.

If you were 18 years or older, to be entitled to welfare, unemployment, Social Security, food stamps, student loans, or any other government subsidy, you had to be a registered voter. It had never been so easy to become a registered voter. People could just stop at any government agency, gas station, or convenience store and fill out a simple form a fifth grader could understand. If you couldn't understand that, someone working for a welfare check was there to assist.

Together you could fill out the form, then drop the completed form into a mailbox, or simply leave the form where you picked it up. If you called to complain to a federal or state agency that your benefits had been denied, the form was sent to you so you could register to vote. You send it back—you go to work—you get what you're entitled to. Simple.

There was an even better tax cut for the elderly who relied solely on Social Security. So many elderly had such big pensions that they were wealthy, yet complaining about everything while doing nothing. A tax cut for elderly citizens who lived only on their monthly Social Security checks irritated those who were elderly and wealthy. They would complain to their elected official, which was exactly what the President had in mind.

The President was family-oriented, not from the viewpoint of being a parent, but from being a child without parents. He often wondered which was harder—to have children or be a child without parents. It wasn't a question that needed to be answered—it was a question that never should be asked in America.

The President had a bill ready for Congress, a tax cut for families with children up to the age of 18, or 23 if the child was in some sort of higher education. It was obvious that education at any age was very important to the President. He was well aware of how expensive an education was regardless of whether it was public school, community college, or university.

It didn't matter if you were going to be a rocket scientist or a plumber; the country needed both. The tax cut was substantial, but there was one clause: fifteen percent of the savings had to go to education. The child or parent had to be in school or the money would be put into a school savings fund. A very large tax was placed on that money and the lender if it was withdrawn for any reason other then education.

The opposing side didn't like it, but the only ammunition they had was to attack the President's lifestyle. "The President doesn't have any children and it's obvious he and the *First Man to Be First Lady* aren't planning on having little ones any time soon." The President put them in their place with facts. "George Washington didn't have any children of his own, yet he is proudly referred to as the 'Father of his Country'."

The new President wouldn't be bullied. Some in Congress felt that if the government is going to give a tax cut to families, parents should decide themselves what to do with their savings. Giving families a high tax cut then making sure they invested a mere 15% of that tax cut, insured that there was going to be a better way of life for the next generation. "It is a small price to pay," the President said.

The President would do everything to help, but American citizens finally needed to take responsibility for their own future. The President informed the American people, "The next generation will take care of this one. And all of us can see exactly how expensive that is." That really made the country think as they registered to vote and reported for work.

Since America was for everyone, the tax cut could be used to make a better life for those who had already achieved a higher education, earning at least a bachelor's degree. The American dream had gotten so expensive that it had become the "dream that couldn't come true". It took a two-parent income just to pay the rent.

The President made a provision that the 15% education tax cut could go toward a mortgage on a house that the family was going to live in, but not rent out. The whole idea behind the bill was to make a better life for each American. If big business would guarantee the mortgage, they would get the tax cut. That single-handedly put a halt to corporate draw-downs. There would be no headaches come tax time. It was very simple. If you had the documentation, you got the tax break; if not, you didn't. It was just one more line on the form. It had never been so easy to save money.

Congress was still in emergency session behind closed doors. The debates were minimal for a group of people elected to argue. They finally came together, stunned into silence. Approval for the President poured into every elected official's office. No politicians wanted to speak out. If they backed the President, it was political suicide; if they were against the President, it was political suicide. Congress watched and waited for word from the American people.

The country had a gay President and his husband was The First Man To Be First Lady. An African-American woman was Vice President. An Asian woman was the Commandant of the Marines. America was deployed for war. Women were signing up for the draft. The country stood by, ready to follow their leader.

Every time a breaking story ended, the commentators would try to give their opinion, but were interrupted by yet another breaking story. For the first time, America was listening and was hearing it straight from the President. The Christian Coalition prayed for politics. They had wanted honesty. They had wanted a leader they could admire. Their prayers had been answered sevenfold. The country was finally getting rid of sexism in the White House. Women would march just as far as the men would. There was equality in the air coming from the man in the White House married to a man.

"Only twenty-four hours?" Clarke thought to himself. Obviously Michael had known he was going to become President for some time. With a bounce in his step, Clarke walked back upstairs to the private quarters. He glanced at his watch and saw that he had just enough time to grab a notepad and pen. He petted Barney goodbye and almost jogged back down the stairs to the Ground Floor Hall.

The Chief Usher had briefed the entire staff; "The First Gentleman is in full command. If there is ever a doubt, Clarke will be glad to take your letter of resignation." The Chief Usher noted, "Just look at what happened to the ex-Chief of Protocol." There was a genuine sigh of relief.

The Domestic Staff hated the ex-Chief of Protocol. She took care of all the previous First Ladies official duties concerning the White House. She treated everyone as if they were something she should scrape off the bottom of her shoe. "At least she treated everyone the same," Clarke thought to himself.

Right on time, the Chief Usher introduced Clarke to the in-house staff. All of the people who worked behind the scenes cooking, cleaning, scrubbing dishes, doing the laundry, stocking shelves, painting, plumbing, carpentry and so on, lined the hallway to be present for this meeting.

Clarke introduced himself to each person with a warm handshake and genuinely thanked each one for his or her service. Many of them looked at each other in amazement. It had been a long time since a First Lady had been so polite to the household staff. Clarke was animated and put everyone at ease with his professionalism.

He was presented with the menus used at the White House. He made notes and asked about different items, whose specialty was what and why and when he and the President could have the pleasure of sampling their specialties. Clarke toured the main White House kitchen, including the storage areas where the fine china was kept. The tour also included the wine cellars and the industrial dishwashing rooms. Clarke was amazed at the laundry room, with its massive linen pressers.

The Chief Usher took Clarke down to the third sub-basement. With a gesture of his hand, he said, "Straight ahead is where the fallout-shelters were during the Cold War years. Now the area is used to store firewood that is burned in all the White House fireplaces." Clarke noticed there was still a path to the fallout-shelter and that the wood supply was low. Clarke smiled to himself; "It won't be for long." They walked back up to the basement kitchens.

Clarke went the same way as the waiters and dishwashers. He didn't take the main staircase but chose the winding back stairs. He opened pantry doors and cupboards, freezers and walk-in refrigerators and actually walked into the refrigerators. The place was spotless. Clarke noticed that the products used in the White House kitchens were the same products found in kitchens all over America. He was so impressed with the staff. He was actually interested in everyone's job and even learned how to use the dishwashers. The kitchen staff was falling in love with the new administration and they hadn't even met the President!

Clarke was briefed on how the kitchen operated, who the staff was, and who gave the final orders, which, of course, was

Clarke. No one doubted that for a moment. Clarke didn't like the power but realized that the quickest way to politicians' hearts was through their stomachs. It didn't matter what country they were from, how powerful they were, or if they had nuclear capabilities.

Clarke's tour of the White House kitchens was over and the staff was assembled, waiting to hear what the First Gentleman thought of the facilities. As Clarke looked around the room, his smile flattened and became almost a frown. His demeanor grew serious. The staff braced themselves.

"My first change in the White House kitchens," Clarke paused, looking at his pad full of notes. The staff collectively shuddered, as if someone dragged fingernails across a blackboard. He continued, "Is to change the White House coffee." A quiet sigh of relief became a huge smile of gratitude among the professionals gathered around Clarke.

"In Seattle, we brew a good mood, which makes every day good to the last drop." Clarke sounded like a commercial jingle and everyone laughed out loud. Since it wasn't really that funny, Clarke knew that it was a laugh of relief. Getting back down to business, he informed the culinary staff that he had a favorite coffee, a special blend known only to 'Latte Land', a coffeehouse in Seattle, Washington.

Clarke personally called the coffeehouse, where they roasted the coffee beans right on the premises. After the manager had congratulated Clarke on his new position and Clarke had thanked him, arrangements were made to make their special house-blend the official White House coffee. Clarke had always been their most loyal customer and he clearly enjoyed the best. "Just because we live in the White House, that isn't going to change." Everyone laughed once again. By the time the call was over, the coffee was no longer called the house-blend: it was the *White House Blend*. Clarke gave the phone number to the Chief Usher, who would make all the arrangements along with the Secret Service.

Clarke was briefed on the traditions of the White House and what shouldn't be changed. Nuts and mints had filled candy dishes on every presidential table at every State Dinner since the days of George Washington. Although he had never lived in the White House, George Washington started many traditions that have been carried out to this very day. Clarke was going to add to the tradition and see to it that only the finest chocolates were served at the White House.

There was only one place to get those—Hazzels' Candy, located on the West Coast. "One taste and you will see what I mean." Clarke called them immediately. When the White House wanted something, the White House got it. Clarke asked for a sampler box. His favorites were the nuts and chews, but he thought that maybe he should expand his tastes. The management of Hazzels' Candy was so honored that they decided to create a special assortment just for Clarke.

Clarke loved the Northwest. Culinary delights seemed to grow wild there. Clarke's favorite was the blackberry and he had created several desserts featuring them over the many years he had lived there. Clarke gave the Pastry Chef those recipes by memory and asked him to mix it with his expertise to create fabulous desserts for the White House. Clarke knew this man was working on his own cookbook, which would be published once he retired. Clarke would let him have all the recipes he wanted.

Clarke knew that once the White House had endorsed you, you were famous forever—just look at what Jacqueline Kennedy did for the pillbox hat. Clarke didn't go to his office, but took care of things right then and there with ideas from the people who would make them work. Clarke made the White House staff feel they were the most important people on the grounds.

Clarke again shook hands with every member of the staff, thanking them for their time and efforts. He asked what they needed to make their jobs easier and dinners more fabulous. Clarke asked for a list and would see to it that the White House kitchen was the whole country's model kitchen. The Chief Usher raised an eyebrow which Clarke took as approval.

Past administrations had never put money into the White House until their second term. It was always bad press at re-election time but Clarke didn't care. He was going to do what was right for the White House and for all the people who made the house 'work'. Clarke asked the Chief Usher for a list of things the kitchen staff needed but couldn't get funding for. The Chief Usher didn't know what to say, but he did it.

Ms. Deverough

Clarke was never alone. The Secret Service was everywhere, guarding everything. Clarke guarded every word until finally he just gave up and tried to relax. As he and the Chief Usher walked back upstairs, a secretary handed Clarke a stack of messages. Many were invitations for *The First Man To Be First Lady* to give a speech or become a spokesperson for various groups in need of a political voice from the person sleeping with the President. Several requests appeared to be an insult, but there were some genuine invitations. Clarke noticed there was an invitation to be a guest speaker in a small town in the Midwest. The invitation was for the First Gentleman, not The First Man To Be First Lady. The sincerity of the request caught Clarke's attention. He paperclipped the messages together and added yet another line to his 'TO DO' list.

Clarke and the Chief Usher continued their meeting in the West Hall, seated in front of the big arched window. As they talked, both men's lists seemed to grow longer than there was paper. Once again, Ms. Jones interrupted them. Clarke said something to the Chief Usher and they both laughed.

"My name is Ms. Jones." she reminded Clarke, "Not 'the woman who kidnapped you'." Clarke blushed. He didn't think he had said that loud enough for anyone else to hear. Ms. Jones enjoyed seeing Clarke. Clarke enjoyed seeing Ms. Jones. Every time he saw her, Clarke immediately excused himself from whomever he was talking to and followed her.

"There is a Ms. Deverough downstairs making the Secret Service earn their pay."

Clarke was so relieved. "Thank goodness! Ms. Deverough is here."

"Pardon?" Ms. Jones asked.

"Ms. Deverough, she grows on you." Clarke smiled.

"Yes, I can see that. I'm not going to look into her eyes." Ms. Jones said as she escorted Clarke down the main stairs. They turned and stepped off the landing.

The Secret Service, as dictated by regulation, had searched her. They looked at Ms. Deverough. If she was a threat, it must be someone's idea of a joke. Ms. Deverough could sense the jocularity in their brief investigation. "If I were Double 'O' Seven, I'd have a pistol designed into my bra strap." She was seriously searched again.

Ms. Deverough was Clarke's oldest and dearest friend. She had always been there: every opening night, every awards ceremony. She was there, holding Clarke's hand, when his aunt passed. Ms. Deverough was a striking woman, whose trademark was an all-black ensemble. Whether it was a beaded gown for an inaugural event or a sweat suit, it was always black. With her own unique witticism, Ms. Deverough joked that she was in mourning for the lack of taste in society.

Clarke couldn't wait to see her. He was escorted towards the south entrance of the White House but when they got to the oval Diplomatic Reception Room, there she was.

"Ms. Deverough!" Clarke said with an exhilarated, but relieved, tone. Ms. Deverough was the reincarnation of Coco Chanel coupled with a splash of Bette Davis with a European accent. Anyone around her was captivated.

Clarke reached out his arms and they embraced. For old time's sake, Ms. Deverough motioned for Clarke to stand up straight. She took off her gloves as they smiled at each other. Clarke said, "Right this way," motioning for her to come with him. He thanked the staff as he and Ms. Deverough walked down the hallway. They were quiet. All you could hear was Ms. Deverough's expressions of dissatisfaction at the White House neglect.

Not only was Ms. Deverough Clarke's oldest and dearest friend, she was also Clarke's advisor and modeling coach. In private, they would practice a walk and Ms. Deverough would tell Clarke when he needed to stand up straight and put his shoulders back. She told him how to hold his hands and to "not walk ladylike" or "manlike, waiting to penetrate a filly." Ms. Deverough was a true thoroughbred. She loved her horses as much as she loved a good man.

In public, Ms. Deverough and Clarke had a secret code that only they could understand, very much like the signals given in baseball from the pitcher to the catcher. Ms. Deverough would give Clarke a blink with an arched eyebrow, which meant stand up straight and walk with a masculine step. A slight nod, with her chin resting on a poised lady-like hand, reminded Clarke not to flip a wrist. It was classy, simple and tasteful.

When Clarke and Ms. Deverough entered the private quarters, the doors were shut by a uniformed man who still wouldn't turn his back on Clarke. Barney ran to Ms. Deverough, turning in circles and barking.

"How is my shooting star?" Ms. Deverough asked Barney. He acknowledged her with a very wet salutation. To Barney, Ms. Deverough was better than one of Clarke's chocolate chip cookies with extra vanilla. She smiled as she stroked Barney's head, then turned serious. She placed her umbrella in a stand then walked over to the sofa, tapping her hand with her gloves. She sat down and placed her gloves on the coffee table. Barney sat down on the sofa right next to her.

Ms. Deverough didn't waste any time. "Clarke, there is someone I want you to meet." He sat down on a chair facing her. "Now that you are The First Gentleman, you need to look the part." Clarke gave her a look and they both smiled. Ms. Deverough went on as if she were performing Shakespeare. "You must set the tone for the fine events here at the White House. Set a style. Model what every woman wants to see. Wear the envy of every man."

Clarke gave her a look of, "Oh, please!" then suddenly realized she was right. "What do you have in mind?" He asked. He surmised that whoever it was must be about to arrive at the White House, with a commitment to make HER every dream their command.

Clarke could read her mind. Why they ever bothered to talk neither of them knew. "A wonderful designer is just what you need and I have just the one." She flipped her wrist in an exclamation, then continued with theatrical suspense. "Costume design has been their way of life. The lists of credits following this designer are longer then the tour lines at the White House." Clarke was so intrigued he couldn't wait to hear more. There was almost a drum roll. "Beverly Anderson is the finest designer in the world." Ms. Deverough seemed awestruck.

Clarke was so captivated. "Beverly Anderson. A woman to design for the First Gentleman." Clarke loved the thought. "It would shock the world." Clarke said. "Traditionally, designers have always been men."

"Beverly Anderson *is* a man." Ms. Deverough laughed, then grew very serious. "He is not gay. He was married at a very young age and widowed soon after. He has never stopped mourning his loss. Beverly enjoys people for who they are." Ms. Deverough paused. "Clarke, he has some of the most incredible ideas I have ever seen. His designs, your body," Ms. Deverough clapped her hands together. "You are going to be more desirable than the man you're married to." Impossible, Clarke thought. Ms. Deverough heard what Clarke was thinking and they both smiled.

Beverly Anderson arrived, confidently carrying his portfolio. A Secret Service agent escorted him to the second floor. Ms. Deverough introduced Clarke with the elegance of a queen. Beverly Anderson was a tall, dark, and very handsome man with the same type of European accent as Ms. Deverough. Clarke invited Beverly Anderson to have a seat. As they sat, Clarke proudly introduced the area as the West Sitting Hall.

An usher wheeled in a cart complete with a silver tea service and fabulous pastries. Clarke was so impressed he hugged the usher with his eyes. The pastries were beautiful. The pastry chef who had created them was watching from around the corner. He appeared honored by Clarke's expression. The usher politely asked Clarke's guests what they would like and how they would like it then gently poured. After everyone was served, the usher nodded at Clarke, who thanked him, then left the way he came in, shutting the doors behind him, never turning his back on Clarke.

Clarke put down his cup and saucer. He couldn't wait for the coffee shipment from Seattle! Beverly Anderson handed Clarke an open leather-bound portfolio. His designs on paper were fabulous. He had really *drawn* his homework. The drawings even looked like Clarke. As Clarke looked through the portfolio, he noticed that the formal designs were titled *Beverly Ann's*. Gentlemen's dress suits and coat designs were called *Anderson's*. The sporty look was called *Andy's*. Clarke smiled. The titles were perfect.

Beverly was a man who knew exactly what he wanted and how to get it. "Clarke, I would like to see your style and my designs catch the world off-guard. Set yourself apart from the men and women in politics. Show the world that while your husband is taking care of the nation, you are taking care of your husband. Politicians wear stuffy suits and plain ties; go with a vest, add a sparkle to a cufflink. Your signature spectator shoes are fabulous. And, may I add, Franklin D. Roosevelt would love them on you, as much as he did on himself." Clarke loved this man's style and it had nothing to do with clothes.

Clarke had some ideas that were captured by Beverly's illustrations. Clarke would still look like a fine gentleman from the turn of the 20th century, but with a splash of new ideas, making him totally 'today'. He was so fascinated by Beverly Anderson's designs that their meeting continued like the thrill on Christmas morning. Clarke shrieked with excitement as he looked at each drawing over and over again. Ms. Deverough calmly sipped her tea. She was so happy to see Clarke finally relax.

Suddenly Clarke dragged himself out of the moment and became very somber. "This is all so wonderful and I agree completely on the importance of an image, but this is all very expensive. There will already be so much bad press with the President's and my lifestyle, without adding the cost of such a wardrobe." As Clarke began to thank him for coming, Beverly blushed. He looked as if he had just been caught doing something wrong. Clarke looked at him with concern, ready to ask if he was all right.

"Clarke, I have been in wardrobe and costume design for many years. I've worked in Hollywood with all the greats. My dream is to have my own designs become famous and be *the* name in the fashion world. The best way to do that is to outfit the First Lady." Beverly corrected himself with an embarrassed smile. "*First Man...*" He paused. "*To Be First Lady.*" They all smiled. "Everyone the world over will be watching you. I will design fabulous clothes for you at no expense to you or the administration. The only thing I ask is that I remain your only designer, putting our ideas into fashion with the respect your new position deserves. In turn, I could become the success I have always dreamed of being. Your clothes will not have a price tag nor will my fame."

Beverly was so sincere; Clarke felt his honesty with every word he spoke. "Your drawings *are* incredible." Clarke was looking through the portfolio as he talked. "If I can look half as good as these, I will be the finest-dressed man in the world." Clarke paused. He shut the portfolio and laid it on the coffee table. "I must be as honest with you as you have been with me. If I don't like something, I will say so, and I will *not* wear it."

"Agreed." Beverly said with a nod, then surprised everyone with his next comment. "I want to see your husband elected to office." He smiled. "I have some great ideas for an inaugural ensemble." Ms. Deverough and Beverly Anderson smiled at each other. Clarke nervously chuckled, then looked at Beverly Anderson. This man was a real gentleman and it felt as if they had been friends for years.

"Beverly, if everything works out as we hope and the nation is taken by storm with a sparkle to their cufflinks, would you promise me just one thing?" Beverly looked concerned. "If you start your own couture shop and begin mass-producing your incredible designs, would you choose factories here in the United States, creating jobs for America? Please treat your employees right and be an example of how employers should be." Clarke was asking politely but Beverly knew without a doubt that it was the only way Clarke would agree to work with him.

"Agreed." Beverly said with a broad smile. They shook hands, a gentlemen's agreement that would prove to be more binding than the most legal of contracts.

Ms. Deverough immediately took command. "Let's get to work."

Beverly took out a measuring tape and asked Clarke to remove his vest and shirt. Beverly was impressed with Clarke's physique. He asked Clarke how he kept such a great shape. Clarke blushed at all the attention and said, "I just try to keep up with the President."

Beverly motioned for Clarke to stretch his arms out. "Beverly," Clarke paused, waiting for Beverly to write down his measurements. "My schedule is filling up so fast already. I seem to belong to every reporter and television news camera. I don't know when I would be able to schedule fittings and alterations." Clarke loved a tailor-made suit, but knew how many annoying fittings they took from start to finish.

"I've taken care of that." Beverly said as he measured Clarke's waist. He asked Clarke to remove his shoes then measured his inseam. "I am having a mannequin made to your exact measurements. It can expand and contract, so it will always be your size. Also, a model will be hired with your exact height, weight, and measurements. That way I can see how the ensemble looks while walking and dancing." Clarke looked over at Ms. Deverough. He couldn't believe how quickly all this had come together since it had been barely twenty-four hours since he had arrived at the White House!

As Clarke was being measured, he informed Beverly he would need to be investigated by the FBI, which would include a full background check in order for him to enter the White House without an interrogation every time. Beverly assured Clarke that not only had he never inhaled, he'd never even tried it. His only addiction was chocolate: anytime, anywhere. Beverly rolled his measuring tape as Clarke got dressed. Clarke was thoroughly intrigued by this man. But he could see that Beverly Anderson was lonely.

Clarke called for a Secret Service agent. Ms. Jones came into the room, and Clarke formally introduced Beverly Anderson to her. Something magical seemed to happen as the two shook hands. Clarke looked from Ms. Jones to Beverly Anderson, then he looked over at Ms. Deverough. She was thinking the same thing.

Beverly Anderson said his good-byes to Clarke and thanked Ms. Deverough for contacting him. Clarke watched Ms. Jones escort him out of the room. They were going down to the East Wing where all the paperwork would be filled out and his fingerprints taken. It was all just 'routine' for a White House Security Clearance.

Clarke couldn't help but think what a handsome couple they made as they disappeared down the hall. He could tell Ms. Deverough was thinking the same thing herself. Clarke turned to Ms. Deverough, who was pouring herself more tea. There was a glow of satisfaction about her. "He is a wonderful man, isn't he?" She asked as she sipped her tea, giving Clarke a wink.

"Underneath her thick crust, so is Ms. Jones." Clarke said. He and Ms. Deverough looked at each other with a matchmaker's gleam in their eyes.

"Ms. Deverough," Clarke paused and sat down next to her. "The President and I would like you to stay here in the White House with us. We have a room for you here on the second floor. Of course, it's the Queen's Room." They grinned at each other. Suddenly, Clarke had a desperate look on his face. "Ms. Deverough, I need your help. I can take care of the President," Clarke snapped his fingers, "Just like that. But being the First Man To Be First Lady," Clarke paused, looking away, almost in tears, then whispered, "I really need you."

Ms. Deverough took Clarke's hand in a comforting hold, interrupting any embarrassing tears. "That's why I am here." She smiled at his unnecessary fears. "You are the First Gentleman, not the *First Man to be first Lady*." Clarke's smile dried any impending tears. Ms. Deverough gave Clarke's hand a comforting squeeze. "You have been groomed for this position all of your life." With a smile, Ms. Deverough promised, "I will stay as long as you need me."

Clarke's desperate look became a smile of relief. They finished their tea, comfortably chatting about life, then Clarke showed Ms. Deverough to her room. History had named it the Queen's Room. Any time a Queen from another country visited the White House, this was her room. It was filled with handsome antiques but desperately needed redecorating. That was the next thing on Clarke's list.

Ms. Deverough's steamer trunks were delivered before Clarke got back downstairs to take Barney out for a walk. Ms. Jones was directing the moving crew, amazed at all the cartloads of vintage luggage. Clarke laughed. Ms. Deverough was so wonderfully theatrical. How she could read his mind before he even thought of something, he never knew. As Clarke walked Barney down the hall, he wondered how Ms. Deverough had arrived at the White House. A car was never announced. Come to think of it, Clarke had never seen Ms. Deverough arrive; she was just suddenly there, any time Clarke needed her. Not a limousine or even a taxicab was ever seen driving away, just Ms. Deverough with her umbrella and vintage luggage patiently waiting at the door.

Years ago, Clarke had joked with Ms. Deverough as he was about to carry in her bags. He looked to the left then to the right, looking for a limousine or at least a checkered taxicab.

Nothing was in sight. Laughing, Clarke asked, "Ms. Deverough?"

"Yes, Dear?" Ms. Deverough said with an 'I'm-glad-to-see-you' smile.

"Did you arrive via umbrella?" Clarke was waiting for an answer.

"Bumbershoot, Dear." Ms. Deverough smiled, then motioned for Clarke to stand up straight.

Clarke had a questioning look on his face, then remembered that Ms. Deverough always referred to her umbrella as a 'bumbershoot'. Clarke's expression melted into a smile of gratitude. He never gave Ms. Deverough's mysterious arrival another thought and thanked his lucky stars for her perfect sense of timing. There was always something magical about Ms. Deverough's arrival. She was always there when he needed her the most.

Clarke came back to reality as he walked Barney through the Diplomatic Reception Room. Barney was excited to be going out for a walk and kept Clarke hustling along. He took a deep breath and finally relaxed. He never worried about a thing when Ms. Deverough was on the guest list. Clarke consulted Ms. Deverough on everything from voice pitch to questions and answers. Her wit was as sharp as a sword and more powerful than the pistol she packed in her purse. Ms. Deverough was a sharpshooter with anything that could be shot.

The Secret Service was so convinced that Ms. Deverough was one of them that, after a few classes and an official government briefing, they actually authorized her to carry the pistol. The more the Secret Service searched, the less they could find on Ms. Deverough. Through their investigation, it was discovered Ms. Deverough was guilty of being healthy, abundantly wealthy, and extremely wise.

Ms. Deverough was Secret Service, Social Secretary, and Clarke's Chief Advisor all rolled into one. She followed all the rules, while breaking every regulation in the book. No one questioned her presence; everyone thought she was part of the Secret Service.

Brightening Up the White House

Clarke was going to make a home for his husband even though it was in the White House. In his own life, Clarke dressed, presented dinner, and decorated with perfect flair. And that's exactly how he was going to redecorate the Private Quarters. The President had been content to leave that sort of thing up to Clarke. He loved Clarke's ideas and felt at home anywhere as long as Clarke was at his side.

Clarke knew the White House needed sprucing up and he would meet with museum experts and decorators for their approval. After all, the White House was a living museum and any changes to the State Rooms had to be approved by the Fine Arts Committee. That was the law. But the Private Quarters was just that—private.

The furniture that was already there was beautiful, but the upholstery was faded and stained and careless drinkers had left ring marks. The prior First Couple had many problems and their memory was still on the furniture. Clarke loved the pieces and he would add ideas of his own along with having a few of the their own favorite pieces sent from Washington, the state.

The President encouraged Clarke to do whatever he wanted but asked if he would talk to a certain decorator named Charles Wallingford. The President had known the family for years. They weren't friends but were friendly acquaintances. Clarke was happy to oblige. He would meet with the older gentleman, who made quite a name for himself. He was in all the decorating magazines of the rich and famous. Clarke was honored to talk with such a successful man. He was just what the White House needed.

Charles Wallingford was announced and Clarke met him with an outstretched hand and a big smile. The decorator did not seem glad to be there. In fact, he seemed a little put out. He hadn't even brought a portfolio or sketches of his ideas; all he had with him was an attitude. Clarke gave him a tour of the Private Quarters, making festive jokes and remarks about fabrics and ideas that were outdated and, at best, distasteful when new. The man just looked around the room and rolled his eyes at Clarke.

Clarke became quiet. Then said, "Let's hear what ideas you have."

The man looked around the room then to Clarke. "I have a contract that needs to be signed. I will take a money order."

"For what?" Clarke asked.

"You will use my services. I will be paid for those services. In advance. You know my work. I am the best in this business. If you don't like it, then you don't have good taste."

Clarke stared at him. "I would like to see your ideas." The man just huffed at Clarke, who was trying hard not to laugh. Instead, he smiled a big smile. "I *will* see what my home is going to look like before I pay for it."

"I will see the President," the man said flatly.

"You are not hired without MY approval." Clarke looked the man straight in the eye. Then Clarke looked around the room, wondering if this man was someone's idea of a dumb joke. The man was irritatingly funny. It was like watching a phony actor on the late, late show. Clarke choked back a chuckle. "Unless you have some ideas and, I might add, very dazzling ideas, and drawings of those dazzling ideas, you will not be hired for this job."

"I will see the President. Do not make me repeat myself." The man looked at Clarke and asked, "Do you know who I am?" Barney hopped off the sofa. He walked up to the decorator and started to sniff him. The man's attitude was almost as big as his ego. "I have been in every decorator's magazine in the world. Why, *Architect's Magazine* has featured me more times than any other decorator in its history. Not to mention those ghastly magazines sought after by class-less, no-talent housewives who have given decorators a bad name." Barney started to growl. The man looked down at Barney then at Clarke. "I *demand* you get rid of this beast at once."

Clarke was going to get rid of the beast all right. He snapped his fingers. That was Barney's signal from Clarke to "come, NOW." Barney slowly walked to Clarke, never taking his eyes off the decorator.

The man looked down at Clarke, repeating himself in the same disgusting attitude. "Do you have any idea who I am?"

Clarke realized this man wasn't a joke. "The question is, sir, do I *care* who you are?" Clarke was very blunt. He looked the man straight in the eye. Again. Clarke didn't smile. He wasn't coy. He was simply truthful.

The man looked at Clarke as if he were something that should put out with the trash. "I will inform the President of your attitude toward me. *I demand your apologies at once.*"

"Thank you for coming," Clarke said with the same smile with which he had welcomed the man.

"The President will hear of this." Mr. Wallingford said, huffing for a breath.

"Yes. Yes, he certainly will." Clarke said. Mr. Wallingford started to walk away.

"I wouldn't go through that door." Clarke said, but almost wished he hadn't.

The man stared at Clarke. "I will go through any door I please."

"If you go through that door, the Secret Service will hog tie you, THEN ask questions. Although I see how that may be appropriate, I don't feel it's very hospitable."

Clarke sighed in relief as his favorite Secret Service woman entered the room. "Ms. Jones, Mr. Wallingford is leaving the grounds and will need an escort. I'll give the President your regards." Clarke said to the man, then smiled. "Oh, shall I ring for a butler to help you out with all of your magazines?" Ms. Jones looked for a stack of magazines but didn't see anything. Clarke kindly gestured for the woman to take the man out.

As Mr. Wallingford was led out of the room, Clarke heard the man yell, "I demand you let go of me. You're hurting me. *I demand you stop this!*" Clarke laughed quietly to himself as Ms. Deverough came into the room.

"Who needs the late show when you live in the White House?" Ms. Deverough quipped.

Clarke laughed. "He certainly is a creature isn't he?"

"Clarke," Ms. Deverough said, "I have someone I would like you to meet." Clarke couldn't wait to hear about the next person about to come into his life. "I've already used up my three wishes." Clarke laughed.

"Nonsense." Ms. Deverough laughed with Clarke. Then she smiled and said, with a serious tone in her voice, "I have a decorator who is one of the best. She just happens to be in Washington today. She has some wonderful ideas and has never been in a decorator's magazine."

"She sounds great already." Clarke smiled.

"She is. Her name is Saundra and she is quite a woman. I've seen her work. It looks a lot like you, Clarke."

Ms. Jones interrupted them as she came into the room, thanking Clarke for all the excitement. She didn't need to work out at the gym with all the people she was escorting off the grounds. Ms. Jones stopped and listened to her radio then looked over at Clarke. "There is a woman downstairs named Saundra. She has been escorted through proper channels. I believe she is your next appointment."

Clarke smiled at Ms. Deverough with a 'how do you do that' look. "Please. Show her up."

Ms. Jones talked back into her radio, telling the front desk she would be down and would personally escort Ms. Powers to the Private Quarters. In moments, Ms. Jones introduced herself to Saundra with a professional handshake. Ms. Jones actually smiled without having to wrestle anyone first.

Saundra was a lovely middle-aged woman and quite the lady, with a youthful glow. She dressed in a close-fitting black skirt and jacket suit trimmed with a whisper of faux leopard skin. Her ensemble said she was proud to be a lady. She wore simple stiletto-heeled pumps, attractively trimmed in the same faux leopard skin. Rhinestone jewelry accented her ensemble. She literally sparkled in the sunlight.

Saundra confidentially carried a portfolio, which matched her incredible outfit, trimmed in the same faux leopard skin. If Saundra was a little nervous, no one noticed. She had captivated the entire room. This new administration was showing class one incredible person at a time.

As the two women walked away, the men in the room watched from behind. Saundra's walk told everyone 'how proud she was to make their acquaintance.' Her perky butt bounced to the left, then to the right, then to the left again. One could almost hear a bass drum as she descended the hallway: BOOM da da BOOM, da da BOOM, da da BOOM. At first, one would think they were hearing her high heels against the marble floor, but the floor was carpeted. The men in the room couldn't believe it. The press was right: this new administration WAS showing class one incredible person at a time. With one last BOOM, da da BOOM, Saundra was escorted around the corner and up the grand stairs.

As Clarke and Ms. Deverough were chatting, a beautiful woman with red hair appeared through the doorway as if she were about to be presented to the queen. Ms. Jones led her in.

Ms. Deverough commanded the moment. "Saundra, dear, how are you?"

The woman was obviously comfortable with Ms. Deverough. She cocked her head, commenting how nice it was to see her and that she was amazed that Ms. Deverough knew exactly where she was staying while in Washington.

Ms. Deverough didn't waste a moment with her introductions. Saundra was honored meeting the First Man To Be First Lady. Clarke's handshake immediately put her at ease. Ms. Deverough introduced Saundra to her 'shooting star'. Barney sniffed at Saundra, then sat at her feet. It was the sniff of approval.

Clarke invited Saundra to sit down. The same usher came in with a teacart and poured the tea. Clarke was getting used to the grand service and enjoyed watching Saundra who was obviously impressed with every moment.

Saundra was suddenly so relaxed with Clarke. She looked at him with a genuine smile. "Dear," The usher handed her tea in a china cup and saucer from the Truman collection. She thanked the usher, and then, with her free hand, clutched her heart. "Oh, I am so sorry." Saundra realized she was so relaxed with Clarke that she had just called the *First Man to be First Lady* 'Dear.'

Clarke interrupted her apologies, "Any time an elegant lady such as you calls me 'dear', I am honored."

"Thank you." She said, still a little embarrassed. She placed her cup on the table in front of her. She had a few drawings and swatches of fabric she was eager to show Clarke.

Saundra spoke to Clarke and Ms. Deverough as she gracefully removed items from her portfolio. "Traditionally, at least since the late 1960's, the West Sitting Hall where we are sitting has been done in a cheery yellow. I'd like to see the traditions remain at the White House, complimented with your sparkle and a dash of the President."

Saundra's enthusiasm spread around the room like a happy, peppy smile. Clarke hadn't even looked at the sketches and already he loved her ideas. Saundra stood gesturing, pointing where there was nothing. As she described her ideas, Clarke could actually see them. Her excitement described them in perfect detail. This woman knew what she was talking about. She knew a lot about past administrations and who had added what and why. Saundra showed Clarke swatches of fabrics that were her own creation. He immediately loved them and passed them to Ms. Deverough.

Clarke had a few ideas that meshed perfectly Saundra's and they both began gesturing with excitement. Clarke described a few pieces in his seaside home and pointed out that they would be perfect here, here, and there. Saundra quickly sketched more ideas as Clarke added color here and a divan there. As they talked, Clarke made a list of what furniture he would have sent in from Washington, the state.

What Saundra and Clarke finally came up with was fabulous. "Do you think the President will like it?" Saundra asked.

"He loves everything Clarke puts his mind to!" Ms. Deverough said.

Once all the excitement of how the Private Quarters would look had calmed somewhat, they again settled down for tea. Clarke realized this was truly a businesswoman and her talents would undoubtedly come with a hefty price tag. Clarke asked for an itemized billing statement.

There was a very long, very still pause. "I don't have a statement or billing." Saundra said. "May I do the quarters for you at my cost, plus travel and a per diem? After we are done, I would like to use your redecorating in my advertising. As you know, mentioned with the First Couple, whether it's fashion or interior design, you are a household name." Then, in a professional tone, Saundra said confidentially, "I've always worked towards having my own design studio."

Clarke put his cup down. He looked over at Ms. Deverough as if she had something to do with it. She did, but you couldn't tell by her expression. She just smiled in that isn't-life-grand smile of hers.

"There are funds available to make sure you receive a salary." Clarke said. He couldn't believe Congress had appropriated over fifty thousand dollars to have the Private Quarters redecorated. And they did that for every new administration. Clarke didn't tell anyone else that, but smiled as he looked at Saundra then to her sketches, "I love your ideas."

"They are mostly your ideas, dear, I just drew them on a pad and added a little splash of Saundra."

Clarke, Saundra, and Ms. Deverough met with the Chief Usher, who told them where workrooms could be set up inside the White House. In the third subbasement, directly under the South Portico, a reupholstering shop was set up along with a furniture stripping area to remove the water stains and ring marks left by the past administration.

Saundra measured for drapes and it seemed a swatch of fabric covered the windows with her excitement. The Private Quarters would be stunning, a place Clarke would be proud to have his husband call home. Saundra called in the measurements for the draperies, proudly announcing they would arrive by the end of the week.

Clarke couldn't believe it. Living in the White House was like a fairy tale.

Clarke offered Saundra a room at the White House, but she wanted to stay in her suite downtown. She would be at the White House first thing in the morning, to personally supervise the work. Saundra was escorted to the East Wing to fill out the necessary paperwork for a security clearance, then to an office where she could make phone calls. She was given an address on the White House grounds, where fabrics and correspondence could be sent. The Secret Service made sure security was tight, right down to the thread.

Clarke made arrangements to have the redecorating start immediately. He was assured that it could be started that very afternoon, but Clarke said first thing in the morning was just fine. He still had several appointments before day's end. The administration's Social Secretary, Press Secretary, and the newly appointed Chief of Protocol were already waiting to meet with Clarke. Clarke armed himself with the best ammunition he had available: himself.

Much to Clarke's surprise, the people in attendance were more afraid of him than he was of them. Each office was there to assist the President and his spouse. After Clarke's introductory meeting, people working for the administration had a completely different opinion of him than what they had heard from the ex-Chief of Protocol.

Morning arrived with the President leaving for the Oval Office before sun-up. Clarke always started his day with the President over breakfast and couldn't wait to crawl into bed with him at night. After breakfast dishes were removed, Clarke dressed and met with the Chief Usher over coffee in the only place there wasn't redecorating mania, the First Couple's private kitchen.

Saundra was already there, directing a work crew in the Private Quarters. A team of men was crating furniture that was to be stored and those pieces to be refurbished were carried away. Draperies were removed and chandeliers were lowered. Carpets were rolled up and taken away. Carpenters had a lot of repair work to do. Electricians upgraded circuits and made safety checks. Fireplaces were scrubbed and chimneys cleaned. Clarke laughed as he thought of Mary Poppins.

Clarke looked around the kitchen. He couldn't wait for the kitchen to be redecorated. It was just too commercial looking for Clarke to feel at home. The flooring was drab and the walls were painted a dull color. Clarke loved to cook Michael's favorites personally. After all, a home-cooked meal was his favorite dinner. Not to mention there would have to be a big supply of chocolate chip cookies for Michael AND Barney.

Clarke chose an appetizing color of red and white floor tile to be laid when new carpet was installed throughout the rest of the quarters. A wallpaper crew would brighten up the kitchen walls with tantalizing designs. After that was done, Clarke would put his collection of refrigerator magnets on the fridge and the White House would be one step closer to being their home away from home.

When Clarke and the Chief Usher walked out of the kitchen, a convoy of plumbers and delivery men were hauling in new fixtures for the Presidential bathroom, complete with a bathtub comfortably designed for two.

"It was the President's idea," the Chief Usher said.

Clarke blushed when he heard that. "How soon will it would be ready?"

As the Private Quarters were being redecorated, Clarke and the President would stay in the Lincoln Bedroom and have their dinner in the Family Dining Room on the first floor. A lit fireplace always warmed any room the First Couple was using. As the President and Clarke were having dinner, Clarke noticed how drab the Family Dining Room was. The room was cold and it had nothing to do with the temperature. Clarke would discuss more redecorating ideas with Saundra as soon as possible but first, the President needed him.

After dinner, Michael and Clarke walked around the White House grounds. Although it didn't seem like it, the White House sat on eighteen acres. The President and Clarke took a different route every night. One team of Secret Service agents was a safe distance ahead of the First Couple, and another team followed safely behind them. Of course, Barney was trotting alongside them, visiting a bush every now and then. Clarke was getting used to the White House privacy, which always included the Secret Service. Clarke didn't even notice them smile when he and the President held hands.

The Private Quarters seemed to be finished almost as soon as they were started. Two weeks had gone by in a snap. The President laughed, wondering what had happened. He recognized the throne-like wingback chairs from Clarke's seaside home and couldn't wait to sit in them. Clarke sat on his lap and Barney hopped up into Clarke's lap. They were one big happy First Family.

Clarke's blue-marble mantel clock chimed the half-hour. Clarke and the President looked over at the clock, which was sitting on an antique credenza. It looked great there, but Clarke wanted the clock to have a place of honor. Suddenly, he knew the perfect spot: the Blue Room mantel! With that, Clarke finally felt totally at home in the White House. He held the President tightly then petted Barney. He looked around the Private Quarters, pleased with the way it had turned out. He couldn't wait to get the rest of the house done. This administration had ideas for entertaining.

The next morning, Clarke and Michael enjoyed breakfast together then Clarke walked the President to the Grand Stairs, seeing him safely off to the Oval Office. Then he showered and dressed in his signature Beverly Anderson ensemble, complete with silk vest and, of course, spectator shoes. Clarke was unbelievably impressed with Beverly Anderson's designs.

Another large shipment of clothes bearing the Beverly Anderson label had arrived. Silk vests, pleated cuffed trousers with matching belt designed from the same fabric, stunning ties in coordinating vibrant colors. Silk-blend French-cuffed dress shirts. Beverly had thought of everything. Cotton underpants and T-shirts for the President. Silk boxers and silk tank T-shirts for Clarke. Simple dark socks for the President. Coordinated print socks for Clarke.

For tax purposes, Clarke couldn't accept the clothes as a gift. A pink invoice had 'one dollar' scribbled after the word total. Clarke clipped a dollar bill to it. Beverly left four quarters as change. Clarke was amazed at Beverly Anderson's generosity. It would be some time before Clarke would have to wear the same thing twice.

With a deep breath, Clarke armed himself with a notepad and pen. He met with the Chief Usher right on time. They walked through each State Room before the White House was opened for public tours. Draperies were being vacuumed as marble floors were buffed. The cleaning staff stopped when they saw Clarke. He nodded with a smile and the staff resumed their duties.

Clarke couldn't believe how the White House looked. It was clean, actually spotless, but still very drab, sporting worn upholstery, faded draperies, and frayed carpets. Thank goodness most people didn't see that on their quick tour. Clarke couldn't understand how anyone could entertain and represent the United States with the White House in such ill repair. The Chief Usher commented that the past administration had barely ever entertained.

Clarke didn't believe it was intentional but with alcohol and drug problems, he supposed the continuing White House restoration wasn't a top priority to the former First Couple. Many grand pieces had been rearranged and even placed in bathrooms or powder rooms. Ideas obviously had come from hangovers and perhaps the odd acid trips. Many people on the Fine Arts Committee had resigned in disgust.

As Clarke walked through the first floor, he asked the Chief Usher about pieces he had seen in pictures. The Chief Usher told Clarke about the White House storage areas. They were off the grounds, in a secret area, far from the press. Clarke gave the Chief Usher a list of items he wanted to see while they were at the storage area. Clarke made arrangements for him and Saundra to go "shopping", complete with a White House camera crew. Clarke eventually wanted America to see the redecorating of the White House just as he did.

As the limousine pulled up to the North Portico, the Chief Usher tried to interrupt Clarke's excitement, "I must inform you, I've already sent for the most valuable pieces."

Clarke looked at the Chief Usher and said, "You may go "shopping" with Saundra and me if you would like. If not, you can stay here at the house."

"Very well." The Chief Usher said. He was going to stay at the house.

After a quick trip with a police escort, Saundra and Clarke were soon walking through the warehouse with staff members who were writing down serial numbers and workmen who were busily carting antique pieces to a loading dock. The camera crew was thrilled to be there and became caught up in Clarke's excitement. The Chief Usher must have called ahead with Clarke's requests. Items were lined up in order from his list.

Clarke said, "I'll take this, this, and that."

Saundra bubbled with excitement and said, "Dear, look at this, this, and that."

Clarke said, "We'll take that, too," and helped a workman cart an ornate drop-leaf table to the loading dock. Saundra sketched ideas as Clarke nodded his approval. He picked up a chair, wondering where the others were that matched it. Clarke was having so much fun he almost forgot about his other appointments that afternoon. He and Saundra got back in the limousine and were back at the White House before the vacuuming was done.

Clarke informed the Chief Usher that he was meeting with what was left of the Fine Arts Committee that afternoon, after the public White House tours were over. The Chief Usher looked at Clarke. "Is there a problem?" Clarke asked.

"No, sir." The Chief Usher paused. "None at all."

Clarke didn't believe him. He didn't think the Chief Usher was lying, but somehow Clarke felt that the Chief Usher wasn't being totally honest. It was almost as though the man had something up his sleeve. Clarke didn't give it another thought. He had to choose which room would be the best place to entertain the Fine Arts Committee. He decided on the Green Room. It had more than enough places for everyone to sit and it needed the most work. Clarke would show the committee firsthand just how bad the White House really looked.

Clarke knew the importance of entertaining, but he wouldn't invite anyone to 'their' home while it looked like this! Clarke met with the culinary staff personally, requesting a nice pastry tray for the committee. Clarke had also invited a few members of Congress. He knew the redecorating would be costly and he wanted those who would approve the funds to see exactly why they were needed.

Clarke insisted Saundra be at the meeting. She was busy directing work crews, adding the final "splash of Saundra" to the Private Quarters. Saundra had Clarke's best ideas in mind. She could draw on paper exactly what Clarke was thinking. He wanted the same excitement she had for the Private Quarters to extend to redoing the rest of the White House. Saundra said she didn't feel qualified, but agreed to be there to listen. The White House would soon shine again and all Clarke did was have a light bulb of an idea.

The Chief Usher clicked his pen and put his mini-tablet inside his suit coat. In the previous administrations, he had been ordered to brief the former President on his First Lady's fiascoes. With or without men, drugged, drunk or not. It had been almost impossible to hide the substance abuse problems of the former First Lady.

When she fell down the stairs of Air Force One, the press had a heyday and exposed the administration for what it really was. The whole world was disgusted. Doctors had said that if she hadn't been so intoxicated, she would have really hurt herself, but the First Lady felt no pain. It wasn't long after that the press televised her leaving the White House for good.

While the meeting with the Fine Arts Committee was scheduled for later that afternoon, Clarke was really exited about his next meeting. He was being taken to the White House greenhouses. As Clarke was driven away, the Chief Usher was summoned to the Oval Office. In between political appointments, the President had made time to meet with the Chief Usher. With a few moments to spare, the President stepped outside to smoke his pipe. The grounds were lush. Birds sang from the trees. Squirrel's hippity-hopped across the lawn. The President hummed a show tune from *Camelot*. Then the Chief Usher was announced and the President came back inside and sat down behind his desk.

Sitting behind one's desk is always a subliminal sign of power. The only person it didn't work on was Clarke. It's hard to show power over someone when he's sitting ON your desk. The Chief Usher was a handsome man dressed in a simple dark suit. He carried a radio but looked very different from the Secret Service.

"You called for me, Mr. President?"

"Yes. Yes, I did." The President stood up, taking several pieces of paper that had been neatly folded and placed them back inside their envelope. He walked around the desk and the two men shook hands. The President led him over to the sofas in front of the fireplace and motioned for the Chief Usher to sit down.

The President sat across from him. An usher brought in a silver tea set with fresh hot coffee. It was placed on the butler's table in front of them. The Chief Usher was surprised and honored. The President motioned for him to relax as he poured the man a cup of coffee, then one for himself.

"As Chief Usher, I know you have an incredible responsibility running this house. I also know your job just got a lot harder when Clarke took the office of First Gentleman."

The Chief Usher smiled. He noticed the President was caring and very kind. The Chief Usher felt honored to work for such a grand man. He smiled to himself, wondering which man he was thinking about—the President or Clarke.

"I realize the prior administration really let things go." The President looked around his office; it had faded with use and neglect. "We all know that. The press has done a good job of informing the public of the former First Lady's substance abuse. I must admit I'm glad they haven't told it as it really was."

The Chief Usher nodded in agreement. It had been pretty bad. Smashed alcohol bottles against fine silk wallpaper, thrown lamps shattering into portraits, lit candelabra thrown onto upholstered furniture. Many White House relics had been destroyed in the prior First Lady's drunken rages.

The pieces had been swept up and, for history, it was meticulously documented as to how they were destroyed. Many of the finer pieces had been packed away for safekeeping. With Clarke's idea of turning the drab house into the White House, the Chief Usher had immediately sent for them.

The President continued. "Who knows? Maybe all that made this administration easier to accept. I don't know." Actually, the President *did* know. So did the Chief Usher. "Clarke is a hard one to keep under your thumb. I know that for a fact. The harder you try, the less likely you are to succeed. I know the former President needed to be told what was going on with his First Lady. I have found it better NOT to know what Clarke is up to until he tells me himself." The President handed the envelope to the Chief Usher. In it were the Chief Usher's notes on Clarke's every move and everything Clarke said when the President wasn't at his side.

"I would like you to build a rapport with Clarke and not tell me anything that's going on. I know Clarke will tell me in time." The President shook his head from side to side. "If Clarke doesn't tell me, I don't need to know." Michael started laughing, "Nor would I want to know. Clarke and I would only do what's right for the other." The President's caring expression seemed to convince the Chief Usher, who sighed, a smile of relief blossoming on his face. Excitement twinkled in the man's eyes. The President was happy to see that. The President and the Chief Usher chatted away about Clarke and his charm and the drab house becoming the White House again. The President could see the pride bursting from the man in front of him and it gave the President the boost he needed. He was honored to serve him. "More coffee?" The President asked. The Chief Usher nodded.

The President took the coffee urn and topped off the Chief Usher's cup. The Chief Usher could tell the President wasn't used to pouring. He handled the coffeepot like it was a football. The Chief Usher was so proud to be served by the President and given the order not to be a spy, but rather to assist.

A buzz announced the President's next appointment and informed the two men that their meeting was over. As they shook hands, the President asked where Clarke had gone. He had seen the limousine drive away while enjoying his pipe. The Chief Usher had a questioning look on his face.

"It's okay." The President laughed, gesturing with his hands. "That's not a spying question. I was just curious."

"Clarke is going to the White House greenhouses to meet with the floral designers," the Chief Usher said. The President motioned that that was all he wanted to know, and then he smiled. Clarke and his fresh flowers! As the Chief Usher left, a butler came in, picked up the silver set and wiped the table clean. Another butler took chairs from around the walls and strategically placed them in front of the President's desk.

The President again sat down behind his desk and his next appointments were escorted in. Two men who had advised the former President walked into the room and stopped at the sofas, presuming that's where they were going to be entertained. One raised an eyebrow as he watched the silver set being carried out. The President told them to take a seat, motioning to the chairs in front of his desk. The two men looked at each other, then frowned at the President.

The President found these two men irritating even to look at. They were the kind of politicians who gave the office a bad name and buffet tables a run for their money! But these two men were the tops in their field and the President needed their kind of expertise and experience. It was their bigotry and attitude he was going to do without.

From today's meeting the President would decide if they were to stay on his staff or be escorted off the grounds. The Secret Service was briefed, ready to go. The two men looked at each other again. They had a few rehearsed words for the President. If the President intended to stay in office, their looks plainly said, he would do what they told him.

The man seated in front of the desk and to the right of the President immediately took over the meeting. The President could smell the man's bad breath. "It was political suicide for you to introduce Clarke the way you did. You don't have a chance to be elected to office when this term is up. If you had to, you could have hid Clarke. Other administrations had their escorts."

The other advisor interrupted the man sitting next to him. He gave the President an order with his attitude. "It is imperative YOU keep Clarke out of the public eye." The man bobbed his head as he poked fun at Clarke's title, "*The First Man to be First Lady* redecorating the White House will just add to the stereotype. It will stop immediately."

The President slowly stood and leaned toward the men from behind his desk. The two men shrank in their seats. "*I* am the President. *Clarke* is my spouse." The President leaned toward the man who had sarcastically called Clarke the *First Man to be First Lady*. "His *proper* title is FIRST GENTLEMAN."

The man took a breath, ready to inform the President that *everyone* referred to Clarke as the First Man To Be First Lady. But the President interrupted the man's juvenile response. "I realize that every time the press refers to Clarke, they call him the *First Man to be First Lady*, but I *will not tolerate* that insult from anyone under this roof. Clarke will be shown the same respect as any woman who has held that position before him. HAVE I MADE MYSELF CLEAR?" The Secret Service pounced from the main entrance and side doors of the Oval Office. The two men looked scared to death. They couldn't move. They were afraid to even breathe.

The Secret Service stood by as the President continued talking in the men's faces. "If I want to introduce my spouse to the American people, I will do so when 'I' feel it's necessary and appropriate. If Clarke is in the limelight, then we finally have something handsome to look at."

The President stared harder at the first adviser, the one who had sneered at Clarke. "If Clarke feels the White House needs to be redecorated, then I suggest you take a better look at this drab house and see how misused it has been. I am not interested in what a second-term decision this could make. I am interested in the right decision." The President paused and looked at both men. "At this point, I am wondering if keeping the two of you on my staff is the right decision."

The Oval Office was silent. The President absolutely would not tolerate people on his staff insulting Clarke, either out loud or poking fun at him behind his back. If they did, they had one moment to apologize; if they missed that one moment, the next moment they would find themselves being escorted out of the administration. Both men immediately offered their apologies and sincerely asked what they could do for the First Couple.

With a nod from the President, the Secret Service agents turned and left the Oval Office. The President sat back down and looked hard at both men. "I believe we have an understanding." The President turned his head slightly. His gesture made it clear that he was waiting for an answer.

Both men chimed in with an embarrassed, "Yes, Mr. President."

Michael offered the man with bad breath a mint. Both men took one.

Clarke arrived at the White House's private greenhouses. In 1902, Theodore Roosevelt had the greenhouses moved from the White House grounds to make way for the presidential offices. They were now located in a secret area outside of the city and they were heavily guarded. The limousine stopped and Ms. Jones opened the door for Clarke.

The entire staff of the greenhouses was waiting for Clarke, lined up like soldiers in formation. In their starched smocks and freshly pressed aprons, Clarke was introduced to a wonderful team of very talented people. The floral staff briefed Clarke. Fresh flowers in the White House had been a tradition since the days of President Adams, the first President to live there. Blooming flowers out of season has always been considered something of a status symbol. "It was high society," one gardener drawled. The tradition lived on.

Clarke made it very clear he wasn't going to wear flowers as Mrs. Lincoln did. She wore flowers cascading down her gowns, roses pinned in her hair. Her breasts always blossomed with a corsage. And, to top it all off, she carried a bouquet. Clarke wouldn't even wear a boutonniere but he would make sure fresh flowers announced that class had certainly returned to the White House!

Clarke had many ideas for centerpieces so he donned one of the designer's aprons and actually worked 'hands on' with the designers. Together, they came up with spectacular results. Clarke was as impressed with the floral staff as they were with him. He made them feel that they were the most important people in the administration.

Clarke was really enjoying himself when Ms. Jones informed him they would have to leave soon if he were to stay on schedule. Clarke untied his apron and excused himself all in one fluid motion. He thanked everyone as he returned to the car.

Clarke arrived back at the White House in time to shower and dress for his meeting with the Fine Arts Committee. He was excited about it, but a little nervous, too. It was going to be expensive, but the White House needed to be done. Clarke would like to have used the Blue Room to entertain, but it was sparsely decorated and there weren't enough places to sit. So the Green Room was being cleaned and arranged for the guests. Clarke made sure the draperies were open so the committee could see for themselves the result of the horrible neglect of America's most popular house.

The committee members arrived and were checked through security. Clarke received them in the Green Room. Clarke proudly introduced Ms. Deverough as a new member of the committee. Each guest had been chosen to be on the committee and was honored to be there. As the meeting was about to start, notepads were taken out of briefcases. Clarke noticed one of the committee members, a well-dressed, distinguished man, seemed rather smitten with Saundra.

Saundra was incredibly beautiful. She wore another dark, two-piece suit trimmed in her signature whisper of faux leopard skin. She crossed her legs and gently rocked her foot. The man wiped his upper lip with a handkerchief and dabbed the sweat from his forehead. His body swayed to the beat of her rocking foot. Clarke thought they would make a nice couple, but he needed the man's undivided attention. Saundra didn't notice the man. She looked at Clarke, waiting for him to start the meeting.

"What I want to do is bring the White House back to its former grand state. During the Monroe administration, the Blue Room was red and the Red Room was yellow with Dolly Madison." The people in the room gasped. The committee knew that was historically correct. Their gasp got the attention of the man so smitten with Saundra.

"Of course, the Green Room has always been green so it will stay this way." Everyone laughed as they realized that Clarke was making a joke. The man apologized with a nod.

Clarke smiled at the man and said, "All righty then," and looked at everyone in the room. "I would like to start the meeting with some great ideas and tell you what I'd like to see for the White House." Clarke didn't talk politics or money. Just the importance of how the Presidency was presented to the world. Clarke had ideas for designs and what he wanted to do. Saundra listened and drew as fast as Clarke spoke. The members of the committee listened in fascination as Clarke breathed life back into the dingy rooms.

The committee then toured the first floor to see first-hand exactly what was needed. Clarke explained how rooms that were faded would again be bright with color. Worn furniture would be reupholstered. Rugs that were threadbare and had raveled would be replaced. The committee's tour brought them back to the Green Room where a lovely pastry cart and coffee had been wheeled in. Clarke's guests were so impressed with the Seattle brew and Clarke's ideas that they positively bubbled with excitement over the anticipated new look of the White House.

Clarke was informed that all the money to redecorate the State Rooms came from private donations. It had been a long time since any money had been put into White House decorating, so there was a comfortable budget to work with. Clarke was happy about that. Every room needed something, even if it was just a coat of paint. Clarke didn't want to make major changes; he just wanted to keep the house alive with the memories of those who had served there in the past, so that those touring in the present could feel secure with their future. The committee enjoyed Clarke's tongue twister.

The work was going to start right away, with a very rigorous schedule. One room at a time would be done. Clarke wanted the work done right away so the White House could entertain again. Saundra had put some ideas on a sketchpad. As coffee was poured, she impressed the committee with the same dazzle she had used for the Private Quarters.

She described drapery designs and fabrics, all with a gold metallic thread that would add sparkle to each room. The committee loved it. Clarke listened to her describing his ideas, even though he hadn't even told her yet what they were! Ms. Deverough just sat there quietly, poised as always, holding her teacup. Clarke caught her smile and nodded a thank you.

Saundra stood and talked with her unique, flamboyant flair. "The State Rooms are to remain the fine museum rooms that America has come to expect since 1962, when Jacqueline Kennedy restored them. I will sketch out our ideas as a committee and present them to Clarke. After he has given his approval, they can come back to the committee." Clarke was so honored she said it like that.

Clarke could tell the Fine Arts Committee enjoyed Saundra's speech. As she talked, Clarke watched their reactions. They nodded to each other with approving smiles. Saundra thanked the committee for allowing her to be part of the White House restoration then took her seat and looked to Clarke to continue the meeting.

The man who had been so smitten by Saundra spoke up. "Finally we have some class back in the White House." The committee nodded and toasted Clarke with their coffee cups.

Clarke thanked Saundra, then took over the meeting. "With approval from the Fine Arts Committee, I would like to see the redecorating of the State Rooms start at once. With all the traffic the White House has going through it, drapes, carpets and upholstery all show wear faster then any other home in America. With that in mind, I would like to order double on all the upholstery fabrics. We can have two sets of draperies made. One set to be hung now and the other set put in storage. When the draperies and upholstery begin to show wear, they can be replaced, keeping the White House dazzling without any fuss."

The committee members looked at each other, nodding their heads, almost applauding at Clarke's idea. It was such a positive response that Clarke confessed, "It was Pat Nixon who had the original idea and did the same thing."

A museum expert from the Smithsonian was so intrigued by Clarke she said, "Great First Ladies think alike." Everyone laughed. Clarke enjoyed having coffee with his guests. As the afternoon began to slip into early evening, Clarke rose and thanked all of his guests for coming. Clarke seemed to effortlessly step right into the position of First Gentleman. The press still referred to him as *The First Man To Be First Lady*, but

Clarke didn't mind the subliminal insult. He loved being close to Michael, actually living with him.

Clarke could tell the stress of the job was really getting to Michael. Michael had been chopping a lot of wood, but now that he had so many meetings scheduled, and it was nearly impossible to chop wood and talk politics at the same time, he did the next best thing. He took his private meetings out on the lawn, with a baseball and glove. It may have looked like Michael was just playing ball, but a comfortable meeting on the lawn playing catch threw Michael's adversaries off guard. While they played ball, Michael knew he was getting the truth and, at the same time, much needed exercise.

Many of his meetings were about the illegal drugs attacking the United States. The President vowed to step up the war on illegal drugs. That put a hefty terrorist price on Michael's head, which made Clarke very nervous. While the President was busy running the country, Clarke knew that, for his own sanity, he would need to keep just as busy. He needed something to take his mind off of worrying about Michael. Taking care of Michael and making the President's house a place America could be proud of would serve to keep Clarke very busy indeed. The days ahead were going to be very hectic and Clarke was looking forward to them.

Saundra designed the room on paper for the Fine Arts Committee, and then it went to Clarke for his approval. Once approved, the crew went into action. Just when Clarke thought one room was going to be started, a problem with draperies would come up or a new piece of furniture or artwork was donated. Of course, the new piece would be perfect and that changed ideas here and there. Clarke enjoyed not knowing what was going to happen next. One thing for sure, the White House was going to be spectacular and something the United States could be proud of again.

When the work started, Clarke donned a pair of painter's trousers speckled with paint, pulled on work gloves, put on a baseball cap turned backwards, and climbed the scaffolding with the crew. Newspapers reported that the *First Man To Be First Lady* was not only redecorating the house, he was also helping to paint and wallpaper it. Clarke hauled furniture around as if he were on the payroll. America hadn't seen a First Lady work like that since Eleanor Roosevelt, although she was never photographed painting the White House.

If something didn't look right, Clarke would take one end of a sofa and a member of the work crew would heft the other and it was moved. The press recorded it all. Americans saw it happening right before their eyes, in magazines at the grocery store and at every newsstand. Each article proudly reported that not one tax dollar was being used, that every cent came solely from private donations.

The first room to be finished was the Blue Room. The last time it had been redecorated was by Mrs. Clinton. The years had not been kind. It was secretly Clarke's favorite room and it was rumored that he shared that with Mrs. Lincoln. Clarke soon set the press straight. "Mrs. Lincoln's favorite room was the Red Room. Her family used it as a music room, complete with a grand piano. There has not been a piano in the Red Room since. And, to answer your questions, we are not going to put one back in there now." Clarke said with a smile.

The Blue Room wasn't for sitting in. Traditionally, the President had used it only for receiving guests. After greeting the President, guests would then enter either the Red Room or the Green Room. The Blue room was the first room one saw when entering through the North Portico, the main entrance of the White House. Since one never gets a second chance to make a first impression, the Blue Room would be the finest room in the house.

Although it was labeled the "Blue Room", over the years blue had only been an accent color. Clarke determined to put the "blue" back in the Blue Room. The bluest skies you've ever seen are in Washington, the state, and that's what inspired the new color for the Blue Room. Silk paper in a refreshing sky blue, accented with vibrant border prints with the shine of gold, covered the walls. Clarke had the chandelier that had hung in the Blue Room during the Kennedy administration moved from the Yellow Oval Room and put back where it belonged.

He ordered a new rug. It was oval, the same shape as the room and designed in the same sky blue with the border the same as the gold in the border print of the wallpaper. The furniture had been refinished and reupholstered. Pat Nixon had designed draperies that were fabulous. Clarke had them recreated with his flair and Saundra's fabric with the metallic thread.

As Clarke stood on the scaffolding holding one end of the draperies, he looked out the window to the beautiful view of the Washington Monument. Then Clarke noticed the President playing catch with someone. They were just throwing a baseball. A man took off running with Barney, then Michael threw the ball. He threw it so far it went past the man, who ran for it but wasn't fast enough to catch such a powerful throw. Barney retrieved the ball but didn't want to give it back, so Barney and the President played tag. Clarke smiled as he went back to the job at hand and hoisted his end of the drapery.

From the scaffolding, Clarke noticed that although the Blue Room was spectacular, it was sparsely decorated. It had beautiful furniture, but it needed something. Clarke called Saundra over to take a look. Saundra had such a bass drum of a walk. When she got to the scaffolding, it was apparent she would have to climb up to see what Clarke was talking about. Without missing a beat, Saundra pulled up her skirt and climbed up to Clarke.

The man on the scaffolding turned his head so hard, Clarke thought he had been yanked by the hair and viciously slapped. The workmen couldn't take their eyes off Saundra's legs. Clarke couldn't take his eyes off the barren room. It was missing something. Clarke just couldn't put his finger on it. Saundra climbed until she was eye to eye with Clarke. She reached over and pulled off his glasses. She put them on so she could see exactly what Clarke was talking about.

Saundra agreed. She handed Clarke back his glasses. The room needed something. Saundra climbed back down the scaffolding and walked to the center of the room, measuring with her feet. She placed one foot delicately in front of the other until she had measured an imaginary object. The work in the room stopped. The men were just staring at Saundra. Some were sweating; others appeared to stop breathing, while some couldn't seem to catch their breath. Clarke climbed off the scaffolding and followed Saundra's footsteps with the same idea.

They added a table designed in the unique oval shape of the room. A tablecloth, made out of the same fabric as the draperies with the same border print that framed the room scalloped along the bottom of the tablecloth and, of course, detailed with Saundra's gold metallic thread, would flow gracefully to the floor.

The room shined and once again became known as the most formal room in the White House. It was Clarke's favorite room. The color was soothing and Clarke's rare blue-marble mantel clock proved that this was indeed his home. The book, *The White House, An Historic Guide,* would picture the room before, with Clarke assisting with the restoration, then the finished room, and, finally, Clarke's favorite, a photograph of the President and Clarke receiving guests in the Blue Room.

The press continued to report that Congress had not appropriated money for the redecorating, reiterating that all money spent came from private donations. It dumbfounded the American people. Just when they thought Clarke was a "Dapper Dan", spending too much of the taxpayer's money, it turns out he hadn't even spent a dime of it. Any leftover funds would be put in a trust to keep the White House America's pride. The press loved it. They were inside the White House, watching and reporting on the most famous man in the world and didn't even need to see the President.

Since the Green Room and the Red Room could be entered through the Main Entrance Hall, through their own doors or through either side of the Blue Room, Clarke wanted to see continuity among the rooms. Saundra had the perfect idea. The drapes were accented with the same gold satin fabric in all three rooms. The Fine Arts Committee loved it.

The Red Room was decorated the same, but was on fire with color. The new silk wallpaper was bright and gilded with gold. The draperies were the same design, but made with Saundra's fabric and the gold accent that matched the Blue Room. The only thing Clarke changed was the rug. In past administrations, the rug that was used in the Red Room looked like it belonged on a back porch. Clarke's new rug was alive with vibrant reds. Flames seemed to dance from floor to ceiling.

Clarke and another workman were putting Dolly Madison's sofa in place. Clarke was eyeing the sofa, making sure it was centered with the painting, when something outside caught his eye. He noticed the President throwing the baseball again although the shrubbery blocked whomever he was with. Clarke noticed again how happy the President looked and how much fun Barney was having.

The President had removed his jacket, loosened his tie, and rolled up his shirtsleeves. Knowing the President, he was in a meeting with whoever was going to catch the ball. Michael was never one to sit behind a desk. Clarke laughed when the President looked to the sky and a baseball landed in his mitt. Saundra, saying, "It needs to go over just a bit, Dear," interrupted Clarke's show. Clarke on one end and a workman on the other followed her command and moved the sofa over just a bit.

The room that took the most effort and caused the biggest headaches was the Green Room. Pat Nixon was the last person who really did anything major to that room. It was beautiful when she finished, but Clarke hadn't even liked it then. Instead of redecorating the room, past administrations just kept adding more furniture. The room was filled with fine antiques, although worn, too much artwork nailed to the walls, and spectacular drapes shabby with age. The bottom line was that way too much was squeezed between those four walls.

With all the furniture stacked in it, one still couldn't find a place to sit. The Green Room was to become a sitting room that would resemble a fine parlor of the early 1800's. That was the law and the law was very clear: "The first floor would be decorated in the late 18th to the early 19th century only." Clarke loved how Mrs. Kennedy had decorated the Green Room. He had the drapes that Pat Nixon had designed for the room copied and splashed with his own special flair. The wallpaper they chose for the room was an emerald green silk. Matching emerald drapes were accented with the same gold satin that hung in the Red and Blue Rooms.

Clarke had most of the furniture removed and only select pieces were brought back. Before 1962, past administrations could do whatever they wanted with furniture that was in the White House, including keeping it. In 1962, a law changed all that. Anything bought for the White House with taxpayer's money or donated to the White House that was not being used by the First Family in office had to be stored. It could not be thrown out or become private property of the President. American taxpayers loved that. The only person who didn't was President Johnson. When he left the presidential aircraft for the last time in

1969, he ordered all china, silver, crystal, and any furniture not bolted down be taken off the aircraft as a gift to himself.

Clarke loved the White House history and found himself daydreaming of First Couples past. Clarke came back to reality in the middle of the Green Room. Saundra had designed the perfect fabric for the Green Room furniture. Since the walls and draperies were dark, the furniture would be upholstered in a refreshing champagne color. The same emerald green of the drapes and Saundra's metallic thread would run through the upholstery in a thin pinstripe. Clarke had the chandelier hung lower. It was simple in design, compared to the Blue Room, but one couldn't enjoy it so high up. A new rug in emerald green framed the entire room. Clarke was proud to point out that the Green Room displayed the White House's most valuable paintings.

Stunning was the only word that could describe the finished Green Room. It was the room that had needed the most attention and it got it. Making its debut on St. Patrick's Day, the Green Room was photographed by and featured in all the decorator's magazines with as much fanfare as an Irish Parade.

The State Dining Room was repainted. Of course, Clarke was there rolling paint and wiping up drips. Since the major portion of the work was done, Clarke started on the trim work around the window. He just happened to look out and saw something flying right towards him at warp speed.

Clarke screamed, "Everyone hit the floor!" The horror in Clarke's voice caused everyone to panic. Clarke couldn't move fast enough. His world went into slow motion. Clarke grabbed the person next to him and threw him to the floor. The work crew stumbled off of scaffolding, trying to cheat an imminent death. Clarke covered the person next to him as a horrendous crash drowned everyone's screams. Secret Service poured into the room with their guns cocked, ready to shoot. Everyone lay motionless.

The Secret Service immediately secured the area. Ms. Jones picked up the assailant's weapon, tossed it into the air and caught it with an attitude. "It's a baseball," she calmly reported to the paralyzed work crew. Ms. Jones knew exactly who threw it. So did Clarke. Clarke helped up the person he had thrown to the floor. Clarke was embarrassed by his hysteria and nervously laughed an apology. The work crew stood, trying to shake off their fear.

"If these windows are bullet proof, then they should be baseball proof," a furious Ms. Jones said. Clarke didn't know what to be more scared of, something flying through the window at warp speed or Ms. Jones really angry.

"The President has quite a throwing arm," Clarke said, trying to calm a very tense moment. Clarke's heart was still pounding. He looked back at the broken window and the puddle of paint. Clarke had safely landed on the paintbrush, which he peeled off of his overalls. Just then the President came into the room with Barney trotting along, looking for his baseball.

"Is everyone all right?" the President asked as he looked around the room. Everyone was still a little shaken, but finally laughed with relief. Ms. Jones tossed the baseball to the President.

Clarke was still laughing at his own embarrassment. The whole room laughed at their own embarrassment. The President apologized as the maintenance crew came in to measure new glass. The President left, with everyone still wondering why a baseball was thrown through the State Dining Room window.

As a cleaning crew swept shattered glass into a pile, Ms. Jones explained the mystery of the baseball to the workmen. "Whenever the President has a private meeting, he grabs the baseball mitts, tosses one to whomever he has a meeting with, and they conduct their meeting while playing catch." No one questioned this and the work in the Dining Room resumed.

Clarke was so shaken up that he could barely hold the brush. Saundra came into the room and announced, with outstretched hands, that the fabric for the State Dining Room chairs had just arrived. Saundra never questioned the broken window or the pile of shattered glass. Clarke left the paintbrush soaking in turpentine and bounced down the stairs, telling Saundra the story.

Clarke was still laughing about the baseball coming through the window, but it wasn't a laugh of jocularity, it was a laugh to mask his fear. Michael warned Clarke that in the months ahead he would be leaving for a drug summit being held on foreign soil. For security reasons, he would not let Clarke go with him. Clarke read between the lines and that terrified him.

Thank God Clarke had the White House redecorating to keep his mind off Michael's safety.

As Clarke unrolled the fabric, Saundra took command and bubbled at Clarke, "The chairs will be reupholstered in gold lame." Saundra paused as she brushed her hands across the fabric. "Clarke, their sparkle will put the finishing touches on the fine dining you have brought to the White House." Clarke smiled at Saundra's excitement.

The East Room was painted as well. Carpet had been laid in past administrations but Clarke had that taken up and new flooring put down. It was the same kind of flooring that would have been used when the White House was originally built; even though the White House was occupied, it was years before the East Room had been finished.

Clarke was fascinated with the history of the East Room. Mrs. Adams had used the East Room to hang her wash. During the Civil war, soldiers were on guard and used the East Room as their barracks. Clarke would make sure that the room would dance with history. How the East Room would look when Clarke finished with it is how it would have looked when the White house was new and still smelled of fresh wood and paint.

The Lincoln Bedroom was America's favorite room in the house. Many people from around the world offered to pay millions to spend the night there. It, too, had really shown its wear. The upholstery had faded and the draperies had almost rotted away from their hooks.

Clarke kept Mary Todd Lincoln in mind with the room's restoration. It was she who chose the furniture, not Abraham, so it took research on Mary Todd Lincoln, not President Lincoln, to make that room sing with authenticity and HER flair. The room was complimented with a whisper of Abraham's masculinity and Clarke's eye for the metallic.

Grace Coolidge favored the Lincoln Bedroom. While her husband was in office, she personally crocheted a coverlet for the bed. Clarke had the room photographed with it but the crocheted piece was only put on the bed when Barney would not be around to lie on it. Whenever Barney wasn't with the President or Clarke, he was sound asleep on Lincoln's bed. Clarke gave up on trying to train Barney not to lie there and had Mrs. Coolidge's coverlet folded away.

New red carpets were designed for the entrance hall. Dignitaries and Heads of State entered through the North Portico, the front door of the White House, which opened to the Main Entrance Hall. Now, when the Marine band played, they read their music from fine, hand-carved, wooden music stands. In the past, the metal music stands looked like they had come from an elementary school band room. It was the first thing Clarke had changed. The Marines loved it and said thank you with perfect tone.

The Diplomatic Reception Room stayed the same but it needed the film lifted off. It was the room where guests other than heads of state entered the White House. New upholstery brought the furniture back to life. Wallpaper was cleaned and touched up until it looked new. The carpet had faded, so Clarke had an exact replica made, but a tiny bit smaller so that everyone entering the White House could enjoy the exquisite craftsmanship in the marble floors.

Clarke wanted to redecorate the Oval Office, too, but he wanted it to be a surprise for the President. As Clarke and Saundra were going over sketches, Clarke saw Michael outside throwing the baseball. Clarke shrieked to Saundra, "HE'S OUTSIDE!" Saundra closed her portfolio just as Clarke grabbed her hand. Hand-in-hand, Clarke and Saundra bubbled with ideas as they ran down the main hall then outside across the pillared colonnade to the Oval Office. Secret Service effortlessly ran along, talking into their radios, informing the West Wing staff that Clarke was on his way.

Clarke and Saundra barged into the West Wing. A security guard Clarke had never seen was sitting behind a desk. The guard stood, trying to be intimidating. He ordered Clarke to stop. Clarke and Saundra just trotted on by. The guard walked from behind his desk rudely pointing at Clarke. "You can't go in there. The President is out of the office." The guard said in a very rehearsed, but condescending tone. "The only person who can go in there without the President is the First Lady."

Clarke stopped dead in his tracks. Saundra thought Clarke had smacked into a brick wall but there was nothing there. Clarke knew exactly what the guard meant by his patronizing tone. Clarke slowly turned around. Saundra stepped back and braced herself. Clarke walked towards the overgrown man.

Calmly, Clarke asked, "Exactly who do you think tucks the President in at night?"

The security guard had never met Clarke, but what he heard about the First Man To Be First Lady was obviously true. The man nervously stuttered, trying to babble an answer. Just then Ms. Jones walked around the corner. Clarke looked at her and said a simple, "Ms. Jones." She knew what Clarke was thinking and nodded in agreement. She escorted the man away.

Clarke and Saundra walked into the Oval Office and shut the door behind them. Saundra looked at Clarke. Clarke looked at Saundra. They both burst into laughter. Clarke laughed so hard tears came to his eyes. When Clarke finally caught his breath, he took a handkerchief out of his pocket and removed his glasses. Clarke wiped off his glasses as he explained to Saundra what he wanted. "The Oval Office is going to be the most spectacular room on the grounds." Clarke looked through his glasses, making sure they were clean, then put them back on and folded his handkerchief away. "The decor must say, 'power sits behind this desk'." Saundra nodded. Clarke and Saundra measured and quietly talked to one another. The Secret Service was standing guard. Clarke was going to keep this a secret until just the right moment.

Saundra had the perfect idea. Again. As her voice bubbled, she clapped her hands. "Let's do something fabulous with the carpet." She cocked her head to one side. "It will take some time." She paused. Her expression said it would be worth the wait.

Clarke interrupted her pause with an anxious, "What? What do you have in mind?"

Saundra whispered behind her shielding hand. "Lets do the rug in a deep royal blue with bright gold leaf trim." Saundra smiled with a sparkle. "The Presidential Seal will be designed right in the middle of the carpet." Saundra stopped whispering. She gestured where there was nothing, but clearly had *something* in mind.

"We'll put a glass-topped coffee table between two kidney-shaped sofas that will be facing each other." It was absolutely perfect and best of all Clarke immediately loved it. "Of course, the rocking chairs will stay right where they are."

Saundra said. "But I have some great ideas for matching upholstery." She winked at Clarke.

The rocking chairs had become a personal favorite of the President. Clarke had designed and bought matching rocking chairs to be used by the First Couple whenever they were together in the Oval Office: one for the President and one for Clarke. The chairs were made of mahogany with a soft rose glow one would appropriately call burgundy. The chairs were the perfect his and his set. The President's rocking chair had a taller back. Clarke's rocking chair had a fluffy cushioned seat.

The only time Clarke would allow the chairs to be side by side was when Clarke and the President were sitting together in the Oval Office watching the evening news. The President wanted to make sure he saw the same news reports as the American people. The First Couple's schedule was so tight that when they watched the evening news together, it was more like a date.

For the time being, the Oval Office would just be spruced up. Then, when the time was right and the carpets done, Clarke would surprise the President with all new furniture and a totally redecorated office. Clarke and Saundra left the Oval Office and continued with the White House redecorating.

Clarke saved the room that would cause the worst press for last. The China Room. The room was going to be splendid, as smooth as the china itself. Clarke and Saundra were both surprised that one of the White House's most treasured china pieces, the rococo-revival very tall pedestal punch bowl from the President Franklin Pierce administration, was put on a window sill. Not only was it fabulous, it was an enormous, flamboyant piece of priceless porcelain. No wonder Clarke loved it so. The punch bowl was extravagantly huge. Reluctantly Clarke agreed. There was no other place for the punch bowl to be displayed, but the windowsill. The cabinets that lined the China Room were big, but still way too small for such a grand piece.

The cabinets that held china from past administrations looked like something from a farm kitchen—perfect for a farmhouse, but not at all suitable for the fine museum pieces of the White House. Clarke had the entire room remodeled so that everyone touring the White House could see America's most treasured relics. Saundra designed all new cabinets, each with their own lighting, and complete with adjustable shelves.

The doors were made of beveled glass and went from floor to ceiling. Clarke had the finest wood carvers in the United States carve the American Eagle into the wood that framed the glass. The cabinets were stained in a burgundy hue that seemed to glow under the subdued lighting. New carpet and velvet draperies complimented the room.

Hysteria exploded from the press: *The First Man To Be First Lady* had ordered china for the most controversial First Couple in White House history! Clarke met with American designers for china proudly made in the USA and working together, a brilliant idea was transformed into an exquisite china pattern. In past administrations, color was used in the Presidential China. The Truman china was designed in green. President Wilson had china designed in blue. Of course, the Reagan's used the stunning Reagan Red. Clarke didn't choose a new color. He had his china designed in a champagne color to enhance the china already being used in the White House.

Instead of an eagle pattern, in a painted or a raised design like all the other Presidential China, Clarke had the eagle design artistically carved out and beveled along the rim of the plates. The china had the fragile look of lace but was designed with durability for White House entertaining. One thing all Presidential China shared was that all services had been trimmed in gold. Keeping with that tradition, Clarke had the eagle beveling etched in the same bright gold. Clarke could still accent table settings with the china of Presidents-past with their true colors showing through his stunning pattern.

The press viciously reported *The First Man To Be First Lady's* china was the most expensive pattern the White House had ever purchased. The publicity surrounding Clarke's enormous china acquisition made Nancy Reagan's china fiasco look like an imaginary spill at a child's tea party. To Clarke's favor, his selection of china was the most elegant china pattern the White House had ever seen.

The press shocked the world when they finally admitted that not one penny of the taxpayer's money had been spent on The First Man To Be First Lady's china. Every single cent came from private and corporate contributions. So much money had been donated that Clarke had many pieces designed for the place settings, including a luncheon service. The President liked the china. He was glad Clarke had designed the coffee cup with a handle big enough a man could put his fingers through.

For the first time in European history, royalty envied the china made in the United States. The Royal Family had the same American china company design a pattern for their own Palace. Their ideas mimicked Clarke's china pattern, although adapted to their royal flair. When that hit the press around the world, no one ever again questioned the price of the White House China.

While sweeping up the pieces of the bad press, one evening news anchorman summed it all up, "With the dignity of a Queen, Clarke, *the First Man To Be First Lady*, has brought the elegance back to White House." The President reached over and lovingly squeezed Clarke's hand.

The First Ball of the Season

It was a national tradition for the President to throw the first baseball of the season. Michael was really looking forward to that. Every time Clarke looked out a window, he saw a baseball flying by it or through it. So far the press hadn't heard about the broken window. The media loved the Sportsman President. With all the publicity, America couldn't wait for opening day.

It was obvious the President loved all sports. His favorite was football, with baseball being a close and almost-tied second. The President never said that publicly but Clarke knew it, and so did anyone else who had watched the President watching football. The closest Clarke got to a football was the other white meat. During football season Clarke did what every other wife in America did—planned time with his husband around a football game.

The President played catch with anyone who would don a mitt. He practiced throwing the baseball so many times that the scent of his cologne was Ben Gay. Clarke liked rubbing the President down anytime he could, Ben Gay, or not. With the anticipation of a child trying to sleep Christmas Eve away, opening day finally arrived. It was guaranteed to be the most watched TV event since who shot J.R.! Of course, not too many people remembered that one anymore.

The President wanted Clarke there in the stadium with him. Clarke couldn't think of any excuse not to go and started to think of all the great reason for going. He wanted to share any excitement with the President. Clarke gladly looked forward to its being over. Clarke would be at the President's side, just like every other First Lady. Beverly Anderson designed an outfit that said Clarke was true, like the red, white and blue. The press reported that, for a baseball game, Clarke was overdressed, but for the game of First Man to Be First Lady, Clarke was a home run with bases loaded. Clarke was in his signature vest ensemble and, of course, his spectator shoes.

The President arrived in a convoy that said, "Let's play ball." The President was so happy he was grinning like a little boy on his first day of little league. America could see his excitement. Applause roared from the stands as "Hail to the Chief" was played. Television cameras zeroed in on Clarke. Thousands stood in the stands trying to get a closer look with a flash of a camera.

Clarke stopped on the sidelines with the Secret Service contingent. The President was escorted out onto the field and stood in line with the players, surrounded by more Secret Service Agents. The National Anthem was sung by one of the greatest American opera singers, Mrs. Elizibette McManion, accompanied by a famous trio of overweight tenors.

It was performed beautifully and literally moved the viewing audience to tears. The crowd cheered at their performance. For many in the stands, it was the closest they would ever come to an opera. From that moment on, Mrs. Elizibette McManion and the three overweight tenors were known as the Star Spangled Operas.

Michael was so excited. He looked back at Clarke and winked. This moment, to the President, was like an afternoon tea to Clarke. Clarke nodded back a smile for good luck.

Dutch Peterson, the sports announcer, complimented the performers over the loudspeaker, which surprised Clarke. Dutch Peterson never had a good word to say about anything, from sports to life in general. The public tuned in to hate him. He deserved it almost as much as he enjoyed it. His sports predictions were always right. If he said an athlete was up and coming, the athlete was up and coming. If he said a player was finished, the player was finished. HE WAS ALWAYS RIGHT, which was one of the reasons people loved to hate him.

Dutch was his nickname; no one knew why, or what his real name was. He was "Dutch" when you agreed with his choice and you sneered and used his last name, "Peterson," if you didn't. But deep down, you knew he was right. Dutch Peterson was arrogant, pompous, unattractive, and irritating to the point you wanted to pull the trigger. America liked that in their villains and would tune in just to hate Dutch Peterson a little bit more.

Surprisingly enough, "Dutch" loved the President and insisted on announcing the game from the field so he could meet him personally. He never said one bad word about President Michael Arthur Kent. And Dutch Peterson never said a good word about Clarke. After all the applause, the performers left the field. The President was given his cue. Clarke was escorted to where the President was standing. It was time. Michael removed his jacket and handed it to Clarke.

He stepped up to the pitcher's mound and Dutch had the honor of tossing the President the first ball of the season. The President caught the ball easily then positioned himself so he could throw the first pitch. No one was going to bat at it. The President knew it was just a tradition, but he wanted to show the world what a great pitcher he was.

A drum roll began. The President took his position in a stance that would make Babe Ruth proud. He was wearing a baseball cap signed by the greats for the evening. The President was almost the happiest Clarke that had ever seen him, which made Clarke happy and very proud to be at his side. The drum rolled on. Michael turned his cap around like any other man playing baseball. The audience cheered. The President wound up and threw the baseball as cameras flashed. America cheered then stood and clapped.

It was a perfect pitch, right over home plate, within the strike zone, landing right smack dab in the catcher's mitt.

The umpire sang out, "STRRRRIKE" and motioned "He's outta there!" with a gesture. The catcher saluted the President's perfect pitch and the crowd went wild. The President waved to the crowd, turned his baseball cap around and walked over to Clarke. Clarke helped him on with his jacket. That proud smile was still across Michael's face and Clarke couldn't help but smile himself.

As the First Couple was escorted to their assigned box seats, Dutch Peterson asked for everyone's attention on a squealing microphone. Clarke thought it was to report how fast the President had thrown the ball. Clarke was as anxious as the rest of America to hear the "stats". Clarke didn't know much about sports, but he did pick up the lingo here and there. Dutch Peterson didn't have any "stats", but he did have an incredibly pointed devilish streak.

"Ladies and Gentlemen," Dutch Peterson went on. "Since this is an administration of firsts, we'd like to continue the tradition here on the field." The President almost thought he was going to pitch for the opening inning and would have loved it. Dutch Peterson wore a devilish smile that Satan himself would be envious of. "We would like to have the *First Man To Be First Lady* throw the ball." He smirked as he looked directly at Clarke.

The Presidential entourage knew that whenever a public figure or the press referred to Clarke as *The First Man To Be First Lady*, it was meant as an insult. He was rarely referred to as First Gentleman or the President's husband. Instead, he was always "politely" insulted with the title of 'The First Man To Be First Lady.' It was a constant subliminal attack on Clarke's masculinity. Clarke never faltered. The President alone saw the horror of humiliation in Clarke's eyes but Clarke's smile hid the degradation to the rest of the world. The First Couple had come so far with acceptance. This could destroy everything they had achieved.

Clarke agreed with a nod to Dutch Peterson and turned to catch the ball. Since the baseball the President threw would be auctioned off for charity, a fresh baseball right out of the package was thrown to Clarke. Dutch Peterson took pleasure in tossing the baseball with a masculine and over-exaggerated throw. Clarke caught the baseball with both hands. The force of the throw almost hurt him. Clarke honestly didn't know if you dribbled the ball or if it was made of pigskin, all he knew for sure was that all of America was watching.

Thousands of people were in the stands and millions were watching on TV. The field was incredibly quiet. A drum roll began. The look on many people's faces was one of horrid humiliation and sympathy for Clarke, knowing he was going to throw a gutter ball. They almost wished he had stayed home with an imaginary illness. Mrs. McManion and the three overweight tenors grabbed each other by the hand and silently prayed for Clarke. Millions stood by their TV's, ready to laugh and call the First Man To Be First Lady a fag. The President was ready to punch Dutch Peterson in the mouth.

The drum roll continued. No one was standing at home plate. Clarke looked at the President, then over at Dutch Peterson. Mr. Peterson was walking backwards toward the outfield, teasing Clarke with a gesture to throw the baseball to him. Clarke had a new enemy and Mr. Peterson was at the top of his list. Clarke looked over at Ms. Deverough. There was no secret code, no signal, and no advice this time. Ms. Deverough just smiled, but Clarke could tell she was angry. She had a loaded pistol for Dutch Peterson when it was all over and, knowing Ms. Deverough, she was anxious to use it.

Clarke positioned himself just as he had seen the President do. The drum rolled on. Clarke wound up ready to throw. The drum rolled on. For luck, Clarke had an angel on his shoulder and a penny in his pocket. The drum rolled on. Clarke followed through. The drum rolled on. Time ticked in slow motion. The drum rolled on, louder and louder.

Clarke threw that baseball higher and farther than any baseball had ever been thrown before. It was like watching an eagle grace the sky. The stands were silent as spectators watched, dumbfounded at the strength and talent The First Man To Be First Lady had in throwing a baseball.

Now time went from standing still and began to gain momentum to slow motion. People in the stands were caught on camera, flabbergasted looks on their faces. Everyone watched, heads slowly turning, following the baseball. Spectators sprang to their feet to get a better look. Arched eyebrows of disbelief were captured on film. Then cheers deafened with applause. Dutch Peterson ran, trying to catch the ball, but Clarke had thrown the ball way out of his reach. The President just stood there bursting with pride. Ms. Deverough smiled.

A cheer in a double syllable, "Cla-arke" sang from the stands, started by Mrs. McManion. The three overweight tenors laughed with such relief they were almost in tears as they clapped. The crowd wanted more Clarke. They were almost out of control, chanting Clarke's name. Ms. Deverough just smiled and danced to the beat of the double syllable.

Clarke moved closer to centerfield. The marquee blinked the word 'Clarke' in rhythm to the crowd's chants. Clarke waved from centerfield. Secret Service surrounded Clarke in a big circle. Clarke felt as if he were playing Farmer in the Dell and blushed at all the attention. Cheering crowds delightedly watched Clarke looking like an actor who was genuinely surprised he had won an Academy Award. Clarke waved another shy thank you all around the stadium.

He walked back to where the President was standing. The smile on Michael's face said how proud he was of Clarke. The First Couple looked over at Dutch Peterson, huffing and puffing and out of breath. He had run back from the outfield, and was requesting that Clarke autograph the ball. With a nod, Clarke said a simple, "Mr. Peterson." His tone thanked Dutch for being such a jerk. Clarke signed the ball, "Clarke, THE FIRST GENTLEMAN." Mr. Peterson was silent, feeling stupid and knowing he had been humiliated on camera.

Michael enjoyed watching the ballgame from their perfect seats. He rooted for each ballplayer, not a particular team. Clarke sat poised as if he were sitting for a portrait. He enjoyed watching Michael having so much fun. In a live interview with cable sports, the President proudly said, "I'm the guy who came to the ballgame with Clarke."

Later that evening, as the First Couple was getting ready for bed, Michael watched Clarke. All the negative press, the humiliation, the nasty televised opinions about Clarke's masculinity, none of it seemed to bother Clarke. As Clarke got into bed, he looked up and saw the Michael smiling at him.

"Caught in the act," Michael said.

Clarke knew what Michael was thinking and snuggled up close. In a breathy, romantic tone Clarke said, "We owe the big guy a lot for this one." The President reached over and turned out the light.

As the sun rose, Michael rolled over. Clarke was already up and about. Normal. Clarke was always the first one up. If the President didn't get up and shower, Clarke would bring him breakfast in bed.

Today was a day for celebration. It had finally arrived. Clarke was already at the breakfast table. Rehearsed. Ready. The Family Dining Room was a great place for the First Couple to start their day. The room was elegant. A warm fire softly danced. The First Couple were freshly showered, comfortable in woolly bathrobes and the world was completely shut out. Except for the occasional interruption from the Chief Usher.

Today at breakfast, Clarke was going to prove to the President that he had made it in the fashion world. In that world, Clarke was a brilliantly polished diamond reflecting fire in any light. Michael was a diamond in the rough. Strong. Resilient. Powerful. The fashion magazine had really outdone itself with a wonderful cover pose of the President. Clarke knew all about it, but had kept it a secret from everyone.

Clarke had the first magazine hot off the press. He was going to surprise the President. Clarke poured coffee into a china cup nestled in a fragile saucer. It had been a few weeks since Clarke had to prove his masculinity by throwing a baseball and he was finally back to being Clarke again.

"Clarke, could I have a mug? Please?" The President asked.

An usher handed Clarke a large mug. Clarke filled it with a smile. The Chief Usher came into the room, interrupting with a bounce, waving the first issue of *Sport Magazine*. The President had always dreamed of being on the cover of *Sport Magazine*. When he was handed the issue, he looked dazed.

Clarke looked at the President. "Are you all right?" Clarke was ready to call for help.

He looked over at Clarke and smiled from ear to ear. "They got the best man for the cover." He turned the magazine so Clarke could see it for himself. There was Clarke, in a very masculine pose, throwing the baseball. With a frown Clarke tried hard to smile. He knew the President was disappointed he wasn't on the cover but could also tell he was amazingly proud.

The President started laughing at Clarke's reaction. Clarke was genuinely disappointed that the President wasn't on the front cover, then noticed that Michael was on the back cover. The press always had a way of subliminally wondering who was on top. Clarke was ready to say how sorry he was when the President said, "As long as I'm not on the cover of a fashion magazine, I'll be just fine." The President thought that was a great joke and laughed as he said, "Me. The rumpled President, married to the best dressed man in the world, on the cover of a fashion magazine." He really howled at the impossibility.

As Clarke laughed with the President, he secretly rolled the magazine in his hands, still hiding it beneath the table. The magazine really liked the rumpled—what they called "relaxed look"—of the President. Thanks to Clarke, the President of the United States had been voted the second-best-dressed man in the world.

An Interview with Mrs. Waters

Mrs. Waters was THE name in television interviews. Like her name, Mrs. Waters could be cool and calm, as relaxing as a lazy summer day. But, as mysteriously as the sea, her interviews could become wild, with uncontrollable waves of fury. You would watch her interviews carefully, like a meteorologist tracking a hurricane. You never knew which direction her devastation would turn. You tuned in to be shocked and, above all, grossly entertained. One thing for sure, Mrs. Waters earned her million-dollar paycheck with every word.

In the White House, it was a typical interview day. Clarke and Beverly Anderson were putting the final touches on Clarke's ensemble. The President was in the Oval Office, trying to officially stay away. He was waiting for anything that might be more important, including a chat about the weather with the cleaning crew!

Tonight, America would see exactly how the President and the First Man To Be First Lady lived and where they slept. That's what America really wanted to see—where the First Couple slept. Clarke was glad to give them a tour. The Private Quarters was absolutely stunning. Clarke had often thought about doing some of the formal entertaining there, but the State Rooms were so full of history that Clarke wanted the present to enjoy the past. Up till now, the Private Quarters had not been photographed for the public or seen through the eyes of a television camera. After the interview, their "home" would be photographed by *Architect's Magazine.*

The Private Quarters was a kaleidoscope of color. Ornate furniture was upholstered in jewel tones, mostly in burgundy, and accented with sapphire and emerald green. Rooms sparkled with Saundra's trademark metallic gold thread whispering through the fabric. Artwork would be re-hung so the camera angle would be perfect and the backdrop exquisite. Fresh floral arrangements were still in the cooler. New, unburned candles had been placed in all the candelabra.

The President's outfit was pressed and ready to go, his tie tied and shoes polished. Typical. Clarke's ensemble was given a once-over, then pressed with a steamer while it was still on the mannequin. Clarke was at ease on stage or in front of the television camera but like every good actor, Clarke psyched himself up for an award-winning performance.

Clarke insisted that, if he and the President were to give a personal interview, all questions to be asked would be pre-approved. Mrs. Waters strictly forbade that, which was fine with Clarke—he flatly refused to do the interview. Clarke would not agree to any interview unless he knew exactly what was going to be asked. However, through the bargaining process and with the advice from every political advisor to the President, along with a personal request from Michael, Clarke finally, although reluctantly, agreed to the interview.

Clarke was given a list of three hundred questions; twenty would be asked and only Mrs. Waters knew which questions would actually be asked. That was fine. Clarke had nothing to hide and neither did the President. The questions asked would appear to be candid, trying to catch the First Couple off-guard.

The President had done everything he could to avoid the interview, including walking Barney. He finally gave in when Barney led him back upstairs. Ms. Jones opened the door for him and Clarke informed Michael that it was time to get ready. The President dressed.

Clarke gave Michael the once-over, adjusting the knot of his tie. There wasn't anything wrong with his tie; it's just something you do, like putting a period at the end of a sentence. One adjusts their husband's tie. The President looked very handsome. Refusing any more fuss, he clicked the remote to cable sports. He wasn't going to watch anything, but it was something HE did. Like putting a period at the end of sentence.

They were alone in the Presidential Suite. Michael looked over at Clarke and smiled. Clarke had quite a masculine physique. He was toned and tanned. But Michael was the only one who knew that. Clarke was sexy and America needed to see it; maybe then some of the nasty press about Clarke's masculinity would stop.

The camera crew arrived and began setting up their equipment. A cleaning crew vacuumed around them. The staff put out the fresh flowers so the camera could get the perfect shot. Candles would be lit just moments before the cameras went on. Saundra was giving the director and his staff a private tour of the White House. Ms. Deverough was going to take care of Barney while the interview was being taped live. It hadn't been discussed whether Barney was going to be interviewed or not, so he would be on the sidelines, waiting with Ms. Deverough.

Ms. Deverough always enjoyed her 'shooting star'. If Barney were left with the Secret Service and Michael and Clarke were in the next room, Barney would play havoc with anything and everyone until he was rescued. So tonight, to keep the Secret Service calm and Barney at bay, he stayed with Ms. Deverough.

Clarke had showered and dressed in everything but his shirt and tie. He would part his hair and slick it down after he was dressed. But for right now it was all combed back. Clarke was dressed in the Beverly Anderson label, of course. He was wearing a bright yellow silk tank top that matched his silk boxers. His triple-pleated trousers were dark—you couldn't tell if they were a dark emerald green or black, and, of course, he was wearing spectator shoes.

Clarke looked as though he should be a model for trendy masculine cologne. He wouldn't even consider being photographed in anything but what his position required. Even though he was the First Gentleman, there was one thing Clarke shared with the ladies who were there before him—it wasn't a position where one was photographed topless. Clarke felt that if America was going to make fun of him, they were going to make fun of the real Clarke. A well-dressed, classy fellow who the press constantly referred to as, "The First Man To Be First Lady."

Clarke was right on time, with a few moments to relax. He was finally excited about the interview and bounced around like a sunbeam. As he was pulling open the double doors to leave, he turned and yelled back to Michael, "Darling, did you want a sandwich before the interview?"

Clarke continued through the doorway and suddenly stopped dead in his tracks. He grabbed at the door and tried to hide. He quickly looked to the right then to the left. There was the entire interview staff with cameras rolling. Everyone in the room began to clap. Clarke was so embarrassed. Then he saw the President and smiled. Knowing the joke was on him, Clarke looked at Mrs. Waters, "The President and his surprises."

Clarke was very poised, as elegant as America expected and everything they wanted to see in a man. Mrs. Waters asked her first question of the evening, "Will you ever forgive the President?" She smiled, almost laughing at Clarke's expression.

"Of course I will forgive the President." Clarke paused, "With revenge." Clarke said, singing the word "revenge" with a laugh. He continued, "We agreed on seven o'clock and I am going to honor that. If you will excuse me?" Clarke made eye contact with the entire crew as he excused himself and walked back through the doorway he had just come out of. The President had already left the room and was back to watching cable sports. As Clarke shut the doors behind him, you could hear him yell in the same loving tone, "Darling, *did* you want a sandwich before the interview?"

The President did so Clarke whipped up a sandwich for his husband, then finished dressing and styled his hair. It was seven on the dot when the First Couple emerged from behind the closed doors. They took a seat on the sofa, facing Mrs. Waters. Clarke could smell the fragrance of the fresh floral arrangements. Even though the camera lights were bright, lit candles seemed to cast a romantic glow about the room. Clarke was a little nervous. Butterflies. His sign of good luck. The President smiled at him.

Mrs. Waters had a script in front of her. She had a very unusual style that America had come to expect. Her interviews were a bit choppy, but genuine. A red light appeared on top of the camera. Mrs. Waters started her performance, looking first at Clarke. "Tell us about a trick YOU'VE played on the President."

Clarke thought for a moment, then smiled and looked at the President. They both laughed as one does when the joke's on them. It may not be funny to the rest of the world. It's just funny to them. That's all that matters for their joke. "Well, we have this great coffeemaker that was a gift many years ago. It's an oldie…"

"But a goodie." The President said. He wasn't interrupting but rather sharing a moment with his husband. "It makes the coffee boiling hot and keeps it bubbling all day if you'd let it. I take my coffee, black, thick, and hot!"

Clarke was having just as much fun with Mrs. Waters' question. "Which is why we've always had his and his coffeemakers." Mrs. Waters smiled and obviously wanted to laugh. The camera caught it and so did Clarke. So what? "Michael can't wait for the coffeemaker to brew a full cup. As soon as there's enough coffee for half a cup, he plays tag with the coffeemaker. He has his cup ready. He's poised. On the count of three," Clarke leaned forward, using his hands, trying to look like a man his man was. "He does this quick grab-pour-and-put-back thing."

"And without loosing a single drop." Michael added. He snapped his fingers with pride.

Clarke leaned back on the sofa, close to the President again. Clarke was laughing, tears ready to stream down his face, "The coffeemaker has an automatic stop, but I've never told him." Clarke looked at the President then back to Mrs. Waters. "It really starts my day." The First Couple burst into laughter.

The President continued, through Clarke's laughter, "But what Clarke doesn't know is, I disconnected the automatic pause years ago." The First couple just howled, enjoying talking about their life and how special it was for the two of them.

Mrs. Waters just sat there. The crew was quiet. One could almost hear crickets in the Rose Garden as the first couple laughed at their own personal joke. It wasn't funny to anyone but the people it mattered to most, the First Couple.

Mrs. Waters was hoping to entertain America but she ended up showing America just what love was, first-hand, with the First Couple. If Mrs. Waters thought she was loosing control of the interview, she wasn't. On the contrary, the interview was taking on something special. A real-life relationship with the most powerful man in the world, in love with his husband, the most watched man in the world.

Mrs. Waters looked at Clarke. He was stunning. "You are setting the trend of what men and women are wearing. You wear a vest—America wears a vest, men and women both. You wear French cuffs with dazzling cufflinks and all across America, men and women are suddenly wearing French cuffs with dazzling cufflinks. You wear spectator shoes, America wears spectator shoes." The camera zeroed in on Mrs. Waters' shoes; she was wearing a pair of spectator shoes with a high-heel. "What do you think of that?" she asked.

"I've always felt that imitation is the best form of a compliment." Clarke answered. Mrs. Waters didn't even look down at her list of questions. She was asking questions that were not on the list, professionally making them up as she went along. Clarke was very well aware of that but it didn't matter. Clarke was comfortable on stage or in front of a camera, and she wouldn't catch him off guard.

Mrs. Waters seemed to love Clarke's candid responses. She crossed her legs and continued with the interview. "The press, the tabloids, all Americans are asking about the First Couple's sex life." Mrs. Waters paused, choosing her words carefully on a very touchy, politically incorrect subject.

Clarke took advantage of her pause to finally put that subject to rest. "I will say this and only this: I am, and always have been, abundantly fulfilled with our sex life." Before Mrs. Waters could ask the President the same inappropriate, unauthorized question, Clarke continued, "And I know the President is, too." The camera never left Clarke, not even to get a nod from the President.

Clarke was ready to stop the interview. He was prepared for questions like this and had briefed Ms. Jones to have the Secret Service stand by if the interviewing staff needed to be escorted off the grounds and the film legally confiscated. Secret Service agents had surrounded the room like panthers ready to pounce at a moment's notice. Everyone stood motionless, clearly waiting for orders from Clarke. The President was calm, knowing that Clarke would not be bullied. Mrs. Waters looked down at her tablet and, with a turn of the page, changed the direction of the interview. As she went on with the next pre-approved question, Clarke gave a small nod to Ms. Jones. At her direction, the Secret Service agents disappeared.

Mrs. Waters wouldn't be intimidated. She was in control. Her next question would prove that. "Clarke? If the United States had a female President in a heterosexual relationship, her husband would be referred to as the First Gentleman." Clarke knew what was coming and armed himself with a smile. "You are referred to as, 'The First Man To Be First Lady'. Many have said this is a polite insult, an attack on your masculinity." Mrs. Waters looked at Clarke. She hadn't asked a question but clearly expected a response to her comment.

Clarke said simply, "I am the First Gentleman," answering her subliminally insulting question with the same attitude he would have if she had asked him his favorite color. It was clear to everyone watching that the press, good or bad, didn't bother Clarke. Michael smiled, trying hard not to laugh at Mrs. Walters' expression.

Mrs. Waters continued. "We know disagreements come about in married life. Arguments. What do you fight about, or maybe a better word would be, what do you argue about?"

"What the President will wear and how he will wear it." The President and Clarke said at the same time; they looked at each other and smiled. The President answered her question in depth. "We've argued over that, but I've learned to just listen and take his advice. He's right," The President looked at the camera, then back at Clarke, "When it comes to that." The President and Clarke looked at each other and laughed again.

Mrs. Waters looked at Clarke as if she wanted him to say something, so he did. "Married couples are individuals who come together as one; they don't always agree. How they disagree is what makes their relationship special."

Mrs. Waters finally continued the interview with the questions that had been agreed upon. She looked down at her list then looked at the President, "We know you're busy but when you have a free evening, what do you watch on TV?" There was a short pause. Knowing that the President was an avid sports watcher and Clarke wasn't. So, in mid-sentence, Mrs. Waters redirected her question, "What do you watch on TV, TOGETHER."

The President didn't even have to think about it. "I love a good ballgame. Clarke loves a good movie. Needless to say we don't watch too much TV together."

Clarke agreed. "No, we don't. We see the movies that come to the White House Theater. It's rare that we have an evening of free time." The President nodded. "But when we do, he loves an action movie; I like a good romance."

Mrs. Waters led off from that to her next question. "What is your favorite movie?" She looked at Clarke.

Clarke answered, "I have several, but I really enjoy *'Somewhere in Time'* with Christopher Reeve and Jane Seymour." The President nodded. He liked that one, too.

"Who's your favorite team?" Mrs. Waters asked the President.

"I like any good ballgame. I've really never had a favorite team. I played for the Navy at the Academy so there's a special place there, but I like a good ballgame regardless of who's playing."

"And you?" She looked at Clarke.

"I like a good halftime show during the Super Bowl. That's as close as I get to watching any sports." The President laughed, his expression saying it was true.

Mrs. Waters continued as she looked at both of them. "You are avid tennis players." The First Couple nodded. "Who wins?" Footage of the President and Clarke playing tennis was dubbed in at this point in the interview. Clarke and the President, both wearing Beverly Anderson sportswear, were playing a hard match, sweating in the sun, not caring about the camera. It was the first time America had seen Clarke's hair messed up.

"It all depends who needs to." Clarke smiled.

Mrs. Waters took the interview to a more serious note. She looked at Clarke. "When the President took office, the first thing he did was introduce the First Gentleman. You were shocked. Tell us about that."

Clarke was just as serious as Mrs. Waters. "We had never talked about it. It never entered my mind at any political level to be the 'in-the-limelight spouse.' We were together in a special relationship that was private but never hidden. It was our lives, not the tabloids." Clarke looked at the President. "Ours." He looked back at Mrs. Waters. "We would go on a vacation and the time together, whether it was seven days or seven hours, was completely ours. The memories would last, along with the anticipation of our next visit."

Mrs. Waters went on with her next question. "The White House is alive with flowers. The Rose Garden and the entire grounds are blooming, such as we've only seen in years past. What's your favorite flower?"

Clarke was quick with an answer. "Anything picked out of the garden with love."

"The Rose Garden?" Mrs. Waters smiled.

"Not necessarily. A child can pick a handful of dandelions for its mother and they are the most beautiful flowers that mother has ever received."

"And yours?" Mrs. Waters looked at the President.

"I like a red rose."

Mrs. Waters looked at the First Couple. "America has a homosexual President. His First Gentleman has captivated the entire world. We haven't seen this sort of captivation since the early 1960's. Tell us about that."

The President just looked at her. "America has a homosexual President. Clarke is my husband and is loved by the world. Is history repeating itself?"

Mrs. Waters couldn't bully the President or the First Gentleman. Mrs. Waters looked at Clarke. "You met while you were an actor in the live Broadway production of Disney's *Beauty and the Beast*. Tell us about that."

The President answered that question. "He was performing just for me. Then I found out the people sitting next to me, in back of me, and in front of me thought he was performing just for them. I have never experienced anything like it from the stage since."

The President looked at Clarke, then back at Mrs. Waters. "There was a back-stage party following the production. The actors made a brief appearance in costume then, as the hors d'oeuvres were served, they left and later came back dressed in party clothes. I wasn't sure who was who, but once again that same man who had captivated the entire theater in costume was illuminating the whole room with his smile. I had to meet him." Michael looked at Clarke with deep eyes that seemed to echo. "And I did."

Clarke happily interrupted with, "And we've been together ever since."

Mrs. Waters looked at the First Couple. "You have been quoted as saying you are married. You had a private ceremony in Vermont when it became the first state to make same-sex marriages legal." The President and Clarke both nodded. This one wasn't on her list of questions, but Mrs. Waters asked it anyway. "You don't share a last name. Why?" The President smiled at Clarke. Michael had wanted Clarke to share his last name.

Clarke was quick to answer. His response didn't sound rehearsed but one could tell it was very well thought out. "That's a decision each person who gets married must make and the decision they make is unique to them. We have seen hyphenated last names for women for many years and even men are now hyphenating their last names. That is their choice. My choice was to keep my family name. That doesn't mean in the future I won't take my husband's last name."

Mrs. Waters smiled. "If you did take the President's last name, you would be Clarke Kent." The First Couple smiled.

"He's a superman regardless of his last name." The President laughed. So did Clarke.

The camera zoomed in on Mrs. Waters as she was experiencing the obvious true love between the First Couple. She had only experienced this with the Reagan's many years ago. But with the President and Clarke, there was something more. It was obvious by watching them. They didn't hold hands or kiss in public. There was something you couldn't see, but felt when you were in the same room with them.

"Clarke?" Mrs. Waters said. Clarke looked at her. He knew it was going to be anther question not on the list. "Why don't you wear a wedding ring?"

"I do. I wear a wedding ring all the time. It's right here." Clarke took off his big vintage ring and with a fisted hand showed her his wedding ring. Underneath you could see the tan line from where the big ring had always been.

"A tan line never lies," she commented.

She looked at the ring with an odd expression. "Did you have this ring designed for you?" The President and Clarke looked at each other with that same special smile they had been sharing throughout the interview.

"No." The President said. "I would like to have a ring designed for Clarke, but he doesn't want one. He wants this one."

When the President paused, Clarke took the opportunity to interrupt with the story of the odd ring. "We were walking together shortly after we met. We saw this sparkling gold ring shining in the seam of the sidewalk, obviously a ring someone had lost. Michael picked it up and said, 'It's a miniature notebook binder ring.' We looked at each other. Michael took my left hand and said, 'I want you to be my partner forever.' He slipped the ring on my finger, saying: 'Not even in death shall we part.' I've worn it ever since. I put my other ring over the top so I won't lose it." Clarke moved his hand and you could see the binder ring was loose. Clarke put his big ring back on. "The jewelers won't size notebook binder rings."

"Why have you kept it a secret all these years?" Mrs. Waters asked.

The President and Clarke looked at each other then back to Mrs. Waters. Clarke said, shaking his head, "We haven't kept it a secret. You are honestly the only person who has ever asked. I love the story and the ring, and there's never been anything to hide. The ring has always been there. A tan line never lies." Clarke repeated Mrs. Waters' comment.

Various photographs, taken of Clarke since the day the President took office, were blown up and, sure enough, there was the ring. No one had ever noticed it. No one had ever asked.

"And your wedding ring, Mr. President?"

"I'm allergic to many metals and gold is one of them; that's why I use a pocket watch. I don't wear my wedding ring on my finger, I wear it around my neck between my undershirt and dress shirt." The President reached under his collar and pulled out a chain with military dog tags and a gold wedding ring. "Its been coated for protection. I've always worn it. You are the first person to ever ask about it."

Mrs. Waters looked at it closer. "It's engraved."

"Yes, it is." The President looked down at the ring, reading the engraving to himself. "It's engraved with the date I originally placed the ring on Clarke's finger. I've worn this ring ever since we were married in Vermont."

"Is that your dog tags from your Navy days?"

"No. It was my father's. He was wearing it the day he died. I've worn it ever since. The dog tags and the wedding band represent the two men I've loved most in this world. I wear them close to my heart." Clarke looked at the President, then looked down at the dog tags and wedding ring. It was a very touching moment. Suddenly Barney jumped from out of nowhere. He hopped up on Clarke and licked him from cheek to cheek. Clarke looked at Barney, then over at Mrs. Waters and back to Barney.

"Barney, what's the matter?" Clarke peered around Barney, looking at Mrs. Waters and the camera crew. "I'm really sorry about this." Clarke looked back at Barney. "Barney, what's wrong?" Barney just sat there wagging his tail and licking Clarke. Then he started barking. "Oh, my gosh!" Clarke said.

"That's right!" The President said as he and Clarke looked at each.

Mrs. Waters just looked at them. She had lost control of the interview. "How do you know what he wants?" She asked.

Clarke looked at Mrs. Waters with apologetic eyes, "Today is Tuesday." She looked at Clarke with an expression that said, 'So?' "I promised Barney I would bake him a batch of chocolate chip cookies and I haven't yet." Barney hopped down and started turning circles and barking. Barney's actions told the whole crew Clarke was right. "I am sorry. It will only take a few moments to whip up a batch. I'll bake them in the morning, but Barney always gets to taste the dough before I chill it."

Mrs. Waters was shaking her head, dumfounded.

"Follow me," Clarke said with a reassuring but commanding voice. "We can continue the interview in the kitchen." The cameraman hoisted a camera onto his shoulder. The lighting man carried a portable light and followed Clarke, who was following Barney as he trotted into to the kitchen. Mrs. Waters just stood back. Clarke reached for an apron and tied it on. The apron was dusty with flour. It was nothing fancy, just special.

"Barney, what kind of walnuts would you like?" Clarke held up a package in each hand. Barney took his paw and batted one of the packages.

"Of course it's English Walnuts." Clarke smiled.

Mrs. Waters looked at Barney then back to Clarke, then back at Barney. "How does he know that?"

"You'll have to ask him." Clarke said. He looked at Barney and laughed. Mrs. Waters looked at Barney then back to Clarke, then back to Barney. The camera picked up how comfortable Clarke was in the kitchen, just like any other man whipping up a batch of chocolate chip cookies for his dog.

Clarke took the yellow package out of the cupboard and started to mix a batch from memory. Clarke went from one end of the kitchen to the fridge then back to the cupboard, balancing butter and eggs and a box of baking soda and brown sugar. He put them all down on the counter and grabbed for the eggs as they were rolling away. He caught one but the other egg met its fate on the floor. Clarke quickly cleaned up the broken egg then walked back to the fridge and plucked another one from the tray in the door.

He didn't bat an eye. He was so obviously at home in the kitchen and he sure wasn't ashamed of it. He reached into a drawer and pulled out measuring cups and spoons. Just like everyone else did at home when his hands were full, he shut the drawer with his hip and carried on. Barney was licking his chops and watching Clarke. Mrs. Waters watched Barney watching Clarke. Clarke took out a mixing bowl and started to measure and pour, all from memory.

"It's an old family recipe." Clarke laughed. "It's the famous chocolate chip cookie recipe," Clarke showed Mrs. Waters the recipe on the back of the package, "but my recipe is made with three-quarters cup more flour and half butter and half butter-flavored shortening.

The President was chatting with the crew. "They are the best chocolate chip cookies I've ever had. And I usually have to fight Barney for them. Thank God Clarke always makes a double batch."

The cameraman took full advantage of this very private room. The camera zeroed in on the 'his and his' coffeemakers. Then to the fridge covered with magnets. A cookie jar sat on the counter, one cookie and some crumbs left in it. It was clear glass, not crystal, and had a lid that wobbled, as though it might not have come with the cookie jar. Mrs. Waters looked at the cookie jar.

Clarke saw her look. As he was stirring, he took the bowl and walked over to Mrs. Waters. "The cookie jar was a gift from a dear friend. Regardless of where I live that cookie jar will always be on the kitchen counter, filled with homemade cookies."

Mrs. Waters looked at the fridge. "What is your favorite magnet?" Mrs. Waters asked. America had been in love with refrigerator magnets for years but no one dreamed the First

Couple did anything so ordinary, at least not while living in the White House.

Clarke didn't stop what he was doing. He stirred and flour seemed to fly. "Whichever one I've been given as a gift. It's like a greeting card. Usually people spend a lot more time choosing the card than the gift. You have in mind what you're going to buy so you go to a store and get it. A card, you search for. Same with a magnet." Clarke had the cookie dough all mixed up and asked Mrs. Waters to hand him the chocolate chips. It was the grand finale and Clarke stirred the ovation.

Mrs. Waters said, "I stopped baking chocolate chip cookies years ago. I never knew when they were going to come out flat."

"Follow this recipe and they won't." Clarke smiled. Barney couldn't take his eyes off Clarke. Clarke took a glob of the dough and rolled it into a ball then gave it to Barney. Barney chewed, swallowed, and calmly trotted out of the room. "There." Clarke said, washing his hands. "We're all done and back to normal. Would you like some cookie dough?" Clarke asked Mrs. Waters and the camera and lighting crew. They all took a glob. "There. Now we're all happy."

Clarke took a glob and ate it, then covered the bowl with plastic wrap and placed it in the fridge. Clarke put everything away and placed the dishes in the sink to soak. Then he took off his apron, looked into the camera and said, "Lets go find the President."

Barney was on Michael's lap. The President was looking at his pocket watch. He closed it, looking up at Clarke. "I think you've broken another record." He looked over at Mrs. Waters. "It's too bad you won't be here in the morning, when they're hot out of the oven. There's nothing like it."

"You *bake* someone happy!" Clarke said with exclamation as he sat down next to the President.

"It's true." The President said, laughing. "If we could only get Congress to bake." The President had Congress's support like no other President in history. It was amazing. Washington seemed to agree with the man in the White House who was married to man. If it was twisted, it was twisted in the right direction and that is exactly where the country was going.

As the crew was winding cords and clicking trunks shut, the producer looked up at Mrs. Waters who looking out a window. "It was a great interview," he said walking towards her.

"It was the best interview I've ever been involved with," she laughed, "And it hasn't even been edited." She never looked away from the window. "I had no idea what was going to happen next."

"Don't you normally get your subjects crying?" He asked.

"It's always been my trademark." Mrs. Waters said with her head cocked. "I thought I was going to have Clarke in tears. Then Barney came in. God! That was the best chocolate chip cookie dough I've ever tasted."

"We have the exclusive on the recipe," he said in consolation.

"Good." Mrs. Waters said as she walked away from the window. "What an incredible interview." She paused, "What an incredible man."

The President's Dinner

The front page boldly spelled it out in huge letters: The White House. It's as grand as the First Man To Be First Lady. Clarke put the paper down. He agreed. It was time to carry on The White House traditions, with as much press exposure the world could print, tape, and view.

Since the era of the Kennedy's, the President's Dinner had become a national tradition. This would be the very first State Dinner the new First Couple would host. Clarke choreographed the entire evening, right down to the dinner forks. It had been a long time since the White House had entertained and Clarke insisted that everything be perfect.

This was the one event to which Clarke invited every American via the press and approved cameras throughout the evening. It was most unusual for a First Couple to actually enjoy the press, but with this First Couple right on the screen in front of the whole world, ugly rumors couldn't be substantiated and Clarke knew that. He put a new swing to an old saying, 'MYSTERY Loves Company'. So he invited the press to take the mystery out of the First Couple.

If Clarke had his wish, the world would be so full of the President and the First Man To Be First Lady that they wouldn't bother to tune in any more. But he knew that would never happen and so he set another place at the table for all of America to come and join the party. The President was too busy with every snap and a flash, but Clarke was as genuine as his smile. Before they realized it, America had fallen in love with Clarke and was at odds with anyone who hadn't.

For the President's Dinner, Beverly Anderson insisted on creating a new ensemble for Clarke. He designed a new look in an elegant basic black tuxedo. A jacket was designed a bit longer than normal, tailored with an athletic fit. Clarke's dress shirt would be black silk with a matching bow tie. Of course, Clarke would be wearing his spectator shoes and a black silk print-on-print vest. The vest had become Clarke's trademark, just as the pillbox hat had been for Mrs. Kennedy. It wasn't planned that way, but the press loved the likeness. Clarke was elegant in his simplicity, which made him the most radiant person in the room.

The new dinner menu was perfect, right down to the dessert, and would become a favorite for many White House dinners to come. Clarke had all the menus chosen for official State Dinners prepared for him and the President first. That way, if there was a problem in the kitchen or it didn't look right on the china or was cumbersome in the serving, appropriate changes could be made. It was an enlightening dress rehearsal and the staff enjoyed the performance almost as much as Clarke.

On the night of the President's Dinner, each former President and First Lady would sit at the head of a round table surrounded by eight guests, people who had made their administrations sing. They would be served from the china purchased by their administration, accented with the new china and crystal Clarke had chosen for the White House.

Not since Mrs. Kennedy had new stemware been purchased for the White House. Clarke had new stemware designed with his trademark, 'elegant in its simplicity.' Clarke wanted each place setting at the White House dinner table to be a work of art. He worked side by side with American designers and together they came up with a crystal stem that was somewhat taller, its design simple, with an etching of gold trim. It would not take away from the china but rather would add to the complete place setting. It was certainly elegant on its own, as unique as the artist who designed them and as elegant as the man who chose them.

There was a lot of stereotypical press about Clarke and his china. Clarke knew the importance of entertaining world leaders. Until this administration, foreign press reported that "fancy dinners in America was like watching cowboys eating grub around a campfire." If Clarke was going to be made fun of for making the White House grand, then he was going to be made fun of! With a smile, Clarke thought about that for a moment. "The more the press poke at me, the less they poke at the President." Clarke grinned from ear to ear. That made him enjoy his position as, to quote the press, *the First Man To Be First Lady*.

Clarke was ecstatic that the press was covering every minute of the President's Dinner. At no other time in history had so many Presidents been alive so long after office making such an event possible. Nancy Reagan, Clarke's favorite First Lady and idol, was first to RSVP. She even enclosed a personal note of thanks. She was the only former First Lady to send Clarke a hand-written letter when Michael was sworn into office.

She had brought the White House up to spectacular standards herself. The country was in a horrible recession and history showed that her husband had brought it back. "Perfect timing is an essence," she wrote. "You and the President are perfect timing for our nation. Please continue to use perfect timing in your favor with all of your adventures at 1600 Pennsylvania Avenue."

When her husband's administration left the White House, she made sure the next First Lady wouldn't have to do a thing to upgrade a single room or purchase so much as a fork. The House, the grounds, the Private Quarters, all were spectacular. Nancy had assisted the new First Lady the only way she could: with a spectacular home.

Beatrice Pyne had never appreciated it and never said another word about it after her initial comments following the First Lady's White House Tour. Beatrice said with a wobbly smile, "Nancy made the White House sparkle." Nancy did and that was the last America heard of it. The press made sure everyone saw Beatrice as "grandmotherly" and never commented on any money she spent on the White House or her clothes. Beatrice Pyne was the last to RSVP. She accepted the invitation to attend the President's Dinner at the White House most graciously. Clarke noticed that she signed it 'The Silver Fox' and was reminded that it had been her nickname during her husband's administration.

Clarke and the President were enjoying the evening news together as if it were a date. They were all alone in the Oval Office, sitting romantically close. The Secret Service surrounded the building. It was the closest thing to privacy the First Couple had since Michael took office. Clarke started to breathe heavily as the news reported on the up-coming Drug Summit. He began to shake. He was scared to death. Michael could sense Clarke's fear and reached for his hand.

After a commercial break, the newscast continued with a fun and entertaining segment. The White House Chef was being interviewed on primetime national news, introducing his new elegant, guilt-free, fat-free cookbook.

Clarke always worked closely with the White House culinary staff. Menus traditionally used at the White House were full of fat and calories. Granted, those are the best kind, but Clarke wanted to make sure he and the President kept their shapes. Clarke and the culinary staff came up with wonderful, fat-free, low-calorie recipes to be served when the First Couple was dining alone. Then, when the First Couple entertained guests, they could splurge with a full-fat, full-calorie menu. Those really *are* the best kind.

The White House Chef was now a household name and he explained, during the special news report, Clarke's reasons for the fat-free, low-calorie entrees and how Clarke had encouraged him to go public with his recipes. The Chef was a natural television celebrity. When he was asked by the news anchor, "What's next for the most popular chef in America?" the Chef proudly said, "To take care of the First Couple." Clarke and the President smiled at such a special comment.

To Clarke's enjoyment, the news anchor continued with a word from a prior First Lady about the upcoming President's Dinner. Clarke couldn't wait to see which prior First Lady it was. When almost all of her appeared on the wide-screen TV, Clarke was surprised that it was the Silver Fox. Eager to hear what she thought about the upcoming event, Clarke actually leaned towards the television.

Beatrice Pyne started off with rude comments about Clarke's worrying about the President's fat intake. "Fat intake is all in The First Man To Be First Lady's head," she said with her chins wobbling.

Clarke leaned farther towards the TV and thought, "And on your thighs, you … you … YOU SILVER RAT." He thought it so loud that the President could have heard it. Clarke couldn't believe she was so rude. Beatrice referred to all of the prior First Ladies by their first names but when she referred to Clarke, she always sneered, "*The First Man To Be First Lady.*" Although they knew quite well that Clarke's proper title was First Gentleman, the press still poked at Clarke with the title, "First Man To Be First Lady." And now, so did Beatrice. She went on and on and on. The reporter kept talking to her as if she had the greatest news known to humanity. Clarke couldn't believe it. He was flabbergasted that the Silver *Rat* could be so mean and public about it. Former First Couples never said a bad word about the First Couple currently in office, since they had once been there themselves.

Clarke knew the real reason she was so nasty about Clarke and her undertone of rudeness to the President. Her son had been in the running to be appointed Vice President or so SHE thought. Before the official announcement for Vice President was made, she had commented, on national news, "Like Abigail Adams herself, I will be a president's First Lady and mother of a president." She was dumbfounded to find that her son hadn't been even in the top ten of the preliminary choices.

Beatrice Pyne continued, on live television, airing her distaste for the man in the White House—not the President, his husband. Her tone obviously said that she was sure that if Clarke weren't in the White House, the President wouldn't be gay. Her smile was as fake as her pearls and she was getting nastier with every pound. Beatrice never got over the humiliation of her husband's non-existent second term, not to mention his overwhelming defeat to a Democrat.

Clarke leaned back and stared at the TV. Beatrice looked like America's grandmother but she was everything America wouldn't admit she was. Clarke knew she was bigoted, close-minded, and a snot, not to mention incredibly flabby. "Grandma Flabby Nasty Snot"—what a lovely, appropriate name for her. Clarke smiled. The President took Clarke's smile to mean everything was okay. It *was* okay, because Clarke had an idea.

The President had a serious look on his face. He realized how much her comments in the press would bother Clarke. The President put his arm around Clarke. He knew Clarke didn't let the press bother him. Michael watched Clarke watching the news, but not seeing the TV. Clarke rarely said a bad word about anyone, but Michael realized that Clarke rarely said a good word about her.

The days ahead were very busy. Clarke was working very closely with a camera crew, spotlighting even the smallest detail. He wanted to make sure the televised White House Tour with the President's Dinner would be perfect. A tour of the White House would be televised just as it had been with Mrs. Kennedy and Tricia Nixon. Mrs. Kennedy started the White House restoration and took America on a tour during her accomplishments.

Mrs. Nixon was the First Lady in history to redecorate the White House on such a grand scale. Mrs. Nixon didn't like the personal publicity, so it was her daughter Tricia who took America on the tour. Clarke loved the White House history and worked with the director very closely, splicing, cutting footage, and re-taping. Mrs. Kennedy took the televised tour through the State Rooms, and Tricia through the private quarters, but Clarke was going to do both, and with those who had done it before him.

With the miracle of TV, a tape showed Mrs. Kennedy walking through the Blue Room and going through the doorway into the Red Room, but it was Clarke taped live entering the Red Room and continuing the tour. Footage never seen of Tricia Nixon walking from the Red Room into the doorway of the State Dining Room had Clarke entering live from her exit. America would love it. It was great footage of the White House, both then and now. The director graciously thanked Clarke for the idea. It would be a night of entertainment for all of America to enjoy.

In the redecorating of the White House, Clarke had two very important areas of the White House renamed and fabulously redecorated. These would be unveiled at the President's Dinner before the former First Couples and the nation. The ground floor corridor that housed all of the First Lady's portraits had been renamed the First Lady's Hall.

The entrance cross-hall that housed the President's Portraits had been renamed the President's Hall. In honor of the Presidents attending the dinner, Clarke had their portraits hung in order of terms in office served. Special lighting had been installed, placing each portrait in the spotlight, one not being more important over the other, but shining together.

The evening's televised tour would begin in the President's Hall, with the former First Couples viewing the portraits. Then would move downstairs to the First Lady's Hall, with each First Lady's portrait proudly hanging with accomplishment and a few surprises added. The former First Ladies live reactions would be caught on camera. This would become a National Geographic Video for sale to benefit the White House Historical Society.

Each invited former President and First Lady had agreed to be part of the video. Each one thought it was a great idea and were glad to help. Even the prior President who resigned the office to Michael was happy to help and felt honored to be invited back to the White House. His ex-wife, who was his First Lady, also felt honored to be invited as well. They would arrive separately but had agreed to be gracious to each other for the evening. She had successfully gone through rehab but still hated her ex-husband. Ironically, visiting the White House would be her first public appearance since she had left there.

With preparations well underway and the evening planned down to the second, Clarke called for the Chief Usher. Clarke told him that some minor redecorating would need to be done before the President's Dinner. The Chief Usher thought that was odd and knew Clarke well enough to know something was up. He loved it. Not only had savoir-faire returned to the White House, it had come back with a lot of fun. Clarke made all the arrangements for the minor but very important subtle redecorating to be done the day of the President's Dinner.

The minor redecorating had been carefully mapped out on paper. Once the President left for the Oval Office, Clarke and the Chief Usher went into action. Clarke could almost hear the theme song from the old TV show, *Mission Impossible*. Clarke, the Chief Usher, and the work crew silently but very carefully moved portraits around. Clarke stood back and eyed the changes. The look was just right. Clarke wanted to make sure no touch-up painting was needed. He knew it wasn't a permanent move and, at the right moment, they would be put right back the way they should be. The President would see it the same time America did and all would watch the lovely sneer on the face of the Silver Rat.

The day of the event, television cameras were invited far behind the scenes so America could see what it takes to put on a State Dinner. From the setting up of tables to the pressing of the tablecloths to the Pastry Chefs in the kitchen, America would see first-hand why it took one hundred and three full-time employees to keep the White House running smoothly.

There were approved camera crews both inside and outside the White House. Every inch of footage was carefully scripted and would not leave the White House grounds without

Clarke's approval. Clarke had promised the former First Couples that the press would not bombard them. The cameras were there only to make a movie as it happened. This would be a professionally edited video with a script, background music, and recorded live reactions.

Floral arrangements for the State Dining Room were spectacular. A large rose arrangement was the centerpiece with four tall candlesticks placed around it. Saundra loved the arrangement. She turned the vase to get the best angle. Clarke was so caught up in the preparations, he was actually humming the tune "*Be Our Guest.*"

Clarke saw Saundra's smile and continued reciting the schedule for the evening. "After the initial toast by the President to the former Presidents, I will give a toast for the former First Ladies. The stewards will remove the large centerpieces and replace them with the smaller ones." Saundra nodded her agreement.

Clarke insisted that the evening be absolutely perfect. Smaller centerpieces looked too small and out of place when one first walked into the room and looked even smaller on camera, so for theatrics, Clarke had the larger centerpieces done for show and the smaller ones for actual use. The larger centerpieces would be taken to the East Room and used to decorate the stage.

"This event is going to be spectacular." Saundra said, clapping her hands together. "Dear, I have a surprise for you. I wasn't going to tell you, not with all the excitement of tonight's event, but I simply must! Everything has been delivered for the Oval Office. Everything." Saundra winked at Clarke. She had something up her sleeve and he thought he knew exactly what it was.

"I will call you the minute we can put the Oval Office together," Clarke winked back.

The dinner was taking place on a Friday night. It would begin with Clarke's White House tour. Then, the Former Presidents and their wives would enter through the North Portico and would be formally announced and escorted by Marines in dress uniform straight ahead to the Blue Room, where the President and First Gentleman would formally receive them.

With an up-bow, the noise and chitchat in preparation for the evening came to a halt. The event began. The Marine Quartet began to play the Presidential March. An announcer's voice boomed: "Ladies and Gentleman, The President of the United States Michael Arthur Kent and his First Gentleman, Clarke." The President and Clarke posed for the flash of the cameras, then walked to Blue Room. A television crew followed, filming every step.

The President and his First Gentleman stood in the center of the Blue Room with an incredible nighttime view of the Washington Monument and Jefferson Memorial as their backdrop. It was spectacular. All the White House chandeliers were set to a romantic glow. A roaring fire danced in every fireplace. Candles lit all the State Rooms. Former Presidents would say their greetings, then move on to enjoy cocktails in the Red Room. The President winked at Clarke. Clarke really made the White House sparkle.

Each former President and First Lady, or the widow of a President, arrived in order of time in office through the North Portico. Other guests would arrive through the South Entrance and would enjoy cocktails in the East Room while a group from the Air Force Band, called the Strolling Strings, walked around the room, entertaining guests with upbeat songs one could tap their feet to.

When a former First Couple left their car, they walked directly to the North Portico. Marines in fine uniforms snapped to attention. Once the former First Couple had entered the White House, they paused for the flash of the camera. Then they were announced and escorted to the Blue Room. The next former First Couple's car pulled up. It was like a professional dance step. No one missed a beat. This was choreographed and rehearsed over and over again, not with the former Presidents in the backseats, but rather members of the staff. Clarke's direction approved the choreography.

Each former President and First Lady greeted the First Couple. They were genuine with their salutations. It was in front of the camera and looked great. Clarke knew it was real. Clarke was captivating the entire evening by just being himself. Ms. Deverough was just a nod and gesture away. Her smile said she thought Clarke was magnificent. Clarke was comfortable with his position as First Gentleman, but didn't get too proud that he didn't worry about something stuck in his teeth or hanging out of his nose. In fact, Clarke had secretly had a small mirror designed into his place setting. That way he could nonchalantly smile, while looking into the mirror for any discrepancies. No one ever knew. Even the press never found out.

Right on cue, President Pyne and the Silver Rat arrived, just as they were supposed to. They never seemed to walk side by side or sit close to each other. The only time you saw them touch was when the former President swatted Beatrice away from his dessert. Mr. Pyne looked great. He had a smile that made you want to throw your arms around him and give him a great big hug. Beatrice had a sneer that made you want to push her down and bob her head up and down in the front fountain. Michael said he would let everything go but a water fight.

Beatrice was gracious to the President, giving him a pleasant smile. A cold handshake went to Clarke. Clarke thought maybe she had smuggled in a cold fish, but it was just the woman herself. Clarke combated the denizen of the deep with a gracious smile and class fit for a queen. Somehow Clarke felt that he had natural revenge.

Gunther and Beatrice Pyne walked into the Red Room where the prior administrations were already chatting and admiring the redecorated rooms. Even with the subdued lighting, it was obvious that Beatrice clashed with the room. The only thing that matched was her white hair and that needed at least combed, if not styled. Clarke loved to see Beatrice and Nancy together. Nancy was the size of Beatrice's right thigh and when they were photographed together, it made Beatrice look so rotund. Clarke, of course, insisted on pictures.

After receiving their guests, the First Couple walked into the Red Room. Michael and Clarke were each served a cocktail. After taking his drink, the President turned to his guests and said, "I would like to propose a toast." The room silenced. "I would like to quote President Kennedy from a toast he gave at the State Dinner given in honor of the Nobel Laureates on April 29, 1962." President Kent looked around the room. "It was appropriate then and I find it even more appropriate today. I quote President Kennedy, 'I think this is the most extraordinary collection of talent, of human knowledge, that has ever been gathered together at the White House, with the possible exception of when Thomas Jefferson dined alone.'" The

President smiled at Clarke, then at their guests gathered around the room. He raised his glass, "To the men and their women AND..." The President looked at Clarke, "...their man, who's leadership has made our country the greatest nation in the world."

"Here, Here!" was heard as crystal was clinked together. Clarke didn't drink alcohol but always tipped his glass. Beatrice set her glass down on the table. An usher immediately placed a coaster under it. Clarke gave him a nod of approval as the Silver Rat sneered in her annoyance. As cocktails were enjoyed, the President very fondly introduced Clarke: The First Gentleman. Nancy started with an ovation and the rest of the room happily followed. Clarke smiled, blushing in embarrassment at the attention. Then he looked over at Beatrice. He imagined that she couldn't get her fingers out of the dip. Clarke's blush of embarrassment turned into a smile at the thought. He wasn't serving dip.

Clarke announced that the taping for the live broadcast was about to begin. The staff came in, removed glasses and tidied up the room. The camera crew came in, measuring light. A makeup crew was assisting everyone with last minute touch-ups. In moments, everyone was ready. There was such excitement in the air.

A bright red light glowed on top of the television camera and Clarke started the tour, looking directly into the camera. "As Mrs. Coolidge said, 'The White House is a home rich in tradition, mellow with years, hallowed with memories'." There was a pause. Everyone was silent, remembering those who had come before. The solace wasn't planned which made it all the more special. Clarke thanked everyone for coming and for their gracious support in the restoration of the White House during their administrations and for participating tonight in the live White House tour, which would benefit the White House Historical Society.

He began the tour with the President's Hall. The cameras followed as each President walked with their wives and those who were widowed walked alone. The Marine Quartet played selections Clarke had specially chosen as background music. Mrs. Carter commented on the new music stands. Beatrice commented to Gunther what a waste of money THAT was.

132

The First Gentleman went first, with the President at his side. Clarke had memorized the artist who had painted each President's portrait as well as that President's term of office. Each former President was honored as his portrait was shown to America. "And Cut." The director instructed.

The cameras were turned off. The President escorted those who needed to use the elevator while Clarke escorted those who used the stairs. Everyone arrived in the Vermeil Room. This room was virtually unknown to most people. All through White House history, the Vermeil Room had been decorated in a rather bland style, perhaps as an afterthought. Clarke proudly dedicated the refurbished Vermeil Room as a museum to the elegance of the First Ladies. A bust of each First Lady had been commissioned and was proudly displayed. This was a total surprise to the former First Ladies. The busts were artistically sculpted, showing how First Lady looked during her time in the office. Clarke's bust would not be started until this administration left office.

The cameras still rolling, the tour continued downstairs. The First Ladies portraits had been re-hung so that each could be televised with their own portrait. Clarke had the camera pick up the chitchat among the Presidents and their wives. It really was an historical evening. Clarke was so proud of Michael. And Michael watched proudly as Clarke gracefully handled such a grand position. Clarke was on top and the President wore a huge smile, but this night was for the former Presidents and their First Ladies. Clarke made sure each one there felt the importance of their contributions toward making the United States great.

As the tour continued, no one noticed whose portrait they had or hadn't seen; they only noticed their own. Beatrice was nasty with her silence. Clarke could feel her glare and took it as a sign of success. He continued with the tour, pointing out interesting artifacts from First Ladies of centuries past.

The President finally noticed that there was something different about the Hall but couldn't put his finger on it. He looked at Clarke, knowing very well that Clarke was up to something. Michael's thoughts were happily interrupted as he watched a former President and his wife remember a special time they had shared while they had been in office. Even those who had lost their spouse enjoyed a special memory.

No one seemed to notice that Beatrice's portrait was not in view. Nancy looked at Clarke. She not only noticed, her smile said she approved. Beatrice had been very nasty in her live quotes to the press about Nancy's choices and the money spent on china and in redecorating the White House. Nancy just wanted to get it done. She knew her timing was not good, but realized even more how Beatrice's big mouth matched the rest of her.

As the tour was winding down, the President escorted those in the elevator who found the stairs a physical challenge. A White House Usher led the other guests upstairs to the Green Room, where the cameras would take their final footage of the tour. Then the First Couple would escort the former Presidents and their First Ladies to the East Room to mingle with the other invited guests.

Clarke was going to be the last one up the stairs and Beatrice stayed behind on purpose. Clarke saw the rage in her face and was prepared for a cat fight. She outweighed Clarke ten to one, but Clarke never faltered. White House Ushers had started to freshen up the restrooms, not realizing that Clarke and the former First Lady were still in the area. Ushers quickly stepped out of sight but stayed within hearing range. The Chief Usher wasn't about to miss any of this! He knew Clarke would want the big dog there if a cat fight did break out.

Beatrice sneered at Clarke and demanded, "What have you done with MY portrait?" Clarke never thought eyes could bulge like that without popping out of one's head.

Clarke was very matter-of-fact. With the class of a queen he stated, "It hangs in the powder room right in front and to the left of the entrance of the first stall." The Silver Rat looked Clarke up one side, then down the other, ready to call him a fag. Clarke would have agreed, then asked how her son was and continued the conversation by asking if he had finally admitted he was gay or was he still keeping himself in the closet for re-election?

"Enjoy your portrait, dear." Clarke said. "The men in the White House certainly do." Clarke smiled at her sneer. "Don't forget to flush." The Chief Usher flushed a toilet for theatrical sound effects and to hide his laughter.

Beatrice left enraged, climbing the stairs so quickly they didn't even have a chance to creak from her weight. Clarke smiled. He would have done a high five with the Chief Usher, but wasn't sure how! Clarke had made the winning point and should have been slapped on the butt.

Clarke bounced up the stairs a safe distance behind Beatrice. He paused at the top of the stairs, making sure he was in order before he met with his guests. With a grand entrance, Clarke walked into the Green Room. The cameras captured the real Clarke: genuinely radiant. The President noticed Clarke smiling like the Cheshire Cat and couldn't wait to hear what happened.

The camera crew was right there and America could see it all for themselves. Clarke smiled and thanked everyone for a totally successful evening, even though it had barely begun. Clarke went directly to the President and, together, they escorted their guests in to the East Room. After a few moments of mingling and more cocktails, the dinner bell rang. The Air Force Strolling Strings gathered all the guests together and led them to the State Dining Room with a peppy tune.

Clarke had made arrangements for the First Ladies Hall to be put back in order once dinner had started. No one would know what had transpired between Clarke and Beatrice. If she brought it, up the evidence would be hanging in Clarke's favor. Clarke was given a nod during dinner from the Chief Usher; everything was back to normal. Clarke commented to the President what a perfect evening it was. Nancy, who was sitting next to Clarke, agreed as they looked at Beatrice, who was asking for another dinner roll.

While dinner was being enjoyed in the State Dining Room, the East Room was transformed into a performance hall. Clarke would have enjoyed dancing, but many of their guests were older and, although they would not admit to it, very frail. Clarke wouldn't embarrass their guests by offering dancing to those who, at best, had difficulty walking.

Clarke still wanted to make the night extra special. The perfect idea came to him as he planned the grand finale. Instead of the East Room being set up theater-style, with all the guests facing the stage in tidy military rows, Clarke had a round stage designed and placed in the very center of the room directly under the center chandelier. Rows of chairs were set up in a circle all the way around the stage.

As a string quartet played, the stage turned very slowly. It was a life-size music box that fairly bloomed with fresh floral arrangements. Chandeliers were aglow. A romantic flame from the candelabra added a special touch. Flames from the fireplace seemed to sway to the beat of the music. Everything down to the smallest detail had been well planned. Clarke even made sure the air conditioning was on so it wouldn't get too warm.

The entire evening was everything one could imagine a fairytale White House event to be. It was a long night for many of the guests of honor. Many years had passed since they were in the White House and they showed their age with tired, but approving smiles. The First Couple's guests were genuine as they expressed their thanks and their appreciation for all the work that Clarke had done in the White House. They praised the President, too, for doing such a fine job. The President and Clarke saw each of their guests to the door, just like any other couple who had hosted a dinner party.

Later that night, the President came into the bedroom all ready for bed. He was shirtless, wearing only flannel pajama bottoms. He still didn't wear slippers and loved to go barefoot through the White House. Clarke thought that was such a sexy look for the President. He was spreading lotion on his hands, sitting on the side of the bed, waiting for Michael to lie down.

"What a night!" The President said as he crawled under the covers. He shook his head from side to side. "You sure have a way of making history happen." That was the First Couple's way of saying goodnight. Daily, something big always seemed to go on that topped the events of the day before. Clarke put away his hand lotion and closed the night-table drawer. He crawled into bed and scooted over to snuggle with the President.

Michael smiled and put his arm around Clarke. "Did you see how Beatrice clashed with the Red Room?"

Clarke said he hadn't noticed, with a smile, but commented how nice she matched the Green Room. Like a good dessert that saves a bad dinner, Clarke knew having Beatrice photographed matching the Green Room would end the tour on a sweet note. That was Clarke's way of showing respect for those who had held the office before them. "Originally, we were going to have cocktails in the Yellow Oval Room." Clarke said. "It was easier for the camera crew to use the first floor. Maybe Beatrice didn't get the message?"

"Boy, she was madder than a hornet when she come up the stairs after the tour." The President looked at Clarke. He wondered if Clarke knew what happened. The President was waiting to hear all about it.

"Maybe she was just winded from having to climb back up the stairs. She didn't wait for the elevator." Clarke said with a smile. Clarke thought the President had found out everything and was going to give Clarke a good talking to. Not that she hadn't deserved it!

"I don't know." The President said. Michael knew very well that Clarke knew exactly what had happened and he also knew very well that Clarke wasn't going volunteer any information. Michael had said many times, 'being married to Clarke is like an *I Love Lucy* episode that never ended.' And that didn't change just because they had moved into the White House. "She didn't even grab for her husband's dessert tonight." Michael laughed. Beatrice always ate his dessert. If Gunther wanted it, he had to fight her for it. He never won. The President laughed again and hugged Clarke. "I just wonder what happened."

Clarke quickly changed the subject. "I had a great time." Clarke said as he reached up and turned off the light. "I can't wait to see the video." Clarke wondered why he and Michael slept in a king-size bed since they were always snuggled up like two spoons. The first State Dinner of the new administration had been perfect and finally Clarke could relax.

Suddenly Clarke sprang out of a sound sleep. He reached over and grabbed for the Michael. Michael stirred. The President was just fine, fast asleep. Clarke looked around the room. Washington was having an earthquake! No. The only thing that was moving was Clarke. It was his heart beating. Clarke thought his heart would beat right out of his chest. It was the same morbid dream. Clarke got out of bed and stood a moment, watching the President sleep. Michael was sleeping so sound. Clarke tied a robe around his waist and stepped into furry slippers. He walked in to the sitting room and turned on the TV. What Clarke needed was a big, giggly dose of the Tonight Show.

"Hey," Jay Leno said. "Did you all see the televised President's Dinner tonight?" The audience roared with applause. That made Clarke feel pretty good. Jay Leno continued, "You know they say behind every great President there is a great First Lady. I guess that's more apparent now than in any other administration." The audience burst into uncontrollable laughter, hysterical at the sexual metaphor. Clarke started laughing. He laughed so hard he could hardly take a breath. Clarke had no idea why he was laughing so hard. The joke wasn't that funny, not to Clarke anyway. He stopped laughing, took the remote and clicked the TV off.

Out of desperation, Clarke decided to take a walk about the house. Everything was quiet. The staff was asleep, just a buzz away. The Secret Service was on duty at their guard posts on the edges of the house. Floodlights from outside peeked in through the drapes, lighting a path for Clarke. He found himself in the Blue Room, looking out at the spectacular view. All he could think about was the drug summit.

The cold war was a thing of the past and the Middle East kept things too exciting and the military constantly on alert. But the world was seeing more illegal drugs then ever before. The drugs were in every nation destroying fine citizens of all ages from the inside out. A war fought with guns and tanks could be seen and heard. A war on drugs was still. Silent. Fought from within.

The President was right. Rumors had finally been proven true. It was the demons of the Middle East who were supplying drugs to the world, using the Panama Canal as their decoy. Strategically, it was the villain's most powerful weapon.

The economic heartbeat of the world would arrest without the Panama Canal. Illegal drugs would be a thing of the past if the canal would dry up. Holding the summit there accused the Panamanian Government without saying a word. If need be, the Panamanian government could easily be overthrown and the United States could take over the big ditch, but the President wanted a peaceful solution.

Clarke felt the comfort of a big fuzzy hug as Michael put his arms around Clarke. In a breathy tone, the President spoke into Clarke's ear. "I've noticed you've been melancholy this evening." It was so out of character for Michael to talk that way that Clarke started laughing. Then silently he reached up and held Michael's hands, snuggling up to his furry chest. Together they shared the view. They didn't talk, just gently cuddled. Clarke didn't tell Michael about the dreams. He just held on tight so he couldn't get away.

The President turned Clarke around. "I am going to be just fine. Security is so tight, *I* don't even know what's going to happen next." Clarke smiled. The President knew everything, right down to when he'd take his next breath.

Clarke's tone was apologetic. "I've been so busy with the President's Dinner I forgot all about you leaving." He perked up as a great idea occurred to him. "If I could just be with you."

Michael interrupted Clarke's enthusiasm with a smile. "Clarke, you know you can't go." Gently, he turned Clarke, holding him by the shoulders, "Besides, none of the other wives will be there." Clarke started laughing then grew very serious.

He took a deep breath, then let it out. "I'd feel so much better if they didn't have to measure you for a bulletproof suit." Michael held Clarke in a loving, very tight embrace and wouldn't let go.

Clarke knew there was a terrorist price on Michael's head. The press hadn't discovered what the CIA had. And even if they did, Michael was still going to the drug summit. Clarke caressed Michael's hand. The President was going to go, regardless who said he shouldn't. The President wouldn't back down.

After a long silent embrace Michael led Clarke back to their Private Quarters. A sleepless night changed to dawn, announcing the day Clarke had so feared. He was scared to death. But the President assured him that with all the security surrounding him, he was safer at the summit then any other place in the world. But Clarke didn't buy it. Not when the President dressed in his bulletproof suit.

Clarke watched the evening news. Like a big prehistoric bird, Air Force One swallowed his husband and flew out of sight. It was only a decoy. While the world thought the President was well on his way to the drug summit, unbeknownst to everyone, the President was well hidden inside the White House. He left late that evening, long after Clarke had gone to bed.

The President secretly left through the tunnels off the old bomb shelters. Everyone including the press had forgotten about those. Lyndon Johnson used that same exit when he wanted to dodge reporters and Vietnam War demonstrators. The tunnels led to what looked like an old tool shed in Lafayette Park, directly across from the White House.

The President emerged from the shed dressed in grubby overalls and dirty work boots. He was made up in dark wig and full beard, complete with a beer gut. He looked like an old dirty hippie from the 1960's. To complete the masquerade, he got into a beat up VW bus vintage to that era. He was taken to a private airstrip and boarded a private plane with no markings, no flight attendants, and a full military escort.

Sweet Dreams

Daffodils hugged tulips as they reached to the sky, gently kissed by the sun. Spring was a welcome guest. Clarke could smell the bouquet of roses given to him at the airport. Crowds lined the streets, trying to get a glimpse of the First Couple whom they had only seen on magazine covers and the six o'clock news.

The breeze felt good as the convertible drove through the streets. The sun was bright and the temperature was rising. Clarke waved to the chanting crowds lining the streets. A young family of four caught Clarke's eye. The young father picked up his child and placed him on his shoulders so the little one could see the Presidential car go by. His young wife held their baby close as the man gently put his arm around her. Clarke waved at the family. The young child caught Clarke's smile and looked at his Mommy and Daddy as if he realized what the excitement was all about.

Suddenly the woman screamed. Clarke felt something slump into him. He was suddenly covered in blood. For an instant, Clarke couldn't tell what was lying in his lap. The man he loved was unrecognizable. In horror, Clarke realized the President had been shot. He was gasping for air. The elegant black car raced down the highway as Clarke sprang to his feet, holding his own head in morbid disbelief, screaming, "They've shot the President! They've shot the President! They've shot the President!" Suddenly a bright light blinded Clarke.

Men and women clutching guns, ready to shoot, ready to kill, burst into the room and found Clarke standing up in his bed holding his head, screaming. Tears streamed down his face. Clarke was gasping for air, exhaling like a machine gun in a whisper. His silk pajamas clung to his body. He was soaking wet.

Clarke looked at everyone staring at him. Secret Service agents, out of breath from the adrenaline rush, stood strategically around the room. Clarke slowly dropped his hands realizing it was all a bad dream—a horrid, morbid nightmare. Clarke sobbed as he stood on the bed, wet and shivering. The bed was soaked. Clarke didn't know if he wet the bed and didn't care.

It was all a dream, a bad dream. Clarke was helped down off the bed by a Secret Service Agent and asked how they could help. Ms. Deverough came into the room tying her silk dressing gown, summoned by a very caring Ms. Jones. Ms. Jones motioned for the Secret Service to leave the room. She followed the last one out and shut the door behind her.

Clarke was shivering. Ms. Deverough sat down in a chair, looking first at the drenched bed, then at Clarke. "Another dream about the President's death?" she asked.

Clarke stared at her. Her smile was gentle but the lines in her forehead said she was concerned. How she knew he was having nightmares and exactly what they were about he would never know. Ms. Deverough looked at Clarke. His hair was matted to his head, wet with sweat. His silk pajamas clung to his skin. He was cold. Clarke sat down, still shaking from the nightmare. Shaking from the cold. Shaking from the fear. Clarke stared straight ahead at nothing and whispered a simple, "Yes." He paused. "Another dream about the death of the President."

"Shall I call him?" Ms. Deverough asked even though she already knew the answer.

"No. He'll be home tomorrow." Clarke said, trying to comfort himself.

"Are you afraid for Michael because you are not there to protect him?" Ms. Deverough asked.

"No." Clarke said in a hushed voice. He smiled. *Someone like me protecting someone like Michael*, Clarke thought to himself. "Of course not." Clarke paused then tears began flowing down his cheeks. "Saundra and I are redecorating the Oval Office tomorrow. It's a surprise for Michael."

"That's lovely, Clarke." Ms. Deverough knew there was more to this story.

"Jackie Kennedy had the Oval Office redecorated for her husband while they were away in Dallas. President Kennedy never saw it." Clarke sounded like was talking through hiccups as his head jerked with every breath.

"Clarke," Ms. Deverough scolded. "History is not going to repeat itself."

The press was always comparing this administration to the Kennedy's. Tasteless editorials always had Clarke drawn in his signature vest and spectator shoes, topped by Jackie Kennedy's pillbox hat. Clarke and Ms. Deverough were interrupted by a knock on the door.

A uniformed staff member came in and asked if he could freshen the room. A young lady followed him, carrying fresh bed linens. The White House nurse offered Clarke a sedative. He waved her off, protesting that he was fine adding that he shouldn't eat so much garlic before bedtime. Clarke hadn't eaten garlic. In fact, Clarke hadn't eaten anything. He was loosing weight. It was noticeable to everyone close to him although it was never mentioned.

Clarke excused himself to freshen up. As he peeled of his pajamas, he realized he had indeed wet the bed. Clarke was embarrassed. He felt like a young schoolboy. As he showered, he realized he was shaking. He was so scared. Clarke had such a feeling of impending doom. He started to cry again. The dreams of the President dying were really getting to him. All he needed was a big hug from Michael and everything would be okay again.

Clarke turned off the water and grabbed a fluffy towel. He dried off and slipped into clean pajamas. It felt good to be warm. Clarke tied his robe as he walked back into the bedroom. He was tired but didn't want to go back to sleep. In his dreams there was always death.

Ms. Deverough interrupted Clarke's thoughts. "The President will be home in less than twenty-four hours, safe and sound. Just in time for the First Couple to be honored at the finest event Washington has seen outside the gates of the White House." Clarke smiled.

Michael was being honored. He was the first President in history to have an above-ninety-six-percent approval rate since the day he took office. Since Clarke was his spouse, the press made it sound like *The First Man To Be First Lady* was invited just to tag along. Clarke looked at Ms. Deverough. She was so caring. Just having her in the same room comforted him. He not only appreciated her advice, without fail he always took it. She was never wrong. But Clarke still had an uneasy feeling. Something bad was going to happen.

Ms. Deverough tried everything within her powers to comfort Clarke. "The President is just fine." Clarke nodded. "Clarke," Ms. Deverough continued, "The most precious gift of life is living one day at a time." An usher came in pushing a teacart. Ms. Deverough had ordered tea—for one. She always thought of everything. Clarke smiled. The tea was decaffeinated. Ms. Deverough walked the usher out of the room, leaving Clarke all alone. The fire danced in a comfortable step. The room was warm and the hot tea felt almost as good as a big hug.

Clarke sat in a wing back chair facing the fire. Ms. Deverough always knew what Clarke needed, and a crackling fire hit the spot. As he sat there, he remembered the last words the President said, trying to calm him. "No, Clarke, you can't come. No other wives will be there."

Clarke watched the flames dance the night away. The dreams, actually nightmares, of the President dying while in the White House were becoming more frequent. Clarke tried hard to shrug it off. Maybe the public opinions and the nasty editorials about The First Man to Be First Lady's homosexuality were finally getting to him. But that wasn't it.

Clarke could care less what people thought of him or what the press wrote. If it was the truth, it was good. If it was nasty, it was someone's opinion who hadn't yet met the man whom the press still referred to as *The First Man To Be First Lady*. To know Clarke was to love him. Plain and simple. The more the press got to know Clarke, the more the world loved him.

Clarke just couldn't get over the nightmares. Maybe there was a vitamin deficiency in his diet. No, that wasn't it. Maybe he needed more exercise. No, that wasn't it. Clarke had even had the water supply checked at the White House. That wasn't it, either. Clarke actually felt fit as a fiddle. Maybe it was his research on prior First Families. It seemed that the most famous administrations had ended in tragedy. Clarke had privately asked for more Secret Service people to guard the President, but the President had to approve that. Clarke had received a stern but loving talking to by Michael.

Talking to Ms. Deverough had helped. Thank goodness she could keep a secret. Clarke was so glad Ms. Deverough was there. She kept him from going nuts. Clarke didn't mind his fashion sense going to the press, but he wanted to make sure the nonsense stayed right where it was.

Talking about the dreams with Ms. Deverough seemed to calm him. That and knowing there were more Secret Service people around the President. The President had finally given in and put more on duty. Michael would do anything for Clarke. The President himself was so worried that he had more Secret Service agents assigned to Clarke. Clarke never noticed.

The President wasn't going to be gone more than twenty-four hours, but they were the longest twenty-four hours of Clarke's life. The next day started long before sunup. Clarke, Saundra, and a work crew were going to completely redecorate the Oval Office. Knick-knacks on shelves were packed and the boxes taken out of the room. Pictures on the credenza behind the President's desk were packed and taken away as well. Furniture was carted off and the chandelier was lowered. Draperies were taken down and hauled away. Carpets were pulled up, rolled, and carried out. Clarke was so preoccupied he didn't even think of Mary Poppins when the fireplace and chimney were cleaned.

The walls and ceiling were repainted. Electric heaters and rotating fans were brought in to dry the paint. Clarke, Saundra, and the work crew worked hard. Lunch was brought in and everyone sat together enjoying each other's company. As soon as dessert was eaten, they were all right back to work. Saundra's designer carpet was laid. New draperies were hung and tied back. New furniture was delivered. Clarke's favorite pieces that had been in the Oval Office had been reupholstered and put back in their place.

Pictures were re-hung. Knick-knacks were put back on shelves. Clarke had ordered a new credenza to sit behind the President's desk. It was impressive, with a marble top and hand-carved wood stained to match the burgundy hue of the rocking chairs. Personal pictures were placed in the same order Michael had them.

The work crew looked around as if they were lost. The room was finished. It was amazing how much had been accomplished in such a short time! The last workman left the room, looking at his watch, still wondering how they had accomplished it. Clarke looked around the Oval Office. Saundra fluffed a pillow. They looked at each other and gestured, "The

Oval Office is spectacular." Clarke laughed uncontrollably. Saundra smiled. She didn't know what was so funny but enjoyed the moment.

The royal blue rug, complete with the Presidential Seal, was incredible. The Oval Office was accented in a spectacular dark ruby. The drapes were dark ruby and lined in the same stunning gold that accented the State Rooms. New kidney-shaped sofas were striped in white, dark ruby and gold. The rocking chair cushions were reupholstered to match the new color of the room. The fabric used in the cushions was the only place Clarke used Saundra's metallic thread.

Clarke was so worried about the President he made sure he was briefed on the President's whereabouts on the hour. Clarke knew the exact moment the President flew into United States airspace. Clarke wasn't going to meet Marine One on the South Lawn. He had been so shaken up about the conference and the nightmares he didn't know how he would react when he saw Michael safe and sound. The President had a meeting scheduled with his advisors the moment he landed and they were already waiting outside the Oval Office.

Clarke watched Marine One land from the Blue Room. He wished he could see the President's reaction when he saw his office. Clarke would wait and see it in the President's eyes when they could finally be alone. Ms. Deverough informed Clarke that it was time to get ready.

Ms. Deverough should have been a drill sergeant. She kept Clarke in step and on time. Clarke smiled and reluctantly agreed. He walked to his quarters as Ms. Deverough looked on rather puzzled, as if she sensed there was something wrong. Clarke turned the corner and was out of sight.

When Clarke came out of the shower his ensemble was on the valet pressed and ready to go. Beverly Anderson had delivered Clarke's ensemble for the evening. It amazed Clarke how Beverly could pop into the White House, leave a fabulous outfit and pop out. Beverly had the security clearance to enter the White House unescorted. The staff was so used to him being there and always honored his request not to make a fuss.

Clarke's dressing room looked like a fine gentleman's salon. Racks of clothes hung in order, shortest to tall, darkest to light and, in spite of the press he was getting, he really didn't mind wearing the same thing twice. But he very rarely did, and if he did, the front page spelled it out stitch by stitch.

Clarke noticed the handsome scroll on the *Beverly Anderson* label. Beverly had become quite the name in the fashion world. *Beverly Anderson* boutiques dotted every fine fashion lane in America. His advertising budget was zero. *Beverly Anderson Fashions* were in every magazine, on every television channel, and proudly worn by the First Man To Be First Lady. Beverly saw to it that Clarke was always the finest dressed man in the world. It seemed that everyone wanted to dress like Clarke, right down to the Beverly Anderson label.

Clarke took his ensemble off the valet, which just happened to be the same height and width as Clarke. The ensemble had been freshly pressed and crisply creased. Clarke thought about it as he dressed. He had become America's fashion consultant and the whole world looked on. Suits were worn only for work or for being buried in. In political office, they were one in the same.

The President was always in a dark suit, right along with his contemporaries, but the jacket was the first to come off and shirtsleeves were rolled up high. Clarke wasn't going to change the world; he was simply going to be comfortable in it and Clarke wasn't comfortable in a dark suit.

Clarke loved the way Beverly Anderson designed his clothes. His vests always had a bizarre lining, in bright pinks or greens and some had unusual patterns. It was almost as though Clarke had a secret, which made him laugh. His only secret was the color in the UN-traditional lining of his vest. Clarke thought about that for a moment. "Gee, what a boring secret," Clarke said out loud.

The President of the United States was being honored tonight at the finest dinner to be given in Washington and all Clarke had to do was be a guest. Dinners out were always Clarke's favorite. He enjoyed being the traditional host, which was the official and traditional duty of the spouse of the President, but it wasn't a night out. Clarke would see to it the event in at the White House was perfect, but it took very careful planning.

America watched as the White House began entertaining again and wanted to follow the leader. Dinner parties across

America, whether they were private or for hundreds, became elegant events. Florists TV commercials featured the new dinner party bouquet designed to be the perfect guest at your dinner table. If a dinner party was announced, a floral arrangement was delivered. Fresh flowers and lovely china decorated America's tables from coast-to-coast.

Entertainment, live or piped-in, was expected like a good dessert. American fine china companies reported the biggest sales increase since the early 1960's. Demands for dinner music CD's soared. Even if the United States didn't want to be just like the First Couple, they surely wanted to entertain like them.

The President's meeting was running late. He would have just enough time to shower and dress. Clarke laid out his tuxedo with all the accessories. It was the same simple tuxedo Michael always wore. Clarke wasn't going to give in on dressing up the President. Clarke looked in the mirror, turned from side to side, then adjusted his tie. He was all dressed and ready to go. He decided to pass the time by taking a walk through the White House. Barney had a different idea, and Clarke decided on a walk outside along the shrubbery instead.

The Washington night was crisp and Clarke enjoyed the walk. He let Barney be tour guide. Clarke found himself seeing little nooks and crannies in gardens one would only see while walking their dog. After a complete tour, Barney walked Clarke back upstairs.

As he entered their bedroom, Clarke could hear the President arguing with his bow tie. Suddenly a pair of hands came around the President and Clarke tied the tie perfectly, the first time. They looked at each other, cheek to cheek in the mirror. The President gently caressed Clarke's hands. They were a handsome couple. "Welcome home," is all Clarke said.

Clarke contained his excitement. He was so relieved to see Michael safe and hold him close that he forgot all about the big surprise. As the President held Clarke, he said that his meeting had been a complete success. "And to top it off," Michael turned and looked at Clarke face-to-face, "The Oval Office sparkles." Then, with a cocky attitude, he exclaimed, "It is the finest room in the White House."

Clarke looked at the President and casually said, "We thought you would like it."

The First Couple walked down the Grand Stairs. The Presidential limousine drove up to the North Portico like a choreographed move for the Cinderella story in Camelot. The First Couple left in their finery with a convoy of police and Secret Service.

They arrived with a welcome of the type only extended to a famous starlet. As they walked inside, Clarke seemed to float in a bubble of his own design. The world not only wanted to imitate it, but also to protect it from popping.

As the First Couple was escorted to the head table, Clarke noticed all the beautiful flowers and lit candles. The room was stunning. The itinerary for the evening was simple. The President would speak after dessert and coffee, then there would be light mingling among the guests. An elegant dinner was served. The entire hall enjoyed the entree. Music was upbeat. It made one happy to be a part of such a grand affair.

Clarke reached over his plate to get a drink of water. The stemware was stunning. Its deep cut glass cast prisms on the table linens. Nonchalantly, Clarke glanced over at Michael. He suddenly had a horrid look on his face and was turning an odd shade of blue. Instantly Clarke realized Michael was choking.

The stemware crashed off the table as Clarke sprang to his feet and placed himself behind the President. The audience screamed in horror. It looked like The First Man to Be First Lady was romantically involved with the President. The Secret Service sprang into action with their guns cocked, surrounding the President. A thousand cameras snapped a flash catching the morbid look on Clarke's face.

The President was choking and with all his might Clarke was performing the Heimlich Maneuver. The President could finally breath again. Clarke thought he would never breath again. It was Clarke's quick thinking that saved the President's life. In the panic of the moment, the pictures looked like Clarke was a filly mounting a stud.

Ms. Deverough had cocked her gun but it wasn't aimed at anyone. She gently un-cocked it, blew off the end of her pistol as if there were smoke from a fresh firing, then ever so gently, she placed the weapon back in her beaded clutch purse. With the elegance of a queen, she took her stemmed glass in a ladylike gesture and toasted the moment in one gulp.

It was the first time Ms. Deverough had drawn her gun since she was sworn in as a Secret Service agent and, of course, on the payroll. Normally a lady with Ms. Deverough's background was Social Secretary for the Administration. But it was an investigation on Ms. Deverough's background that had gotten her appointed to the team of IN-HOUSE Personal Secret Service agents to the First Gentleman.

Ms. Deverough was calm, as if she had rehearsed the moment. She enjoyed everyone's overreaction. The President had choked and no one saw it but the man next to him. The Press reported that without Clarke's quick thinking and fast maneuvering the President would have died. The President regained his composure and Clarke started to breathe normally.

With a nod from the President, dinner continued. Coffee flowed with dessert. Clarke was fighting tears. He was poised and most gentleman-like, but he simply couldn't eat. He had a lump in his throat with no threat of choking. He just pushed his food around his plate to make it look nibbled on.

The President got up to make his speech. He stood behind the podium and, as he did every time he started a speech, unbuttoned his jacket. No one noticed this but Clarke. The President was comfortable. Clarke took the President's unbuttoned jacket as a sign everything was okay.

Calmly the President began to speak. "I choked tonight and I must admit, it's times like this you're glad to be married to a man."

The audience sprang to their feet with applause and admiration, chanting Clarke's name in a double syllable. The clapping and cheers caught Clarke off-guard. He was bright pink with embarrassment. The guests loved it. Ms. Deverough inconspicuously danced to the beat of Clarke's name in the double syllable. Clarke sat there with a humble smile, trying desperately to keep the tears back. He forgot all about the tears when he saw Ms. Deverough chanting the loudest and, of course, leading the crowd.

Clarke nodded "Thank you" over and over and was finally called to the podium. The President knew that would calm the crowd. Not prepared for a speech, Clarke just said a simple "Thank you." He squeezed the President's hand, then walked back to his seat. There was one more gestured "Thank you" and

Clarke sat down with the rest of the room. The President's speech was like no other, the ovation more than topped the one Clarke had received—it seemed to bounce off the moon.

After the scheduled mingling with guests, the First Couple was given a nod by Ms. Jones. This was their subtle notice that it was now time to leave. Security was so tight that Clarke never knew how he and the President would leave. It was usually out the back door and through an alleyway. Clarke hated that. The finest President since the days of Washington and for security's sake, Michael had to leave through the back door. But tonight Clarke didn't care. He wanted to leave. He wanted to get home. He wanted the President all to himself, safe and sound.

The First Couple was escorted through the kitchen, then down a long corridor. Hundreds of people lined the hallways. Routine. Normally, crowds chanted the President's name and clapped but for the first time, Clarke heard genuine remarks about the First Man to Be First Lady.

There was applause for the First Couple. Then someone yelled out Clarke's name and everyone started to clap and chant Clarke's name in a double syllable. Usually Clarke heard words like "fag" and "prissy homo", but tonight the crowd was friendly and seemed to genuinely like Clarke. Clarke smiled and blushed at all this wonderful attention. Cameras flashed like strobe lights and didn't stop until the presidential limousine drove out of sight.

Clarke was usually chatty on the way home. Not this time. He was quiet.

"I'm just fine and I'm going to stay that way," The President said, scolding Clarke in a loving tone. That's all that was said all the way back to the White House. The presidential limousine drove to the North Portico and stopped. A staff member opened the door and Clarke and the President got out of the car and walked to an open door, entering the White House.

White House staff mingled in the Entrance Hall when the First Couple returned from an event or dinner that was held away from the White House. Clarke was so enthusiastic about his evenings out that he intrigued the whole staff with his excitement. Clarke would often get great ideas, add a sparkle of his own creativity, multiplied by the talents of the White House staff, and start planning the next White House event right then and there.

But tonight, the First Couple walked quietly to the Grand Staircase and climbed out of sight. The staff had never seen Clarke so solemn. They looked at each other as if they had never met the man who just walked away. Ms. Deverough briefed the staff on Clarke's heroism.

Clarke walked to his dressing room. He started to unbutton his vest. For some reason the section of his dressing room where black suits and black vests hung caught his eye. They had hung there since the first shipment of Beverly Anderson's designs were delivered to the White House. Beverly had thought of everything. He had a wardrobe, appropriate apparel for mourning, immediately available.

The President found Clarke in his dressing room staring straight ahead. "Do you want to talk about this?" Michael asked.

Clarke was silent. He tried to shake off the bad thoughts and continued to undress. He placed his clothes on a hanger, then wrapped a robe around himself.

"I'm all right," Michael said. He was calm but very worried about Clarke.

Clarke was very careful about tears, even in private, but he couldn't control his emotions and started to cry. It broke Michael's heart seeing Clarke like this. Michael knew it was the pressure of being the First Gentleman. The subtle insults of the press calling Clarke the First Man To Be First Lady, the editorials, and the constant news media. Michael felt responsible for every bit of it. Clarke knew what Michael was thinking, and took his hand in his own.

"Darling, I'm scared for you. Tonight brought to life how vulnerable you are, and not only from being attacked, but just by being human."

"I can't change that," The President interrupted. He took Clarke in his arms, holding him tight. "Clarke!" He pulled Clarke away in a tight hold and looked him straight in the eye. "You're shaking."

"I'm fine," Clarke said looking down to the floor.

"Clarke, it's okay!" Michael was pleading with Clarke. "NOTHING is going to happen to me."

"Damn it! Darling" Clarke interrupted, tearing himself away form the President. Clarke was drowning in his tears, fighting for a breath. "I was wearing a blue vest lined in pink." Clarke was dumbfounded. "Don't you get it?"

The President didn't get it. He looked at Clarke with deep concern.

"Jacqueline Kennedy was wearing the same colors in Dallas." Clarke crumbled. He was sobbing with a morbid tone to his cry.

"Clarke!" The President scolded again. "History is not going to repeat itself."

For a moment, Clarke was comforted by Michael's concern and laughed through his tears. "That's exactly what Ms. Deverough said."

"She's right. Clarke, I know you're under a lot of pressure, but I am just fine." The President grabbed Clarke and held him tight. He wouldn't let him get away. Suddenly Michael pushed Clarke an arm's length away, holding him by the shoulders, "Clarke, you're burning up with fever." Michael was deeply concerned. "Clarke? What is the matter?" The President looked at Clarke, then reached for the house phone to page the doctor.

"White House operator," a cheery voice said, ready for her command.

Clarke grabbed the phone and placed it back down. He realized that was a stupid thing to do. They both paused, knowing the Secret Service would be inquiring about their safety. Any time a phone was picked up and not answered, the Secret Service was there in a snap. Clarke walked a few steps, folding his arms as if he was giving himself a hug. He wasn't in the mood to be interrupted.

Right on cue came a knock at the door. "Mr. President, are you all right?"

"Yes. I'm fine." The President commanded, not taking his eyes off of Clarke.

"We're both fine. Thank you." Clarke answered before he was asked. It was a nice way of saying get out. In a more rational tone, still shaky from crying, Clarke looked at the President and said, "I'm sorry. I'm just coming down with something. I'll see Maddeline tomorrow." Clarke paused. He took Michael by the hand. Clarke wanted to let it all out. He wanted to tell his husband everything. Clarke started to say something to Michael, "Darling . . . I . . . " He stopped. He was trying to find the right words. Clarke sniffled. The President reached in his pocket and pulled out his handkerchief. He wouldn't let Clarke go, not even to get a tissue.

"I want you to see a doctor tonight," the President commanded.

Clarke interrupted him with his official itinerary. "I have an appointment with Dr. Maddeline at Bethesda Naval Hospital at eight a.m. tomorrow. I'm going to have a complete physical. She'll give me something for this bug I have, then I'll be just fine." That seemed to calm Michael as he took Clarke in a caring embrace.

Clarke was embarrassed, but had to admit letting that the tears flow while his husband held him made everything "all better." It was like a "cookie will cure it" cry, a ton lifted from his shoulders. Clarke's eyes were red. He had cried so hard, his eyes stung to the touch. After a long, caring, and much to Clarke's pleasure, romantic embrace, Clarke went to take a shower. Michael watched him until he turned down the hall. Clarke walked into the bathroom and turned the shower on full blast. He let the room steam up. Clarke was still shaking, and a hot shower felt so good.

Maybe it was all just another horrible dream, but this time, Clarke was wide awake and scared to fall asleep. Now Clarke was having nightmares while he was awake. When Clarke got to the bedroom, the President was already in bed. Clarke must have taken a longer shower than normal. He was a little ashamed of himself for overreacting and blushed and smiled at Michael as he crawled into bed. As usual, the President was reading something official. Clarke nestled up close and was out like a light.

The President put his arm around Clarke. He felt Clarke's face. Clarke was still burning with fever. Michael reached for the telephone but he noticed that Clarke was sound asleep and decided to let him rest. Michael was worried. He couldn't concentrate on what he was reading. In one motion he closed the folder, put it on his nightstand and reached up and turned out the light.

Clarke was up early. The newspaper was already read, folded back neatly as if it had never been opened and sitting next to the President's plate. The First Couple was quiet. The President looked at the newspaper. It was headlined with a photograph of Clarke mounting the President from behind with the caption, "Brute strength of the First Man to Be First Lady saves the President's life."

America had always wanted to catch the First Couple in a romantic pose. The issue of the President being married to a gay man was always on the public's mind. It seemed the press was constantly inquiring about the sex life of the President and his First Man To Be First Lady. The President closed the paper with a smile. The picture was certainly suggestive. They smiled at each other. Clarke laughed at the President's arched eyebrow, then looked at his watch. Clarke was a little disappointed they were on such a tight schedule.

Clarke poured the President more coffee. "Could life get any better?" Clarke asked with a big smile, looking at the President. The President looked up at Clarke. They burst into laughter. Last night seemed an eternity away. Michael reached for Clarke. Just as the moment was theirs, an usher announced the President's Chief Advisor. Clarke excused himself with a nod and a smile. He had an appointment with Dr. Maddeline.

The Doctor

The examination room was as cold as its polished metal looked. Even after Clarke dressed, he could still feel a chill, but it had nothing to do with the temperature. A husky nurse, who still felt it proper to wear a nurse's cap, assisted Clarke. He looked around the curtain at the doctor silently scribbling something in his chart.

Maddeline was incredible. She was a debutante with a brain and wore a stethoscope to complete her ensemble. Clarke always said Mother Theresa could learn bedside manner from this woman. Maddeline looked up and saw Clarke looking towards his chart. "When you're ready, we'll talk in my office." Clarke noticed what a beautiful smile she had.

Maddeline's office was clean and fresh, decorated with a feminine flair. A lovely bouquet of springtime flowers graced her desk. The Secret Service entered the room first. There was a man and a woman. They did a quick once-over then motioned to Clarke. When he was safely inside, they left, standing outside the only door into or out of the office. Maddeline took her seat behind the desk and folded her arms over the desk blotter. She stared at Clarke. Her expression said it all.

Clarke's world shattered. "Dear God." was all Clarke said.

Maddeline couldn't look at Clarke but somehow managed to look through him. "The tests are all positive." Maddeline looked down at the test results, then back to Clarke. She paused for a long time. Clarke looked straight ahead. Maddeline was so caring. She cocked her head slightly to one side and leaned towards Clarke. Her smile begged Clarke to let her help. Maddeline waited patiently for Clarke to say something, anything. She waited for Clarke to show some type of emotion. The results were devastating. Maddeline knew Clarke was a trooper, but everyone had a breaking point, even the First Gentleman.

There was so much nasty press about Clarke, about his clothes, his spectator shoes, the stereotypical remarks about redecorating the White House. The press constantly belittled Clarke's genuine smile but he never commented on the bad press. In fact, it was as if he never knew the bad press was there. Maddeline knew it would all take its toll eventually.

Maddeline was ready. She watched Clarke very closely, not through the eyes of the press, but through the lens of a microscope. Ever since Maddeline had been appointed private physician to the First Couple, she had consulted with the finest psychiatrists in the land. Any normal person would crack under the extreme negative pressures. Maddeline personally made sure Clarke would stay in one piece. No one on earth had taken the ridicule Clarke had and certainly no one could handle it like Clarke did.

Maddeline watched Clarke for any signs of repression, depression, or substance abuse—for anything out of the ordinary. The results were always negative. The only astonishing lab result was Clarke's cholesterol level. It was so low. For a man who loved chocolate as much as Clarke, Maddeline found herself repeating the test. Inside and out Clarke was the epitome of health. Until today.

She looked at Clarke. He just stared straight ahead. No tears. No emotion. She wanted Clarke to open up and let it all out. Finally, Maddeline stood and walked around her desk and sat down next to Clarke. She took Clarke by the hand, "I'm so sorry." She searched for words of comfort, but they weren't there.

Clarke slowly turned and looked at Maddeline. His voice was quiet. "Who else knows about this?" He asked.

"No one. Your tests were done anonymously. A team of physicians has reviewed your test results. The lab work we took this morning and that we repeated as a precaution this afternoon confirm it. You and I are the only two who know."

"I will tell the President. This will have to be handled with such care. Maddeline, we're so close to running for election."

Maddeline interrupted Clarke. She was angry. She wanted Clarke to let it all out, but it was Maddeline who had a hard time keeping it all in. Maddeline's voice was loud and to the point. "This has nothing to do with running for election. It has to do with your life. This is no different than someone shooting at you. You have been shot at from inside, and it will kill you if we do not act immediately."

Clarke looked at Maddeline and smiled at her caring hysteria. "Of course." Clarke said. Then calmly asked, "What are our options?" Clarke wasn't fighting tears. It hadn't sunk in yet. But it would. Clarke was a pro. He had the charm of Jacqueline Kennedy and the balls of Eleanor Roosevelt. The press had never been so accurate in all their literary days.

"Surgery, chemotherapy, then radiation, in that order. Then we go from there." Maddeline said.

Clarke had all the faith in the world in Maddeline. He would do whatever she said, whenever she said it must be done. "When do we start?"

"First thing tomorrow morning." Maddeline said in her authoritative doctor's tone.

Clarke's voice returned to its normal chirp. To Maddeline's surprise, Clarke's smile returned. "Make it tomorrow afternoon and I'm all yours." When Clarke gave his word he kept it. "I'm giving a speech at a prayer breakfast tomorrow morning, but I have the afternoon free." Clarke's tone said clearly, 'that's the way it is going to be.'

Reluctantly, Maddeline agreed. "Okay."

She briefed Clarke as to what to expect and the discomfort involved with the surgery. She also briefed Clarke about the possible side effects of chemotherapy and radiation. She gave Clarke the same written information to read later once everything sank in. At Clarke's invitation, Maddeline would brief the President that evening at the White House. With nothing left to be said Clarke left her office with a thank you handshake.

On the outside Clarke appeared to be his usual self. On the inside, however, Clarke was numb with the news. He walked towards the limousine like a robot, borne of routine, sandwiched between Secret Service agents. The entire team was dressed in the same type clothes as the First Gentleman. Even Ms. Jones was in trousers and a silk vest. The theory being that an assassin wouldn't know exactly which person was Clarke. He looked around the team of Secret Service agents guarding him as if he knew some Top Secret information. Maddeline was right. Clarke had been shot from the inside but no one knew it. No one was treating him any differently.

The Secret Service was there to protect the lives of the First Couple. Clarke was there to protect the President—from the press. The press made such an issue out of the First Couple's sex life. How do they do it? What do they do when they do it? When do they do it? How often do they do it? Now this.

The limousine door was opened for Clarke. He sat down, still sandwiched between the same Secret Service agents. "Just for once," Clarke thought to himself "I would really enjoy a window seat." The click from Clarke's seatbelt prompted Ms. Jones to speak into her radio. The motorcade drove off.

The Secret Service agents weren't a chatty bunch. Ms. Jones looked at Clarke as if she thought he was about to say something. Clarke smiled at her then looked straight ahead at nothing, and thought about everything. Everyone in the car was quiet. Clarke asked for the stereo to be turned on. Music always cheered him up, but this time, the classical piece didn't help.

Clarke grew deeper in thought as the limousine drove on. "Wasn't it enough that just this very morning's headlines had us in a suggestive pose?" Clarke shook his head from side to side. "Now this." As Clarke thought about it, he suddenly seemed comforted. He had never hidden from the press or the camera and he wouldn't start now. Clarke asked for a swing CD to be played. In a moment, Clarke was snapping his fingers and wiggling to the beat. The Secret Service agents looked at each other with a nod; The First Man To Be First Lady was back to normal.

It was late afternoon when Clarke got back to the White House. The President would be busy for the next couple of hours and wouldn't be back in quarters until late. Clarke excused the chef and started dinner for himself and the President. Clarke whipped up the President's favorite dessert. Clarke met with his staff to organize an army to take over his daily chores. Their meeting was held in the kitchen as Clarke mixed up several batches of his famous chocolate chip cookies. Barney licked his chops, watching a cauldron of dough became a mountain of cookies.

The meeting moved to the President's dressing room, where Clarke picked out the President's clothes for the next several weeks. He even tied the President's ties. All of them. Clarke left a big loop so all Michael had to do was pull the tie over his head and cinch up the knot.

The staff worked out a calendar. Clarke went over what would need to be rescheduled. Not canceled. Clarke called for Saundra. Many private tours of the White House had been scheduled with Clarke as tour guide. He asked Saundra to take his place, but only for the time being. He didn't go into detail.

Ms. Deverough peeked in and noticed all the staff in the Private Quarters. She knew Clarke had a doctor's appointment. She also knew Clarke wasn't well. The staff around Clarke wondered if there was a problem, but honored Clarke's wishes that he would talk with the President first. With the idea of running for election, things around the White House were hectic, but for the next few weeks, everything in the White House was scheduled to be surprisingly calm.

"The President is in the hall," an usher bellowed.

Clarke laughed, "You know, a simple, 'Lucy, I'm home' would be fine." That bellow was everyone's cue that the business day was over and to get out. And they did. All of them. All at once. The days were long and the First Couple's private time was theirs, and no one would take one second of it away.

Clarke made sure the smell of dinner—roast beef spiced with cloves and ginger—permeated the Private Quarters. It was the President's favorite. Of course, there were generous helpings of creamed gravy poured over smashed potatoes. All served with Clarke's flair and his homemade bread.

The President would forget to eat if Clarke didn't put a plate down in front of him. He drew in a deep breath. "Whatever it is, I'll take seconds." Michael said as he walked through the doorway. An usher, who still never turned his back on the First Couple, shut the doors.

Finally they were alone. Clarke couldn't wait for his 'welcome home' kiss. A wiggling Barney interrupted their embrace. Michael took off his tie with the same force one would use to remove a snake that had coiled around his neck.

"What a day! I'm going to shower before dinner."

"Do you need a snack to tide you over?" Clarke asked as he reached for Michael's tie and rolled it so it wouldn't wrinkle.

"No, but I might need thirds." The President gave Clarke a quick peck on the cheek. "I'll be out in a minute," Michael said almost jogging out of the room. Barney followed him. "I'm starving," Michael said to his best friend as they trotted along.

Clarke was going to make sure Michael was so full he'd burst with the next bite. Clarke knew Michael would take it hard. But as long as Clarke was ready to face it, the President would be, too. When Clarke heard the water running, he called for Barney. Barney's favorite Secret Service man was going to entertain Barney around the grounds while Clarke talked to Michael over dinner.

Clarke set a lovely table complete with fresh flowers and lit candles. The President came to the table barefoot, wearing string tied pants and a big sloppy athletic jersey with his favorite numbers on it. The President became more handsome with every passing day. Clarke presented dinner to him and fixed a plate for himself. Clarke didn't have much of an appetite. Lately, Clarke just pushed food around his plate to make it look like he was eating.

"How was your day today? May I have the salt?" Michael asked.

Clarke passed him the salt and pepper "Great. I always love to see Maddeline." Clarke said making conversation.

"How's her nurse?" Michael asked.

Clarke laughed. Michael had a defensive tone to his voice. The President wasn't scared of anyone, but if he were to start, Maddeline's nurse would be the first in line. Clarke was trying not to laugh but finally gave in, which got them both laughing. "Still crabby, but she cracked a smile."

"God, this is great," the President said. It was just simple meat and potatoes.

"Would you like some more?" Clarke already knew the answer.

"Please! I don't think I had lunch today." Clarke knew he hadn't.

Clarke went the kitchen and filled his plate. He took his own plate to make it look as if he was going to get seconds, too. He came back with a heaping third helping for the President and a little bit for himself.

"Clarke, this is so good." He looked at Clarke, knowing he had something up his sleeve. "You made this yourself, didn't you?"

Clarke nodded. "Make sure you save room for dessert. It's coconut cream pie. And there's a lot of it." The President moaned. Clarke had made sure the cookie jar was so full, life would be easy for everyone.

Michael was so hungry that he talked with his mouth full. "The Chief Usher said you've been baking ever since you got home. You okay?" Clarke passed him the basket of homemade bread and nodded another yes. He felt good. It was his test results that were bad.

"You bet. I just wanted to get ahead of my baking and stack the freezers full. I think I'm the first person to hold advisory meetings in the kitchen with everyone standing back, out of the way." They both smiled remembering the time Clarke whipped up a chocolate cake and the mixer came out of the bowl while it was still beating on high. Everyone was covered in batter.

The President was chatty about life. Clarke smiled but looked lost, trying to find the right words. Michael finished his dinner. He saved just enough room for a big piece of Clarke's coconut cream pie. It was his favorite. Clarke picked up the dinner plates, then cleared the table. All that was left were the lit candles and the arrangement of fresh flowers.

Clarke came back to the table with a mountain in a pie plate. He served a big piece to Michael and cut a sliver for himself. He knew it was bad luck to eat dessert alone. He took a bite. "This is great," Michael said taking another bite. Clarke was glad there were two more pies in the fridge.

They ate as the fire dwindled to almost a glow. When the President had eaten his last bite, he leaned back and thanked Clarke with his eyes. Clarke said, 'You're welcome,' with a smile. Michael got up to poke at the fire. Sparks raced up the chimney. The President hung the poker back up. Clarke got up and walked over to him. The President took Clarke in a 'thank you again for a great dinner' embrace and said, "Now will you tell me what's wrong?" He looked at Clarke and would hear the whole story.

Clarke looked the President straight in the eye. "The lump is malignant." The President caught himself as though he had been hit with a ton of bricks.

"I have testicular cancer and I have a bilateral orchectomy scheduled tomorrow afternoon. Chemotherapy starts

Thursday." Clarke was blunt and to the point. He had rehearsed it every other way, but that's the only way it would come out.

The President had a look of horror on his face. He tried to swallow but the lump in his throat wouldn't let him. His voice cracked. "Are you going to die?"

Clarke tried to be animated. He smiled a big smile but his lips quivered. "Someday, but not because of this. We are going to take the bull by the horns, although this bull won't have any dangles." Clarke smiled at his own joke.

The President looked away. Tears filled his eyes. He was trying to catch his breath. Clarke couldn't take the thought of Michael's tears and choked back his own. In a whisper, Clarke said, "Darling, millions of Americans have cancer. Now I do, too. Millions fight and win and so will I. I'll be better before you know it. I have to be. We are going to run for election." Michael pulled Clarke close and held him tight. Clarke had never before talked about running for election. This was the first time he had agreed to four more years.

Michael released Clarke. "Why didn't you tell me this afternoon?" Clarke knew Michael felt deceived.

"Everything has been taken care of, right down to a press conference with Maddeline after surgery." Clarke's attitude said that it was no big deal. "It's a one-day surgery at Bethesda Naval Hospital." Clarke motioned with his hands as if he were performing from the stage. "The medical staff is arranging the chemotherapy to be done here at the house. Your closets are organized right down to your favorite socks. We are ready. Beverly Anderson is coming over tomorrow to make sure the First Gentleman still looks great with or without hair." Clarke laughed at his own joke. The President wasn't amused. "I laid out your clothes. You have a meeting with your staff. The Vice President doesn't know why. Maddeline is on her way over to brief both of us on what to expect. Just for precautionary measures, her staff is going to put a hospital room together here in our quarters. We're gonna fight this thing and win. Besides," Clarke almost had a cocky attitude with his sly smile. "I want to win the election." Clarke really didn't, but his husband did, and Clarke would do anything for Michael.

Clarke said something good about running for office again and it seemed to give the President the boost and reassurance he needed. Clarke dressed and cleared the table and tidied up the kitchen. After an emotional meeting with Maddeline, the President went to the Oval Office and Maddeline went through the quarters with her staff while the Secret Service stood guard. Barney stayed with Clarke.

The First Couple didn't sleep that night; they just held each other. The morning started before sunup. The work crew was there, making an extra bedroom into an impromptu hospital room. Furniture was taken to storage. Beverly Anderson was so devastated by the news that he was trying hard not to cry. Clarke was directing the work crew when he and Beverly made eye contact. Beverly burst into tears. He looked away, trying to hide his emotions. Clarke walked to him with a big comforting hug.

"I'm not dead, so don't bury me. Just keep me looking great for the President." Beverly burst into nervous laughter, sniffling through his tears. Michael was always Clarke's number-one concern. Clarke could have cared less about the Presidency; he just wanted to make sure that Michael was taken care of.

If Clarke didn't look his best, the President would think he was even sicker. The smile, the clothes, the look, Clarke's home-baked chocolate chip cookies, it all had to be the same. Ms. Deverough informed Clarke that it was time to get ready. Clarke went to his scheduled meeting. He gave a speech that brought the entire room to their feet in a standing ovation. Television news cameras loved to film the ovations following Clarke. They were becoming the beginning and the end to many newscasts. Clarke left with a skip in his step and a smile that spread around the room. The audience had no idea what was about to happen.

Clarke was taken by limousine to the Bethesda Naval Hospital and prepped for surgery. The President was on his way via Marine One. Michael insisted on being at Clarke's side when he was given the anesthesia. When the President came into Clarke's room, Clarke was a little groggy.

The President walked up to Clarke's bed. Michael didn't know what to say so he reached for Clarke's hand and just held it. Clarke smiled and squeezed his husband's hand. Clarke was tired and lying on the bed waiting to be wheeled into surgery relaxed him even more. Dr. Maddeline came in, interrupting their moment.

"Mr. President, if we could have you stand over there please." Madeline motioned for him to stand aside.

Michael stood out of the way as the nurse started an IV on Clarke. A gurney was wheeled into the room and parked alongside Clarke's bed. Clarke scooted over on it and the side rails were lifted. Clarke felt like he was incarcerated. He was wheeled away, the President walking beside him.

"I'm sorry, Mr. President. Authorized personnel only." The President didn't know who said it, but he followed their orders. Clarke was wheeled through the double doors leaving Michael to stare at the shut doors that kept him away from Clarke. Big red letters marked the doors, SURGERY-DO NOT ENTER.

All across America, television networks preempted regular programming. "Please stay tuned for a special news report." An anchorwoman was in front of a sign that proudly read Bethesda Naval Hospital. "Network news has learned Clarke, the First Man to Be First Lady, is presently in surgery for removal of a cancerous growth. We will take you live to the briefing room here at Bethesda Naval Hospital where Dr. Maddeline, Clarke's personal doctor and surgeon, is holding a press conference."

Maddeline walked to the podium. She had a prepared speech that was quick and to the point. The room was quiet. "I want to assure all of you that Clarke is comfortable and out of surgery. His husband is at his side. We discovered testicular cancer and had to do a bilateral orchectomy. Clarke will go through chemotherapy followed by radiation treatment. We caught the cancer early, but this type of cancer it can spread fast. Therefore, we must take all precautions. We are confident the First Gentleman will fully recover. We also placed a shunt into Clarke's left arm where he will be receiving chemotherapy. Inserting a shunt is routine and involves a minor surgical procedure. It's like an IV that can be connected and disconnected without having to put in another needle. This will give Clarke the freedom to move around as much as possible and the medical staff will be able to control the chemotherapy with better accuracy. The millions of people who have had cancer and have gone through chemotherapy know what I am talking about. We would like to open the floor for any questions."

"Why was this hidden from the American people?" A reporter asked.

"It wasn't and isn't. The cancer was detected yesterday. We repeated all blood work and tests for confirmation and they all came back positive. Clarke asked for a press conference after surgery. The President agreed. Clarke just found out yesterday and the American people know today."

"How is the President holding up?" Another reporter asked.

"Great!" Maddeline said with a big smile and a cheerful voice. Maddeline grew serious. "He is very concerned for his spouse, as anyone one of us would be, but Clarke is a trooper and, as usual, is upbeat and says he will beat the cancer. I agree with him."

The President's Chief Advisor stepped towards the podium. "The Vice President has been briefed. Business is as usual." He stepped back, giving Maddeline complete charge of the conference.

"Why isn't the President briefing the nation?"

His advisor stepped in. "The President will address the nation within twenty-four hours. This is standard protocol. The President is with his spouse. The Vice President is standing by; again it's business as usual."

Maddeline took over. "The First Gentleman has cancer. Millions of Americans themselves or their loved ones have been diagnosed with cancer. This is all quite routine and it happens every day around the world. Until it hits you at home, you don't feel it. Clarke will be receiving chemotherapy at the White House. There is an around-the-clock medical staff scheduled to meet with him. The chemotherapy will last approximately fifteen days, and then there will be five days of radiation. Again, this is routine. I urge everyone at home, if questions do arise, to contact your doctor or local Cancer Society for information. This is all the information I have at this time. Clarke and the President would appreciate your prayers. Thank you."

Clarke was coming out of the anesthetic and was taken by stretcher to Marine One. Clarke still had an IV and a complete medical staff was wheeling the gurney. The President held Clarke's hand. The press was standing by with news cameras, but the First Couple could barley be seen. Marine One lifted off the ground, heading for the White House.

It would be a short ride. The President looked out the window of Marine One toward the White House. Already it seemed that hundreds of flowers had been placed at the gates. Many people were standing and looking up towards the helicopter, holding signs that read, "Get well soon, Clarke." Hundreds of floral arrangements were being delivered to the White House, all going through special security. For the most part, pictures were taken and the note card cataloged so Clarke could send a thank you.

The same medical team lifted Clarke's gurney out of Marine One, releasing the legs of the gurney so they could wheel Clarke inside with the President at his side. Clarke was still a little groggy and soon fell back to sleep. He slept until they transferred him to his bed. Vital signs were taken and Clarke was put on monitors. Every precaution known to medical science was being taken. Clarke would start chemotherapy in the morning.

Secret Service and Clarke's staff, who had followed Clarke to his room, were escorted out. The only people left were the President, Dr. Maddeline, her nurse and, of course, Ms. Deverough. Clarke was coming to and asked to be alone with the President. Everyone left the room.

Michael scooted a chair up to Clarke's bed. "Hey," Michael smiled. "How are you feeling?"

"Good." Clarke was weak but he reached for Michael's hand. Michael took Clarke's hand and gently held it. Clarke fell back asleep. Michael sat quietly, holding Clarke's hand and watching him sleep.

Clarke woke up early the next morning. The medication he had been given made him feel fuzzy. He looked at Michael, who had never left his side. He was wearing the same clothes and had quite a five o'clock shadow. As Clarke looked at him, he noticed how handsome Michael was becoming as the office was adding an aged look to him. Clarke knew that chemotherapy was going to make him sick. He just wanted to relax and enjoy the moment. He finally nudged at Michael.

Michael's first words were, "Clarke, are you OK?"

"I'm just fine." Michael knew Clarke didn't like the word fine. Fine was like lukewarm, plain yogurt. That was fine.

You had to add something to it to make it great. "It's still early. Would you like to cuddle up for a while?" Clarke asked with a begging smile. Michael crawled under the covers fully clothed, like a cautious bull in a china shop, trying not to break anything. Clarke informed him that he wouldn't break or even chip.

"Clarke, I'm really scared," Michael admitted in a whisper.

"About what?" Clarke asked. It was obvious what Michael was talking about. "Everything is organized right down to what tie you're wearing for the next three weeks. Dinner menus are made up, press releases have been written, and my staff is standing by. There aren't any State Dinners planned for the next three weeks. There's nothing to be scared of." Clarke reassured Michael with a gentle caress.

"Clarke, that isn't what I meant." His look said, "and you know it."

"I know. But this is all routine." Clarke said nonchalantly.

"But it's not routine for you, and that's why I'm scared." Michael took Clarke's hand and kissed it.

"Don't be. I am going to be better before you know it, and back to irritating the whole world. You better shower," Clarke nuzzled up to Michael's face. He loved the whisker stubble. "We have a press photo shoot from the Truman Balcony scheduled for this morning, before the chemotherapy starts. Your clothes are labeled and don't forget, your tie has already been tied."

Michael couldn't believe it. Clarke was organized all the way down to the velvet robe and silk pajamas he would wear to greet the press. Clarke was sick and the world knew it so it was completely appropriate to wear pajamas. It was amazing what Beverly Anderson could do with Clarke's ideas.

As the President showered, Clarke also showered, assisted by his male nurse. Even though Clarke had just had surgery, he could move around with minimal assistance. Considering that it was a man's major body part, it was really a very minor surgery. The incision bothered Clarke more than the actual orchectomy. Clarke looked great in the velvet robe and coordinating pajamas Beverly had designed for him. They would be taken off as soon as the press left and would be replaced by an ugly hospital gown with no back. Then the chemotherapy would start. There would be no press inside the private quarters during that time, no photographers, and no scheduled appointments, just medical staff.

The First Couple walked through the Yellow Oval Room out on the Truman Balcony with Barney trotting along. They faced the South Lawn. The air was crisp and the morning sun was bright. The Washington Monument added a beautiful backdrop. Clarke was a little weak from surgery and took advantage of holding the President's hand in public.

The First Couple was too far away to hear any questions being asked, but there were a lot of cameras and a lot of people waving. Clarke and the President waved back. Clarke's big smile told the world he would be just fine. Then the First Couple and Barney turned and walked back inside the White House.

The President was going to stay with Clarke, but much to his surprised disappointment, Clarke asked Michael to excuse him and the medical staff. The President stared at Clarke in disbelief, then finally complied with his request. He said a simple, "By the way." Whatever that meant, it made Clarke shine brighter than gold. Clarke whispered the same words back to Michael. With Clarke's reassuring smile, the President left for the Oval Office.

Clarke was escorted back to his room. He removed his robe and satin pajamas and put on the ugly hospital gown with no back and sat down. The shunt in his arm was for the chemotherapy and another IV would be started for medication to keep Clarke from being too nauseated. The first IV didn't take, so they had to poke Clarke again. The IV began to drip slowly, then Dr. Maddeline pushed a knob and it started to flow. Clarke could feel the coolness entering his arm. He looked to the right, then to the left. He had an IV in both arms. The one IV dripped very slowly, just enough to keep the vein open. If Clarke need emergency IV medications, the medical staff was ready.

At first, Clarke was going to have the Yellow Oval Room made into a bedroom as it had been during President Jackson's administration but decided against it. He wanted everything to be as normal as possible for Michael. Plans could be put into action if Clarke was to be bedridden. Clarke always dreamed of being bedridden with Michael, but in all of his fantasies there was never an IV pole or medical staff.

The medical staff was incredible. They were so "chippy chirpy" all the time. Dr. Maddeline insisted that one particular nurse be on staff who would be Clarke's personal nurse. Audrey was an oncology nurse who also specialized in psychiatric care. She was totally professional. Clarke respectfully referred to her as Miss Audrey. She was a tall, shapely woman with beautiful platinum blonde hair she braided into a loose bun on the back of her head. She didn't wear a traditional nurse's uniform; instead, she wore comfortable shoes, a white skirt of modest length and brightly colored blouses. The fabric of her blouse was always a subtle pick-me-up: flowers with ladybugs and smiling bees, buildings with an animated design, happy faces on beasts of the jungle and, Clarke's favorite, dancing music notes.

Miss Audrey taught Clarke how to laugh at his disease. He was convinced that cancer cells hated laughter and that the more he laughed, the faster the cancer would leave his body. But even with "chippy chirpy" laughter, the chemotherapy made Clarke more nauseous with every drip. If he read a book, he threw up. If he moved, he threw up. If he lay down, he threw up. An ugly hunk of a recliner was brought in. Clarke reclined. Someone joked that all Clarke needed was a beer and a remote. Clarke laughed as he secretly hid the remote behind the cushions. Clarke didn't care for beer.

Every day started with a walk from the Presidential Suite through the Yellow Oval Room. Clarke felt so regal being escorted by Michael. Clarke insisted, rain or shine, that they walk to the Truman Balcony to greet the press, who were waiting below with cheers and flashing cameras. Clarke hadn't noticed, but the crowds grew larger everyday.

As the chemotherapy continued, Clarke was getting weaker and paler. His hair started to thin out. The walk from the Presidential Suite to the Yellow Oval Room was taking its toll and finally a wheelchair had to be brought in. The President pushed Clarke to the French doors with Maddeline and Miss Audrey barley a step away. The medical staff stood by. Then, Michael would help Clarke out of the wheelchair. Clarke stood, Slowly gaining his composure. Miss Audrey took Clarke's pulse and smiled at the cancer cells. Her smile spread to the President and Clarke. Beverly made sure Clarke's ensemble was perfect. Ms. Deverough was just a nod away.

A gloved White House staff member would first open the drapes, then the French doors. The First Couple walked out on the Truman Balcony with Barney calmly trotting alongside Clarke. The President almost had to hold Clarke up, but no one could tell by Clarke's luminous smile. All of this was against doctor's orders. Maddeline always stood by with a pain shot.

The press was quick to comment, "Even while deathly ill, The First Man to Be First Lady never falters." Beverly designed the most beautiful velvet robes and silk pajamas for Clarke, which was like a pick-me-up greeting card. The fabrics were colorful and the designs were unique. There was something new every day. The press loved it and so did Clarke. Even though he was sick, Clarke still kept his sense for fashion.

Get well wishes poured into the White House by the ton. Flowers were sent and displayed on the south lawn so Clarke could see them from his room. The White House floral staff even sent Clarke a huge arrangement of beautiful fresh flowers. Clarke could smell them the minute they were carried into the room and was instantly nauseated. Miss Audrey held a pan for him to throw up in. He had the dry heaves. To his horror, the scent of fresh flowers was making him sick.

"Maddeline, why are the flowers making me sick?" Tears streamed down his face.

"Clarke, that's just a side effect of the chemotherapy. Don't worry, it will go away."

"Promise me that!" Clarke demanded.

"You have my word." Dr Maddeline said in a comforting tone. She looked at Clarke's IV then smiled at him. Miss Audrey took the pan away. Dr Maddeline's smile reassured him. She handed Clarke a tissue and held his hand. "I promise."

While Clarke was talking to Maddeline, Miss Audrey went downstairs and, with Ms. Jones' assistance, took close-up Polaroid's of the flowers. Then she glued a stick to the snapshots and arranged them in a big vase. Miss Audrey set them on the table next to Clarke's recliner. It was the most beautiful arrangement Clarke had ever seen and he immediately burst into tears. He couldn't stop crying. Miss Audrey informed Clarke that the tears were just a side effect, and *that* side effect meant he was getting better! That made Clarke smile and cry all at the same time. The staff remained so "chippy chirpy" that Clarke's tears finally stopped. Miss Audrey's smile flooded the room and those cancer cells seemed to leave with every happy face.

Clarke insisted on watching the evening news with the President. It was a busy married couple's idea of a date. The First Couple sat close together. Nightly news always started with Maddeline telling the world the wonderful progress Clarke was making and how she and the medical community expected a complete recovery.

Everyone tuned in to watch the incredible doctor, whose beside manner made even them feel better. Maddeline was such a down-to-earth woman with an inner beauty that radiated outward to everyone watching. After the first week of Maddeline reporting to the country on Clarke's chemotherapy, she was offered her own medical newsbreak during primetime news. She agreed to the stardom but only after Clarke's chemotherapy was over.

The First Couple enjoyed their nightly date: Clarke in his recliner, Michael in a rocking chair and the oncology staff an IV-drip away. The staff was so touched as they watched the First Couple. Michael would hold Clarke's hand until he had to make a note of something he heard, and then he would immediately put his pen down and reach for Clarke's hand once again. The First Couple was genuine. Even with all the medication and a hospital room just a diagnosis away, the love between them was tangible.

The chemotherapy seemed to drag on, second by second. Not only was Clarke nauseated by the smell of fresh flowers, the smell of food also incapacitated him. His personal diet was so simple he could literally see through it. He was very weak and getting weaker. Another side effect. Walking from the recliner to the bathroom exhausted him. He couldn't walk to the dining room, so Michael had his dinner brought in to Clarke's room.

Clarke knew Michael wouldn't eat unless they were together. A staff member removed a silver dome from the President's plate. Clarke could see that Michael was hungry. As the smell of good food wafted through the room, Clarke couldn't take it. He tried to breathe through his mouth, but he could still smell the food. He turned green, his eyes watered and he felt a wave of saliva roll across his tongue. Clarke stood, holding his mouth. Miss Audrey hurried into the room to help Clarke to his recliner.

The President had a horrid look on his face. He sprang to his feet as he barked orders at the nurse. "Help him. Now! What are you doing just standing around when Clarke is so sick?"

Miss Audrey assisted Clarke with his pan. He was trying to concentrate on aiming into the pan, while walking to his recliner and keeping an eye on Michael at the same time. Clarke was relieved it was only the dry heaves again.

"Don't just stand there holding a pan! Help him, DAMIT IT!" The medical staff was trained to know the President was displacing his anger and was feeling helpless all at the same time, so they weren't offended. You could hear Michael yelling all through the Private Quarters. "Did you hear what I said? *I SAID HELP HIM!*"

Ms. Deverough came in and tried to escort Michael out. "Michael, why don't you come with me and let the medical staff help Clarke?" But Michael wouldn't budge. Maddeline came in to comfort Clarke.

"Dr. Maddeline, DO SOMETHING!" The President demanded that Clarke be taken care of immediately.

Clarke finally made it to the recliner. After the spell of nausea, Clarke reached for Michael, "Darling, I am going to be just fine. Stop yelling."

When Clarke was comfortable, Maddeline walked the President out of the room. She explained that the nausea was a normal side effect and reiterated that Clarke would be just fine.

"Expect Clarke to feel a lot worse before he gets better." Maddeline took Michael by the hand. "He will get better."

Michael watched Clarke from across the room. The medical staff was assisting Clarke as he suffered more nausea and throwing up. "Dr. Maddeline, I am so sorry for acting like this. Please forgive me?"

"There is nothing to forgive." She held Michael's hand. "Promise me you won't give it a second thought?"

Michael nodded. Maddeline squeezed his hand, then let go. She went to Clarke and relieved the nurse. Clarke could hear Michael apologizing for his behavior and Miss Audrey comfort the President. That made Clarke feel so much better. Clarke begged Maddeline to give him something for the nausea so he could be with Michael at dinner, but Maddeline was reluctant to give Clarke any more medication. She was stern in dealing with Clarke's pleading. "Clarke, the side effects of that medication will knock you out. You said you didn't want to be out like that."

Clarke interrupted her, "Maddeline, I'm worried about Michael. He won't eat unless I'm right there."

"And I'm worried about you." Maddeline shot back.

"Please, Maddeline." Clarke grabbed for her hand, begging. She finally agreed. It was a simple IV dose that dripped during dinner. There was idle chitchat between the First Couple. Clarke smiled and watched everything Michael ate. He was eating well. At a nod from Clarke, the staff took the President's empty plate away. Michael walked Clarke back to the recliner. Maddeline was right—the side effect from the medication knocked Clarke out. As soon as Clarke sat down he was out like a light. Michael kissed Clarke, tucked a blanket around him and then sat in his rocking chair next to the recliner. Barney was at Clarke's feet.

As days stretched into the next week, Maddeline was so happy with the results of the blood tests that she reduced the chemotherapy dosage. Miss Audrey had proven that laughter really was the best medicine. Clarke never doubted her for a minute. He started to feel better. The nausea almost went away. He could handle the smell of food and even asked for a small helping of dessert. He could only handle half a bite but that was a strong step forward.

With the assistance of Miss Audrey, Clarke was walking a little bit more and a little further every day. Miss Audrey asked Clarke if he would like to venture to the first floor. Clarke's expression said that was a great idea. The wheelchair was wheeled in but Clarke waved it off. He was ready to walk. Ms. Deverough helped Clarke into his satin robe. She adjusted his pajamas and tied a silk ascot around his neck. Miss Audrey pushed the IV pole alongside Clarke.

Together, Clarke and Miss Audrey took the elevator to the first floor and walked toward the Blue Room. Clarke looked into the room as if he had never seen it before. He walked slowly over to his mantel clock and checked his watch with the time. He reset his watch. Clarke escorted Miss Audrey into the Red Room and out to the Main Hall. A White House photographer asked if he could take a picture of Clarke and his nurse. Surprisingly, Clarke agreed. After a snap and a flash, they walked to the Green Room. It was a wonderful tour. Clarke didn't even notice the time of day, but he noticed the White House staff and was so glad to see the familiar faces.

When Clarke got back upstairs, one of the IV's was taken out. Clarke felt so good that he felt he could fly. Clarke had read that Mamie Eisenhower held staff meetings from her bedchamber, decked out in frilly pink bed jackets dripping in diamonds. Clarke didn't drip in diamonds, just chemotherapy. Clarke enjoyed his staff and wanted to meet with them. He was feeling so much better he invited the press into the meeting.

It was important to Clarke to show the world he was going to be just fine. Maddeline took that as a good sign and took the last IV out, leaving just a plug in Clarke's arm. That way, if he needed medication he wouldn't have to be poked with a needle again.

In the Yellow Oval Room, Clarke and the White House staff, with pad and pen in hand, made the final arrangements for Thanksgiving and Christmas. Clarke talked about menus and the floral arrangements.

Maddeline was watching Clarke from the back of the room. She looked at Miss Audrey. "This is another step forward." Miss Audrey agreed. The staff commented that both holidays would be quite gala in the White House. Clarke was concerned that the White House staff wouldn't be able to join their families for the holidays and was assured those who were on duty had requested to be there with the First Couple.

Ms. Deverough was always just a whisper away. Barney was still at Clarke's feet. Michael didn't breathe until he knew how Clarke was feeling. Clarke started his day with the President on the Truman Balcony waving to the press and every well-wisher. The White House tours always started with a briefing on how Clarke was feeling that day. Many tourists left flowers and get-well cards.

Clarke's favorites were the handmade cards from the children. A table was set up in the East Wing lobby, where the White House tours started. Crayons and paper for little ones were available if they wanted to leave a note. Adults even left pictures and well-wishes written in crayon. These were presented to Clarke daily. He loved them, reading each one with a smile.

Time flew by once the chemotherapy was done. Clarke went for daily radiation at Bethesda Naval Hospital. He was always escorted by the Secret Service and, of course, Miss Audrey. Clarke was much thinner and very pale. His hair had really thinned out, but he wasn't bald. He was feeling better and showed it with every snap and flash of the camera. Beverly had seen to it that Clarke's wardrobe was fabulous, as usual.

With Clarke feeling better, the President was now ready to announce his candidacy for a second term. The elections were less than a year away and his political party needed to know if President Kent was going to seek another term. Clarke wasn't sure if it was a medical setback making him sick or the idea of four more years. There was never a doubt that Clarke would do whatever Michael wanted. Michael wouldn't want it without Clarke.

Michael took Clarke by the hand. He was so sincere. "Clarke, I can't do this without you." Clarke smiled and agreed to the campaign trail.

It had been four months since Clarke's surgery. His public appearances had started out very slowly. Proper protocol had a nurse on board an aircraft any time the President or First Gentleman flew. With a nurse on board, Maddeline and Miss Audrey both felt Clarke didn't need to be accompanied by the oncology staff any longer. It was sad saying goodbye, but Clarke felt so good about getting better that he grinned from ear to ear. As he grew stronger, his campaign trail gained momentum fast. He also insisted on scheduled stops at cancer wards and research centers.

Since Clarke had been afflicted with cancer, he was going to do something about it. There was hope and the world needed to know that. So did the President. The press followed Clarke like a honeybee on a springtime flower. He would not give a political speech from cancer wards, but he did talk with the sick. He offered a hug where there seemed to be no hope and a smile where there was pain.

Months passed like a speeding train. Like every other political campaign, there was a lot of mudslinging. But this campaign was different in that there was no mudslinging by Clarke or the President. The nasty press followed the wife of the other candidate like a hound chasing a bitch in heat. She always wore a snug dress to show the world she was a real lady. The press was quick to comment that she just couldn't pull it off, not when Clarke was on the airwaves looking so elegant.

The First-Lady-wannabe's comments about the First Couple were always nasty. She spoke of religion and the Bible. She always talked as if she were on her way to a prayer meeting.

"Maybe she was." One reporter said with a raised eyebrow. "With scandals of sexual misconduct from her husband's campaign trail, it wouldn't be long before she was on her knees."

Clarke never commented about anyone unless he could say something nice and he never commented on any of their opponents.

The press reported, "*The First Man to Be First Lady* is sincere. Clarke holds children long after the cameras are gone. He holds the hands of the elderly." Even with Election Day only weeks away, Clarke still wouldn't comment on politics; instead he offered only words of encouragement.

As Clarke boarded his plane to return to Washington the city, he thanked his hosts of the day. A reporter sarcastically asked, "Who are you going to vote for President?"

Even though Clarke had his testicles removed, he still had balls. Clarke turned to the reporter with a smile and a song to his tone. "I am going to vote for the man who's been doing a great job for the last one thousand days and will continue that great job for the next four years." Applause seemed to roar from the crowds. Clarke turned and walked up the stairs listening to chants of "FOUR MORE YEARS! FOUR MORE YEARS!"

Matt Robinson

The campaign trail had been well walked, run around and flown over. Clarke was traveling with the advice from Doctor Maddeline NOT to. Even though the President had the popularity vote, the polls said it would be a very close race. Clarke's homosexuality was the issue. The attitude was one of if Clarke wasn't married to the President, the President wouldn't be gay. It was as simple as that.

It amazed Clarke how a supposedly well-educated religious leader could say and write such a thing. But Matt Robinson did. Even more amazing was the fact that people still followed that kind of idiotic teaching. Matt Robinson always wore a sly grin, which made people wonder if they could trust him. He was a very small man. If he wore a green hat and buckled shoes, people would follow him looking for a rainbow and pot of gold. The producers of the Matt Robinson show were surprised when Clarke agreed to a television interview, in their studio, live in front of their cameras and so close to Election Day.

Clarke met the enemy on their own turf. He insisted on that. It made the enemy feel as though they had already won the battle without using any ammunition. But Clarke didn't need ammunition—he *was* the ammunition, the President was convinced of that. Political analysts had the opponents packing for the White House and November was still days away. Halloween was in the air and it was Clarke's turn to say "Trick or Treat."

It was rare that the President and Clarke were on the political trail together. It was felt they could do a lot more for the campaign if they each had their own agenda. Clarke, knowing cancer firsthand, continued his tours of research centers. He visited oncology wings at hospitals. Clarke didn't like politics or the campaign trail, but happily did whatever his husband wanted.

So, while the President was hiking the campaign trail gaining votes and leading the nation into his next term, Clarke was shining the spotlight on a horrible disease that in one way or another affected nearly every American in the United States.

Reporters followed Clarke just as much as they followed the President.

Today the First Couple started their campaign trail together. With the pride of an American eagle, Air Force One gracefully landed deep in the heart of Texas. The aircraft taxied down the runway, then came to a complete stop a short distance from cheering crowds. Screaming jet engines silenced to a purr. The band started to play. Thousands of people lined up behind heavily guarded fences waiting to get a glimpse of the First Couple.

Michael and Clarke released their seatbelts and stood up to stretch. There was idle chitchat about the smooth landing. The President and Clarke were given the once-over. Clarke, in his signature vest ensemble and wearing spectator shoes, looked great. He brushed off the President's suit, as any wife would do. Although briefed and comfortable with today's agenda, the President and Clarke waited for instructions from their campaign managers. As usual, everything was organized down to the second.

The staff people flying with the President were amazed that the First Couple didn't talk politics. They *were* politics. They were partners who had a life together and that life didn't require public opinion or national polls to tell them how to live. The President affectionately took Clarke by the hand and said, "Be careful and don't hurt anyone." Clarke smiled at him.

The front door of Air Force One swung open. Everyone onboard could hear the band playing. Clarke paused for a moment as Ms. Deverough removed a piece of lint from his lapel. The President didn't know Clarke had stopped and he continued to walk outside the aircraft on to the platform. There was loud applause. Michael stopped when he realized Clarke wasn't at his side. He turned and reached for Clarke. Clarke stepped out the door. The crowd went wild, clapping and cheering. In an instant, the double-syllable chant, "Cla-arke" began. Ms. Deverough danced to the beat, looking ready to twirl the man next to her.

Clarke was so touched. There were so many bald people in the crowds. Those people whose chemotherapy took their crowning locks had come to see the man who inspired them with a smile. As the First Couple walked down the stairs, the crowds kept chanting Clarke's name in that double syllable.

The President looked at Clarke and said, "I wonder why you invite me along." Clarke smiled and concentrated on walking down the stairs.

"Clarke looks great." The Governor's wife bubbled in an uppity Texas drawl. She was more interested in watching Clarke and the President walk down the stairs from Air Force One than the television cameras in front of her. Being a Southern Baptist, Cheryl Anne didn't understand Clarke and the President.

She also didn't understand why Jesus made the water into wine only to have her preacher condemn the vineyards. Cheryl Anne wore the biggest diamonds anyone had ever seen. She was a cowgirl at heart and proudly said her most cherished possession was a saddle that had belonged to her Granddaddy. Cheryl Anne watched the President. She didn't know any cowboys who didn't want a cowgirl.

Cheryl Anne had never met Clarke, but she adored him from the airwaves. The Secret Service motioned for Cheryl Anne to come forward. It was time to greet the First Couple. She gushed with excitement. "The sparkle in Clarke's smile could jump-start the sun on a cloudy day." She grabbed her husband by the hand and left the interviewer talking to himself.

Clarke was enjoying the cool breeze when he noticed the Governor and his wife walking towards them. Clarke had seen Cheryl Anne's televised interviews and mentally braced himself for whatever was going to hit the fan. She was quite a woman. Cheryl Anne could verbally yank you by the hair and twirl you like a Texas twister. Why she wasn't in politics no one knew. The Governor and Cheryl Anne introduced Texas to the First Couple. Clarke immediately noticed how beautiful Cheryl Anne was. Her smile was genuine and as big as Texas itself. She presented Clarke with a dozen yellow roses.

Clarke was so surprised and felt honored. He happily took the flowers. They smelled of spring. They were the biggest roses he had ever seen. Only in Texas, Clarke smiled. He noticed there was another rose. A red rose for luck. Under it was a handwritten card, not in an envelope. "Thirteen has been good luck for this country since the colonies. Don't forget there were twelve disciples with Jesus, and when you count them all together that makes thirteen. For women everywhere, knock 'em down with one blow." Clarke looked at Cheryl Anne and they both smiled a Texas-sized smile.

The First Couple walked towards the podium, shaking hands with dignitaries from the area. The President walked to the podium and Clarke stood at his side. The Governor and Cheryl Anne stood next to Clarke. TV was live with every camera in the city trained on the First Couple. The President gave a wonderful speech that could have elected him to office right then and there. But there was Clarke standing right beside his husband, resting the flowers in his arms like a Miss America contestant.

After his speech, the President thanked the cheering crowds with a wave. He was a great speechmaker and the world always listened. When the leader of the United States said he was going to do something, he did it. But he also did Clarke. Thunderous applause continued as a limousine pulled up. Michael waited for Clarke to sit down, then shut the door behind them. The limousine slowly drove away, surrounded by a police escort.

The President didn't have an opinion on Clarke's going live on a religious program. Political advisers always ended in argument as to how it would or would not benefit the campaign. Surprisingly they did agree one thing: at best, it could destroy it. The President's opponents had seen to it that this show would be broadcast live, not only on cable, but had paid billions of dollars for it to be broadcast only days later, the night before Election Day, on all the major television networks. This was their ace, they thought, their landslide win.

The country would see the sin the First Couple was committing and vote against it. The opposing side had an ironclad contract: the show would air exactly as it was live. There would be no edits. No background music dubbed in. No special lighting. Nothing. It was a billion-dollar guarantee not be edited, screened, and under any circumstances, preempted.

While Clarke would be in the studio, the President had a speaking engagement and hands to shake. Some things in politics never change. Women forgot the President had a man. Men thought a night with a good woman could turn the President around. For the first time in television, a political speech got higher ratings than *I Love Lucy* in her famous chocolate factory episode. It was simple. The world tuned in to be turned on.

Matt Robinson turned off his TV. He was watching the First Couple on the very channel where he would later humiliate the *First Man To Be First Lady*. Matt Robinson was ready. The *First Man To Be First Lady* would be condemned to eternal flame and Matt Robinson was going to strike the first match. He had his Bible in one hand and an attitude in the other.

There was no need for Matt Robinson to prepare for this interview. He'd had Clarke's opponent, the First-Lady-wannabe on his show just days before. The studio had prepared for a crowd, but few showed up. The interview went like a piece of cake at a church supper. The First-Lady-wannabe was a nasty woman and many people thought that she might have ancestry dating back to a pillar of salt in Sodom and Gomorrah.

Matt Robinson's producers warned him about the First Man To Be First Lady. America had watched the most popular man in the world beat cancer and he was their hero. "I've got God on my side. That man never would have been punished with cancer if he was living right with God," Matt Robinson boasted with a thump on his Bible.

"You better watch it," the producer threatened with a pointed finger at the preacher. "All of your viewers have been smitten with cancer in one way or another. You go saying anything like that on the air and we will be canceled, just like that!" The producer snapped his finger so loud there was an echo. "Just like that," the man repeated. Matt Robinson didn't care. "Did you hear me?" His producer asked. He snapped his fingers again so close to the preacher's face it made him blink. "Your ratings are already so low."

Matt Robinson's attitude interrupted the man. "A few quotes from the Bible and my God will strike *The First Man to Be First Lady* dead, live, on my very own show." Then he turned and walked away. He left the studio for a private pre-congratulatory lunch. A feast to bask in his own greatness. The producer just shook his head. He walked away throwing his hands up in the air.

Secret Service agents and their teams of dogs and guns had gone through everything in the studio and surrounding auditorium. There would be over a thousand people in the audience and millions watching from all over the world. It was reported that the Pope would be interviewed live after the broadcast for his views on the biggest argument in religion.

Clarke arrived at the studio and was met by the producers of the show. Across the highway a small crowd was carrying signs scribbled with Bible verses. A few people yelled unflattering names at Clarke about his sexuality. On Clarke's side of the highway, mobs of well-wisher's squirmed behind roped-off areas.

Armed police patrolled the perimeter. The crowd lining the red-carpeted walkway was filled with women chanting Clarke's name in a double syllable. Clarke smiled as he walked into the studio. The Secret Service had given the place a final once-over and escorted Clarke to his dressing room. The room was packed with fresh flowers and well-wishes from all across the country.

Just as with any interview, an outline was given to Clarke, along with a list of questions that would be asked and topics discussed. It was all fundamentalist propaganda that tried to make the world a better place through bigotry and hatred. It was all in the name of the Lord, so it was considered religious. Clarke looked at the questions, then put the paper down. He was ready.

Clarke and Ms. Deverough left the dressing room to practice poise and voice diction. Just before they turned and stepped out on the stage, a loud argument erupted among several of the stage technicians. Clarke and Ms. Deverough stopped. It wasn't a violent argument. It was more like watching a passive, G-rated war movie photographed in pink instead of black and white.

The argument was sided by who was for the President and *First Man To Be First Lady* and who said they were for family values. A man, whose wife had just had twins and adored his wife, also adored freedom. He felt freedom was for all people not just those who were married to a woman.

"You want your kids to grow up to be faggots? Hey, they too could be President." A man with his belly plopped over his belt laughed from across the room.

"Hank! Be cool." Someone said to him from the back. "The President made America great again. Go tell THAT to your kids."

"Yeah and tell your kids that's why the FIRST FAG got cancer. That's God's punishment and you know it." Hank was really stupid and tried to hide it by stirring up trouble.

Someone sang from the sound booth, "If you condemn something loud enough on the outside, no one knows what you really are on the inside." Everyone started laughing at Hank, who was the only one insulting The First Man To Be First Lady. The argument sounded like it was coming from young boys in a middle school locker room, although there was still no swearing. Clarke thought that, for a Christian fundamentalist show, there were a lot of opinions on right and wrong.

A man sitting behind a camera leaned towards Hank and laughingly said, "Coming from a man who got off welfare because he didn't want to have to work, that ain't saying too much." America now had to work for a paycheck and there were still a few who didn't like that.

Timmy, the assistant stage manager, was very thankful for the President and what he was doing for the families of the United States. Timmy was very proud of his wife and new babies. He wasn't going to let anyone insult the President or the First Man To Be First Lady. He looked Hank straight in the eye. "You know, if God was handing out cancer as punishment for our sins, then you would be the first in line." He looked around the room at the other technicians. "And so would the rest of us." He continued with fact. "Look at the criminals in prison who rot there, sentenced to life in prison because they murdered or raped someone. But they live to a ripe old age. No! That's not the way MY God works."

"You're right, Timmy," the man leaning from behind the camera said. Many in the room agreed out loud. Others nodded their heads.

"Hey! A brass tack is a brass tack." Hank said, bobbing his head. He turned and walked away, trying to put his hands in his pockets with an attitude. He had gained so much weight his hands wouldn't fit.

"And the First Man To Be First Lady is sharp." Timmy continued. "I want MY children to grow up and be who they are."

Hank stopped. He turned and walked towards Timmy who was trying to have an adult conversation. Hank spit his chewing tobacco into a Styrofoam cup. His hands wouldn't fit in his pockets so he did the next best thing to show his masculinity. He doubled up his fists. "Your old lady needs a real man."

Those were fighting words to Timmy. He was breathing fire when the rest of the crew stepped in to separate the two men.

"ALL RIGHT! THAT'S IT!" The stage manager yelled as he came around the corner, pushing people out of the way. He got right in Hank's face, then into Timmy's. "We have the spouse of the President of the United States here and I want this stopped. You both got it?" The stage manager looked at Hank, then over to Timmy. The two men agreed.

"Keep it to yourselves. This studio is in a free country and people can be who they are. Got that?" He turned to Hank, knowing very well who was picking the fight. Timmy apologized with a handshake. "I want every crew member in a tie by the time I get back. Got it?" The stage manager snapped. The crew had already been told they were to look sharp, but so far no one was wearing a tie.

When the stage manager walked out of the room, crewmembers started clipping on ties. Timmy tied his own and offered to help Hank clip his tie on. They weren't a polished bunch, but they wanted to look their best. Ms. Deverough looked at Clarke. He never faltered. Clarke slowly turned and walked back to the dressing room. Ms. Deverough looked out at the technical crew, then turned and joined Clarke in the dressing room.

Security was extremely tight. Matt Robinson had to go through a security gate and was almost arrested when he tried to resist. Security gates were placed at every entrance. Armed guards in uniform were lined up, ushering people to their seats. Policemen in plain clothes sat pretending they were part of the audience. There was standing room only, and there wasn't enough of that. Hundreds of people were turned away.

The audience was all dressed up like it was a special holiday. Many of the ladies were in frilly dresses and wearing soft white gloves. Those women in pants were wearing a matching vest and sporting spectator shoes. It was like an Easter Parade but in late fall. Men were in dark pressed suits and polished shoes. Usually people had on their Sunday best to see the preacher, but today they looked positively grand.

The house lights dimmed and Matt Robinson came on stage. The audience politely clapped with the normal, rehearsed standing ovation. He was shocked to see how pretty everyone looked, even the men. With a surprised smile, Pat Robinson exclaimed, "My Lord, with everyone looking so pretty, it's like the garden of Eden in here." The audience laughed a thank you. Suddenly Matt Robinson became grossly serious. The lines on his face deepened. His eyes became parallel slits. He quieted everyone with an authoritative hand gesture, telling the congregation to sit. The studio went silent. Normally, with instruction from cue cards, the applause went on and on. But today the crowds wanted to see more. Matt Robinson started out in the usual way, with a prayer.

Clarke was summoned and surrounded by a team of Secret Service agents as he and Ms. Deverough walked towards the stage wings. She wished him good luck. Butterflies were always Clarke's sign of good luck and the butterflies were certainly applauding today. Clarke was standing in the wings silently saying a prayer. He was ready. He was very comfortable in front of the camera, or a firing squad, and many times, they seemed one and the same. Clarke was ready to meet his maker and his maker was *not* Matt Robinson.

Suddenly, Clarke felt very much at ease. He realized something he had totally forgotten in all his studying and preparation for this interview. He and Matt Robinson had something very important in common—they worshipped the same God. And that same God had seen to it that Clarke's husband had become the President of the Untied States. Clarke's thoughts were interrupted by Matt Robinson's voice announcing,

"Ladies and Gentleman, The First Man To Be First Lady, Clarke."

Clarke walked onto the stage. The audience sprang to their feet in a thunderous ovation. Clarke was shocked. He was honestly touched and blushed at such a welcome. He hadn't known what to expect, but he surely hadn't expected this. And it was obvious that neither did Matt Robinson. Then the audience began chanting Clarke's name in double syllable. Naturally, Ms. Deverough was in the wings dancing inconspicuously to the beat.

Clarke thanked everyone with a smile as he was led to a seat beside the desk where Matt Robinson sat. As Clarke gave one last look at the crowds still chanting he nodded, then sat down. Suddenly the room went quiet. There were only muffled sounds and rustles as people sat back down. The audience didn't want to miss a thing. A television camera rolled towards Clarke like an electronic beast going to battle. Another television camera gracefully moved towards Matt Robinson.

"Thank you for coming, Clarke." Matt Robinson said with a sly smile.

"Thank you for having me." Clarke looked towards the audience. "It's great to be in Texas." The crowd cheered with a whoop and a holler, Texas-style. Clarke's expression showed that he really enjoyed it, so the crowd cheered an encore.

Matt Robinson wasn't enjoying any of this. He thought God would have already smitten Clarke down. But Clarke was charming. Matt Robinson had remarked in his opening dialogue that, "With everyone looking their best, the studio was as pretty as the garden of Eden." Now the forbidden fruit was sitting next to him. Clarke sat there calmly, waiting for the first question. Ms. Deverough was in the wings in full view of Clarke. She winked with a nod. Matt Robinson began to sweat. Once again, he calmed the audience with a hand gesture.

The audience grew silent. Matt Robinson looked down at his desk then looked up at Clarke. "Our nation is about to vote for a President." He paused, choosing his words very carefully. "We have never seen anything like this administration in history." He had a serious look on his face. "We want God back in this nation. We want our children to grow up with family values." Matt Robinson paused to swallow a burp.

Clarke took Matt Robinson's gastric pause as his turn to speak. "Family values have never been stronger. More people are attending church or a synagogue of their choice. And they're doing it as a family, thanks to the President of the United States." The crowd cheered. Again.

Matt Robinson wanted to show the world that the President breaking the very commandments God set forth had destroyed family values. This time Matt Robinson didn't try to calm his audience, he just interrupted them with what he had to say.

"The Bible tells us how to live. Since Moses was given the Ten Commandments by God Himself, we know what is right and wrong." He looked at Clarke as if he was ready for Clarke fall to his knees and repent.

Clarke shook his head in agreement. Then, with a comforting smile, he said, "Jesus himself said the two greatest commandments are, Love one another and love the Lord thy God with all your heart and soul and mind. Just think if everyone followed those two commandments."

Matt Robinson thought about that for a moment. So did the audience. The interview was not going the way Matt Robinson wanted it to go. He had to bring the ball back to his court. "Our country started out that way. Our forefathers founded America for the teachings of God." He picked up his Bible. "And that's why God's people came to this land." Matt Robinson got loud, "FOR THE FREEDOM OF RELIGION FROM THIS BIBLE." He looked towards the audience expecting hysterical applause. No one clapped. No one cheered. The auditorium was completely silent.

Clarke became serious. "Unfortunately, our forefathers brought many people to this country on slave ships, which had nothing to do with religious freedom, or any other kind of freedom. Now their descendants have said enough is enough. Freedom shall be for all people, for all nationalities, from all walks of life. Our constitution guarantees that. Finally, hundreds of years later, we are saying that we demand our constitutional rights. African Americans, those of Asian nationalities, those of Indian descent." The congregation sprang to their feet in an ovation, cheering to almost hysteria.

Stagehands tried to quiet the audience with cue cards and hand motions. Clarke smiled. Matt Robinson also smiled at his audience as he motioned for them to sit down. But they wouldn't. The double-syllable, "Cla-arke" started, but stopped when Clarke continued talking.

"Our country is going to excel as bigotry and hatred is stomped out. We all learned the golden rule back in kindergarten. Treat others as you want to be treated yourself. It sounds an awful lot like, 'Love thy neighbor as thy self.' If we don't agree with our neighbors does that mean we can't love them? Don't try to change that person. Pray for that person. Our churches and synagogues need to set the example of God's love. The Constitution guarantees the right to worship freely. It does not give freedom to prejudice. If you feel people are wrong in their interpretation of the Bible, instead of arguing with them, pray for them." Clarke looked at the audience as he continued to speak. "If someone felt you were wrong with your interpretations, would they be able to sway you?"

The camera was on the audience. Many were shaking their heads no. The lines in their faces said they were really listening and thinking about what the two men were saying on the stage. Clarke looked at Matt Robinson. "They would not be able to sway you. We all know that praying for them is more powerful than the double-edged sword."

"This guy is sharp," a technician said. He turned a dial so Clarke could be heard in the sound room. Clarke was very calm. He was very much the "class act" the press reported him to be. The producer of the show just shook his head. " I knew this was going to happen. I just knew it." He wrung his hands.

A technician sitting next to the producer drawled, "I'll bet you the hole in a donut that Clarke has something up his sleeve."

If Matt Robinson was going to publicly humiliate Clarke, he was going to have to do it now. Matt Robinson's devilish streak was as sharp as his pitchfork. He wanted a fight. He wanted to win. And he would make it look like it was all Clarke's fault. Matt Robinson smiled and one could almost smell the brimstone.

"Besides health, enough food to eat, and a roof over our heads, what do you want for America?" Matt Robinson was ready. He leaned in towards Clarke. Gay men always bring up freedom of choice and acceptance of homosexuality. The preacher had his Bible marked and ready to shove in Clarke's face. He leaned towards Clarke. The demons of his attitude chanted "Say it. Say it. Say it!" The preacher could feel the evil chant with each heartbeat. As a coiled snake hypnotizes its prey, Matt Robinson stared deep into Clarke's eyes. The preacher's eyes widened, shattering the windows of hell.

Clarke thought for a moment, then calmly said, "I want to see all American citizens get the education they deserve." Clarke looked out at the audience. "An even higher education than what is required by law." He looked back at the preacher. "As you know, Pastor Robinson, with education comes knowledge. From knowledge comes understanding. And from understanding comes acceptance." Clarke looked at the audience. "With acceptance, bigotry and hatred are a thing of the past."

As if an angel had poured water over a burning soul, silence extinguished the moment. With one simple paragraph, the audience watched Clarke reduce the preacher to ruin. The director was giving the wrap-up sign. Matt Robinson had to end the show. He thanked Clarke for coming. Clarke smiled. The preacher bowed his head. He was embarrassed by how he had wanted the show to be and was honored with the way his show had gone.

With disappointment in his eyes, followed by a blank expression, Matt Robinson looked at Clarke. In a flat tone, he said, "I don't agree with your lifestyle." Lines appeared in his forehead. Clarke noticed that the preacher was deep in thought, searching for the right words, "But may I say how honored I am to have you on my show today."

Matt Robinson looked right through the camera and out to the audience. "Our country is getting ready to hold an election. The President, Michael Arthur Kent, is the best man for the job. He has my vote." The audience cheered, chanting, "FOUR MORE YEARS! FOUR MORE YEARS!" Clarke stood and thanked the preacher with a handshake as the audience continued their chanting and applause. Clarke looked at the audience with a smile and thanked them as well.

Matt Robinson stood and walked towards Clark and they shook hands again but Matt Robinson didn't let go. He proudly yelled over the audiences' chanting, "Ladies and gentleman, The First Gentleman." The preacher, still holding Clarke in a handshake, put his other hand over their clasped hands. It was the closest thing the preacher ever thought he would get to a hug for the First Man To Be First Lady.

The crowd sprang to their feet clapping and chanting Clarke's name in a double-syllable. Clarke thanked Matt Robinson once again and released their handshake. He left the stage, escorted by the Secret Service, through the side wings. Ms. Deverough joined him with a look that said, "I knew this was going to happen." Somehow, she always knew. Clarke was escorted out the side door and got in the shiny limo. Ms. Deverough just smiled at Clarke as they were driven to the airport to meet the President.

Campaigning an Election

The nation had traveled far down the bigotry road but that road had a lot of pot holes and exit ramps. The country was headed in the right direction, but it still had some hills to climb. The President knew that. This was an election where the biggest turnout in the history of the vote was expected.

Every state in the union had adopted a policy of voting by mail. It was like an absentee ballet. Many people across the nation had such long commutes that they were on their way to work before the polls opened and even if they rushed home, the polls had already closed.

Then there were those who were shut-ins, or worked at home and couldn't get to the polls. Not to mention the people who were so busy they couldn't stand in line. There were those, as well, who just wanted to vote by mail. Ballots could be mailed thirty days in advance. It didn't require a stamp and could be mailed from anywhere in the world. The ballots could be counted as they came in, but local results could not be announced until the polls closed for that state.

Once the polls had closed in that state, officials could announce the results as they were counted for local issues and candidates. National results could not be announced until one hour before the polls closed on the West Coast. This brought a lot of national debate, but it was fair to every voting citizen across the nation.

If you didn't want to vote by mail, you could go to any voting poll convenient for you, whether it was in your home state or not. You just needed to present the ballot you received in the mail. It was scanned for authenticity, along with your voter's registration card. Thanks to Microsoft, the scanner could also detect if you were stuffing the ballot box.

Both political parties worked very hard to get everyone registered to vote. For the first time in the history of television, there were more commercials about getting people to vote than there was election-year mudslinging. The world knew about Clarke and the President. Those who cared, cared. Those who didn't, didn't. It was voter turnout that would ultimately make the decision.

The President's record spoke for itself, in a very loud shout. He deserved an ovation for his accomplishments and got it wherever he went. The President was a highly decorated military man and a war hero. His opponent had never signed up for the draft. The President was honest; just look at his relationship with Clarke.

When it's among children, it's called arguing. When it's presidential candidates, it's called a debate. The presidential debates won respect for the President all over again. After his horrendous debate defeat, the President's opponent publicly criticized the relationship between Clarke and the President, "If it's Camelot, it only has to do with a double humped ride. And that has nothing to do with Egyptian wildlife."

The President's opponent made quite an issue of the President and Clarke's sex life. It wasn't until his own campaign trail extramarital affairs turned the weasel of a candidate's philosophy on fidelity into a carnival road show. To her horror, the press exposed the First-Lady-wannabe's nickname, initialed only as C-C, to stand for Cotton Candy.

One could only think of the President's classless opponent. The press reported that it was a man like him that got the President, a homosexual male married to the *First Man To Be First Lady*, appointed to office in the first place. He was the Secretary of Defense, commonly called the Secretary of Defiance. He had thought for sure that he was a shoe-in for the Vice Presidency. When Michael Kent was chosen, the man had acted like a bully and quit. In fact, he was so enraged that he even changed political parties, just so he could run against President Kent in this election.

He was divorced at the time, but married the past administration's Chief of Protocol, the very first person President Kent fired. Their campaign for office was vindictive. Revenge was the name of the game. But the President had something his opponent didn't and that was spelled C-L-A-R-K-E.

Every church in the Bible Belt held debates over one sin against the other. The President was never mentioned in any argument. His opponent's dishonesty was the longest list in history. But there were still those in the nation, and a lot of them, who felt gay was nothing to be happy about and they couldn't vote Clarke back into the White House.

The former President, who had appointed Michael to be his Vice President, now President, spoke against President Kent and his homosexuality. Michael was ready for that. He would not pardon the man for his crimes once discovered after he resigned his office. America rallied around President Kent's decision. When the former President spoke against his appointee, the other side quickly realized it was just another vote to elect President Kent.

The former First Lady had successfully gone through rehab and was a spokesperson for the war on illegal drugs, as well as the legal drug that killed the most—alcohol. She was honest and candid with her genuine remarks. She made no secret that she thought Clarke was grand and wished she could have been a First Lady like him.

For the first time in history, the gay community visibly worked in politics to get the American people to vote. Gay Pride Parades with bra-less "Dikes On Bikes" and Drag Queens with big hair had always been on America's hit list. Now the gay community was showing the world what life was all about. It had nothing to do with men in high heels or butch women in leather. It was about real people who are the people next door. Gay men and women proudly went door to door in rough neighborhoods that were filled with bigotry and hatred. Small towns in the Bible Belt were hit the hardest.

The President spoke of direction and purpose, country and freedom. That was still a big issue, but the opposing party seemed to be sleeping with everyone. That didn't look good and the Bible Belt was tightened. It was going to be a very close race. The President used everything he had. Clarke did everything he could.

Strategy really hit the fan. The President had a whirlwind tour by himself to states that marginally accepted him. In those states, most statisticians felt that, without Clarke, the President would be straight. The Vice President went where she could best use her influence. She was a woman. She was African-American. She was a retired U. S. Army General, and one of the most fascinating women the country had ever met. The Vice President went to states where the women's vote was needed the most. Not only did she hit those states, but she also talked of freedom and how there was finally a voice in the highest office for all Americans.

Then there was Clarke. Clarke went to areas where he could really move the people. And move them he did. As awful as it is to say it, Clarke's cancer came at the perfect time. It brought one nation back to God with its prayer for healing. The fundamentalists thought God would smite the administration with AIDS, but He didn't. You couldn't very well say the First Man To Be First Lady's cancer was a punishment from God, not when thousands of parishioners had cancer. If God had smitten Clarke, he had also healed him. There was no argument. The sympathy vote was the President's and Clarke was happy to help any way he could. The opposition always reported on Clarke's cancer. They said Clarke was using it to get the sympathy vote. If that was true, it worked. But it wasn't true. Clarke still hugged the sick long after the cameras were gone.

The military as a whole didn't approve of their Commander-In-Chief being gay. Clarke would not allow his plane to land on military bases until he was invited to visit their hospital cancer wards. That brought a lot of press to the base. If the truth be known, and the press made sure that it was, under President Kent's leadership the military was the strongest it had ever been. Maybe because a woman was in command of the toughest branch of the United States Armed Forces and the other branches of the service wouldn't be outdone. The Armed Forces were lean and with all the women recruits, one heck of a fighting machine.

The opposing side searched hard, but the more they dragged President Kent's policies through the mud, the more the American people realized what a great President he was. There was only one thing the opposing side could do and that was to attack his husband, *The First Man To Be First Lady*. Their campaign managers laughed. "That is going to be as easy as winning this election." C. C. and her husband just smiled at each other. They were already packed and ready to move to 1600 Pennsylvania Avenue.

As Clarke visited cancer floors and met with hundreds of patients, doctors, and nurses, the press presented a healthy Clarke to the nation as a fine gentleman, a debutante. The opposing

First-Lady-wannabe couldn't hold a candle to Clarke's class. She could only wish her masculinity did as much for her as Clarke's femininity did for him.

The First-Lady-wannabe was told by her husband and ordered by their campaign manager to visit the sick to achieve the same positive press Clarke did. Clarke was genuine with every hug for the sick and seemed to have the celestial help of an angel's halo. It was obvious that the closest the First-Lady-wannabe was to an angel's halo was the doughnut she ate for breakfast.

"It is true," the news anchor said, reporting live from her campaign trail, "Clarke, the First Man To Be First Lady, is more woman than C. C. will ever be, and more man than she will ever have."

That comment infuriated the First-Lady-wannabe. Enraged, C. C. ordered her campaign to search and destroy the *First Man To Be First Lady*. Within hours, network news was reporting that her campaign managers were under FBI criminal investigations for breaking into confidential documents and exposing Clarke's investment portfolio. But it was too late. All the documents had already been made public.

Clarke had invested in American companies that just needed a chance. Clarke gave them that chance with his investment dollars. Those same companies had become Fortune 500 companies. Nonetheless, the First-Lady-wannabe tried to drag them through the mud. It backfired on her like a tour bus needing a tune-up. Those Fortune 500 companies went public with their distaste for the President's opponents and their favor for the President and his First Man To Be First Lady.

C. C. refused to stop there. She doubled her fists and clinched her teeth and ordered her cronies to Clarke's little town. The seaside village was prepared for battle. They had their weapons and they were loaded with Clarke. It was immediately uncovered that Clarke's estate was a self-supporting farm. After expenses, food from vintage fruit orchards and yearly crops went to feed the needy. Any profits made from the estate went to scholarships for local children and adults.

Clarke's hometown rallied with how good Clarke and the President were. They didn't care if they were gay, straight, black, or white. Clarke and the President were good people, and good people needed to be in the White House. The press watched and happily reported, "The more the First-Lady-wannabe and her husband search and try to destroy The First Man to Be First Lady, the more good they do for President Kent's Campaign."

But there were still many in the United States who thought, and publicly said, that the President wouldn't be gay if it wasn't for the *First Man To Be First Lady*. But, knowing there's not much one can do with that kind of thinking, the President fought for a better life for all Americans with Clarke proudly at his side.

Clarke continued their campaign in cities where the President had the best followings and loved Clarke the most. There, Clarke had more speaking engagements than the President did. When the President was out west, Clarke was back east and the Vice President was down south. During the final days of hysteria before Election Day, that all switched around. Against all advice from Dr. Maddeline, Clarke still kept his rigorous campaign schedule.

Even on last-minute campaign stops, Clarke insisted on visiting cancer centers and research facilities in the area. He would not let the cameras follow him inside. The stop wasn't for political reasons, but to genuinely give his support to the ill and to personally thank those who were trying to stomp out the disease.

With the hysteria that accompanies the evacuation of a rapidly sinking ship, Election Day finally arrived. Clarke and the President were exhausted. The President and his First Gentleman cast their ballots. They were televised coming out of the voting booth with genuine smiles. Then the First Couple took a much-deserved day off.

Back in the Private Quarters, Michael surprised Clarke with a romantic bath for two. The Jacuzzi jets turned the bubble bath into a mountain of whipped cream. Only their heads poking above the mounds of bubbles, the First Couple looked like two cherries on top of an ice cream sundae. Champagne was delivered in a silver bucket. In a quiet gesture, the First Couple toasted one another. After their bath, a very relaxed President cuddled Clarke in a mid-morning nap.

Clarke woke up refreshed. He looked at his watch. This was becoming the longest day of his life. He got out of bed, dressed and went to the West Sitting Hall. Clarke tried to relax and enjoy reading a good book. He never turned the page. Michael tossed and turned. He decided to get out of bed and finish up some paperwork in his private study. Clarke met the President for lunch but neither of them ate. They didn't talk. Even Barney seemed nervous, chewing on whatever he could find. Clarke made sure there were a lot of chew toys.

The day slowly ticked by. After lunch, Clarke tried to read again. He finally gave up and put his book down, then went looking for the President. He smiled as he looked around the room. Clarke knew exactly where to find Michael and Barney. Whenever the stress of the job got to the President, he would walk to the shed, commonly known as the woodshed, and grab an ax. Then he'd chop wood.

Clarke walked out to the woodshed. He sat quietly on a log and watched the man he loved. Barney sat next to Clarke, chewing on a tennis ball. Even though it was a crisp November day, the President was hot. He was shirtless. His muscles bulged. He was shiny with sweat. Whack. The ax split the log. The next whack cut the wood to fit the fireplace. Michael knew Clarke was watching him but he didn't look up.

"I'm so glad you're here, Clarke." There were almost tears in his voice. Whack. The wood flew like bowling pins in a strike.

Whack. The log split. The force the President was using to chop the wood almost scared Clarke.

"You know Clarke, I really want to win this election. I want to be voted into office, just once." Whack. The log split in two. "I couldn't have come this far without you." Whack. Clarke smiled but the President didn't look at him. He just kept chopping wood. Michael said he wanted a good supply of firewood for the White House but Clarke knew it was the anxiety of Election Day.

As the sun went down, the President finally hung up his ax. He was dirty with wood chips and sweat. His blue jeans clung to his body. His boots were dusty and dirty. He threw his shirt over his shoulder as he put his arm around Clarke. Clarke snuggled up close. The First Couple left the woodpile and walked to the house with Barney trotting along.

As the President showered, Clarke laid out his clothes. When Clarke heard the water shut off, he met the President as he came out of the shower. Clarke knew he would be sore from all the wood chopping and locked him in their bedroom for a rubdown. Clarke rubbed the President down like a fine masseuse as Michael went on about the election. He listened to the Michael talk but Clarke's mind was nowhere to be found.

As Clarke massaged the President, he thought about the election. Clarke knew very well that the gay issue was the only point against the President. Even though it was the President's idea to introduce Clarke to the world, Clarke still felt totally responsible. The press publicly said it was *The First Man To Be First Lady* who brought savoir-faire back to the White House, inside and out.

It was *The First Man To Be First Lady* who brought style back to America. Men and women were dressing for success, dressing just like Clarke, right down to his French cuffs. Clarke didn't mind one bit that he took all the bad press for all the good that was the President. The White House was a symbol of class. THAT was Clarke's doing. The White House was a symbol of power. THAT was the President's.

"CLARKE, PLEASE! You're just a little bit rough." Clarke had really done a workout on the President. The President dangled on the side of the bed, wondering if he was sore from chopping wood or from Clarke's massage. Michael laughed at Clarke's apologetic look and held him close. Ms. Deverough quietly knocked on the door, informing the First Couple that it was time to get ready. They reluctantly broke their embrace to dress.

The political team had set up for election results to be reported from the White House grounds. Typically, the First Couple would go to their home state and watch the results come in. The President didn't have his own house outside the White House, and Clarke's home in Washington, the state was so far off the beaten path that the President was advised to stay in Washington, the city.

Television cameras were poised and ready. When the First Couple walked into the room, it could be seen live from all the major networks. Clarke's smile hid his disbelief when he looked around the room. The elegant briefing room was unrecognizable. All the furniture had been removed. A horrid dark rug had been laid on the floor to protect the carpet and hide the cables that snaked through the room.

Priceless portraits had been removed from the walls and taken away. In their place were video equipment and television monitors. The monitors stood on tall stands and could be seen from all over the room. Each monitor was tuned to a different major news network. The election staff from both sides received the results just moments before the major news networks reported it live. Clarke could smell the scent of good coffee wafting through the west wing. He poured a mug for the Michael. The Vice President was across the room and saluted a hello with her coffee cup.

Due to the new voter policy that national election results could not be announced until one hour before the polls closed on the West Coast, it was going to be a late night. It was 11:00 p.m. Eastern Standard Time when the first results were released. Once released, election results would flood the electronic equipment from almost all fifty states.

The room that was blustering with chatter moments before became instantly quiet. The first results were in. Hearts pounded like a drum roll. A woman on the election team stood as she read the results to herself, then flatly said, "The Carolinas went to the opponent's side. There was no recount." She put the paper on her desk then sat back down. There was never a question. They wanted a new President.

The President wasn't surprised but the Vice President was crushed. She had rallied hard in those states. With anticipation, the results from the next state came in. With a sigh of disappointment it was announced Rhode Island went to the other side. That surprised the President and the political analysts who were sure Rhode Island was a shoe-in for the President.

Disappointment grew. Smiles were forced at best. No one wanted to look at the President, but Clarke did. He could see the hollow look in his eyes, but his man never faltered. The room filled with anticipation as results were announced from Vermont. Shoulders dropped. Heads shook in disbelief. Vermont went to the other side. Clarke's heart sank. It didn't matter what HE wanted. Clarke wanted Michael to have what HE wanted. He wanted to win.

Suddenly printers seemed to rip through the paper as more election results poured in. Bells from computer screens rang as results began to flood the room. Clarke looked from side to side at all the electronic commotion. Disappointment turned to bubbly excitement as results were announced with all the enthusiasm of a Miss America contestant. Massachusetts was the first to announce that all twelve of their electoral votes went to the President. Everyone in the room screamed.

Florida wanted to start its day with the President. Its twenty-five electoral votes were the President's. The President had the senior populace vote all over the nation. That was never in question. He had done more for the senior citizens of this country than any other President in history. They had a loud voice and all the President needed to hear was a whisper.

Clarke had arranged for a buffet table of good and hearty hot comfort foods. The television cameras zeroed in on that first thing. With the first results, everyone seemed to have lost their appetites. But when the results came in for the President, appetites took over, but everyone was too busy leave their desks. Clarke had the election staff served. A man took a bite of his sandwich then yelled with his mouth full, New York was proud to the core to vote in the President with their thirty-three electoral votes.

West Virginia's five electoral went to the opponent's side. They still didn't like the idea of a gay President. Virginia said with their lucky thirteen electoral votes, 'Mr. President and Clarke, please join us for a mint julep on the verandah.' Suddenly there was a happy scream. After a computer re-count, New Hampshire went to the President. Georgia, proud as a peach, said they had thirteen luckier votes for the President. Delaware went to the President, and so did Connecticut. Together that was eleven more electoral votes. New Jersey was proud that their fifteen electoral votes wanted the President for four more years.

Analysts said the dreaded Bible Belt would be the hardest for the President to win, even with Clarke's triumph with Matt Robinson, but the Bible Belt loosened up. They were praying for the President to win. And their votes said their prayers had been answered. Texas was in a recount and that surprised everyone. Oklahoma sang with its eight electoral votes for the President. Ohio was 'O' on the ends, 'HI' in the middle and gave it all to the President. So did Illinois. That made the Vice President feel a lot better. Indiana was the President's, too. Michigan was in a recount, and the Vice President held her breath. North and South Dakota went to the President. All six electoral votes passed a heaping second helping to the President.

The Vice President could breath again. Mo-Town drove Michigan to the President. So did Missouri. They showed all eleven electoral votes for the President. Their only recount was for their state governor. Maryland's recount came through for Clarke with their ten electoral votes. They loved the President, too. Kansas was hit hard by a whirlwind of politicians but came through for the President. And Toto, too. Or was that Clarke? Everyone laughed.

The people in the briefing room were excited. It was becoming the party Clarke planned it to be. Barney was enjoying the hors d'oeuvres as the results continued to come in. Kentucky and Tennessee picked their music and picked the right man for the job. They voted for the President. Pennsylvania finally made up its mind. Bells rang for the President. The Dairy State 'got milk' and served all eleven electoral votes to the President. The President wanted and needed the thirty-two electoral votes from Texas. He got every one of them on the third and final recount from deep in their heart.

The southwestern states shined bright for the President and cast all of their electoral votes for the President and Clarke. As the night went on, California, with its open mind and surfing spirit, was in a recount. "Better to be in a recount than go right over to the other side," the President said. The President wanted to win California.

It was quite a decision—a gay man or a crook voted into the White House. America really had to think about that one. And Washington State did. Washington deliciously picked the President. Utah was salty in their words for the President's life style, but shriveled up his opponent like a slug. Utah's vote went for the President. California was still shaken up about the Presidency. After all, that was the opponent's home state.

Wyoming and Montana said the President was a wood choppin', Wrangler-wearing cowboy at heart, and lassoed in their six electoral votes with a hoop and a holler on a recount. Oregon was in a re-count. They were tight with their vote, but not as tight as Idaho. Idaho finally peeled their vote and French-fried it for the President. Clarke had fought hard in Oregon. So did the President. But that state was so against homosexuality that it was politically a loosing battle. But the First Couple never gave up and neither did the Vice President. All of Oregon's seven electoral votes went for the President. Applause deafened the room. California was moving and shaking for the President with all of its fifty-four electoral votes.

The final results were not announced until the very late hours of the night, and in many parts of the country it was the wee hours of the morning. The President and the First Man To Be First Lady had won. An openly gay man proudly living in the White House with his husband, married in the first state of the union to legalize same-sex marriages, was voted into the Office of President of the United States by the majority vote. The President vowed he would never let the country down.

A congratulatory telephone call from the other side interrupted the President's bear hug with Clarke. A staff member put the call on speakerphone. One could hear the conversation via telephone or watch it from the monitors. Every news station was reporting live as it happened. Everyone was quiet.

The President still had his arm around Clarke. The opponents were proud of their fight and wished the President and Clarke all the best and good health. That was really nice, but they had made such an issue of AIDS and Clarke's cancer that everyone knew what they really meant. Old stereotypes never die. They just keep on going like a pink bunny with a great battery.

After receiving their good luck wishes, the President passed the phone back to an aide who hung it up. Thinking they were off the camera, the President's losing opponents shook their heads in disgust at their overwhelming defeat. The First-Lady-wannabe stared at her monitor that was showing the President holding Clarke in a big bear hug. Bobbing her head in sarcastic exclamation, C. C. barked, "Long live the queen." Everyone watching heard her.

The crowds gathered around the President and his First Gentleman stood motionless, watching for Clarke's reaction. A millisecond turned into an eternity. No one wanted to comment on her rude statement. It had turned out to be such a victorious night that no one wanted to start four more years of ridicule. Suddenly, and almost uncontrollably, Clarke burst into laughter. Holding on for dear life, Clarke happily returned the President's bear hug. It was a grip that should have broken the First Couple in two. The room cheered. The President was so happy he twirled Clarke around the room in what looked like a choreographed dance step.

Cameras flashed like a Midwest lighting storm. Everyone clapped. Television camera crews pranced around the First Couple trying to get every inch of their embrace on camera. Newscasters flung themselves at the First couple for their first reactions on their spectacular win. They interviewed the President with his arm still around Clarke. The Vice President stood next to the First Couple. Clarke was quiet. He just looked at the President with pride. Barney sat at their feet.

Champagne flowed. Everyone had a glass, even the camera crew. The President, gazing into Clarke's eyes with his arm still around his First Gentleman, made a short speech that said it all,

"To four more years."

With his head slightly cocked to one side, Clarke smiled back at Michael. Pride burst from every inch of his body, "To four more years."

Following the First Couple, glasses clinked together. In a theatrical exclamation, some threw their glasses into the fireplace. Many filled their glasses and toasted the victory once again.

"You did it." Clarke whispered, oblivious to the crowds and cameras around them. Clarke was so proud of the Michael.

"*We* did it, Clarke. I can't do this without you." The President said with a smile that made Clarke's heart skip a beat.

The Vice President yelled, "Three cheers for the First Couple." They chanted so loudly, it actually vibrated the room. The White House staff wheeled in a cake. The Pastry Chef knew who the winner would be and outdid himself with a fabulous four-tiered cake. Clarke was so surprised that the Pastry Chef fairly bubbled with excitement. He loved to please Clarke. Clarke noticed Ms. Deverough in the back of the room. She nodded with that, 'I-knew-it-would-happen' smile of hers. Clarke nodded back.

The President and Clarke cut the first slice with a big sword, accompanied by deafening applause. Cake was served and coffee poured. Television cameras and monitors were turned off. Champagne continued to flow, toasting the victory. The party lasted for some time. Music was piped in. Ms. Deverough danced as young men lined up to be her partner. The Vice President led the Conga Line. The Presidential announcement came very late and after a victory like that, who could sleep?

The best man for the job had been elected to office, with his husband at his side. The First Couple of the United States were the most admired couple in the world. Only whispers talked of their homosexuality. It didn't matter. Religion, sex, race, sexual orientation, even though it dangled in front of them, it was all behind them. Everyone had predicted at best it would be a close race, with a win for the other side. It was amazing. It was a super landslide for President and First Gentleman, Kent.

It was a gala with a sense of accomplishment and relief all rolled into one. There was so much euphoria it seemed to have exhausted each person in the room. The President was worn out. Clarke felt dazed. The First Couple thanked everyone for their hard work. Saying their good-byes, the President and Clarke left the party hand in hand. Barney trotted along. The President beamed a smile from ear to ear. There was a glow about Clarke, but he was quiet. As the First Couple walked through the White House Clarke smiled but the hollow look in his eyes was mystifying.

Clarke's Inaugural Gown

The President woke up startled as if from a bad dream. He reached for Clarke but Clarke's side of the bed was empty. Michael was a little bewildered as he looked around the room, wondering where Clarke was. Barney wasn't in the room either. The President sprang out of bed and walked out of the bedroom into the sitting room. No Clarke. He walked down to the West Sitting Hall, Clarke's favorite spot to relax. No Clarke.

The President went looking for anyone. As he looked down corridors and through doorways he could feel his heart skip a beat. He was breathing heavily. The President asked the first person he saw, an usher, where Clarke was. The usher looked at the President. It was very early and obviously the President had just woken up. He was wearing only flannel pajama bottoms. His hair was all tousled and he was barefoot.

The usher looked down. He paused, trying to select his words carefully. The President was worried and so impatient he was ready to shake the answer out of the man. The usher looked back up to the President.

The usher smiled, obviously trying hard not to laugh at the President's fuzzy look. "Clarke is with Beverly Anderson being measured for his Inaugural ensemble." Relieved, the President smiled, patting the man on the back. Michael started to breathe normally again. He had no idea why he was so concerned. The usher led the President to a closed door.

Michael wanted to sneak up on Clarke. He ran his fingers through his hair, not that it helped. Ms. Jones walked by with a smile. Michael knew that whenever Beverly Anderson was in the house, so was Ms. Jones. He nodded a good morning as she walked by. The same usher returned with a bathrobe for the President and held the robe as the President reached in with each arm. Michael tied the robe excusing the usher with a thank you.

The President opened the doors without being noticed. He was quiet as he watched, leaning against the wall with his arms folded. Michael was enjoying Clarke relaxing with the people he loved. Beverly Anderson was busy measuring Clarke.

Ms. Deverough was going through drawings of Clarke in an incredible tuxedo. Barney was at her feet chewing on a tennis ball. Ms. Deverough added a few suggestions. Michael smiled when Clarke bubbled with excitement.

The chemotherapy had really taken Clarke's shape. Although he wouldn't admit it, Clarke was still weak and couldn't work out as he was used to. He missed his firm body and big chest. He looked at Beverly and said, "I want something to really make my chest look bigger." The President laughed out loud, startling Clarke and Beverly. They turned in time to watch Barney run over to the President with a lick for luck. Beverly and Ms. Deverough immediately gave the President their congratulations. Ms. Deverough said it wasn't any surprise to her. Beverly said it was the first time he really wanted to vote. Barney just wagged his tail.

Beverly Anderson apologized for calling on the First Couple so early. The President nodded that it was okay as an usher served him a mug of coffee. Michael sat down next to Clarke. The same usher poured fresh coffee for everyone else from a silver coffee urn. Barney was still chewing on his tennis ball.

The President knew with an Inaugural Ball comes the Inaugural *Gown*. Clarke never wore a dress, but mean editorials and comics in poor taste had depicted him wearing one. Some cartoons were fabulous, copied from Beverly Anderson's designs; others were just an ugly stereotypical insult. Thanks to Clarke's wearing Beverly Anderson designs, this year's formal wear was the finest anyone had ever seen.

Beverly explained their drawings to the President. America wouldn't dream of missing neither the Inaugural Ball nor the fanfare that went with it. As if by the stroke of a magic wand, Clarke would go to the ball with his handsome prince and would leave with both slippers. Clarke took the traditional idea of a tuxedo, added his own flare, and designed by Beverly Anderson. It would be something everyone has seen before but never after six and certainly not off the rack.

Beverly would also design a fabulous tuxedo for the President and explained that the First Couple's tuxedos would be made out of the same fabric but in different styles. The President smiled and said he would wear whatever Clarke laid out for him.

Beverly took a measuring tape and asked the President to remove his robe and stand with his arms stretched out. Clarke helped the President off with his robe and laid it over the arm of the settee. Clarke sat back down and watched the President with a smile. Ms. Deverough sipped her tea as she watched Clarke enjoying the moment.

"Mr. President, may I design a vest for you?" Beverly asked while measuring the President's chest.

"No," The President said concentrating on being measured. Then he smiled at Clarke. "Clarke wears the vest in the family." Everyone laughed. Beverly took the measurements and scribbled down numbers on a sketchpad. The President didn't care for being measured but Clarke was really enjoying it.

As Beverly measured the President's inseam, he calmly asked Michael what side he dressed on. The President had no idea what Beverly was talking about. Clarke happily chimed in with, "the right." Beverly jotted that down and continued with the next measurement. Clarke smiled at the President. The President still had no idea what Clarke and Beverly were talking about.

As Beverly was winding his measuring tape, Michael excused himself, explaining he had to get ready for a very busy day. A gloved staff member, still never turning his back to the First Couple, shut the doors behind him. Beverly went back to measuring Clarke. He pulled the tape a little tighter. He looked at the tape, then at Clarke, then back at the tape again. Clarke had lost quite a few inches.

With the chemotherapy, then the campaign trail, Beverly had been consistently tailoring Clarke's clothes. He made sure nothing dragged, bagged, or sagged. With a knock on the door an usher came in and announced that breakfast was served. Clark invited his guests to the Family Dining Room to join him and the President for breakfast.

A drawing of the First Lady's gown had always been released to the press long before the Inaugural Ball. Clarke's Inaugural ensemble was to remain top secret until the moment Clarke was on camera wearing it. Many people were annoyed about that, but their anticipation gladly took over. The day after the Inaugural Ball, all secrets would be released to the press, including everything from types of fabrics to waist and inseam sizes and even the cost. It was the same cost for similar items found in Beverly Anderson's fine men's wear salons. Beverly insisted it would all be a donated gift to the First Couple. The First Lady's gown was always a gift from the First Lady to the Smithsonian.

January twentieth came quickly. It seemed Clarke had just taken the Christmas tree down and put the Blue Room back to normal. The Presidential box had been erected along Pennsylvania Avenue with the White House as its backdrop. Clarke loved a parade. Clarke's husband would be sworn in to office for a second term with Clarke at his side. Clarke beamed with pride as he walked through the White House.

Clarke had organized a lovely reception before the swearing-in. Of course, guests were received in the Blue Room, then enjoyed a buffet brunch in the State Dinning Room. For the President's new term, Beverly Anderson designed a new look for Clarke. Since all the politicians would still be in suits, Clarke would need to stand out, but still have the professional look his position required.

After the early morning festivities, Clarke went to the Private Quarters. Assisted by Beverly Anderson, he dressed for the swearing-in. Clarke and the President left through the North Portico where the presidential limousine was waiting. Hundreds of people lined the streets, yelling cheers and waving signs congratulating the First Couple. The President and Clarke arrived at the Capitol for a lovely reception hosted by Congress.

A chime rang throughout the reception signaling that the swearing-in was about to begin. The room emptied as dignitaries left for their assigned seats. Clarke and the President were escorted into a private area. Beverly Anderson and Ms. Deverough gave the First Couple a complete once-over.

Ms. Deverough straightened the President's tie. Beverly Anderson had really out-done himself. Clarke was in a suit, but with the pizzazz Beverly was known for designing. Clarke's suit jacket went only to his waist. Naturally he was wearing his signature vest, but designed this time to be tucked in. The look started another craze, second only to Clarke's spectator's shoes.

The First Couple was ready. The President embraced Clarke and whispered a loving, "Thank you." Clarke smiled with deep eyes that said 'I love you'. The door opened and a voice interrupted, saying, "Mr. President, it's time." Clarke's heart began to pound.

Together the President and Clarke were escorted through the halls of the Capitol. Everyone was quiet. All that was heard was the tap of footsteps against marble floors. A man and woman, both in uniform, opened the outside doors to chanting cheers for the President. The First Couple stopped.

Michael looked at Clarke. Clarke looked at Michael. Clarke was so proud of him. Michael wouldn't do the job without Clarke, and the country had voted the First Couple into office for four more years. There was a feeling of pride in the air. The Marine Band began to play "Hail to the Chief."

The First Couple walked to the podium as the cheers grew louder with each step they took. The crowd quickly silenced as the Chief Justice faced the President. Clarke held up the Bible. The President placed his left hand on top of it and Clarke placed his hand over the President's. It was the same Bible Michael has used when he took the oath of office for Vice President, then the oath of office of the President of the United States for his appointed term. It was the same Bible Michael's mother had carried down the aisle on her wedding day. Clarke had secretly placed a penny in the Bible for good luck, just like Michael's mother had on her special day. Clarke looked at Michael as if he had never seen him before. Pride continued to radiate as America stood silent, watching the man they had overwhelmingly voted into office with his husband at his side.

The world was silent as Michael repeated the oath of office after the Chief Justice. Clarke could feel the cameras watching them with a panoramic view. Pride swelled up in Clarke as he looked at Michael. Then Clarke thought of what the next four years meant—four more years of ridicule; four more years of living in the fishbowl; four more years of all the press. Then Clarke had to control his smile. He thought of four more years of going to bed with his husband. Four more years of waking up beside him. Four more years of being with the man he loved.

Pride burst like a surprise rain shower over Clarke and a tear streamed down his face, followed by another, then another. He never faltered. He was not ashamed of the tears. Many of those watching from their homes were touched by such a moment and reached for a loved one's hand. Spectators in the stands were moved to tears. The camera got it all on tape.

Traditionally the President and First Lady kissed after the oath was taken. Clarke and the President hugged. It was a long hug. The President, feeling Clarke's tears, whispered "I love you" to Clarke. The tender moment was shared with each American watching. Cameras continued to capture the moment in panoramic view showing the world how proud they were of their elected First Couple.

When the First Couple broke their embrace, they gazed into each other's eye, then hugged again to thunderous applause. After their embrace, the First Couple held hands and waved to the crowds. Today Clarke didn't mind the whole world seeing the First Couple holding hands.

With a big smile and tears still streaming down his face, Clarke continued to wave to the crowds. Michael reached in his pocket for a handkerchief and handed it to Clarke. Just what any other husband would do for his husband after taking the oath of office of the President of the United States.

Clarke sat down in his assigned seat, holding the Bible on his lap, never taking his eyes off Michael. No one noticed the penny Clarke had hidden in the Bible for good luck fall to the ground. A very poised Clarke sat in his assigned seat listening to Michael. The President gave a speech that brought America to its feet with a sense of hope and future.

The First Couple were driven down the parade route in the presidential limousine. Secret Service were hysterical with the President's request, then direct order, to have the top down so America could see their First Couple. Secret Service walked alongside the car. Between the Secret Service agents who were walking along the limousine was a motorcade of motorcycles. Law enforcement officers lined the parade route. Security was tight. No one could see the First Couple from the parade route, but millions were watching from all over the world, via a television camera poised high atop a vehicle driving in front of the presidential limousine.

The limousine drove to the Presidential Box and the President and Clarke were escorted to their seats to watch the parade. A Washington January is crisp if not bitterly cold. Today was no different, but Clarke was warm inside. He was so happy for Michael.

Clarke was completely surrounded by the people he loved. The President, holding his hand, sat beside him. Sitting on the other side of Clarke was Ms. Deverough, then Beverly Anderson, then Saundra; every one of Clarke's dearest friends. Barney was brought to the Presidential Box to watch the parade and he loved all the excitement. Behind the First Couple, the Presidential Box was crowded with political people and their families.

The world watched the bands marching in spectator shoes. Many waving from floats were wearing vests, both men and women. Clarke was so honored. Imitation is the best form of compliment, and Clarke said thank you with every smile. The photographs of the President and the First Man To Be First Lady and their dog were on the front page of every newspaper across the globe.

It was a grand day. As the sun set, it proudly introduced the night of the Inaugural Ball. The press was invited into the Private Quarters to photograph the First Couple in a private congratulatory toast. There were no television cameras, just candid snapshots. A fire crackled from the fireplace. Candles were lit, offering a romantic glow. For the finishing touch, Beverly Anderson had designed smoking jackets for the President and Clarke.

The idea of the smoking jacket swept the nation. These smoking jackets were traditional, as one saw in the art deco period. The jackets were striking, designed out of black cotton suede, with a rounded satin lapel.

The smoking jacket was such a surprise and the only place America would be able to buy them was with Beverly Anderson's label. Millions would be sold before other manufacturers could make crass imitations. After a snap and a flash, the press was escorted downstairs. The First Couple was finally alone. They didn't talk. Just held each other in a simple dance step. No music was heard. Just felt.

A knock came at the door, and Ms. Deverough informed Clarke that it was time to get ready. After a kiss for luck, the President left to finish dressing for the evening. Clarke had laid out the rest of the President's ensemble. When the President finished dressing, he waited in the Blue Room. The First Couple was going to have a private photo shoot with a professional photographer for a 'government official' photograph. Beverly helped Clarke dress. He wanted to make sure every stitch was perfect. Clarke's tuxedo was impressive. At first it looked like a Nehru jacket but just a little longer. Then on a closer look it was something from the Gone with the Wind era.

Clarke looked thinner and that made his outfit more smashing. The jacket buttoned along one side, not down the middle. The same matching covered buttons decorated the opposite side of the jacket. Clarke kept it buttoned to the top, then Beverly Anderson unbuttoned the jacket and it opened to a triangle securing to the side, revealing a bow tie and signature vest ensemble. The vest had a deep V cut exposing sparkling diamond studs. In a word, Clarke was dashing.

To Beverly Anderson, there was never a doubt the President and Clarke would win this election. Beverly worked closely with artists from Tiffany's in New York and tuxedo studs were designed in the shape of shields, brilliant with diamonds, bright with color. The cufflinks matched the shield shape with a carat that would fill Bugs Bunny's appetite. The jewelry was only on loan for the evening. It was worth more than the President would make during his entire administration. Facsimiles were made up, one as a gift for Clarke and another to be donated to the Smithsonian.

Clarke was so thankful for Beverly and his generosity. Beverly just looked at him. "I owe it all to you, Clarke. Everything." Ms. Deverough informed Clarke it was time to go. Clarke nodded. He turned and walked out of the Presidential Suite. As he walked down the hall, it all hit him again, that same case of fever and chills. His husband was voted President of the United States. Clarke was his First Gentleman.

As Clarke reached the top of the Grand Stairs, he stopped and turned around. Beverly Anderson and Ms. Deverough were watching him, almost embracing each other as they stood side by side. Beverly was bursting with pride. Ms. Deverough smiled with a twinkle in her eye. They looked at each other then back to Clarke as if they had a secret surprise. Clarke turned, ready to walk down the stairs to meet the President in the Blue Room.

Clarke stopped. He thought about all the other First Couples who had been there before them. The First Lady in her gown as it trailed behind her walking down these same steps. As he took the first step, walking down the center of the Grand Staircase, he felt the pride the White House commanded. With each step, Clarke was humbled at such a position, proud to bring the White House traditions back and to make it a place America could be proud of.

As Clarke carefully took each step, he imagined the spirits of First Ladies past lining the stairs. Mrs. Adams, the first First Lady to live in the White House; Dolly Madison, a buxom woman and a First Lady who was the exception to all the rules; Mary Todd Lincoln in her famous hoopskirt; Grace Coolidge with her beautiful white dog. He heard their lady-like clapping. Many fanned themselves in ovations. In their day, a proper lady did not clap.

Clarke slowly descended the Grand Staircase. Eleanor Roosevelt had a hard look but a genuine smile for Clarke. Mamie Eisenhower stood tall and clapped the loudest. Clarke stood proudly, nodding to their ovation, as chandeliers sparkled in an encore.

Tonight Clarke was the finest gentleman in America. As he reached the landing, he turned and walked down the last steps to the main hall. He imagined a very poised Jacqueline Bouvier Kennedy giving an out-of-character aviator's "thumbs up." Clarke smiled at his fantasy. Suddenly the surprise of a thousand cameras captured the elegance of Clarke with a flash.

Clarke stopped but never faltered. He was radiant. He stood poised for the cameras. He had never been so honored to be the First Gentleman. The cameras seized the moment. As Clarke looked into the crowds, acknowledging the cameras and press, he saw the President. Clarke cocked his head slightly. His broad smile was replaced with an, 'I love you' sparkle. Like a strobe light, the flash of the cameras went wild. The President went to Clarke and held out his hand. Clarke took it and the President escorted his First Gentleman to the Blue Room.

No one missed a First Lady's gown with Clarke on stage and Beverly Anderson outdoing himself on the Vice President's gown. Her gown was beaded all black and a matching beaded cape with a white satin lining. It framed her like a full-length portrait, but she never took one stitch of attention away from the First Couple.

As the First Couple went from Inaugural Ball to Inaugural Ball, they were met with ovations and deafening cheers. The President proudly introduced Clarke as the First Gentleman. The Ballroom became hysterical, chanting Clarke's name in the familiar double syllable. Michael Kent was the most popular President the country had ever known and to many it was because of Clarke. The First Couple didn't get a chance to dance with each other or anyone else. There had never been so many Inaugural Balls in Washington's history and the First Couple went to every single one of them.

Exhausted, Clarke and the President returned to the White House via the Presidential Limousine. As the car entered the gates, the Chief Usher gave the White House staff a nod. With anticipation of yelling, 'SURPRISE' at the Birthday Boys, exhilaration became muffled chitchat as each person took their place. Everyone stood motionless. The Entrance Hall was quiet.

The entire staff was dressed in their uniform finery: Maids in starched aprons, chefs in tall white hats, ushers in fine suits. They stood in two rows, forming an aisle between them. Two Marines dressed in fine military uniforms opened the White House doors with gloved hands. As the President and Clarke walked into the White House, thunderous applause came from the very people who made the house work.

Cameras flashed. The First Couple stopped, dumbfounded. The President and Clarke looked like two figurines that just walked off the top of a wedding cake. Clarke looked over at Michael, thinking this was another one of his surprises, but the President was just as shocked. Clarke looked at the staff, then back at the President, then back at the staff once again. Clarke was so honored that tears filled his eyes.

Michael was so touched he put his arm around Clarke and pulled him close. Ms. Jones was so moved by the reaction from the President and his First Gentleman, she began clapping right along with the rest of the staff. Clarke and the President took the time to shake each one's hand and to personally thank them for all their incredible service.

Clarke was so graciously radiant and the President so handsome in his basic black tuxedo. As the President and Clarke

215

made their way down the aisle, they turned hand in hand. Once again, the First Couple offered their sincere thanks to more deafening applause. Still holding hands, the First Couple walked up the Grand Stairs to their Private Quarters.

The President had a surprise for Clarke. He had made arrangements for him and Clarke to spend their first night as elected First Couple in the Lincoln Bedroom. A fire danced in the fireplace. *Of course, where else would it be?* Clarke smiled to himself. Already-lit candelabra added a romantic touch. The most beautiful arrangement of wild flowers Clarke had ever seen was on the table. A box of Hazzels candy had been flown in, packed in a special box hand carved by the President. To Clarke, the simple, from-the-heart expressions of love were the most beautiful. Clarke had a new pocket watch specially designed for the President, inscribed, "'By the way', Our lives will be ours FOURever'

Life After Election

The campaign trail can wring a man and his spouse out like a limp rag, but this trail brought the First Couple even closer, to the point of being inseparable. If the country was going to have a President in love with a man in love with the President, they voted it for another four years. Historians would write that it was perfect timing that made this administration the great one it was.

If Mother Nature did anything to help elect the appointed President into office again, it was giving Clarke cancer when she did. Clarke was fit as a fiddle. Somehow it was the happy-ever-after-story America had always read about. The cancer that had afflicted the First Man To Be First Lady took the issue of being gay out of the campaign. It was Michael's brilliance as a leader that got him elected to office.

The President was proud to be elected to the office, but he refused to get an attitude about it. In gratitude, he was working harder and doing what was 'right for America, not right for politics.' That was the promise he made when he took office. Keeping that promise voted the sexiest and most respected man into office.

Clarke's schedule was full for the day, but due to a surprise late-night Washington snowstorm, Clarke's first appointments had been rescheduled and today he had the morning free. He was dressed for the day and decided to relax in the West Sitting Hall. He was looking at a magazine dedicated to the First Couple's time in the White House. Clarke was surprised it even included an inaugural photograph.

On the opposite page was an advertisement from the Franklin Mint. It was a set of porcelain dolls, The First Couple, Michael and Clarke, in their Inaugural Ensembles. The dolls were a perfect likeness, right down to how much taller Michael was than Clarke. Beverly Anderson, complete with his signature of authenticity, had even designed the doll's clothes. Clarke gently removed the order form. He wanted a set. Clarke couldn't believe how the Franklin Mint could have designed the dolls so quickly. Clarke smiled. Beverly Anderson and Ms. Deverough were quite a duo.

When he turned the page, he noticed the pictures of Michael. The office had aged him. He was getting more handsome with every year and looking more distinguished. Nothing could make a gentleman look finer then wearing a woolly cardigan sweater and smoking a pipe. It was Clarke's favorite pose.

The President interrupted Clarke for a surprise coffee break. Clarke put down the magazine and happily joined Michael. Clarke never said how he felt about winning the election. His job was to be at Michael's side, wherever that was. The President knew he had a really tough job.

Clarke was still taking all the ridicule from the press. He was the most admired man in America and in the most recent Good Housekeeping poll, was the most admired woman. Clarke really had a good laugh about that. Everything a perfect First Lady should be, Clarke was. Like a fairy tale, The First Man To Be First Lady was the most admired person to ever hold the office and his husband was the most popular President since the days of Washington.

Michael adored Clarke. He would do anything in his power to make Clarke happy. Even with their rigorous schedule, the President always found time splash with Clarke in a bubble bath. When Clarke needed romance and to be with his husband, Michael would surprise Clarke in the East Room with the chandeliers set on a romantic glow and Clarke's favorite music piped softly in over the loudspeakers. When the President requested the East Room to be set up for him, the news spread like wildfire among the White House ushers. The staff loved to secretly watch the First Couple dance.

As usual, the Chief Usher was working very late. There weren't any State Dinners or White House functions, so he took advantage of the time to catch up on his paperwork. After a yawn and stretch, he turned off his desk lamp then grabbed his briefcase and coat. As the Chief Usher walked down the Grand Hall, he noticed that the service entrance to the East Room was open. He thought that was odd and decided to close it on his way out. When he went to close the door, he saw several of the staff peeking in at the First Couple through a slightly opened door.

The staff was quiet, almost stacked one on top of the other, trying to get a closer look.

The music scratched over the loudspeaker. It was the First Couple's favorite dance music and they had worn out the CD. The Chief Usher looked on with the staff. The President turned the First Gentleman and Clarke twirled with a theatrical step. The First Couple enjoyed each other, as privacy will let any married couple do.

The Chief Usher finally stood back and whispered, "Let's give the First Couple their privacy." A few of the staff nearly jumped out of their skin, being caught in the act. The Chief Usher waved off their fear and motioned at the door. Reluctantly, one by one the staff left. One staff member stopped and turned to the Chief Usher, who was still watching the First Couple. He cleared his throat, "Chief?" The Chief Usher looked at him holding the door waiting for him to leave. They both smiled. The Chief Usher quietly shut the door behind them as the First Couple danced the night away.

With ease, the First Couple settled into the White House routine. Clarke planned the largest State Dinner the White House had ever hosted. It was to be held in the East Room. The State Dining Room just wasn't big enough. This State Dinner was in honor of all the State Governors and their spouses.

Clarke made sure those who had really rallied behind the President and helped to get him elected were seated with those who hadn't. Seated at the table with each governor and spouse was a famous person—an actor, actress, writer, singer—but they weren't from that Governor's state. It made perfect dinner conversation.

After dinner, but before dancing, guests were escorted into the State Dining Room, which had been set up for after-dinner drinks and conversation. A light jazz combo entertained the guests. This time was also used for restroom breaks and freedom to walk about the first floor of the White House. The Air Force Strolling Strings entertained guests as they comfortably enjoyed America's home.

Secret Service was poised about the hallways and, of course, Saundra was tour guide for anyone who had a question about the White House. While after-dinner drinks were served, the staff miraculously reconfigured the East Room for dancing.

Once again Clarke, with his staff, had planned the perfect evening.

Flowers in the Rose Garden bloomed; their fragrance introduced spring. The famous Easter Egg Hunt on the White House lawns had the First Couple hunting Easter Eggs with the children. Television cameras tattled on the President as he showed little ones where they might find a surprise from the Easter Bunny.

As the days followed, Clarke planned fabulous luncheons held in the Rose Garden. It all started with the Senate spouses, then another for the Congressional spouses. One couldn't call them wives anymore. They had to be called spouses. Never before had so many women been elected to office.

The nation had come a long way with acceptance, but the press kept informing the nation there was still a ways to go. Clarke's seating assignments always had him sitting next to the person who was most verbal in the press about the First Couple's sexuality. It may have been uncomfortable, but Clarke loved to watch them squirm. By the time the luncheons were over, Clarke invariably had a new friend.

The White House was known as the busiest home in the nation. There was a State Dinner or formal luncheon three times a week. Beverly Anderson had a new suit waiting for Clarke for every Rose Garden luncheon. Clarke wouldn't wear the short-waisted jacket after six, but for lunch it was the perfect ensemble, complimented, of course, with his signature vest, tucked in, and spectator shoes.

Rose Garden luncheons became America's favorite spectator sport. Everyone watched from their own backyard barbecue to see what the First Man To Be First Lady would serve and, of course, what he would be wearing. In a whisper, spring turned to summer. A summer day in Washington can be hot.

As the days grew too hot for Clarke to wear a jacket and vest, Beverly Anderson stunned the world by dressing Clarke in linen trousers and bright white shirts. Clarke insisted they be long-sleeved with French cuffs. He wore brightly colored ties, but still retained his signature vest in a very lightweight fabric and, of course, spectator shoes. With an outfit like that, one could only expect croquet.

The event was everything a White House luncheon should be. Peacocks roamed freely about the grounds and guests challenged the First Couple to a croquet match. Teams had cute names like 'the whippets' and 'the mallets'. If you were called a wooden ball in Congress it meant you could take a hit from a mallet and still keep rolling.

A six-o-clock news anchor described a tax bill going through Congress using croquet symbols. "A wood ball hit by the mallet went through the center of the whippet." It was mind-boggling but every American knew the tax bill had gone through Congress without a hitch. Manufactures couldn't make croquet sets fast enough. For the first time in history, more croquet sets were sold in America than baseball bats

At a White House luncheon it was announced that Clarke had been chosen to be the national poster person for the American Cancer Society. In his impromptu acceptance speech, Clarke summed it all up in five important words, "Early Detection—The Best Cure." It became the motto to live by.

In between State Dinners and Rose Garden luncheons, Clarke loved to surprise the tourists who came to Washington for a tour of the White House. Sometimes Clarke would walk along with the tour guide, other times Clarke walked the long lines and shook hands with people who were patiently waiting for the tour.

One day in late fall Clarke sat behind a table autographing, *The White House, An Historic Guide*. It was a booklet for sale, photographed by the artists of *National Geographic*. Clarke was proud to autograph such an elegant book. The idea of the White House guide had started in the early 1960's with Jacqueline Kennedy and had been growing strong ever since.

As the long lines came to an end, Clarke noticed an older couple quickly walking to catch up to the end of the line. Since it was a weekday and tourist season had passed, Clarke guessed they were newly retired. They were as American as apple pie, comfortable in easy-to-care-for polyester, chubby with success. Clarke smiled at how charming the couple was.

They were the end of the line, followed by a Secret Service agent who held the door open for them. The woman proudly thanked the agent and the man decided to return what he thought a favor and motioned for the Secret Service man to go ahead of him. Clarke could see the man and the Secret Service agent chatting then the man walked in behind his wife and the Secret Service agent followed.

As they walked to the table where Clarke was sitting, the woman stopped. She just stared. "Oh my!" She gasped. She held her face and screeched, "It's the First Man To Be First Lady." The man looked at his wife. When he realized she was okay, he held out his hand to Clarke and introduced himself. Clarke politely stood. "I'm Harold and this is my wife, Edith." Clarke shook the man's hand.

Edith just stared at Clarke, "I never thought I would ever see the Blue Room and here I am shaking hands with the First Man To Be First Lady. I watched the televised White House tour over and over."

Her husband, Harold, interrupted her, laughing, "She wore out the tape, then cried for a week when it wouldn't work no more." Edith lovingly swatted at Harold, but she didn't deny it. Clarke was so impressed with these two people that he couldn't help but ask where they were from. They were from the same little town where Clarke had given his first speech as First Gentleman. They didn't mention his visit. Neither did Clarke.

The Secret Service motioned to Clarke that tour hours were almost over and these people were far behind the line that was almost finished. Clarke motioned with a hand gesture that it was okay and congratulated Harold on his recent retirement.

Edith beamed with pride when she looked at Harold, "Forty long years at that plant," she bubbled, never taking her smile off of Harold.

Harold looked at the booklet Clarke had in his hand and asked, "What do you have there?" Clarke explained it was *The White House, An Historical Guide* envisioned and created by Jacqueline Kennedy. "Page by page, it follows you on the White House tour." Clarke handed it to Harold as he told him how much it cost and that the money it raised went to keep the White House decorated with America's finest.

Harold put on his thick-rimmed, half-lens reading glasses. He held the book an arm's length away. Edith looked on. "Robert would love one of these." Edith said as she turned the page. She looked at Clarke. "Our son, Robert, thinks you're keen. He buys all the magazines with you and the President in them." She seemed about to burst with pride as she described her son to Clarke.

"He dresses like you, in a vest and those spectator shoes." She looked down at Clarke's shoes and smiled when she saw them. "He wears his hair just like you do. He talks just like you do. You're all he ever talks about." Edith smiled then looked at Clarke in the way an elderly woman looks at a newborn. "You and my Robert are just five months apart," Edith proudly said.

"Yep. He's just like you." Harold joined in with a twinkle in his eye.

Edith looked up at Harold. Harold looked down at Edith. Tears filled her eyes as Harold wrapped his arm around her tight. They discovered the family secret. Edith caught a tear and looked at Clarke. Her voice was shaking as she swallowed hard. "Would you autograph a book for Robert?"

"He would like that." Harold said as he handed money to a woman with the cash box. The woman made change and, out of habit, quietly thanked Harold.

Edith looked in her purse for a pen. Harold reached in his pocket and pulled out a handsome pen. Clarke already had a pen but happily used Harold's. Scrounging around in her purse, Edith couldn't find a pen, but she found a car window sticker from Indiana. Joy returned to her face. "Look Harold. I found it." She held up the sticker, proving it to Harold. He was just as happy.

Harold looked at Clarke. "We get a sticker from every state we drive through then put it on our suitcase."

Finding the sticker was almost too much excitement for Edith. She interrupted Harold, waving the sticker in exclamation. "We've had that sparkly emerald green suitcase ever since our honeymoon."

"And now it's got a sticker from everywhere we've ever been." Harold smiled, then looked down at Edith. "You can't even tell what color that suitcase is anymore." There were a lot of special memories carried with that suitcase. Clarke could see that in the way Harold and Edith looked at each other. Edith was still a little shaky about their new discovery and sniffled through her excitement.

"Who shall I write this to?" Clarke asked ready to write a note in the booklet. "To Bobby." Harold said.

"No," Edith interrupted, shaking her head from side to side, "He likes to be called Robert." Harold agreed with a nod.

A Secret Service agent politely interrupted in an authoritative tone. "Folks, the White House tours are winding up." Normally Clarke would agree and thank the tourists he was talking to, then he would politely motion for them to join the tour.

Clarke looked at Edith and Harold. They were obviously trying to hide their shock about Robert. Clarke wanted to give them a big hug and tell them everything would be just fine. Instead, Clarke found himself asking Harold and Edith if they would like a private tour.

The Secret Service agent started talking code into his radio. Suddenly Secret Service agents came out of the woodwork like cockroaches in the dark. Edith didn't know what to say. Harold answered for both of them with a smile and almost sang, "That would be Jim Dandy."

Clarke stood up and walked from behind the table. He handed them their booklet and motioned for the Secret Service to escort them. Harold and Edith, with Clarke as tour guide, went a different direction than the normal White House tours. Together they walked to the Private Quarters. Barney met Edith and Harold and gave the sniff of approval. Clarke offered his guests a place to freshen up and said they would tour the Private Quarters, as the tour was finishing up downstairs.

Clarke could see the relief in Edith's face. An usher showed them through the Lincoln Bedroom to the bathroom. Edith didn't look at the Lincoln Bedroom too much. She needed a ladies room and was thankful Clarke had been so thoughtful.

After a few moments, with a refreshed, relieved Edith, Clarke continued the tour. Edith remarked on the kitchen, telling Clarke how much she had enjoyed the Mrs. Waters special. Clarke offered them a cookie. Harold gave his cookie to Barney. Clarke offered Harold one for himself.

Clarke enjoyed these people. The couple talked of their five children and thirteen grandchildren. Harold talked about Bobby and how much he would enjoy seeing what they were seeing. All Edith could talk about was how Clarke and Robert were so much alike. Edith was accepting the truth about her son with every step of the tour.

Edith and Harold jumped as they heard someone yell, "The President is in the Hall."

"Oh, my." Edith said as she patted her fingers through her hair and smoothing out her pantsuit. Harold reached for her hand as the President walked in the room.

"I heard Clarke was receiving guests and I couldn't wait to meet them," the President said with an outstretched hand to Harold. Harold introduced Edith. She made as if she would curtsey but stopped herself. Like Clarke, the President was instantly charmed.

The two couples chatted away as if they had been friends forever. The President excused himself and removed his tie. Edith laughed and said Harold was the same way. She looked at Clarke, "The only time I can get Harold in a tie is on Sunday, and that comes off before he starts the car for the ride home from church."

"I'm with you, Harold," the President laughed.

Clarke continued the tour. Barney trotted along. The President walked to the cookie jar then caught up with Clarke.

The scheduled White House tour was long over and the staff was putting carpets back down that had been rolled up not to be walked on. Edith commented that she used the same vacuum sweeper at home and agreed with the maid, the furniture polish she was using was the only thing to make wood shine. Edith was awestruck at the brilliant sky blue of the Blue Room. Clarke invited her and Harold to sit down. Edith sat down with such care.

"Oh, my." she said as she rubbed the silk fabric on the armchair. As the tour continued, Edith noticed the ornate blue-marble clock on the mantel. Clarke proudly told her that the clock had belonged to his Aunt and they had it sent from his seaside home when the President first took office. Harold and the President were a few steps behind Edith and Clarke, chatting about football.

The President insisted that Edith and Harold join them for dinner. "Nothing fancy," Michael said, "just dinner." Ms. Deverough and Beverly Anderson were invited to round out the party. Dinner was served in the Family Dining Room. Right before dessert was served, Edith asked if she could take everyone's picture. She took a cardboard disposable camera out of her purse and was ready to get up.

A staff member asked if he could take the picture so that Edith could also be in it. Clarke then asked for a White House photographer as well and told Edith he would be glad to send her a copy of all the pictures that would be taken.

Dessert was enjoyed in the Blue Room in front of a roaring fire. As the staff removed empty plates, Michael, Harold and Beverly went out to the South Portico for a breath of fresh air. Edith showed Clarke and Ms. Deverough pictures of her grandchildren she carried in her wallet. The Washington night air was crisp and sent a chill through the room when the President held the door for Harold and Beverly. The three men warmed themselves in front of the crackling fire as Clarke was commenting how cute their grandchildren were.

Harold said he was getting tired. Edith knew that meant it was time to go. They said their good-byes to Ms. Deverough and Beverly. The First Couple escorted them to the North Portico. As Clarke requested, an Usher met them with a small package in hand. He handed it to Clarke. Clarke thanked him and turned to Edith. "I thought you would like a copy of the unedited videotape of the White House tour. There's a lot more behind the scenes and more on the Blue Room than was televised." Edith's eyes welled up with grateful tears.

Harold looked at the President and said, "Now she's gonna start blubbering." That was Harold's way of saying that was the greatest thing anyone had ever done for his Edith. Their car had been brought to the front of the house. Edith beamed with pride when she said again how much her own Robert was 'just like Clarke'.

Edith and Clarke hugged each other good-bye as the President shook Harold's hand. The car door was open by Ms. Jones and the elderly couple got in. Michael put his arm around Clarke. As Harold drove the car away, Edith turned and waved a good-bye. The First Couple waved back and watched as the car left through the gate.

As the days passed, thousands of letters continued to pour into the White House, most of them worried about Clarke's health. Clarke wanted a project that would compliment the administration, make the country a better place, and at the same time, assure the American people he was just fine. Clarke would start on his new project as soon as he got back to the White House. He was meeting with Maddeline for yet another checkup that would be complimented with a clean bill of health.

Bethesda Naval Hospital was used to the First Gentleman. He received a nod from the staff just like any other patient who had been there before. It really was a great place but it still had that hospital smell. Clarke adjusted his tie and walked out of the exam room and into Maddeline's office. He was exhausted after so many 'routine' tests, x rays, and needle pokes. Just when Clarke thought they were through, there were more tests and needle pokes.

The tests were still reported under an anonymous code for security reasons but, more importantly, for Clarke's own privacy. Maddeline walked into her office and sat behind her desk. She had all the results neatly organized in a manila folder. Clarke sat down in front of Maddeline's desk. He noticed how her plants had grown, full of life. The sun streamed through the office windows. Maddeline and Clarke were the only two in the room. Secret Service was just outside the door.

Maddeline took a breath. "Clarke." An eerie presence fell over the room.

Clarke knew at that moment what she was going to say and interrupted her search for the most comforting words.

"How much time do I have, Doctor?" He asked.

"Six months to a year. Eighteen months at the most," She said in a professional tone.

"What determines how much time I have?" Clarke's questions were automatic.

"You. You will tell yourself when it's time to go. Your body will only give you eighteen months tops. The cancer has spread throughout your entire body." Helplessly, Maddeline folded her hands and looked through Clarke.

There was a long pause. Nothing was said. Nothing could be said. There was nothing to say. Clarke took command. "I will tell the President."

"Do you want me there when you tell him?" Maddeline asked. Her comment made Clarke realize this wasn't a dream. He was wide awake, but living a nightmare. Clarke didn't look at her. He looked through her, staring into space. His expression was blank. He didn't cry. He didn't shake. He just stared. "Who is going to take care of Michael?" Clarke said to himself. Maddeline was waiting for any type of hysteria, emotion, anything.

Clarke started to shake his head from side to side. "I don't know when I'm going to tell him."

Maddeline got up from behind her desk and sat down next to Clarke. She took his hand and held it. "Don't you think it's best to tell him right away?" Clarke's expression said he didn't know. They were both silent. Clarke still didn't cry. He didn't demand to know why. He sat there. Quiet. Maddeline held his hand tightly. Clarke was hanging on for life.

After a very long silence, Clarke turned and looked at her. Then he smiled and whispered a simple, "Yes." The Clarke Maddeline knew looked at her and said in a positive tone, "Yes. I think it's best. If your life was going to be over, but you were to go on living, would you want to know when the end was?" Somehow that made a lot of sense.

"Our lives have never been normal." Clarke continued. "Being in the White House is just icing on the cake. My husband runs this nation and should live as normally as the fishbowl on Pennsylvania Avenue will let him. Let me live as normal a life as I can. If that means this is our secret, then please," Clarke gently squeezed her hand, "let it be our secret."

Maddeline just looked down at their hands. Clarke let go. "If the ball was in your court what would you do? Maddeline just looked at Clarke and they both burst into laughter. "Okay. If the tables were turned, what would you do?" Clarke smiled.

"I don't know." Maddeline answered.

Clarke smiled. Once again he took Maddeline's hand and held it. "All I know is, the balls aren't even in the court. I want to live. I will tell the President when the time is right."

Maddeline nodded. "I will respect your wishes. Your test results will never leave this office. The hospital staff is ready to stand by when you need us. Here or at the White House."

"I will remain at the White House," Clarke commanded.

Maddeline nodded. She agreed that was the best place for Clarke to be. He had become a national treasure. The world would be at his side right along with the President. "Clarke, the cancer will continue to grow. Without any warning, the pain will suddenly become unbearable. Medication is available but, to be honest with you, it will knock you out to the point of making you unconscious."

"We will cross that bridge when we come to it." Clarke said as he let go of her hand and stood up to leave. There was a cumbersome pause. Clarke said a simple "Thank you" with his charming smile.

He immediately started thinking of all the medical appointments there would be. He would have to rearrange his schedule to meet with specialists, X-ray machines, and IV pokes. Clarke almost smiled. Maybe he would finally turn the Yellow Oval Room into his fantasy of a big Yellow Oval Bedroom. As Clarke reached for the door he turned and said to Maddeline, "When did you want to see me again?"

Maddeline walked up to Clarke and put her arm around him. "Call me when you need me." As if an arrow shot a bulls-eye through his heart, it finally hit Clarke that nothing more could be done. With a nod and a smile, Clarke turned and left her office.

Clarke was silent. He didn't notice anything on the drive back to the White House. He was so surprised by the test results. He felt fine. He was a little tired, but his schedule kept him so busy. Maybe it was a mistake. Of course! It was all a mistake! Doctors' make mistakes all the time. But in his heart, Clarke knew it wasn't a mistake. There was a hollow ache in Clarke's heart. He thought about Michael. Clarke could feel himself breathing heavily. He was angry. In his thoughts, he demanded to know who was going to take care of Michael. Clarke took a deep breath and slowly let it out. Clarke didn't bargain with God. He simply prayed that God would take care of Michael.

As Clarke thought about it, he could hear Maddeline's voice over and over, getting louder and louder. "The pain will suddenly become unbearable. The Pain will suddenly become unbearable. THE PAIN WILL SUDDENLY BECOME UNBEARABLE." The voice was so loud in his head, Clarke wondered if the Secret Service could hear it. He calmed himself once again. He still didn't feel like someone who was ill, just tired.

Clarke was surprised when the limousine stopped and a White House uniformed staff member opened the door. He was home. He entered through the East Wing, quietly acknowledging the staff around him. The White House was beautiful and smelled of fresh flowers.

An usher took his coat and welcomed him home. Still in shock, Clarke couldn't feel the floor beneath him. With the robotics of routine, he placed one foot in front of the other and walked down the hallway. Clarke felt as if he was seeing the mansion for the first time.

The White House was a mansion, smaller than most, but with an enormous feeling of home. The house was surprisingly quiet. If there weren't hundreds of people buzzing around, you never noticed the twenty who were. Clarke didn't want to see anyone, but there was one he should. He wanted to live but he knew he wouldn't. He wanted to cry, but he couldn't.

Ms. Deverough was watching him. She sat down without him noticing she was in the room. Clarke had walked to the Blue Room and stood looking toward the Washington Monument. It had started to rain and suddenly a feeling of comfort fell over him. Clarke knew Ms. Deverough was in the room and he hadn't even seen her. Ms. Deverough almost wished she hadn't been part of Clarke's moment, but knew she was needed. Neither of them said a word.

"How long have you known, Ms. Deverough?" Clarke quietly asked.

"As long as you have." She was staring at Clarke's reflection in the window, looking for any emotion.

"Does anyone else know?" Clarke was really asking if the President knew or even suspected.

"No." Ms Deverough shook her head from side to side.

Clarke looked at Ms. Deverough, "Good. This will be our secret."

"You're not going to tell the President, are you?" Ms. Deverough already knew the answer.

"Not until the time is right," Clarke assured her.

Their conversation was interrupted as the President was announced in the hallway. Clarke looked towards the door. When he looked back towards Ms. Deverough, she was gone. Disappeared. The President came in, reaching for a hug from Clarke. His staff told him Clarke was home and he let everyone with an appointment wait.

"How was your doctor's appointment?" Michael asked, holding Clarke by the shoulders.

Clarke just looked at him. Then took a deep breath ready to tell the President. Then to his own surprise, Clarke smiled. "Here's to four more incredible years."

The President was so glad to hear good news that he grabbed Clarke in a bear hug, lifting him off the floor and twirling him around the room. Ms. Deverough was in the hall looking in as the First Couple twirled. She saw the President's relief in his smile and the tears streaming down Clarke's face. The President had no idea and Clarke was going to keep it that way.

The State Dinner

When the President finally put Clarke back on the ground he asked Clarke for a favor. Clarke looked shocked. The President knew Clarke would do anything for him—anything. So for Michael to ask Clarke for a favor, it could only mean there was something of grave importance. Clarke looked worried.

Michael pulled a gilded chair close to Clarke and sat him down. He walked to the other side of the sofa, lifted another chair and put it down in front of Clarke. Michael sat in the chair and took Clarke's hands in his. The President looked deep into Clarke's eyes. "The President of France and his wife have asked to tour the United States. I would like them to be our guests here at the house, starting with one of your great State Dinners." As if he had asked too much already, Michael smiled with a shy grin. "And a personal request from the First Lady of France," The President held his breath then blurted out, "A Rose Garden luncheon?"

Clarke smiled, then in relief, grinned from ear to ear. He had thought the worst and all the President wanted was a State Dinner and a Rose Garden luncheon. Clarke was so relieved he threw his arms around Michael. Michael was so relieved he hugged Clarke so hard he couldn't breathe. Ms. Deverough just shook her head with a smile. Noting everything was back to normal she turned and walked to her private quarters.

Clarke knew that in the business world the most important decisions are often made over lunch. If you really want to impress a client, you wine and dine them over dinner. Politicians are no different. Clarke's official duties as First Gentleman were to be the official 'hostess'. Actually it was to be the official host. Clarke made State Dinners an event that America was invited to, along with the press and every news channel. There were no secrets. The First Couple had nothing to hide. One could only imagine what it would be if they did.

The President was working hard to make the world a safer place. The Cold War had warmed up to the point it was almost a tropical paradise, but the Middle East was another story.

It was scary. The President wanted a show of force in the region. He already had it on sea and in the air, but he wanted military bases with foot soldiers on land. To be safe, there had to be thousands of troops ready to go.

The President wanted to build up forces in Europe. He had England and Germany, but what he really needed was France. The United States military had been banished from France in the early 1960's. If it weren't for the American dollar keeping their country alive with the fanaticism of fashion, they would have been enemies, possibly nuclear enemies. Air power in Europe was best managed from France. The President of France was leery, but knew that, for the safety of his nation, he needed the United States.

The United States government had always gone too far in promising foreign lands the moon then, when the United States didn't need them anymore, that moon melted like a big ball of smelly cheese. The world loved France, the food, the wine, the fashion, and that romantic language. The President of France was ready to make a deal, and on American soil. It wasn't just for fun that the President of France wanted to tour the United States.

Clarke would impress the French with America. He insisted the White House would not compete with Versailles, nor would they in the kitchen. Clarke calmly informed the culinary staff, "Dinner will be as American as apple pie. Simple." The staff braced themselves. They knew Clarke had very simple tastes. It simply had to be the best. Clarke continued. "After dinner, American entertainment will be enjoyed in the East Room. That will be followed with dancing." The President and First Lady of France loved to dance. Clarke would spoil them rotten with a twist and a turn American style.

The State Dinner for the First Couple of France was rehearsed weeks in advance with up to two State Dinners a week. The Chefs prepared new menus of specialties from the Northwest. Of course, they included salmon as an appetizer and fresh blackberries in a dessert. The Pastry Chef always outdid himself. It would be difficult to choose which dessert would be served to the French First Couple. Many ideas came across the drawing board, but few made it to the table.

Entertainment in the East Room following the State Dinners was a spectacular audition. Clarke and the President loved to dance and the evening always ended with dancing. The President knew Clarke was working very hard. The staff was outdoing themselves with each dinner. Clarke helped cook, spice up the menu, and personally worked with florists on tabletop ideas.

The weeks quickly passed for everyone involved. Tonight was the dress rehearsal State Dinner before the First Couple of France would be honored. With Clarke and the White House staff practicing with so many State Dinners, Clarke insisted that this be the flawless dress rehearsal. After a perfect dinner, the evening turned to a night on the town in the East Room.

The announcer for the evening took the microphone. The orchestra leader lifted his baton. "Ladies and gentleman, by personal request of President Kent, the first dance of the evening will be performed by the First Couple." The President reached for Clarke. Clarke was so surprised and grinned from ear to ear.

Taking his cue from the President, the orchestra leader twirled his baton. Drums introduced a swing beat. The President led Clarke to the center of the East Room. Guests for the evening smiled and clapped to the beat. The President and Clarke started to swing dance as if they were in a dance competition. A spotlight revealed that they were the only ones on the dance floor.

When men and women dance everyone loves to watch the lady's skirt twirl, but no one missed the twirling skirt, not when the First Couple danced. Beverly had designed Clarke's trousers wider in the leg so when he turned his ensemble seemed to whirl with the rhythm. The First Couple was in step like a well-oiled machine. Ladies in stiff hairdos bobbed their heads to the beat. Men snapped their fingers as the First Couple twirled. The First Couple's guests became their audience and smiled as they clapped their hands and tapped their feet.

At a certain point in the song, the President had instructed the ushers to invite the other guests to the dance floor. No one would move. They wanted to watch the First Couple. The oldest Senator in the history of the Senate was so taken with the dance music, and the urging of the staff for others to dance, he almost skipped to the center of the room.

The President led Clarke into a stomping-stomp-step, then they rocked in place to the beat of the orchestra as they watched the old Senator. The Senator took the dance floor as if he was alone on a stage. He moved like he was tap dancing but without taps, known as stomping to the hill folk, native to his southern state.

Clarke enjoyed watching their guest have so much fun. This was the same Senator the President had to fight with for everything. Michael asked Clarke to reconsider inviting him tonight but Clarke insisted, "Even old Senators with narrow views on life needed a good time every now and then." Clarke and the President danced in place, still in a rocking step, watching the old man have such a good time.

The orchestra was so theatrical. The brass section stood and moved their instruments into an imaginary square as they played to the beat of the swing. The Senator stopped his stomp, to much applause, as the President twirled Clarke. Laughter bounced from the chandeliers. Applause was still heard for the Senator as he walked back to his seat. He'd had quite a work out. He took a handkerchief from his back pants pocket to wipe the sweat from his brow as he continued to watch the First Couple twirl.

On the final note everyone clapped, including the orchestra, at the performance from the First Couple. The President turned Clarke in one last dance step and they bowed to their audience with a hand for the Senator. The orchestra played the song again as the other guests made their way to the dance floor.

The evening was perfect. Clarke noticed that the President had walked the old Senator to the North Portico where the valet had his car waiting. As Clarke watched, the old man shook the President's hand with a big smile. Michael put his other hand over their shaking hands. Clarke knew in politics that was the equivalent to a big bear hug.

Whatever transpired between the two, Clarke knew the old Senator wouldn't be a problem for the President ever again. As the last guests left for the evening and the White House was being put back in order, Clarke complimented the staff, "If the State Dinner for the First Couple of France goes half as well as this evening, we can pat ourselves on the back."

The days quickly passed. The State Dinner for the First Couple of France drew closer and closer with every minute. Naturally, Beverly Anderson was creating the perfect ensemble for Clarke. Clarke spoke fluent French but had a tutor come in to polish things up. The tutor was honored but knew he wasn't needed. They rehearsed daily, touring the White House as though Clarke were giving a tour to the First Couple of France. They walked to the Rose Garden, where Clarke could name each flower and leaf in French and in English. They even played croquet, only speaking French.

The Welcoming Ceremony for the First Couple of France would be grand. The Welcoming Ceremony had been invented by the Kennedy Administration and became a presidential tradition. This too would have to top all the rest. The White House lawns were manicured. Flowers were bright with color. Even the blacktop had been buffed to perfection. Clarke was leaving no stone unturned. He was at ease with all the preparations. He was the busiest he had ever been since Michael took office. The motto was, 'This event had to be elegant as France and as unique as America.' Clarke demanded nothing less. Period.

The President was just as busy with his advisors. America was known to give everything in a deal. This time, that would be a last resort, if even then. What the world needed was safety and the President of France knew that. He wanted the security of the United States on his own soil.

The day had finally arrived. The sun was shining as though Mother Nature was putting the finishing touches on all the preparations. The White House Staff was ready. The President was ready. Clarke was ready. The press covered this event with more enthusiasm than any other event in this administration. America was watching with the same fanaticism as France.

The President of France and his First Lady arrived through the main gates of the White House. A full honor guard snapped to attention as the leaders shook hands and greeted each other's nation. After a perfect Welcoming Ceremony and a parade of America's military outfitted in their finest, the Presidents retired to the Oval Office.

Clarke gave the First Lady of France a televised tour of the outside gardens and the inside of the White House. The tour was a request from the citizens of France. After the Presidents' hard day of negotiating and their spouses enjoying the grandeur of the White House, the State Dinner in honor of France would take place.

As scheduled, both First Couples were given a few hours of free time before the party would begin. The President and First Lady of France were guests of the French Embassy in downtown Washington. Clarke went through the White House with the Chief Usher, making sure the finishing touches would make the night perfect.

Clarke walked up the Grand Stairs to put the final touches on Michael. After what seemed only seconds, a chime rang through the Private Quarters, signaling that the First Couple of France had arrived via limousine. Michael and Clarke held hands as they walked to the front door, which was opened by a gloved staff member.

The First Couple of the United States met the President and First Lady of France on the North Portico. Military dressed in formal uniforms escorted the First Couples into the White House. The President and Clarke then escorted the First Couple of France to the second floor for a private cocktail party where soothing music from a harp was accompanied by a string quartet.

The guests invited to the private cocktail party with the First Couples were carefully selected. All the guests had been at the White House for a State Dinner and were comfortable with their surroundings. Actors, actresses, political people, writers, all known to be personal favorites of the First Couples of both France and the United States. Everyone there had one thing in common: the press had dubbed each to be "America's finest".

The President of France and his First Lady talked to Clarke in their native language as the President of the United States lit his pipe and wondered what they were saying. Clarke didn't talk politics but he surely could play the game. He was winning with all of France watching. The President of France was so impressed with Clarke that the First Lady was almost jealous. She wanted Clarke all to herself while the men talked business. Meanwhile, Michael was ready to call for Barney so he would have someone to talk to.

A chime rang, the signal for all guests to go downstairs. Gloved butlers collected glasses as guests were escorted downstairs by more White House staff. The First Couples were alone. A few moments were put in the schedule so the First Couples could freshen up. The First Lady of France and her husband freshened up in the suite of the Lincoln Bedroom.

The President and Clarke walked to their bedroom. Michael sat down and Barney hopped on his lap. A boy and his dog, Clarke thought as he walked to his dressing room. Beverly Anderson had designed a fabulous pair of spectator shoes for Clarke and the first pair off the production line was waiting there.

Clarke couldn't wait to wear them. The leather was soft. The style complimented the elegance of the First Gentleman. The shoes were designed for comfort and, of course, dancing. He put the shoes on and walked around his dressing room, turning and pivoting.

Ms. Deverough interrupted Clarke, telling him it was time to go. She commented on his new shoes. Clarke bubbled how comfortable they were. Clarke met the President and walked to the Yellow Oval Room. There they met the First Couple of France. Both couples were quiet, humbled by the power shared in the room. The head of the Color Guard marched into the room. He snapped to attention with a salute. "Mr. President, may I take the colors?" The President gave him a nod.

The soldier did an about-face. He ceremoniously walked to the Color Guard. Quietly but with a stern tone he called them to the military position of attention. They immediately snapped to and marched slowly.

The President and Clarke and the President and First Lady of France walked behind the Color Guard who were carrying the flags of the United States and France. In ceremonial step, the First Couples walked from the Private Quarters, down the hall, and to the Main Stairs.

The Marine Band played the introduction to the Presidential March. Clarke's heart began to pound. He held the President's hand as they walked down the Grand Staircase. With a squeeze, Clarke let go of Michael's hand before they turned to the landing. When the First Couples got to the third step, they stopped. The Color Guard marched ahead.

"Ladies and gentlemen, the President of the United States, Michael Arthur Kent and First Gentleman, Clarke, accompanied by the President and First Lady of France."

The Marine Band continued to play "Hail to the Chief." The First couples were radiant. Both countries, proud of their leaders, were watching as the event was televised live. Clarke looked fabulous in his tuxedo, signature vest and spectator shoes.

As they took the next step, suddenly Clarke fell to the floor. The guests gasped with an echo. Clarke was so embarrassed. It was the same gasp one heard while watching an Olympic figure skater fall to the ice. Clarke was up before the next note of the music as if nothing had happened. The President was so concerned that he stopped and took Clarke in his arms, demanding to be reassured he was okay. Clarke's red face said it all.

The Presidential March continued to the Blue Room, where a receiving line would welcome each guest to the White House. The First Lady of France was so concerned about Clarke's health that she asked Clarke if he was all right in English. Clarke was so impressed with her sincerity as he assured her he was just fine in French. She held his hand until they took their places in the Blue Room.

The music continued. Guests lined up in the hall and walked through the Red Room into the Blue Room, shaking hands with the President and Clarke and the President of France and his First Lady. The guests would leave through the Green Room then be escorted into East Room for cocktails.

The first and last guests were always planted. They were staff and Secret Service, dressed to blend in. No one wanted to be first. At the White House it was always follow-the-leader. Ms. Deverough was always the first in line. She commented to Clarke how gracefully he handled himself. He had impressed everyone. She whispered with a smile, "The cameras got it all on film." Clarke smiled. He knew that one would make the front page.

The President and Clarke received their guests as if each one invited for the evening were the most important person in the room. Clarke shook hands and reassured each guest he was just fine. His shoes were better for dancing than walking downstairs. That comment filled Clarke's dance card in a snap.

The Air Force Strolling Strings performed as they strolled from room to room. The last guest, always Beverly Anderson, greeted the First Couple. He smiled at Clarke with a "You-did-it-again" grin. Clarke looked at him and whispered, "I may have bruised my pride a little. Thank goodness, it was well padded." Beverly laughed as he walked through to the Green Room. Clarke noticed that his escort was Ms. Jones, who was wearing another incredible Beverly Anderson original. Clarke smiled at the President. The First Couple knew their secret.

The First Couples enjoyed a cocktail with their guests in the East Room. The Strolling Strings played. From across the room, Clarke received a nod from the Chief Usher. Dinner was ready to be served. Clarke returned his nod just as they had rehearsed. The Chief Usher nodded to the leader of the Strolling Strings. Gloved White House ushers walked among the guests with empty trays, gathering cocktail glasses. The Strolling Strings finished their song. Then in a toe-tapping prelude signaled "Dinner is served."

As the Strolling Strings played, they led their guests into the State Dining Room. Guests found their seats, standing until given the nod to sit down. The Strolling Strings strolled to the center of the room to finish their song. Everyone applauded. The President motioned and everyone sat down. The musicians continued playing as they left the room, covering noise of scooting chairs and happy chitchat.

The President of France gave a toast, then the President of the United States. Glasses clinked together. Dinner was served. It was the moment that had been rehearsed and rehearsed and rehearsed again. The chefs had really outdone themselves. Clarke insisted only on one thing. It had to be the best. And that meant it had to be perfect. Dinner, right down to dessert, was the grandest event ever to be served at the White House.

Dinner started with an appetizer of capered salmon, followed by a leafy vegetable salad with Raspberry Vinaigrette and the plumpest raspberries Clarke had ever seen. The entree followed with Ellensburg Rack of Lamb complimented by an apple-pear chutney and, a personal favorite of the First Lady of France, asparagus tips with Hollandaise sauce. Homemade rolls were served piping hot. Clarke watched the First Couple of

France; they seemed to enjoy dinner and also seemed genuinely impressed.

Dessert was absolutely spectacular. The Pastry Chef outdid himself and anyone else with a culinary title. He designed and created individual edible baskets made of a ground almond confection and filled with homemade ice cream topped with the Northwest's own blackberries. The ice cream was as elegant as French Vanilla but as unique as America. The ice cream was molded in the shape of a rose and sprinkled with an edible candy glitter that made it sparkle in the candlelight. The First Lady of France squealed with delight.

Sauce dishes of blackberries could be passed around the table family-style, giving a sense of home. And, of course, it was complimented with candy dishes filled with fine Hazzels Chocolates. As dessert was served, a harp romantically played a fine prelude to the entertainment that would be enjoyed in the East Room.

When dessert had been enjoyed, the Strolling Strings led the guests into the Red and Green rooms. A cocktail bar was set up in the Blue Room for after-dinner drinks. Many guests took advantage of the opportunity to visit the ground floor restrooms. The Secret Service was poised throughout the hallways and stairs. Saundra was happy to talk with the guests about the relics on display. And, of course, the Strolling Strings played as the party continued throughout the house. It was a grand party and everyone was clearly having a wonderful time. The Chief Usher gave Clarke a nod. The entertainers in the East Room were ready.

Once again, gloved White House ushers walked among the guests with empty trays, picking up cocktail glasses. The Strolling Strings played with enthusiasm. In roaming rhythm, guests were gathered toward the East Room, where entertainment and dancing would capture the night in a grand finale. Clarke had chosen the finest performers for the evening. He wanted America to be represented and enjoyed by their guests. Clarke's favorite news anchorman was the Master of Ceremonies.

There was a brief introduction, and the very lovely Mrs. McManion and the three overweight tenors, known as the Star Spangled Operas, sang the first number of the evening. The show was fast-paced, including acts from opera and ballet, as well as a hoe down complete with clog dancers dressed in checked

241

gingham. It was a grand performance. Even though Clarke had seen the show rehearsed, he enjoyed it as if he were seeing it for the first time.

With the final number, applause bounced off the chandeliers. In an encore, another song began. The cast lined up on stage parted, revealing a candelabrum. Clarke hadn't seen this in rehearsal. When the orchestra started playing "Be Our Guest" Clarke looked over at the President. This was another one of his surprises. The number was incredible. Clarke watched the man playing the very same part Clarke won a Tony Award for. The guests in the East Room tapped their feet, clapped their hands, and sang along.

The First Couple of France enjoyed Lumiere the most. Ever since it was publicly announced that they had been invited to the United States, French television had aired Clarke performing that same number over and over and over. It was a French national obsession. The President had ordered research done on what the First Couple really wanted to see and hear while at the White House and this is exactly what they wanted.

Clarke looked at the First couple, captivated by the cast. Then as the song was in its last note, Lumiere turned around and his costume became the Statue of Liberty, complete with his arm extended. The instant the orchestra stopped, the East Room went completely dark and fireworks shot from the Statue of Liberty's extended arm.

The entire audience sprang to their feet with applause. The President and First Lady of France were so honored. The Statue of Liberty was known all over the world. It was just as well known that the Statue of Liberty had been a gift to the United States from France.

Clarke knew what the President had done and added his own flair to the grand finale. Beverly Anderson had designed the costume so it wouldn't be noticed during the number of "Be Our Guest." After congratulating the stars of the show, the guests relaxed to sounds of the Air Force Strolling Strings, who gathered everyone, including the performers, and led them to the Main Entrance Hall where everyone could mingle with the guests of honor and the performers.

An espresso bar was set up in the State Dining Room as well as a bar for after-dinner drinks. Guests were so glad to have frequent breaks and the freedom to roam around the house. The Strolling Strings played as the East Room was being set up for everyone's favorite pastime, dancing.

Guests returned to the East Room to tables placed around the edges of the dance floor where candles softly flickered out their welcome. Guests were treated to dishes of mixed nuts and trays of Hazzels Chocolates. A sparkle glowed from the chandeliers. The Strolling Strings played one last number as guests took their seats.

With an up-bow, the orchestra quieted the room. The first waltz of the evening began. Just as Michael was reaching for Clarke, the First Lady of France interrupted, asking Clarke to dance. Clarke looked at the President with a smile and whispered, "I'll take a rain check."

The First Lady smiled, then joked with sincerity, "May I lead?" Clarke nodded a yes, and they twirled about the room. The cameras were focused on the First Lady of France and Clarke as both countries looked on. It was obvious the First Lady of France was leading the dance and it was just as obvious that Clarke was charming both countries with each step, pivot, and twirl.

The President of the United States chatted with his guests, leaving politics at the door. As they danced, Clarke and the First Lady of France chatted about the evening and how grand the entertainment was. The First Lady of France bubbled, "The Clog Dancers were my favorite." That didn't surprise Clarke. He had seen her satin shoes tapping right along with the dancer's feet.

The President of France watched his wife and Clarke capture the entire dance floor. He looked at Michael and said, "What do you Americans call it when you tap on one's shoulders and take their dance partner?"

Michael had to think for a moment before realizing he was talking about the American custom of 'cutting in'. "I believe we call that cutting in." Michael said.

The two Presidents chatted for a few moments then the President of France stood up. He walked to the First Gentleman and the First Lady of France as they danced in step. He tapped on Clarke's shoulder. Clarke saw him and was ready for the President of France to take his wife's hand.

In a totally surprise move, the President of France took Clarke's hand and twirled him away to the beat of the music. Clarke smiled when he looked back and saw "Michael to the rescue" without so much as a miss of a beat. Guests in the East Room clapped as the First Couples whirled their partners. On the final note from the orchestra, everyone clapped, including the First Couples. Clarke and the First Lady of France walked the Presidents back to their seats.

After an entertaining prelude, the next dance number began. The familiar beat of the drum introduced a swing tune. It was the moment everyone had been waiting for. Clarke wanted to make sure he and the President weren't the only ones on the dance floor. As rehearsed, Beverly Anderson took Ms. Deverough as his partner. Saundra asked the old Senator to dance. With a childish grin, he proudly led Saundra to the dance floor. The First Couple of France almost skipped to the dance floor and really cut a rug. Clarke and the President continued to dance as White House staff invited more guests to join in.

As early evening turned into late night, the party ended with the President and Clarke escorting the President and First Lady of France to the North Portico where their limousine was waiting. The First Couples said their good-byes. The First Couple of France got into the car as Clarke and the President stood close together, waving good-bye. As the limousine drove away, a national news commentator taping live in front of the White House said, "So ends the grandest event ever enjoyed behind the White House gates."

Clarke crawled into bed. The President read until Clarke was safely tucked in. Clarke snuggled up to Michael as he reached up to turn out the light. Clarke was so happy that everything was perfect. Planned right down to the dinner forks and unexpected as his trip down the stairs. It was as if Clarke's Guardian Angel pushed him down to make everyone live happily every after.

The President and First Lady of France were so impressed with Clarke. He was the only reason they agreed to everything the President wanted, and without a price tag.

"Clarke," the President said, "I think we could have had the same results if we had them upstairs for a cupcake."

Clarke smiled. He knew what the President meant and that meant the world to Clarke.

Stash Your Trash

Like a windstorm, days whirled into months and months spun into years. Like all Presidents, the First Couple traveled all over the world. Clarke saw to it that the White House was spectacularly decorated for every holiday. America saw it with their own eyes, one tourist at a time or in magazines at every newsstand. Snow melted into spring with the anticipation of the famous White House Rose Garden Luncheons.

In the blink of an eye, a world at peace was engulfed in horror. Suddenly, everything stopped. It was only a matter of time. Chemical warfare was imminent. The demonic dictator of the Middle East was proud he had caused such worldwide fear. There were debates as to whose soil, but every world leader agreed on one thing: chemical warfare threatened extinction to every living creature on earth.

It had become impossible to keep peace with the Middle East. All through history those countries had never gotten along. Prophecy from the Bible declared they never would. The President worked long and hard, keeping America and the world safe from their attack. The nations of the Middle East had capabilities to destroy the world in an instant with biological warfare.

The citizens of the Middle East realized if they destroyed the rest of the world, they themselves would go right along with it. Evil dictators promised loyal citizens their fatal efforts would be rewarded in the afterlife. With that kind of logic, terrorism became the war to fight. Surprisingly there wasn't fear as there had been during the Cold War. There was safety in awareness. Thanks to President Kent, America was trained, ready to fight and every American had a weapon. The size of a packaged condom, it was easier to get into and quicker to use. It was also one hundred percent effective. Applied to the skin of any human or animal, it neutralized the biological agent. Just as important as it was to have the Bio Disc on your person and an extra for a friend, it was just as important not to use the Bio Disc until officially instructed to do so. "Caution! Only use the Bio Disc when instructed that the biological agent is present. Even though the Bio Disc is one hundred percent effective, the human body could become immune to the antidote."

The little packets were free and were carried by everyone. Any government agency or those accepting government funds supplied them. Highway markers posted them. Phone booths, on the side of garbage cans, in every public place, there was a supply. When the electric bill arrived, so did a Bio Disc for everyone in the household. Adolescent boys not only carried a condom in their wallet; they also carried the Bio Disc.

Air raid sirens of the 1940's era were brought back into service to inform those not around a TV or within earshot of a radio. It was a simple siren with a loud wavy tone, a much different tone than that of a tornado warning. The siren was blasted at noon every day, including Sunday.

If one was driving when the siren blasted, traffic lights blinked in whatever color they directed traffic. They blinked in the same rhythm of the siren. That way, it wasn't confused with a traffic direction. If one was driving on the freeway, lights on directional signs blinked in the same rhythm. Notification of when to use the Bio Disc was well thought out and comforted the American people with assurance of their safety.

Even with the threat of a biological attack, America was still growing in the right direction, but it kept the President very busy. Clarke realized he himself needed to be just as busy. It's hard to criticize an administration that is doing so much good for the world. The more Clarke was seen in the press, the fewer rumors were printed about the President.

Clarke knew travel had become a pleasure only enjoyed in the past. The future of mankind was viewed as a luxury. With the threat of chemical warfare, people were staying home, wondering if today would be their last. Tourism in every nation was down and so was morale.

Clarke was asked to give speeches all across the country, from cancer research fund-raisers to college graduations to kindergarten promotions. He jumped at the chance to show the world it was safe to travel. Naturally, Clarke made headlines wherever he went. He did everything he could to help the President make the country a better place.

As the Christmas season approached once again, Clarke made sure the White House was decorated, topping the year before. Even though everyone had a Bio Disc on their person, Clarke wanted to make sure America lived life as normal as possible. What could be more normal than a Christmas tree, carols and, of course, Santa Claus with a Bio Disc and eight tiny reindeer?

As the seasons passed, Clarke did everything he could to keep the nation's morale high. With the threat of chemical warfare, this was the scariest time in the nation's history. By showing the country it was safe to leave the White House, Clarke was hoping others would feel just as safe to leave their homes. Clarke was always in the news, live, as he traveled from one state to the next, with or without the President, proving life was still safe. "Just keep your Bio Disc handy for you and a friend," the news anchor calmly said. But the broadcast ended with the same terrifying news: *biological warfare was imminent.*

As graduation month quickly approached, Clarke was asked to speak at so many graduation ceremonies, he almost felt like he had to run to the plane so he could be on time for the next ceremony. Clarke worked closely with his speechwriter and never gave even a hint of the same speech. He never wore the same ensemble to the next ceremony. He actually thought changing his outfit so often might be a bit much, but Beverly insisted. Clarke wouldn't wear the traditional ceremonial robe, but thanks to Beverly Anderson, always matched the school colors with his signature vest and, of course, spectator shoes.

The press made such an issue of it if Clarke wore the same thing twice; they made it look as if he had no fashion sense at all. Clarke was happy to wear the different outfits for Beverly. With the threat of chemical warfare, seeing Clarke in the news gave everyone something nice to see and hear. Newscasts made it very clear: "It's simple; if the President feels it's safe for his husband to travel, then it must be safe for everyone else."

Clarke visited as many schools as he could across the country and always stopped at cancer hospitals, visiting with patients and their loved ones. No other First Lady, or President, in history had been asked to make so many graduation speeches. Clarke was proud of that. He gave a rousing speech for Harvard graduates with the same enthusiasm he gave to Mrs. Simm's kindergarten class. And he always received the same heartfelt standing ovation.

Clarke was amazed at the scholarships that were offered to children, from those who were smart, to those who were great in sports, to those physically or mentally challenged. Clarke thought of all the thousands of single parents, both women and men, who had children in school but were in dead-end jobs and couldn't afford an education. And even if they could, they couldn't afford the childcare. So many parents could be on their way to a better life and a better life for their children if they could get some educational assistance.

An Education Bill had been signed when the President first took office, but the country was going through so much change, America seemed to set it on the back burner. Clarke turned up the heat and started a campaign to help all people in need of a good education. The idea bubbled over so fast, the smoke detector went off.

Millions of Americans rallied their support, including many state colleges who already accepted federal funds. They didn't want to be forced to comply. But it didn't take a rocket scientist to know Clarke could charm his ideas in to Congress, to Presidential support, to instant backing from the United State's citizens. As one reporter put it, "Watch out! Clarke knows how to win the feud and influence people."

Colleges and major corporations volunteered their support and went public with it. The biggest corporations offered incentives, not only to those who went to school but also to those who helped with daycare and, in many cases, 'nightcare'. Study days were given like holidays with pay and even a bonus for 'making the grade'. Large corporations loved the positive publicity, and people didn't even mind that their phone bills went up a dollar or the electric bill was thirty-seven cents higher. Even the National Bake-Off included a scholarship for the winner or a family member in their million-dollar purse.

Milk cartons featured good news about getting a good education and how to pay for it. Clarke was the headline story of every national newscast as he went from state to state, school to school. It didn't matter if it was a university or a community college, high school or elementary. High school students no longer felt that twelfth grade was the end of an education, but rather a stepping-stone to a better future. Dropout rates went down so far that it was hard to keep up with the statistics. If there was a twinkling star hidden under storm clouds, students everywhere were wishing upon it.

Clarke was on the road to getting America back to the classroom. An education became as American as baseball and apple pie. When Clarke traveled by car between speaking engagements, he noticed the trash along the highways. When the President first took office, many on welfare were assigned trash pickup. When those people went from welfare to non-welfare, paying jobs, it seemed there was no one left to pick up the trash.

Clarke knew security was always tight. When he traveled by land, the highways he was to travel were always publicized. Several of them. That way, for security reasons, no one knew exactly which highway or route the First Gentleman's convoy would be taking. Surprisingly, no effort was made to clean up any of those highways. The trash never seemed to bother anyone. Anyone but Clarke, that is. America was beautiful, but it needed a good sweeping up.

America was going back to school with a new motto: "make the grade to reach the stars." America's children saw the importance of going back to school by watching Mom and Dad doing it. Clarke decided to take on yet another assignment that would make America proud.

Clarke remembered what happened to Nancy Reagan when she went from Foster Grandparents of America to "Just Say No." Changing projects to the extreme brought a lot of criticisms. So, when Clarke started a new campaign, he combined the two. "On your way to school *Stash Your Trash*." He started with the citizens who were closest to the trash, the little ones.

"We all want a better life for our children, whether it's our own children or a younger generation full of hopes and dreams. We want a better life, a better America and, ultimately, a better world," Clarke said from the podium.

Stash Your Trash started with the children. It's hard to argue with a little one who says, "Mommy, stash your trash." Americans were not only getting smarter, now they were "stashing their trash." Talking dumpsters were the hit at parades with the slogan, "Garbage Is My Bag" painted on them. The

250

'happy face' was back. It smiled on trash bags and containers everywhere. A smile was piled high on trash pickup days. Annoying trash days turned to happy days. With every great idea in politics comes opposition, but Clarke refused to listen to negative press. When "Stash Your Trash" was attacked, it was combated with: "America the beautiful will *Stash Its Trash*."

It was getting harder and harder to insult Clarke. When people talked with him, the nasty press about him ceased to exist. But exist it did. Clarke knew every fairy tale had its villain. If the Secret Service were there to take the bullet for the President, then Clarke was there to take the bad press. Michael was the world's favorite President, married to the world's most famous man. America as a whole didn't think it was cool to be gay, but that wasn't an issue. And if it was, it was combated with "*Stash Your Trash*."

One local newspaper subtly poked an insult at Clarke with its headline: "The First Man To Be First Lady, America's Peacock in Bloom, will visit our town today."

Clarke gave a speech ending with, "Beauty is understood and appreciated in all walks of life, at any age, even with the birds in nature." Clarke was making reference to the 'Peacock in Bloom'. The audience went wild with their ovations. Clarke's speeches always turned negative press into a positive for the administration.

Clarke's speechwriter, Daffney Velaflor, was so far behind the scenes writing speeches for the First Gentleman that no one ever noticed her. Many didn't even know the First Man To Be First Lady had a speechwriter. Clarke continued his speech and challenged all Americans to do their part. "On your way to school, America," Clarke smiled. "Let's *Stash Our trash*."

The campaign spread like wildfire, with Clarke lighting the match in every corner. He had a rigorous schedule, inspiring America as he traveled. It was all the good news that combated the bad news of impending biological attack. As Clarke boarded his plane and the doors shut behind him, he commented to Ms. Deverough that he was looking forward to getting home and relaxing with the President. He clicked his seat belt together as the plane taxied down the runway and gently reached for the sky.

When the aircraft reached cruising altitude, Clarke changed his clothes. Again. He went over his speech and together he and Daffney Velaflor made the necessary changes. Clarke had one more stop to make before his plane headed back to Washington. He was going to attend a simple school assembly. He was really looking forward to this one. It was a grade school deep in the Bible Belt of America.

It was the same place Clarke had given his first speech as First Gentleman. It was also Edith and Harold's hometown. Their little town had been the first to ask The First Man To Be First Lady if he would come and speak at their school. Clarke smiled. It seemed so long ago. Clarke remembered the debate over the invitation. It may have started out to be a far-fetched request, and maybe even a sick joke, but Clarke was proud to be asked and responded with a hand-written acceptance. The town was genuinely honored to have him.

At the time, the press was more interested in the new President than they were in his husband. There was a small local camera crew and a photographer from the state's big newspaper. That was it. With that first speech, Clarke did more for the press agents and photographers that showed up than a Pulitzer Prize did for their senior comrades.

Clarke's appearing in this little town so early in the administration did more for that little town than all its 200 years of existence. In honor of Clarke's return, today's assembly was going to be much like a Fourth of July parade and Christmas all rolled into one. It would receive worldwide coverage on every major news channel in the country.

The town had been nicknamed "America's First" little town. They never forgot what Clarke did for their town and Clarke never forgot what that little town did for him as First Gentleman. The assembly was humble in size but big in heart. It wasn't the Marines who presented the American Flag, but Boy and Girl Scouts standing proud in their uniforms. There wasn't a grand band, but the sixth grade orchestra who had won first place in the talent show, playing the "Star Spangled Banner" with pride.

Clarke's speech received an ovation like none other ever heard in those parts. Clarke and Edith had corresponded since their meeting, but they hadn't seen each other. Edith was first to shake Clarke's hand. Harold was at her side. Clarke met their son, Robert, and his partner, Mike. Edith whispered, "Just like you, Clarke."

Clarke noticed that both men were very attractive and were dressed in vests and spectator shoes. He saw what a handsome couple Robert and Mike were and how proud Edith and Harold were to introduce them as a couple. Edith handed Clarke a book. It was a cookbook from her ladies' group. Each lady had autographed her recipe with a note.

Edith leaned in towards Clarke and said, "Be careful of recipes from Lilla Jean. She always leaves something out when she writes up a recipe. That way she thinks nobody can cook as good as she can." Clarke laughed a thank you. Edith introduced others in line, then was called away to handle a problem at the bake sale being held in the back of the auditorium. Harold stood next to Clarke. Clarke shook hands with the children and their families. The line snaked along. Clarke insisted he was going to stay right there until he got to meet the last person in line. And he did.

At the end of the line was a lovely family, dressed in their Sunday best and uncomfortably so. They were polished and starched crisp. The mother of the group was proud of that and kept her children's annoyance to a whisper. She had gone back to school, thanks to Clarke and his campaign to get Mom and Dad back in the classroom. When it was this family's turn to meet Clarke, he reached out his hand to the father. Clarke's handshake was firm, shocking the man.

Clarke noticed the man's hands were callused, and Clarke could feel his hard work. The mother beamed with pride and proudly introduced her family, as if they were being presented to the queen. And to them, they were. Clarke didn't know who was more proud at that moment, that mother bursting with pride presenting her family or Clarke meeting them. It was genuine and the cameras flashed like a lightning storm introducing a twister.

A little boy, feeling the pride of the moment and no longer noticing the extra starch in his shirt, tugged on Clarke. He had something important to say and it had to be said to the First Man to Be First Lady. He tugged with such might it almost knocked Clarke over. Clarke excused himself from the youngster's parents and knelt down to give the young fellow eye-to-eye contact.

"Yes, sir?" Clarke said, knowing this little guy had the most important news of the day. In that gymnasium the world quieted, waiting with anticipation to hear what this little American, living deep in the Bible Belt, the future of the country, had to say. Clarke waited in silence, giving the little guy the floor. News cameras were poised. Music went silent. The world waited for the great news this little one had.

The little boy looked at Clarke with big brown eyes, somehow knowing how important this moment was in his life. He spoke with the clarity of a fine gentleman of the third grade. He adjusted his starched shirt and put his hands to his side. He lifted his head and proudly stated with a loud voice, "My Daddy says you're a pervert."

If someone had dropped a pin it would have deafened every human within miles. Clarke smiled as he looked at the young fellow. News cameras zeroed in, first on this family from America's heartland, then to the First Man To Be First Lady. Clarke never faltered. After what seemed an eternity of deafening silence, Clarke, with his charming smile looked at the little boy and said, "What do you tell your Daddy to do with his trash?"

The little boy, knowing very well all eyes were on him, shouted, "STASH YOUR TRASH! STASH YOUR TRASH! STASH YOUR TRASH!"

That roused the whole gymnasium to a cheer that almost brought the roof down. Their chants had nothing to do with litter or recycling. Townspeople looked at the man, yelling at him, "STASH 'YOUR' TRASH!" The man realized his comment was inappropriate. Clarke saw how the man's wife looked at her husband. Every wife, whether it be a man or a woman, has 'the look' that comes with commitment. Her look clearly said that her husband was in deep, deep trouble.

The gymnasium chanted, "Stash Your Trash" as the First Gentleman made his way to the car that would take him back to the airport. It was the best assembly Clarke had ever been part of. Clarke's wit and charm gracefully told that attitude to "stash it" and the entire town chanted along. Clarke did more than clean up litter; he was also cleaning up society. He did it with grace, class, and charm, wearing a vest and walking in spectator shoes.

The President was watching TV in the Oval Office as the assembly was shown live. He chanted along with the nation. As usual, the President took out his pipe and lit it. He sat back and watched the TV. Whenever Clarke was on the airwaves, there was always a surprise attack. Michael's hero flew off into the sunset and would soon come bouncing through the door of the Oval Office as if nothing had ever happened, and everyone would live happily ever after.

The President clamped his pipe between his teeth and grabbed the remote. He clicked the TV off as the news commentary came on the screen with cheers of, "Stash Your Trash." The President knew the newscast was going to end with another briefing about the Bio Disc.

There was always a contagious, cheerful jingle instructing how to use the Bio Disc. It was going to be played again and the President knew that, once he heard it, he would be humming it all night long. The President laid the remote down. "Clarke did it again."

Clarke was taken to the airport via limousine where his plane was waiting to take him back to Washington, the city. Ms. Deverough sat next to Clarke. She noticed that he looked pale but Clarke insisted he was fine. The car drove to the front of the aircraft. Clarke got out of the car, sandwiched between Secret Service agents. As Clarke walked up the stairs, each step seemed ten stories tall.

Rarely did Clarke stay in his quarters on the aircraft, but today he shut the door behind him. Ms. Deverough quietly asked the nurse to keep an eye on him. Clarke wouldn't let the nurse near him, explaining that he was just fine. The nurse honored Clarke's request per orders of Dr. Maddeline.

The flight was bumpy. The Fasten Seatbelt sign was illuminated for the entire flight. Clarke was uncomfortable. It wasn't motion sickness. Clarke felt truly ill. He wanted the President to hold him, but that was still hours away. He wanted rest, but when he lay down, he was sick. He sat in the easy chair with a seatbelt around him and tried to relax. He prayed for a strong tail wind. He just wanted to get home.

A knock on the door interrupted Clarke's thoughts. It was his nurse asking him if he was okay and if he needed anything. Clarke invited her in but, much to her surprise, he didn't get up.

He looked in the opposite direction. The room was dimly lit. Clarke explained that the bumpy ride was making him a little nauseated. She tried to give him something for it, but he refused with a hand gesture. Clarke politely asked the nurse for some privacy.

"Is there someone I can call for you?" She asked

Clarke shook his head from side to side and whispered, "No."

"Clarke, I'm right outside the door if you need anything." She stressed 'anything', knowing very well what was happening to him. She shut the door behind her and went to the telephone to talk with Dr. Maddeline over a secured line.

Clarke had been in pain for some time but there was no need to complain about it. After all, if he kept it to himself then no one else knew it. Clarke smiled as he thought to himself that Ms. Deverough knew. She knew everything. Including how much Clarke wanted his privacy.

Clarke laid his head back and relaxed. He finally fell asleep. The double chime awakened him, signaling that the initial descent for landing at Andrews Air Force Base had began. Clarke got up to ready himself for any surprise press when he left the plane. To his surprise he could barely walk. He was sweating. He looked in the mirror. He looked awful. His color was gone. It hurt to stand up straight. Clarke wanted to call for the nurse, but he sat down instead.

The aircraft softly landed and quickly taxied off the runway. Clarke looked out the window. He was glad to see that there was no fanfare scheduled. No surprises. No press. No television cameras. He would leave the aircraft and board the helicopter for the ride back to the White House. Then Clarke would be home. It was all just a few steps away.

The aircraft came to a complete stop. Clarke was summoned and as he walked to the front door of the aircraft, he noticed that the door was open to the cockpit. Normally, for security reasons, the doors were kept shut and bolted. Clarke knew his nurse had briefed the flight crew of his discomfort and asked for a very smooth landing. Clarke was so grateful he almost walked into the flight deck.

Clarke thanked the flight crew for a safe ride and all of their service. The crew noticed that Clarke was moving slowly and his posture was bent. The pilots just looked at one another then back to Clarke. As Clarke left the aircraft, his favorite flight attendant wished him a good day. The man had been very loyal to Clarke since his first flight from Washington, the state. The man noticed that Clarke looked ill. Ms. Deverough walked very close to Clarke. She was afraid he was going to pass out. Clarke refused any services from the nurse and demanded she understand he was just fine.

Clarke boarded the helicopter. It took off with its normal ease and was soon out of sight. In an instant the helicopter landed on the South Lawn of the White House. Normal. Clarke walked off and went straight to the White House. Normal. Ms. Deverough immediately went to the Oval Office. She interrupted an important meeting between the President and his advisors who were ready to inform the nation that use of the Bio Disc was imminent.

The ushers opened the door for Clarke. With a sigh of relief, Clarke made it. Safely inside the White House, Clarke's energy was gone. Clarke walked into the Blue Room and stood in front of the window. His silhouette was striking as dusk welcomed him home.

Clarke was looking towards the Washington Monument but not seeing anything. This is where it all started. The Blue Room, Clarke's favorite room of the house. This the where the President made his announcement of love for Clarke. The Blue Room, where on their anniversary they renewed their wedding vows. It was the First Couple's only secret from the American people. The press had never heard of it and never commented on Clarke taking the President's last name. Clarke looked at his wedding ring. The Blue Room, this is where the President and Clarke greeted their guests. This was Clarke's room, where the nation had been invited many times.

The President entered the room, thanking the uniformed usher in white gloves for opening the door for him. Ms. Deverough nodded as she stayed back in the Grand Hall, letting the usher shut the doors behind the President. The President knew there was something terribly wrong. Clarke wasn't ready to look at Michael. He was in a lot of pain, but refused any medication. Clarke knew it was time to tell the President.

The President took a gilded armchair and sat next to where Clarke was standing. Michael sensed what was coming and needed to sit down. Clarke continued to stare out the window. After a long silence, Clarke turned and looked at the President. He reached for his hand and held it. "The cancer is back and there is nothing they can do."

The most powerful man in the world was suddenly powerless and knew it as he stuttered, "I'll send for Maddeline."

"No. I've seen Maddeline." Clarke couldn't believe how quickly the time had passed. "She gave me eighteen months almost three years ago."

"And you didn't tell me?" Michael interrupted. He was so angry his voice was shaking.

"And I planned it that way," Clarke interrupted Michael with such a matter-of-fact tone that he knew it was Clarke's wish. Surprisingly, that seemed to calm the President.

The President's voice grew extremely authoritative. Michael was strong and held the most powerful position in the world. Michael stood, taking Clarke by the shoulders. "I'm not going to let you leave me! Clarke, I can't do this without you." Michael's voice grew stern. "Surgery, more chemotherapy...I don't care what it takes." Michael looked Clarke in the eye. "Clarke, you are going to get better." Michael said it again. "I'm not going to let you leave me."

Clarke smiled. "What makes you think I am leaving you?" Clarke was morbidly pale. "I promised you I would never leave you. I will be right here until the day we leave this house." Pain had taken Clarke's smile but it would never take the twinkle out of his eyes.

The President took Clarke in a cumbersome embrace neither of them felt. The President broke their embrace and held Clarke away from him as if he was looking at him for the first time. The pain was unbearable. He wanted to carry Clarke and make his pain go away.

The Vice President was escorted into the hall and was waiting for orders from the President. The doors to the Blue Room opened. Many of the staff members taking care of the house were standing by. Ms. Deverough had briefed the President's cabinet. Everyone seemed to be standing guard in the Grand Hall. Many gasped when they saw Clarke. The President and Clarke walked very slowly. Ms. Deverough briefed the Chief Usher that Dr. Maddeline was on her way to the White House.

The President and Clarke walked towards the elevator but as the doors gently rolled open Clarke motioned a, "No thank you". The staff watched as the First Couple walked towards their Private Quarters. The staff bowed their heads. Clarke looked up at the President. The President looked down at Clarke. The love they shared was captured in their smiles. The Vice President, with Ms. Deverough at her side, stood motionless. The President silently signaled to the Vice President that he was going to get Clarke settled in, then would address the nation when it was time to use the Bio Disc. "Please stand by," the President calmly said.

As America watched nighttime TV, an interruption flashed across the screen. Sports events went into "time out" as large screen TV's silenced coliseums. Live radio broadcasts interrupted songs, asking their audiences to please stand by. Shopping mall loudspeakers asked for everyone's attention. The same announcer was heard over the emergency broadcast system, "Please stay tuned for a special news report." America stopped, watching and waiting to hear if it was time to use the Bio Disc. Hearts pounded an anticipation beat.

Tom Jennings came on the TV. He gave the American people the only facts he knew. "We have learned that the Vice President and the President's Cabinet have been summoned to the White House. Americans have been asked to keep their Bio Disc handy. This may be the time we are ordered to used them." His voice was calm just as normal, keeping his audience calm. "We are standing by to keep you informed on use of the Bio Disc. Again there is no threat of national security, and the National Guard and Red Cross have been activated in all 50 states to assist with the Bio Disc."

People at home reached for their Bio Discs. Wives called their husbands in from outside. Parents called for their children, gathering them together with the Bio Disc in hand. With sports events in time out, Bio Discs were retrieved from seat backs. Movies stopped in theaters as the house lights slowly brightened. The Bio Disc was retrieved from pockets and handbags. Ushers handed a Bio Disc those who either didn't have one or felt better with two.

Airports came to a complete stop, airplane engines silenced, passengers still. Everyone seemed calm. The Bio Disc was available and everyone had been briefed on how to use them. It was simple, like a blink of an eye. Tom Jennings grabbed his ear piece, being briefed on what was happening next.

His expression said he was anxious to hear what was happening.

"We take you live to the White House Briefing Room."

The press had assembled, trying to catch their breath as they took their seats. Television cameras zeroed in on reporters with pad and pencil in one hand, a Bio Disc in the other. This was breaking news, and America was watching as it happened.

Every American was ready to follow their leader with the Bio Disc in hand. Reporters in the pressroom were ready to stand, as the President was about to enter. Everyone was shocked to see Dr. Maddeline walk into the briefing room followed by the President's Chief Adviser. Maddeline stood behind the podium. Her head slightly bowed.

"At 8:27 p.m. Eastern Standard Time, Clarke, The First Gentleman, died due to complications of metastatic cancer."

A hush slammed into the nation.

No one spoke. No one moved. Athletes looked at one another then back to the big screen. At home, people grabbed a loved one's hand. Shoppers stood motionless. No one could move. There were tears of disbelief. Then tears of accepting truth. Then just tears. The Bio Disc was ignored.

The President's chief adviser spoke into the microphone. With assurance but hollow eyes, he said, "The President is with his husband in the First Couple's Private Quarters. The Vice President is here in the White House. The President's cabinet is standing by. Following standard protocol for the safety of our nation and its allies, the military is on alert."

Dr. Maddeline went back to the microphone. "The cancer spread throughout Clarke's body." She made a fist. "It was like taking a handful of popcorn kernels" then she spread her hand "and dropping them. Where they landed was where the cancer spread and continued to grow. There was nothing medical science could do. Clarke died comfortably, but secretly lived in pain for some time. Clarke's wishes that it be kept between him and his medical staff were honored. Clarke wanted a normal life to the very end, and he had one. He himself told the President early this evening."

The Chief advisor again took over. "We will answer any questions you have at this time, but please, a show of hands out of respect for Clarke." He nodded and gestured to a lady sitting three rows back.

"This is a two-part question. Why wasn't Clarke in the hospital and why was this kept from the American people?"

"As we said, these were Clarke's wishes, and they were honored. Clarke knew there was nothing else that could be done. He would not spend his last days in a hospital but at home here in the White House."

The President's advisor stepped in.

"Clarke's request was honored. The President would have to inform Congress of his own medical condition, but it is not law that the First Lady must do so. Again, this was an individual American's request, and it was honored."

Maddeline took over, looked up and into the crowd, taking full command. "It was my patient's request and his dying wish. It was my obligation as a doctor to respect that wish." She pointed to another reporter, who quickly stood and looked angry, ready to attack, "He was America's and we had a right to know."

"And he had a right to his life." Maddeline said, then pointed to the next reporter who, visibly moved, could barely choke out her question.

"Will the President be making a statement?"

The President's advisor took the microphone. "He will address the nation. We do not know when. The President has just lost his spouse and America has lost a national treasure. This will all take some time." He motioned for the next reporter, who stood and very matter-of-factly asked, "Who is leading our nation?" He continued to stand.

The President's advisor answered as he made eye contact with the entire press conference. "The President is in command."

"Why is the Vice President here?" the same reporter continued.

"It is standard protocol." The advisor paused. "Next question." He pointed to someone in the back of the room.

"When will funeral services be held?" The reporter broke into sobs and sat down, not even hearing the answer.

The Chief Advisor was deeply moved and shared in the nation's mourning. "That is to be announced. America will know as soon as possible. That is all we have at this time."

The cameras went back to the reporter in front of the White House wiping his eyes. He was deeply moved along with the rest of the world. Like everyone else, he couldn't speak. The network interrupted with a newscaster behind a desk in a studio ad-libbing, with tears flowing down her cheeks, as she struggled to be professional.

"America has lost a national treasure this evening. Our prayers are with the President. Again, for those of you who just tuned in, Clarke, The First Gentleman, died at home in the White House at 8:27 p.m. Eastern Standard Time of metastatic cancer, a complication of his testicular cancer."

The nation was glued to the TV. Traffic snarled as people tried to get home for comfort from a loved one. Not since the day John F. Kennedy was shot had news stunned, not only the nation, but also the entire world. America stood by, waiting for someone to shake them out of a bad dream. The clock struck twelve. The ball was over.

Ms. Deverough walked down the hallway of the Private Quarters and quietly opened the door. She walked into the Lincoln Bedroom where she found the President with Clarke. He had held Clarke's hand as he took his last breath. He wouldn't let go even though Clarke's body had turned cold. The room was silent.

"Clarke promised he would never leave me," the President said. Tears streamed down his face. "What am I going to do without him?" For the first time, the world's most powerful man was helpless. Ms. Deverough sat next to the President and held his hand.

Then Ms. Deverough took command. "Clarke has planned everything down to the finest detail, including what you will be wearing to the memorial services." The President smiled through his tears. "I have it all right here." She handed Michael several documents. The President smiled again. Michael understood why Clarke idolized Ms. Deverough. The President read the documents as she quietly walked out of the room.

In the papers handed to him, Michael found funeral arrangements, organized and in order. Clarke's request was to be laid out in the Blue Room, not the Capitol, for those who would like to pay their respects. After the memorial service, Clarke's body would be cremated and his ashes were to be scattered in the sea at his home in Washington, the state. The President didn't have to plan the funeral. He just had to read Clarke's requests.

The President finally came out of the Lincoln Bedroom with Barney trotting along. Secret Service stood poised on each side of the doorway. Maddeline's nurse, in a starched white uniform and nurse's cap, asked Michael if there was anything he needed. He motioned a no. The President's staff lined the hallways. Together they walked in silence to the Oval Office. Ms. Jones and another team of Secret Service agents escorted the funeral directors into the White House. With a convoy surrounding the hearse, they took Clarke away.

After briefing the staff that the Bio Disc was not to be used at this time, the President had asked to be alone in the Oval Office. He politely thanked his staff for their assistance, then escorted them out and shut the door behind them. Michael turned and walked across the room. He sat down in his rocking chair next to the fireplace. Barney lay at his feet.

The President slowly rocked back and forth. A roaring fire dwindled to a glow. Michael watched the last spark race up the chimney. The fire was out. The warmth was gone. Once again Michael slowly went through the papers of Clarke's hand-written requests. Clarke had thought of everything. With a deep sigh, the President turned and looked out the window. It seemed late, but actually it was early. The sun was beginning to rise. If America hoped it was just a horrid nightmare, the morning news brought them back to reality.

The President watched the sun rise. As the dew was still deep on the roses, the President and Barney went out and picked the most beautiful flowers in the garden. The Chief Usher found the President holding the flowers, smelling them. His eyes were red. He was in the same clothes he had worn the day before.

The Chief Usher had become the best of friends with Clarke. They had worked so closely together that each knew what the other was thinking. The Chief Usher had to tell the President that Clarke's body had been brought back to the White House. He tried to be professional, but when he started to speak, he just broke down into sobs. The President hugged him as they cried together.

When they broke their embrace, the Chief Usher informed the President that Clarke was at rest in the Blue Room. The President thanked him as he picked up the flowers.

"May I be of assistance?" The Chief Usher asked. The President shook his head as he held the flowers close. Barney was in step, making sure the President was safe.

The President entered the White House through the Diplomatic Reception Room. The White House staff bowed their heads as they watched him. Slowly the President walked to the Blue Room. The doors were closed. An usher, one on each side of the doorway, opened them. The President stepped in then stopped as if he had never seen the room before. Barney sat at his feet. All the furniture had been removed. The draperies had been closed. In White House tradition, the chandelier, dimly lit, was draped in black net. The President, holding the flowers and with Barney at his feet, slowly walked to the casket as the doors to the Blue Room were shut behind them.

The President looked at Clarke. Barney looked up at the President.

"Clarke is in Heaven," the President said. Barney stood on his hind legs and looked into the coffin. Barney looked at Clarke then back to Michael, then back to Clarke, as if to say, "No, he's not. He's right here." The President put his arm around Barney. Barney sat down then bowed in a way that makes one realize how human dogs really are. The President bowed with Barney.

Michael looked at his watch, then over to the dark fireplace waiting for the mantel clock to chime the hour. Clarke's blue-marble mantel clock was gone. The President called for the Chief Usher. The man immediately walked into the room. Michael demanded to know where Clarke's mantel clock was.

"I'm sorry, Mr. President. The clock stopped. It is downstairs being repaired. With the forty-two clocks in the White House, Michael knew the finest clock masters were on staff and wondered why it had not been taken care of instantly.

"We may need to send the clock out, Mr. President. The staff doesn't know what's wrong with it."

Michael ordered the mantel clock be returned to the spot where Clarke had placed it and the hands set to the exact time when the clock stopped. The Chief Usher left the room to personally take care of the President's request.

Michael slowly looked about the room. A beautiful spray of flowers and peacock feathers, designed by the White House floral staff, had been laid on the casket. Michael's simple bouquet of flowers, picked from the garden, was laid next to Clarke. Michael turned and walked with Barney out of the room.

America poured into the White House by the thousands. Flowers were laid all along the White House fence. Thousands and thousands of flowers. Not since the day the world lost its Princess had there ever been such a worldwide cry of sympathy. Millions of letters and cards were delivered to the White House.

As Clarke had requested, the funeral services would be very simple, held in the Washington Cathedral with a lovely mass presented by the ministers from St. Mark's Cathedral in Seattle. They lead the nation in a healing service said by many to be too short to take away their pain.

The Star Spangled Operas were invited to sing "Amazing Grace." It had been Clarke's Aunt Naomi's favorite song. It was sung at her funeral. Clarke had asked that it be sung at his. It was beautifully performed, acappella. On the last verse, everyone in the congregation was invited to sing. Not only did the congregation inside the Cathedral sing, so did those standing outside, and those at home watching the service on television. Matt Robinson had been invited to say a prayer. Tears streamed down his face as he spoke of the fine man that was First Gentleman. As he prayed the flag waved at half staff.

The doors opened from the Cathedral. Thousands of people were standing by. Everyone was silent. News cameras filmed the moment. The President walked out of the Cathedral. Barney was at his feet. No leash, just walking in step. Then came Ms. Deverough, Saundra, and Beverly Anderson. Harold and Edith with Robert and his Mike followed. Next came dignitaries from all over the world led by the First Couple of France. There was no background music. No fanfare. Just a stunned nation. Quietly watching.

The President was driven back to the White House. Barney howled if the President left him alone, so Barney was at his side. In the Blue Room, the President and Barney accepted condolences from dignitaries and their spouses who had come from all over the world. Clarke had planned everything to the last detail, including a luncheon to be served in the State Dining Room.

The President was kept to schedule by Ms. Deverough. The day lasted an eternity, and then suddenly it seemed over in an instant and Michael was alone in the Private Quarters. He paced up and down the hallways, then stopped, staring into the Lincoln Bedroom. The Chief Usher had called Dr. Maddeline. She quietly asked Michael when he had slept last. The restless President couldn't remember.

Michael couldn't tear himself away from the doorway of the Lincoln Bedroom. He was offered a sedative but refused it. Finally the President ordered the Lincoln Bedroom to be sealed and the doors to remain locked. With the doors shut and locked, the President walked to his bedroom. Barney had crawled onto the President's bed and was asleep on Clarke's side. With the robotics of routine, Michael turned and walked to the Oval Office.

When Barney woke up alone he howled so loudly the Secret Service decided to take him outside and let him run around the grounds. Barney's favorite Secret Service agent and another agent opened the doors to the Private Quarters. Barney jumped between them and ran down the Grand Stairs with the Secret Service tumbling after him. Barney ran down the hall.

The Secret Service couldn't keep up and yelled in their radio, "Barney is on the loose!" The doors were open at the end of the hall as a staff member was coming through, and Barney escaped just as it was closed. With the Secret Service running after him, Barney kept running through the pillared colonnade.

Barney started to howl as he ran toward the Oval Office. As the President opened the door to see what was wrong, Barney leaped into his arms. The out-of-breath Secret Service agents explained that they were letting Barney out and he ran away, right to the President. "I even tried to whistle for him, but he wouldn't stop, Mr. President." Michael knew Barney and this Secret Service agent had been the best of friends. If this man was off duty for a couple of days, Barney searched the house for him and wouldn't let him alone once he came back.

The President put Barney down. The Secret Service agent reached for Barney. To everyone's surprise, Barney growled and snapped at the man. Barney sat ON the President's feet and wouldn't budge. The Secret Service man was crushed at Barney's reaction.

Michael looked down at Barney sitting on his feet, then waved off the Secret Service agent and said it was okay, as he petted Barney. Michael and Barney became inseparable. When the President was in the Oval Office, Barney was in the Oval Office. When the President ate, Barney ate. Barney wouldn't go outside until the President went outside. Regardless of where the President was going, Barney was there, too.

Minutes slowly turned into hours and the days slowly passed. The world watched the American President. The satanic dictator of the Middle East waited. He was known for taking advantage of the worse situations to achieve evil superiority. Like a thief in the night, he would steal world peace. The twisted leader had planned to take advantage of the American President and attack in his time of mourning, then quickly realized that the world would do anything for America in her time of loss, including blowing up the satanic dictator. For a man responsible for so much death and destruction, he was terrified of his own demise.

With sincerity, the twisted tyrant requested a Peace Summit with all the leaders of the Middle East. It was scheduled to be on American soil, on the grounds of the White House. The South Portico would be its backdrop. Before the President would let the evil man on American soil, he had to surrender his chemical warfare arsenals to NATO peacekeepers. Military leaders of the United States would command his armies.

If it was too good to be true, the American President was ready. He trusted no one. Not anymore. The United States Armed Forces were on alert all over the globe. The dictator's country was full of American soldiers. If ordered to attack, the fight would be from the inside out. U.S. Armed Forces were in the air and on the sea, ready for their command. CIA flooded their country. The United States was ready with the Bio Disc. With so much as even whisper of espionage, the American President would give the order. While standing in front of the White House, one reporter aptly summed it all up, "The United States is ready for war. If the Middle East does not comply with President Kent's requests, they might as well paint a target on their foot and shoot."

The United States military was on alert, covering every inch of the globe. The President wasn't going to take any chances. If the leaders of the Middle East were in the United States, naturally security would be tight, but Michael made sure there would be no surprise attack on any nation's soil. Every country allied with the United States had their military on alert. President Kent made very clear from the start that any suspicious activity would jeopardize the Peace Summit. Period.

In style of the Kent Administration the Welcoming Ceremony for the Peace Summit was grand. Military bands played each country's anthem as their flag was marched by. Each leader ceremoniously shook the President's hand, then the hand of his enemy. Secret Service surrounded the stage. All President Kent would have to do is nod and they would pounce. The Joint Chiefs of Staff were ready to give commands to the Armed Forces.

Each leader made a speech promising peace throughout their land and the world. An enormous outdoor theater screen had been erected on the South Lawn and showed chemical arsenals being taken apart piece by piece. Chemical weapons were neutralized. NATO peacekeepers were standing guard in each Middle Eastern country.

President Kent promised world peace. "With today's peace treaty, the horror of chemical warfare will only be a horrid nightmare of the past. The United States is committed to assist each country in keeping their promise, and that is my promise to the American people and every human being around the world." This was the most important speech of Michael's presidency. His speech was short, to the point, and brought the longest applause in his political career. President Michael Arthur Kent made sure their honesty was backed with his power.

Ms. Deverough

Time passed slowly. Hours slowly ticked into days and days slowly became weeks. Even with all the peace in the world, the President still couldn't sleep. He would be happy just to relax. The President sat in his rocker. For the first time in his Presidency, the world was finally safe. He gently rocked back and forth. Barney lay at his feet. He should finally relax, but he couldn't sit still. Half of him was gone. The President looked at his watch. His appointments were over for the day. Michael didn't want leave his office. He would have to be alone in his Private Quarters.

He sent for Ms. Deverough. Gently rocking back and forth, he enjoyed the thought of talking to her. She would listen to his loneliness. Her simple comments would comfort him. For a while. A knock came at the door. The President got up from his chair and walked towards the door with Barney trotting along. Michael said a relieved, "Ms. Deverough, please come in." But in walked Ms. Jones.

"Mr. President, we can't find Ms. Deverough. No one has seen her leave the White House, but all of her things are gone, including all of her steamer trunks." Ms. Jones had a lost, bewildered look on her face, which made the President believe her. Ms. Jones continued to brief the President. "Security would have seen her leave the grounds. Secret Service people are checking the surveillance camera tapes as we speak. We have everyone searching the House. With your permission, we would like to search the Private Quarters."

"Of course." The President said as he walked towards his desk, Barney trotting along side him. Barney waited for the President to sit down, then lay down, resting his head on Michael's feet.

Ms. Jones radioed the staff that was ready to pounce on the Private Quarters. There was nothing. No one. She was radioed back. "No one has been here since the President left for the Oval Office this morning." The President heard their radio transmission and was ready to question Ms. Jones.

Ms. Jones assumed an attitude of power as she briefed the President. "There are concealed surveillance cameras poised over every entrance into the Private Quarters." The President had an angry look on his face. Ms. Jones reiterated what she had just said, "Not *in* the Private Quarters, Mr. President, but on the entrances to the Private Quarters."

"Why wasn't I told about this?" the President demanded.

"National security," she bluntly said.

The President gave up and merely nodded. The radio blared that Ms. Deverough wasn't anywhere on the videotapes, just the President leaving for the Oval Office that morning.

"This is the White House. People just don't disappear." The President had a surprising calm in his voice. Then, with an arched eyebrow, he said, "Find her." He got up from behind the desk and walked back to his rocking chair. Barney followed him. "If she didn't leave the grounds, then she is still in the house. Bring in more staff if you have to. I want Ms. Deverough found. Immediately."

"Yes, Mr. President." Ms. Jones left the Oval Office, barking commands into her radio. More Secret Service staff arrived on the grounds. Each room, closet, nook and cranny was searched. Even the secret passageway was searched. When a room had been searched, a Secret Service agent was put outside the door. Video equipment scanned every inch of the White House, both inside and out.

The President wasn't comfortable in his rocker. He got up and sat behind his desk. Barney trotted along. Michael couldn't concentrate so he got up and walked to the window. Barney trotted along. Helicopter searchlights crisscrossed the grounds. Michael walked back towards his rocking chair and Barney trotted along. Michael stopped and walked back to his desk. Barney sat down, waiting for Michael to do the same. Michael stopped. He realized he was pacing and knelt down to pet Barney.

Ms. Jones came back into the Oval office. "Mr. President, Ms. Deverough is gone. We can't even find her umbrella."

"Bumbershoot." The President said with no emotion. "Ms. Deverough always called her umbrella a bumbershoot."

Michael walked to his desk and sat down. He looked up at Ms. Jones, waiting to hear what she had to say.

Ms. Jones looked somewhat bewildered at the President's mundane explanation and changed the subject back to Ms. Deverough's whereabouts. "Mr. President, we went through all the files, checking for Ms. Deverough's private address or family member's addresses. There is no information on Ms. Deverough. The FBI files show she never existed. The Secret Service files are empty. Her file, copies of her personal photograph, fingerprints, I signed the report myself, it's gone." Ms Jones paused. "As if it had never existed."

"Don't be ridiculous." The President's expression said she was insulting him. He stood, ready to go look for Ms. Deverough himself, then stopped. "Of course she existed. Clarke and Ms. Deverough were the best of friends. I handed Ms. Deverough her first paycheck as a Secret Service agent right here in the Oval Office. Clarke made a party out of it." Michael paused, convincing himself Ms Deverough did exist. "For Christ's sake, Clarke always called Ms. Deverough his Fairy Godmother!" There was an eerie silence. The two just looked at each other, then the President slowly sat down in his chair.

"This is the White House. We don't have Fairy Godmothers." He paused, trying not to show emotion. "Not anymore." The President was annoyed. Suddenly he was in full command and barked his next order. "Get me Beverly Anderson." The President calmed himself. "He knew Ms. Deverough like the back of his hand. There is no way you can tell me HE doesn't exist. I'm wearing one of his designer ties." The President pulled at his tie and looked at it, as if he was trying to convince himself he wasn't going mad. Ms. Jones had never been so scared of anyone in her life.

She calmly told the President, "Beverly Anderson is on his way over now. We sent a car to pick him up and search his studio. There is no sign of Ms. Deverough." Just as Ms. Jones was about to go on with the search of the city, Beverly Anderson was announced. The President greeted him with a warm handshake and a pleading look. Beverly Anderson commented on the President's tie. Forced smiles bounced around the room. The President, minding his manners and being a perfect host, invited Ms. Jones and Beverly Anderson to sit down. They sat down on the sofas facing each other, making an effort not to sit close.

The President took his commanding rocking chair. Barney sat at his feet. "Did you know Ms. Deverough?" The President asked Beverly Anderson. He was trying to convince himself that he had actually met Ms. Deverough. Beverly Anderson had already been questioned by the Secret Service. All that was missing from their interrogation was a cigarette and a firing squad. Beverly was really shaken up.

"Of course I knew her, Mr. President, but I have no idea where she lived or where she came from. Ms. Deverough summoned me right after you took office and announced Clarke as your partner. I was watching it on TV when I received her telegram to come to Washington at once. It was an instant friendship and it felt like we had known each other forever." Beverly looked puzzled. "But her personal life never came up. I'm sorry, Mr. President. She wouldn't just leave, not without saying good-bye." There was a pause, and his voice shook with the next question, "Would she?"

Beverly Anderson never thought of saying good-bye. They were soul mates, the Three Musketeers, Clarke, Ms. Deverough, and Beverly Anderson. Clarke was gone, now Ms. Deverough. Beverly Anderson started to cry and couldn't stop. He had shown no emotion when Clarke died. Now it was all taking its toll. He just sat there with his head in his hands and sobbed.

The President slowly rocked in his chair. He didn't know what to do, but he had to do something, so he slowly rocked back and forth. The President motioned to Ms. Jones that it was okay to comfort Beverly. It was no secret that she and Beverly Anderson were seeing each other.

The President got up and left them alone. The search continued for Ms. Deverough but no one found her. She had disappeared as mysteriously as she had appeared. Everything was gone from her room, photos, gowns, and personal belongings. Ms. Jones was right; all of her steamer trunks were gone. Even her special soap was gone. She wouldn't bathe without it. The room looked like it did in all the photos, like a museum that only people looked at, not slept in.

The President stopped the Chief Usher, asking him about Ms. Deverough. "Of course we all knew her, Mr. President. The staff liked her and, quite honestly, were scared to death of her." They smiled at each other. The President excused himself and enjoyed a walk around the grounds with Barney. The night air was still. The grounds, usually dimly lit, were as bright as if it were high noon. There were many more guards on duty. It almost looked like a busy day.

Beverly Anderson said his good-byes as the President walked back into the Oval office. The President sat behind his desk and tried to concentrate on his work. Michael refused to believe in fairy godmothers. He finally gave up and decided it was time for bed. He and Barney walked through the halls of the White House. Each room had a guard outside a closed door. He nodded as they acknowledged the most powerful man in the world. The President and Barney entered the Private Quarters, then sat down together. The President fell asleep on a divan with Barney curled up next to him.

Running For Reelection

Michael Arthur Kent was the best man for the job, every voting American citizen knew that. The President had the speech that had been written for him, informing the nation that he would run for office again. He also had a speech he had written himself. The President enjoyed writing his own speeches, even though he had a staff who wrote them almost as well as he did.

The President prepared himself for national television. He waved away the makeup people. The President was scheduled to address the nation live in just moments. He asked his staff to meet with him before he addressed the nation. They were assembled in the Cabinet Room. The President stayed in the Oval Office.

The President had been a man of action, living up to his every word. He had also been a man of surprises. "Surprise is the spice of life," he had been quoted. He lived up to that every day in office. The surprise was always in good taste, and always surprisingly right for the nation. The First Gentleman let the camera in on their administration and the President kept it spicy. Tonight would be no different.

Even with the months that had passed, the nation was still in mourning over the loss of Clarke, but the President held everyone together. The President didn't smile much. He was always clean-shaven, but looked a little rumpled around the edges. America wanted four more years. The world was safe and wanted four more years. The camera crew was standing by.

The President's Cabinet waited patiently to be briefed. It was rumored the President would announce his candidacy for four more years. It would be the easiest campaign America had ever seen. It was political suicide to disagree with the President.

Unemployment was at its lowest point since records were kept. There was a surplus in money set aside for welfare and that was invested in American companies keeping jobs in America. The money it made was put into a Money Market Account to strengthen Medicare and Social Security. Americans were in school, getting the education they deserved. The entire globe was safe, as America's military was the strongest the world had ever seen. There was no Cold War. The United States military guarded the Middle East from the inside out.

The President took the speech he wrote and positioned it as the cameras pulled closer. Pictures of Clarke were on a credenza behind his desk. Barney was at the President's feet chewing on a rawhide bone. A large red light flashed over the camera as the director pointed to the President.

"My fellow Americans, thank you for inviting me into your homes this evening. This has been a rough time for our nation. We all miss Clarke very much." He paused, then swallowed hard. "As your President, I was proud to be appointed, then elected to office. I strive to do what is right for the United States and the world. It may not be a popular decision, but it is the right decision.

"The decision to run for office again has been thoroughly thought over and it is with great pain I announce to you that I will not seek nor will I accept another term as your President." There was a pause then Michael broke into that comforting smile of his that everyone missed so much. "I would urge all Americans to vote for Olivia Longley, your present Vice President, to be your next President. I will tell you, she has my vote. I am still in office, and will be until the third Monday of January, and you can expect that I will do everything in my power to keep America for the people, by the people."

The Vice President watched with shock as she was catapulted into the running. She called the already-assembled political advisers to announce her candidacy in a press conference that next afternoon. She had just learned moments ago that the President would not run for re-election.

The Vice President didn't have much time to think about running herself, but the President did, and, as always, he knew what was best for the nation. The tradition would live on as the administration of firsts. She had learned much from the President and was charmed by the First Gentleman. She would carry on their dream, as they had become hers. If she won this election, she would be the first African American, first female, first single parent President. She knew the campaign ahead would be tough.

Her campaign WAS tough. Opponents sprang up like cockroaches caught in the light. With the President out of the picture, it was anyone's campaign. Cronies promised to keep the President's vision and with their great ideas make America even better. They had great ideas, but the Vice President had something no other candidate had. The President was behind her one hundred percent.

The President spoke on her behalf constantly, while still running the country with the same excellence the world had come to expect. He campaigned hard for her. Every luncheon, every ten-thousand-dollar-a-plate dinner on her behalf, was getting tougher by the dollar. By the time the President left with handshakes, the people knew who was perfect for the job.

Not since 1877, when Rutherford B. Hayes was sworn into office, had there been such a narrow victory in a Presidential Campaign. His race had been so close he was secretly sworn into office in the Red Room following a private White House dinner. When the votes were tallied, the Vice President broke that record and had won by the narrowest victory in the history of the United States. A re-count proved she was truly the first woman, first African American, to be elected to the office of the President of the United States.

After her victory, the President took the last few months he had left in office and signed many bills that needed to be passed. Some may have been a bit premature, but it would make her transition to office, although tough, a lot easier. History would say she did for President Kent what Lyndon Johnson did for John Kennedy. The President vowed he would never forget what she did for him and Clarke in their own run for office. The President made good on his promises all the way to the end. Politics took on a new slogan. "It's not the popular thing, it's the *right* thing." America was for the people, with or without Bibles, with or without color, with or without alternative lifestyles.

The President signed a document, closed it, and put his pen down. He got up from behind his desk. Barney trotted along. The President went to the office of the Chief Usher. The staff didn't know what to do when the President walked in. So they stood quietly. The President was invited to sit down. He sat in front of the Chief Usher's desk. The Chief Usher sat behind his desk and nervously asked the President how he could be of service.

"I need your help in orchestrating the grandest Ball the White House has ever seen. Make it like one of Clarke's. Really overdo it." Smiles flooded the room. There hadn't been a State Dinner or a party since Clarke died. The President didn't go in for all the frou-frou, but Clarke had made sure every party, every White House luncheon, every State Dinner topped the one before. It would be hard to top Clarke, but together the staff would try.

"Of course, Mr. President." The Chief Usher took a long yellow tablet out of his drawer and started to write.

The President continued, "This is going to be a Ball in honor of the president-elect. It will be totally in her honor. I will be host for the evening with no escort." The President had once made a comment to the Chief Usher that Clarke was always with him and no one ever doubted that for a moment. The President loved to dance but wouldn't take a step without Clarke.

The President had a piece of paper that had been folded in thirds. "Here is a list of people I want invited. It can grow from there. I would like you to take care of the rest. The Protocol Office will work with you as well. Right now the president-elect doesn't know anything about this. I will brief her so we can get her input on the guest list."

"Yes, Mr. President." Excitement seemed to grow in the office as Camelot again began to bloom. The President could even feel it. He knew the Ball would be grand. The Chief Usher had worked so well with Clarke that he knew exactly what the President wanted.

The President continued, "I would like this open to the press." The Chief Usher smiled and nodded his agreement. I would like to be briefed on the plans as they are made. This will be the last grand event I will host in the White House and, without sounding like I've lost it, I like to think that Clarke will also be here, in spirit. So, with that in mind, make it a ball Cinderella would want to attend and her Fairy Godmother, pardon the pun," everyone in the room smiled. "Would wave her magic wand and let Cinderella stay out past midnight.

The Chief Usher smiled. The President stood and everyone in the room, out of respect, followed his lead. The room was quiet as they watched the President leave. The staff missed Clarke. His memory was alive and the staff could see how it tugged at the President's heart. The Chief Usher started making telephone calls. As he dialed the number he realized he was humming "Be Our Guest." He stopped for moment and bowed his head, remembering Clarke. With great memories in mind he smiled, then called his assistant in with a list for the committee. It was going to be a grand Ball.

The Chief Usher, the Protocol Office and Clarke's staff of decorators and party planners really outdid themselves. It was as though Clarke had planned this party himself. But what Clarke did single-handedly, it took a whole staff to do. When the President informed the Vice President what he was doing, she loved the idea with almost a shy, embarrassed excitement.

The White House staff used Clarke's favorite recipes. Floral designers put Clarke's best ideas into the centerpieces. The nation's finest entertainers from across the country volunteered to perform for the President in honor of his Vice President, the president-elect.

Beverly Anderson was invited to the White House for a private luncheon with the President. The Ball in honor of the Vice President would be the President's last duties as official host. Michael asked Beverly if he would design an outfit for him that Clarke would be proud of.

Michael didn't like wearing all the frou-frou but requested it just this one time. Beverly was honored. He had the perfect idea. He fairly bubbled with excitement as he took the President's measurements. Just as Beverly was putting his measuring tape away, an usher announced that lunch was served. The President motioned for Beverly to accompany him to the dining room. Beverly suddenly stopped. With a pointed finger, he informed the President he would personally tie his bow tie the night of the Grand Ball.

The President smiled as they walked down the hall. Clarke always tied the President's bow tie. If not, the President would tie it himself. At best it looked sloppy, "But presidential," Michael would say, teasing Clarke. Michael informed Clarke that Abraham Lincoln was always photographed in a sloppily tied bow tie. Clarke couldn't believe Mary Todd Lincoln let Abraham out of the Private Quarters looking like that. The First Couple always laughed about it while Clarke put the finishing touches on Michael.

Early on the night of the Grand Ball, Beverly arrived at the White House with the President's ensemble. He helped Michael dress and, as promised, tied his bow tie in a perfect knot. He held up Michael's coat and Michael slipped his arms through the sleeves. Beverly gave the President a final once-over. A knock on the door informed the President it was time. Michael thanked Beverly with a warm handshake. The President turned and walked out the door. He nodded a hello to Ms. Jones who was standing guard and walked to the Grand Stairs.

Michael stopped on the landing as the announcer said, "Ladies and gentleman, the President of the United States, Michael Arthur Kent." As the Presidential March played, Michael appeared to the flash of a thousand cameras. President Michael Arthur Kent stood tall in his coat designed with long tails. It was cut away at the waist exposing a beautiful Beverly Anderson original silk vest. The President paused then walked towards the Blue Room as the light caught the sparkle in his cufflinks.

A vintage carriage had been sent for the Vice President. She arrived at the White House like Cinderella after the magic wand. The press had done a wonderful job of covering all the preparations, and the only thing that could top this was the Inaugural Ball and even that was going to be tough.

Beverly Anderson, with the President's agreement, designed a dress for the President-Elect. She was radiant as her flowing gown trailed behind. A full skirt with a scalloped bottom and simple train iridescent with color sparkled like diamonds against her ebony skin. She stepped out of the carriage. Her hair was in an up-do with a headpiece of flowing pearls. One had to wonder if she was wearing glass slippers. She entered through the front doors of the North Portico in step to the music of a Marine Quartet.

Escorted by Marines in full dress uniform, she walked to the President waiting in the Blue Room. A glow sparkled from the chandelier. Flames from the candelabra stood at attention. The president-elect was presented to her host. She reached out her gloved hand and the President took it with a bow. The press was awestruck. America had a queen. Again.

The Vice President now the president-elect, with the Blue Room as her backdrop, cocked her head slightly to the camera's flash. She felt like a queen and, for a day, she was. Then she would be sworn into the highest and most powerful position in the world. It was almost something out of a Cinderella story, but then again, President's Kent's whole administration was.

No one at the Ball was as grand. It wasn't planned that way, but had been secretly hoped would end up that way. Dinner was served in the State Dining Room. The tables were set in a horseshoe pattern for good luck, with the President at the head of the table with the president-elect to his right. The candelabra framed her as a toast given by the President brought an ovation for the guest of honor. The press was sent to the East Room while dinner was served. The china and stemware Clarke had designed was used. Not since President Monroe's administration in 1817 had such finery been commissioned for the White House.

After a wonderful dinner, the President and the president-elect had the first dance of the evening. It was proudly televised. It was the first time the President had danced without Clarke. On a choreographed note, the staff motioned for other selected couples to dance. As the dance floor filled and the President and president-elect danced, Michael asked what he could do for her.

She looked up at him and said, "What can I do for you?" There was a long silence as they danced in step. The President offered to show her how to throw a ball for the first pitch of the season. She reminded the President WHO gave him a run for his money. The President had offered the Private Quarters to the president-elect but she declined and said it was still his and Clarke's until the third Monday in January.

"Are you sure?" The President asked.

His Vice President nodded. "Saundra has everything under control."

After a long silence, The president-elect asked the President, "So what's next?"

"I'm going to enjoy Clarke's home." He stopped and corrected himself. "Our home, by the sea." Michael grinned from ear to ear. "Clarke's will made it very clear." Michael recited word for word from the will: "The estate will remain a place for fine parties and grand cotillions." Then Michael became serious. "I'll write my memoirs and Clarke's." He smiled. "But not in that order."

The president-elect gave Michael a friendly nod. "What a great idea, just a man writing his husband's memoirs." The both laughed out loud. "That sounds like a great title for a book."

"Thank you. I was looking for the perfect title," the President said as he turned his partner to the beat of the music.

"I will have the first autographed copy," she said as she twirled her partner.

"You know the Treasury Department wants me to sign the order to mint Clarke on a coin. It will be the first time a First Lady will be minted on a US coin. It will be my last official duty as President."

"If you don't, it will be my first official duty as President."

There was humbled silence between the two. "Thank you." The President said.

"But after that," Michael said, "I don't know what life is about without Clarke." They were silent as they continued to dance. The dancing couples parted, as they twirled neither knowing what to say, and neither wanting to say a word.

It was the Grand Ball the President asked for. After a full evening of fun, food, entertainment and dancing, the President walked the president-elect to her vintage carriage. She left the White House with as much fanfare as when she arrived. The television cameras zeroed in on the handsome man the lonely President was. The horses clip-clopped as the carriage drew away.

The Washington night was clear and crisp. The President wore full pajamas and pulled on a pair of slippers Clarke insisted he at least wear outside. The President took his favorite pipe, a gift from Clarke, and held it tight between his teeth. Clarke didn't like Michael smoking. He broke him of the habit indoors, but outside was fair game.

Clarke didn't like what smoking could do to the President's health but loved the smell of fine pipe tobacco. Many times it was an aphrodisiac for Clarke. Not that he needed one. The President used to tease Clarke that the only aphrodisiac he needed was ambient air. Clarke knew the truth: all he needed was Michael.

The President and Barney walked to the South Portico. Michael sat down on his favorite rocker and Barney hopped on to his lap. The nighttime view was spectacular. Regardless of how many times the President sat there late at night, it was like he was seeing the view for the first time.

The memories of the White House came alive for him as he slowly rocked the night away. The good and the bad. The political good. The President smiled. The political bad. Michael lit his pipe. The quiet was interrupted when Ms. Jones came out, carrying a mailed package in her hands.

"This came for you, Mr. President. It's gone through security. It is marked "to be delivered at once". There's no return address or letter attached."

The President took it and said, "As long as it's not ticking, we're all right." The President smiled. Ms. Jones was not amused. The President looked at Ms. Jones and said, "That will be all." She left as the President opened the parcel.

Michael pulled the packing paper off, then opened the box. It was a book, spiral bound, in two volumes. The President thumbed through it and noticed it was all double-spaced, a manuscript ready for publishing. He looked at the cover. It was blank. He opened the book. On the first page was a hand-written inscription: "Clarke, The First Man To Be First Lady, was a rip snortin', roller coaster of a ride, and we are all better for having received a ticket. Thank you for my ticket. All the best, Ms. Deverough." The President just sat there.

Some time had passed. He regained his composure. The President thumbed through a few pages then realized he wanted to look at the pictures. There was Clarke and Barney when the President first announced his 'First Lady'. Michael laughed at Clarke's expression. He looked like a deer caught in headlights.

There was Clarke being measured for clothes, making Beverly Anderson *the* name in fashion, not to mention incredibly wealthy. Ms. Deverough was in every picture and, as usual, she was in the background, almost behind the scenes. Michael smiled. In every picture, Ms. Deverough seemed to look right through him. Michael held his pipe in his hand and started laughing out loud. He imagined the picture of Ms. Deverough had actually winked at him. Just seeing a picture of Ms.

Deverough made him feel so good. He turned the page. There was Clarke on the Matt Robinson show.

The next page was Clarke and he on their wedding day in the Blue Room. The press never knew of it. It was the administration's best-kept secret. Not since Grover Cleveland who married Francis Folsom in 1886 had a President been married in the Blue Room. The President and Clarke renewed their vows on the same day they had been legally married. Ms. Deverough, Saundra, Beverly Anderson, the Vice President and, of course, Barney were the only invited guests. There was no publicity, but there was plenty of cake. The Pastry Chef always outdid himself for Clarke.

The President bought Clarke a real wedding ring with baguette-cut diamonds. During the ring exchange portion of the ceremony, Clarke put the big vintage ring on his other hand and put the new wedding ring over his first wedding ring, the notebook ring binder. Clarke loved both rings and wore them together like an engagement ring and wedding band combo.

The President kept going page by page, then back to the front of the book to look at the pictures again. The pictorials were incredible. They looked like they had been photographed by National Geographic. The First Couple's lives, the two of them in the White House. Behind the scenes, which America loved, and in front of the camera, where Clarke loved to show off his husband.

There was Clarke redecorating the White House with a paintbrush. Clarke behind the scenes of the televised White House tour. Most of these photos had never been seen. The President loved Clarke's pose of throwing the baseball. Michael shook his head from side to side. There were photos of Clarke almost bald after his chemotherapy.

Michael laughed out loud at the picture of Clarke falling on the stairs. Clarke had planned the perfect State Dinner for the First Couple of France. Michael was so worried that Clarke had hurt himself. The President was photographed laughing with Clarke when he realized he was all right. Michael heard Ms. Jones come back to check in. He shut the book.

"Is everything all right, Mr. President?" Ms. Jones asked.

"Fine. Everything is," he swallowed hard. "Everything is just fine. I found Ms. Deverough." He said with a smile. He handed the Ms. Jones the book so she could see for herself.

She thumbed through the pages, laughing at the pictures. She didn't know she had ever been photographed with Clarke, but there were pictures from the very beginning, at Clarke's 'kidnapping'.

"I don't know how Ms. Deverough got in every picture," the President said with his comforting smile. "But there she is."

Ms. Jones had a puzzled look on her face as the President took the book to show her the pictures of Ms. Deverough.

"She is in every picture staring right back at you," the President said as he thumbed through the book, looking for proof. Ms. Deverough was not in any picture, no where in the book. The President and Ms. Jones thumbed through the book trying to find proof that Ms. Deverough was really there. Barney hopped off the President's lap and walked to the edge of the balcony. He stood on his hind legs, resting his front paws on the railing, wildly wagging his tail, watching a shooting star over the Washington Monument.

The President slowly closed the book. He was trying to convince himself he was sane. Ms. Jones commented how incredible the book was, insisting on an autographed copy. The President smiled, then asked Ms. Jones to please sit down. This was most unusual but Ms. Jones did as the President asked.

The President looked at her. "I wanted to personally thank you for everything. You and Clarke may have started off on the wrong foot, but it didn't take long for the two of you to become inseparable. Clarke thought the world of you and said so, many times."

The woman with a heart of stone melted right in front of the President. Tears streamed down her face. She apologized for her un-professionalism. The President reassured Ms. Jones it was okay.

Through her tears, Ms. Jones asked the President if she could be so bold as to ask him a personal question. She had wondered something since the day she and Clarke first met. The President looked at her and said a simple yet concerned, "Of course."

"Mr. President, what does, 'By the way' mean?"

The President looked at her, then looked away towards the Washington view, not seeing anything. With a twinkle in his eyes said, "That was our secret code for, 'I love you.'" Ms. Jones nodded as if she should have known that.

After a long silence, Ms. Jones excused herself and left the Private Quarters. Barney hopped back up on the President's lap. Michael gently petted him. The President was glad to be going home. His job was done. He smiled with a sigh of relief. It had been an incredible term of office.

The third Monday in January finally arrived. The President and Barney walked through the Private Quarters one last time. The rooms were bland. Draperies had been taken down and replaced with simple sheers. Carpets had been rolled up and packed. The furniture Clarke had purchased and those pieces sent from his estate had been crated and sent back to his home.

Michael walked past the Lincoln Bedroom just as he had so many times before. But this time he stopped. The door was unlocked and partly open, as if someone had walked out of the room and hadn't latched the door. Michael opened the door and just stood in the doorway. Barney sat in the hallway and wouldn't budge. The President walked towards the empty bed and stopped. He slowly looked around the room, then turned and walked away.

As tradition dictated, the new administration met with the old for coffee in the White House. Naturally it was served in the Blue Room. It was an exciting time but everyone was very quiet. The President missed Clarke. Barney was at his side. The president-elect was excited to take America where no other woman had taken the country before. Coffee was poured. No one seemed to drink, just held the cup like a warm hug. Michael looked at his watch then over to the mantel. Clarke's blue marble mantel clock was gone. Michael smiled. It was packed, already on its way to Washington, the state. Michael looked at the president-elect. She was radiant.

Beverly Anderson had designed a fabulous suit for her. It was a slate blue pin stripe, mid-calf, two-piece double-breasted suit, conservative, yet very feminine. A simple hat made out of the same fabric lay on the back of her head. Not since the 1961 inaugural had a President worn a hat to the swearing-in. The press informed every one of that. The president-elect's signature single strand of mini pearls hugged her neck. Her earrings dangled and told the world she wasn't stuffy at all, but radiant. The president-elect would set a style for women in power. The first woman to be President was ready to take the challenge.

The old with his dog and the new with the bull by the horns were ready to take their traditional walk to the stands together. The President proud of his administration and the president-elect proud to be the first woman, first African American to be voted into the office of President of the United States.

The President walked towards the doors of the North Portico for the last time. Barney was at his side. Barney knew they were leaving and was happy to be going to his home by the sea. He was a spirited puppy when he got to the White House and now he enjoyed staying at the President's feet.

As the President and Barney waited side by side, the President waved the Chief Usher from opening the doors. Michael looked around the room to silent people, many with tears. He said a quiet, "Thank you." He turned and looked down at Barney. Barney looked up at the President. Suddenly Barney looked in the opposite direction, where there was nothing. No one. Barney waged his tail, squirmed, and turned circles. Then he calmly sat down as if someone were gently petting him.

The Chief Usher motioned for the doors to be opened so America could see a boy and his dog one last time. It was the end of an era that had taken the country by surprise. The President, Barney and, with the angelic magic of the hereafter, Clarke, walked out of the White House.

Fabulous recipes compliments of

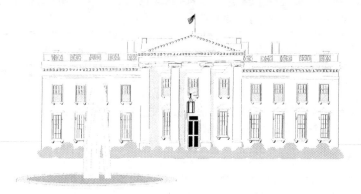

The First Gentleman

Clarke's Perfect Pie Crust

To make a perfect piecrust, just use this recipe.

2 Cups Flour
½ teaspoon salt
2/3 Cup Crisco - ONLY USE CRISCO,
   (Not butter-flavored but the regular white stuff)
6-8 Tablespoons chilled Sprite. Yes, Sprite. **Regular** Sprite, not Diet
   You want all the sugar and carbonation from the regular Sprite.
Before you start anything, pour the 'Sprite' (yes, the 'Sprite') over ice and let it chill while you're gathering all the other ingredients. Even if the Sprite is chilled in the fridge, still pour it over ice. The colder the better!

Combine the flour and salt. Cut in the CRISCO with a fork or a pastry blender. I use a fork and just mash it all together, until it looks like it's all mashed together. The books say, 'till it looks like peas'; I say till it looks like it's all mashed together.
NOW, add the 'Sprite'. (Not '7-Up', **Sprite**'), and mix only till it's all moistened, not real sticky, and not too dry (6-8 tablespoons should be perfect), and you can gather it all up in a 'cling-together glob' to roll out. Roll on a floured area until its about 2 inches bigger than your pan.
 Here are just a few helpful hints to keep your crust perfect:
The more flour you add to the pie dough and the more you roll pie dough the 'tougher' it gets, but don't worry about that too much. The more you bake pies, the better you'll get at it. You will be a Blue Ribbon winner before you know it!
Using SPRITE will cause your crust to brown quicker so watch it in the oven. You will want your crust to be golden, not brown.
You can really mix the flour and CRISCO and salt together, but make sure it's coarse and looks like peas in the bowl. The more uniform-looking the clumps of shortening, the flakier the crust; but you want it to be uniform, not a big clump here or a clump there.
Pies should be baked in a hot oven, preheated to 400 degrees.
Preheating is a must. Piecrusts should bake fast at a high heat. This keeps the crust very flaky.
If you're baking crusts for a cream pie, prick the living daylights out of the unbaked crust with a fork, then turn the pan around and do it again. Otherwise the crust will bubble up and it will be hard to fill and serve.

President Kent's Favorite
Clarke's Coconut Cream Pie

2/3 cup sugar
¼ cup cornstarch
¼ teaspoon salt
3 cups milk or Half-and-Half (*I use Half-and-Half*)
2 large eggs, beaten (just beat the eggs with a whisk or fork until nicely blended)
3 tablespoons margarine
2 teaspoons coconut extract. *This is a must!*
'Just a drop' of almond flavoring. This is an <u>absolute</u> must, but just one drop—any more than a drop and your coconut pie has become an almond pie!
1 ½ cups coconut

Mix the sugar, cornstarch and salt together. Add the milk or Half-and-Half and beaten eggs and stir until smooth. Bring to a full rolling boil over medium heat, stirring constantly while it's boiling, for 1 minute. ****If the heat is too high the milk or Half-and-Half can curdle.* Removed from heat, add the butter, flavorings and flaked coconut. Stir until the butter has melted.
Cool completely in the refrigerator.
Spoon into baked, totally cool pie shell. Garnish with a border of whipped topping and sprinkle with browned coconut.

Here's the easiest way I've found to **brown coconut: pour the desired amount of coconut into a saucepan. Place the saucepan over medium heat, stirring constantly. Coconut has a mind of its own and can burn without notice, so stir it constantly. At first, it feels like you're stirring forever…just keep stirring until the coconut is browned to your liking. If you find a few flakes have over-browned just pick them out. Make sure the coconut has cooled before sprinkling on whipped cream or the whipped cream will melt.
Store your beautiful pie in the refrigerator until serving.

Barney's Favorite Chocolate Chip Cookies

2 ½ cups all-purpose Flour
1 tsp. baking soda
1 tsp. salt
½ cup butter (*not margarine*)
½ cup Butter Flavored Crisco
¾ cup granulated sugar
¾ cup dark brown sugar (To me, C & H has the best brown sugar on the market.)
1 tsp. vanilla
2 large eggs whisked together. (I like large eggs but I've used jumbo and medium sizes, too.)
2 cups Nestles Semi Sweet Chocolate Chips
1 cup walnuts (English Walnuts are Barney's favorite. The more nuts the better.)

Mix the flour, soda, and salt together. In another bowl, cream butter, Butter Flavored Crisco, granulated and brown sugars, vanilla and whisked eggs together until smooth. Add to the dry mixture and mix until smooth. Blend in the Nestles Semi-Sweet Chocolate Chips and English walnuts.
Taste. Taste again. Don't taste anymore. You won't have enough dough to make cookies!
I like to chill the dough overnight, at least 8 hours. Chilling gives this cookie a really nice shine, and brings all the flavors together.

The real secret to this recipe is in the baking. **Underbake.** Bake on an ungreased cookie sheet in a preheated oven at 375° for 8-10 minutes. Bake two cookies first to see how the dough is. If they run a little flat, add ¼ cup more flour and bake two more.

***Bake with the doubt. If you think the cookies are done, they are.
***Once they have cooled, if the cookies are too gooey, place in a freezer bag. When ready to serve, mix with vanilla ice cream and warmed chocolate sauce. Another favorite of Barney's!

****Do not substitute margarine for butter**. Many margarine's have more liquid in them than butter and can cause this cookie to go flat. Play it safe and always use butter. I have used salted and unsalted butter; whichever you have is fine. I prefer the unsalted

Barney's Favorite Chocolate Chip Cookies (continued):

***If you want to "impress" people with these cookies, try this:

Put12oz of chocolate, dark or white, or even peanut butter chips in a microwave-safe bowl. Microwave on high until melted, about 30 seconds, then stir, repeating until smooth and creamy. Dip cool cookie.

This is perfect for gift-giving or just plain impressing someone. The bowl can get hot so be careful.

***You don't have to use English Walnuts. Regular Walnuts will do. But I will tell you this: *Barney can tell the difference.*

Garlic Smashed Potatoes

8 medium potatoes
3 cloves garlic—2 crushed, 1 finely minced
Salt and pepper to taste
Bottled Ranch Salad Dressing (yes, bottled Ranch Salad Dressing!)
Butter to garnish to taste

Thoroughly wash the potatoes. You don't want to peel them.
Place potatoes in a pot and fill halfway with water. (Potatoes do not have to be drowned in the water.) Place the 2 cloves of crushed garlic in the water with salt and pepper to taste. Boil potatoes until tender.
Make sure the water does not boil away. If it does, add more water.
When potatoes are tender, drain off the water.
Add the minced garlic and Ranch Salad Dressing to taste and creaminess. Start with about ¾ cup and add ¼ cup more to desired creaminess.
Smash potatoes with a potato masher.
Remember that you want these to be lumpy and be able to hold a ladle of gravy. Dot with butter. Serve with gravy.

For a Fat-Free treat, use Fat-Free Ranch Dressing and omit the butter.

Clarke's Homemade Bread

If you're going to make white bread from scratch, this is the only recipe you will ever want. It takes time and energy to make homemade bread and rolls but these are the best. So double the recipe and double your fun.

3 cups warm potato water. (You will get this when you boil peeled potatoes.)

1 package active yeast. Check the expiration date on the package.

1 cup mashed peeled potatoes

3 teaspoons plus 1 teaspoon salt

3 tablespoons softened, not melted, butter. You want the butter to melt through the dough.

2 tablespoons sugar

6-8 cups of flour

Cut peeled potatoes in small pieces so they will cook faster, and cover with water. Sprinkle about a teaspoon of salt in the water. Cook potatoes until tender. Make sure you use enough water to get 3 cups. (The water will boil away so use about 4 cups of water.) Drain water, saving it in a bowl, and mash the potatoes.

***Make sure the potatoes and water remain warm but not too hot. A little warmer than a baby bottle, but not hot to the touch.*

Add the sugar to the potato water. The yeast needs the sugar so it can rise. Without sugar, the yeast goes flat.

Add the yeast and let it dissolve about a minute or so, then stir. Make sure all the yeast globs are off of the spoon and are totally dissolved.

Add the warm mashed potatoes, salt, and the butter and beat it together with a spoon. Add half of the flour and continue beating. I use a mixer at this point but the more flour you add, the harder the mixer will have to work, so just beat it with a mixer with about 2-3 cups of the flour then continue to beat by hand.

***Yeast breads usually like to be handled rough at this point and the more you beat them the better they are.*

Add enough flour to be able to knead the dough without it sticking to your hands and everything around it. Usually 6 cups of flour will do the trick, but if not, add a little more. But eight cups should be enough to flour the counter while you are kneading and not make it sticky.

Let the dough rest for about 5 minutes or so, and rest your self 'cause you will be kneading for about 10 minutes. This really is a lot of work but all the effort is worth it because this recipe is so good.

Knead dough for about ten minutes, and then let stand in a warm, draft-free place until double, about an hour. A sauna would be the perfect temperature and humidity for rising the dough, so anything close to that is perfect.

Generously grease two 8"x8"x2" loaf pans.

Once the dough has doubled, punch it down. Yes, it likes this and if you don't do it, your dough will go flat. So enjoy it! Double your fist and go for it. It won't even stick to your fist. Well, maybe a little.
Roll out the dough and fold into the desired shape. If you're making loaves, roll out a rectangle a few inches bigger on both sides than your pan. Rolling the dough will get rid of air bubbles. Then fold your dough into a rectangle the size of your pan tucking the sides in and under to make it the exact size of your pan. Shape the dough once it's inside the pan to hump like a loaf should be. Yes, it will touch the sides of the pan all the way around. Let it rise about 30 minutes, then bake at 350 degrees in a preheated oven.

The loaves will be done when they sound hollow when you knock on them. (If anyone answers, check the expiration date of the yeast again.) Let the loaves cool about 15 minutes and remove them on a pan.
TIPS:
***Always check the expiration date of the yeast.
***Make sure the mashed potatoes are warm not hot.
***Make sure that potato water is warm but not hot.
***Always knead dough away from drafty or cool areas. I preheat the
     oven to get the kitchen really toasty at this point.
***Don't open the oven for the first 15 minutes of baking the loaves.
     Loosing too much heat too fast can cause the dough to fall.
***If you leave the bread in the pan, it will become soggy.
***Always serve homemade bread warm.
    If you're going to use this recipe for dinner rolls, you don't have to roll the dough out in a rectangle unless you need to, to make your shapes. Make sure to always grease the pan you're baking in, and work with the dough the least amount at this point. It shouldn't be kneaded again, and should always be worked in a warm room so it can continue to rise. You name it and you can shape the dough into it. At this point it will work a lot like play dough. But remember that it will rise about double the shape.
***Be on the quicker side when making your shapes.

Creamed Gravy

1 8oz tub of sour cream, which comes out to one cup.
2 Tbs. flour
1/8 tsp. cloves
¼ tsp. cinnamon
Salt and pepper to taste
1 cup beef broth, right from the roaster (without the cloves) OR
**2 Beef Bouillon Cubes melted in 1 cup of boiling water

Mix flour and sour cream in a heavy saucepan. Let this come to a boil
over medium heat. Boil for one minute, stirring so it won't scorch.
After this has boiled, add 1 cup of hot beef broth right from the roaster.
Let this boil for one minute then add ground cloves, cinnamon, salt and
pepper to taste. Simmer.
Serve hot!

**If you don't have enough broth add 2 bouillon cubes to 1 cup of
boiling water and let the cubes melt.

Spiced Roast Beef

4-6 lb. Beef Roast
Whole cloves
Ground cloves, ginger and cinnamon
1/2 cup brown sugar
4 whole onions peeled
1 cup of orange juice

Preheat oven to 325.
Choose a nice roast from your grocery store. The roast should be well marbled, but not too fatty. Remember a little fat gives a lot of flavor. I usually get about a 4-6 pound roast. Remove from the package and place in a roaster. Place the roaster on top of the stove, on high heat, and quickly brown the roast. The roast will be brown on the outside, but totally rare and still cool on the inside. This is done quickly to sear in the juices. Add 1 cup of orange juice to the roaster. Add ½ cup brown sugar. Dot the roast with whole cloves, about 15 on each side.
**Whole cloves are sharp on one side so go ahead and spear them right into the roast.
**I like to sprinkle the top and sides of the roast with ground cloves, ginger and cinnamon, then sprinkle with a little salt and a dash of pepper.
Peel four medium onions, and leave them whole.
**Make sure you cut out the woody stem of the onion Place onion in the roaster as well.
Roast until meat thermometer reads 145 degrees, approximately 2 and one-half hours.
**Turn the roast every half-hour while roasting so both sides get well browned. Remove from the oven.
**Let the roast stand in a covered roaster for 10 minutes. This will make it easier to carve. This is also the time you can make the gravy. Remember the roast will continue to cook as it stands in a covered roaster.
When you are ready to carve the roast, if you see any cloves, remove them and also remove them as you carve.
Slice the roast and arrange the slices on a platter with the whole onions.

**Remember: The gravy is the last thing out of the pot.

Capered Salmon

Buy a salmon that has been cleaned and de-boned. I like to use a
   cooked, smoked salmon

2 cups of fresh lemon juice.
1 cup capers with their juice
1 tsp. prepared Grey Poupon mustard
1 tsp. white pepper
A few cranks of freshly ground pepper
2 stalks celery, finely chunked
Chopped fresh ginger in very small chunks
I small purple onion, finely chunked
Firm Roma tomatoes, chunked

Place all the ingredients, except the salmon, in a container with a tight
fitting lid and shake until well blended.
Place the smoked cooked salmon in a pan and pour mixture over it.
Let marinate for 12 hours, turning every 6 hours. Cut salmon in small
pieces. Garnish with marinated chunks. Arranged on greens.
Serve well chilled.

*** I always chill the greens and freeze the plates before serving the
salmon.

Raspberry Vinaigrette Dressing

1 ½ cup olive oil, extra virgin
1 cup pureed raspberries (puree in blender)
1 Tbs. granulated sugar
½ cup lemon juice
½ cup lime juice
1 tsp. salt
¼ tsp. white pepper
1 tsp. finely chopped parsley
1/4 tsp. finely chopped mint
1 tsp. finely chopped chives
½ tsp. prepared mustard
¼ clove garlic finely minced
Whole raspberries for garnish of individual salad servings

Place all the ingredients in a blender. Blend until well mixed. Let stand in refrigerator no more then 24 hours. Right before serving, add 2 cubes of ice to the dressing and "blenderize" until the mixture thickens to the consistency of medium cream sauce.
**I like to make this the morning I am going to serve it for dinner. This is tart and tangy!
**If you're using frozen berries, thaw completely and drain excess juice before '"blenderizing".
**All herbs should be very finely minced. No chunks other than the whole raspberries you add right before serving.
**Makes about 2 cups.

Serve with your favorite greens in season.

Ellensburg Rack of Lamb

Where else but Seattle would strong coffee be used in cooking a rack of lamb?

1 4 lb. rack of lamb
1 Tbs. Salt
3 Tbs. course-ground black pepper
2 Tbs. brown sugar
3 onions, pureed
1 cup beef broth, warm
1 ½ cup hot strong coffee
1 cup heavy cream
¾ cup warm cream
3 Tbs. flour

Preheat oven to 425°. Rub salt, pepper and 2 Tbs. brown sugar into the lamb. Cover the ends of the rack of lamb with foil so they do not over-brown. Place into roasting pan. Pour pureed onions and warm broth over rack. Roast 30 minutes then skim off the fat.
Reduce oven temperature to 350°. Add hot strong coffee, warm cream and sugar. Continue roasting, basting frequently, for 40-60 minutes.
Transfer rack of lamb to a warm platter.
Transfer meat drippings to a pan through a sieve or puree once through a blender. Mix flour with ¾ warm cream. Shake until all lumps are gone. Pour through sieve. Mix into drippings and bring to a boil. Brush this onto the rack of lamp. This is not a sauce as much as it is a coating.
Return to broiler for 2 minutes—1 minute each side

Serve at once with Apple Pear Chutney (Recipe on next page).

***Make sure when you are adding cream and coffee that it is hot. Hot liquids should be added to hot liquids.
***Peel and cut up onions, then place in a blender until they are pureed and pour-able. Make sure you have a tissue ready.
***When you return this to the broiler, watch it very carefully. You want it to be golden brown, but not too dark.
***Do not cover the roaster while roasting. This can make the lamb tough.
***Use a warm platter. Lamb can cool very fast.

Apple Pear Chutney

2 strips bacon
2 tbs. lemon juice
6 medium tart apples, peeled and chopped
1-6oz. can mandarin oranges
1 large purple onion, chopped
3 cups beef broth
1 cup brown sugar
½ cup golden raisins
¼ cup currants
1 tsp. cinnamon
½ tsp. ginger
¼ tsp. cloves
2 tsp. salt
¼ tsp. pepper
1 clove garlic, finely minced
1 tbs. parsley, chopped
¼ tsp. cumin
½ cup honey
6 pears, peeled and chopped

Fry the bacon with the lemon juice until crisp. Remove bacon from the fat. Cool, then chop fine. Add brown sugar, raisins, currents, mandarin oranges, chopped apple, onion, and beef broth to the fat. Simmer until apples and onions are almost cooked. Add all spices and honey. Mix well. Add pears. Continue to simmer on low heat until pears are tender, approximately 1 hour.
Serve chunky and hot

***Low heat is the key to this simmering pot. Stir frequently to
    prevent scorching.
***If your chutney gets too thick (fresh fruit can do that), add 1 cup
    of hot orange juice. Just zap 1 cup of orange juice in the
    microwave for 2 minutes.
***Mandarin oranges are fragile and cook down to nothing but the
    flavor they leave behind will be heavenly.

Asparagus with Hollandaise

3 large egg yolks, beaten
2 tbs. cold water
½ c unsalted butter, softened
¼ tsp. salt
1 tbs. lemon juice

Combine the beaten egg yolks and water in the top of a double boiler. Beat with a wire whisk over hot water until fluffy and the mixture has warmed. Add butter a few dabs at a time and beat continually until the butter has melted. Add the salt and lemon juice, beating until thickened.

***Remember Holland is the land of butter, so no wonder
   Hollandaise sauce is a treasure from Holland!
***Make sure the water in the double boiler does not boil. This can
   cook the egg.
***Add butter a dab at a time, letting it melt while whisking and the
   sauce gradually thickens. This will make for a more velvety
   smooth sauce.

Asparagus

1 lb. asparagus
1 tsp. salt
½ cup lime juice

Wash asparagus and cut off the woody ends. With a vegetable peeler, gently peel the outside skin. Add the lime juice and salt to about three inches of water. Stand asparagus on end; do not lay flat. Cover. Bring water to a full rolling boil then turn off the heat, but leave the pot on the burner. Let stand covered for approximately 12 minutes. This will make a nice, slightly crunchy asparagus perfect for Hollandaise Sauce.

***Use 3 inches of water in the bottom of your pot to steam the asparagus. Asparagus should be standing in water 1/8 the length of the asparagus stalk.
***If you do not have a lid to cover a steam pot, tightly cover with tinfoil.
***Try not to open the lid of your steaming pot. You want lots of steam with none escaping while the asparagus is cooking.

Almond Baskets

*This recipe can be very tricky, but once you try it and get the hang of it...you will
be making all kinds of beautiful edible dessert dishes*

1½ c granulated sugar
1/3 cup molasses
1 cup cream
1 tbs. Butter
A sprinkle of nutmeg
1 ½ cup sliced almonds with 1 tsp. salt added

Combine the sugar, molasses, cream, butter and nutmeg in a heavy
saucepan. Bring to a boil and continue to boil over medium heat,
stirring occasionally, until a candy thermometer reads 240 degrees.
Mixture will form a ball in cold water. This takes about 40 minutes.
Remove from heat. Add salted sliced almonds and stir until well
blended. Remove from heat. Generously butter 6-inch squares of waxed
paper.

Working quickly spoon a 3-5 inch circle onto the buttered waxed paper.
While this is still hot, but not too hot that it will burn your fingers, drop
waxed paper lined almond mixture into a small bowls so it make a nice
bowl shape. With your fingers, make a nice edge. Let cool. Carefully
remove the waxed paper.
To store baskets, place a piece of waxed paper sprayed with cooking
spray between each basket.
Store in an airtight container in a cool place, **not the fridge**.

***As you get used to making these edible dessert dishes, try dipping
the edges in white chocolate or drizzle with white and dark chocolate.
Your imagination makes the possibilities endless. To me, they're pretty
all by themselves.

French Vanilla Ice Cream

1½ cups whole milk
2½ cups cream
3 vanilla beans
8 egg yolks, whisked heavily
¾ cup sugar
¼ salt

Scald the milk, cream and vanilla beans (Scalding is to heat until mixture comes to a gentle boil.) Remove the vanilla beans. Blend the beaten egg yolks with the sugar and salt. Pour into a double boiler. Stir in the scaled milk a little at a time, beating after each addition.
Cook, stirring occasionally, until the mixture coats the spoon, about 45 minutes. After you have added all the scalded milk to the egg mixture, remove from hot water and cool immediately, stirring occasionally.

Pour the cooled mixture into 13"x9"x2" pans, no more than 2 inches deep. Freeze until mixture is solid.
Remove from pans and place in a mixing bowl. ***Make sure the mixing bowl and beaters are well chilled***
Beat with an electric mixture until very fluffy.
Return mixture to 13"x9"x2" pans sprayed with cooking spray.
Freeze until firm. Scoop into nice balls.

**Cool immediately by placing the top of the double boiler into a bath of cold water and ice cubes. Stir mixture frequently as it cools. You don't want a film layer to develop. That film will take away from the velvet texture.

***Don't forget to remove the vanilla beans!

***Always use a non-flavored, no-flour-added cooking spray.

***I don't recommend lining the 13"x9"x2" pans with waxed paper or foil. This becomes cumbersome when trying to remove the frozen ice cream for the mixer beating or when trying to scoop it into balls. You can get small pieces of foil or waxed paper in your ice cream. Ick!

TIPS:

***Make sure on your final freezing that your ice cream pans lay flat. If it doesn't you can have uneven scoops, making your dessert look sloppy. And after all this work you really want this dessert to look your best.

***Make sure you have a fresh opened box of baking soda in your freezer. This mixture will pick up odors you never thought you had.

***Adding ¼ cup of REAL maple syrup to the frozen mixture during the final beating will make this ice cream an incredible maple dessert.

*****Adding imitation maple** to this recipe makes the ice cream taste hollow.

Blackberries

4 cups blackberries
¾ c granulated sugar
¾ c orange juice

I like to use warm fresh blackberries when serving with French Vanilla ice cream.

Add granulated sugar to the blackberries and let sit until a nice juice forms, about an hour.
Drain the juice from the blackberries into a saucepan and add the orange juice. Bring it to a boil. Remove from heat and let stand to cool just a bit, then add blackberries.

Serve at once, while still warm, over French Vanilla Ice Cream cradled in edible almond baskets, and sprinkled with edible glitter.

***Blackberries are very fragile and can literally melt in hot juice.
***Edible glitter can be found in cake decorating and specialty kitchen stores. Edible glitter can add quite a luster to your dessert. If you cannot find edible glitter, sprinkle with coarsely ground white sugar.
***Frozen blackberries can be used. Thaw and drain well. Do remember that thawed, once-frozen blackberries can be more fragile then freshly picked blackberries.